IN THE Shadow of the Wall

An Anthology of Vietnam Stories That Might Have Been

Edited by Byron R. Tetrick

CUMBERLAND HOUSE
Nashville, Tennessee

To David P Babey, SP4, US Army ☆ John L Carroll, Maj, USAF
Harry G Cramer, Sr., US Army ☆ Lewis E Casner, Jr., 1 Lt, USMC
Richard T Gray, 1Lt, USAF ☆ Robert A Harrison, 1Lt, US Army
Sharon Lane, Nurse, US Army ☆ Carl O McCormick, Lt Col, USAF
George W Morris, Jr, Capt, USAF ☆ Harold L Mischler, Capt, USAF
Mark A Peterson, 1Lt, USAF ☆ Patrick A. Shutters, 1Lt, US Army

And to all those not on the Wall but who also died in support of
their country and comrades.

Published by Cumberland House Publishing, Inc.
431 Harding Industrial Drive Nashville, TN 37211
www.CumberlandHouse.com

Cover design by Gore Studio, Inc.

Library of Congress Cataloging-in-Publication Data
In the shadow of the wall : an anthology of Vietnam stories that might
have been / edited by Byron R. Tetrick.
  p. cm.
ISBN 1-58182-252-9

1. Vietnamese Conflict, 1961-1975—Fiction. 2. Veterans' writings,
American. 3. War stories, American. I. Tetrick, Byron.
PS648.V5 I53 2002
813'.0108358—dc21

                        2002005773

ISBN 978-1-68442-278-4 (hc)

CONTENTS

Introduction 7

50 WPM
Orson Scott Card 13

Long Time Coming Home
Elizabeth Ann Scarborough
and Rick Reaser 27

The Pilots
L. E. Modesitt, Jr. 45

Wallgate
Laura Resnick 53

What's in a Name
Michael Belfiore 69

Black Reflection
Robert J. Sawyer 79

Getting There
Barry N. Malzberg 95

Obsessions
Leah R. Cutter 99

names in marble
Joe Haldeman   *117*

Second Chance
Ralph Roberts   *121*

Blood Bone Tendon Stone
Michael Brotherton   *131*

Reflections in Black Granite
Mike Resnick
and Michael A. Burstein   *151*

While the Band Played
Paul Allen   *167*

The One-Half Boy
Nick DiChario   *173*

Dirty Little War
Michael Swanwick   *189*

The Angel of the Wall
Byron R. Tetrick   *197*

Willing the Child to Return
David Lange   *261*

Contributors   *266*
Copyrights   *270*

IN THE Shadow of the Wall

INTRODUCTION

FOR MANY WHO SERVED, the Vietnam Veterans Memorial is their only thanks . . . a cold, black stone one, at that. Yet this memorial—inanimate though it is—has embraced hundreds of thousands of veterans and their families with outstretched arms, comforting them with a sense of belonging and shared pain. It has become a "magical" place of healing. A common thread woven throughout the stories of the veterans, the ones who carry mental scars more painful and destructive than anything physical for which they received Purple Hearts, is that the Wall or their buddies or God, for that matter, spoke to them. And yes, healed them. Tim Brown, one such veteran and a survivor of a deadly ambush, said, "When you're there [the Wall] you can reach out, touch, feel, and communicate. They can hear you, and you can hear them tell you it's OK." In many respects, the Wall has played a broader role in the healing of our nation, so divided and angry when the war was being fought. It is now the most visited memorial in the country.

Designed by a young architectural student named Maya Ying Lin and dedicated in May of 1982, the "Wall"—as it quickly became known—is 494 feet long, rises to ten feet at its vertex, and is made of polished granite. Etched upon its surface are the names of those killed or missing. The average age is nineteen, and four of every ten men were fathers or about to become fathers. A magical aspect of the Wall's design, with its 58,226 names carefully spaced and etched into the granite in the order of their death, is that it causes one to think first of the individual. Only then does the enormity of the numbers hit home. Laura Parker, in her remarkable book about the letters and poems left behind at the Wall, *Shrapnel in the Heart*, says it best: "Name one child, your own, and each of the names on the wall will break your heart."

There are many fine nonfiction books that bring to life the names of those who died, reminding us—not that we should have to be—that each and every name on the Wall lived and breathed, loved and dreamed, and died much too young. Among them are: *The Wall: Images and Offerings from the Vietnam Veterans Memorial* edited by Brennon Jones and Amy Janello; *Voices From the Wall* compiled by Jan C. Scruggs (founder of the Vietnam Veterans Memorial Fund); and *Offerings at the Wall* by Tom Allen. However, nonfiction can't always go to the places and do the things that fiction is capable of, especially through the literature of the fantastic. Just as nonfiction is filtered through the viewpoint of the one telling the story or is a recapitulation of memories distorted by time, fiction is a story told from the perspective of that author. But fiction does not limit that which is beyond an author's own experience. That is what gives fiction its richness, its ability to pose questions and offer solutions beyond the scope of the few who have experienced it.

And the authors within—professionals all—know that.

And yet, when asked to be part of this anthology, some questioned their right to tell a story "reserved for vets only." The younger authors, who were only children when the war was being fought, wondered what kind of story they could tell, and to what end? Well-meaning friends suggested other authors who were vets as possible contributors, assuming that would be a requirement to take part in this anthology. Such is the power of the Wall. For this reluctance came from the knowledge that the Wall has become a sacred place, and as such, it's assumed by those who didn't serve that the vets have an *a priori* right to its sanctity. At one point in my own story, "The Angel of the Wall," I have *my* character saying: "I feel a rage building in me at their sacrilege. It is *our* Wall!" But another magical aspect of the Wall is that most who visit it come away realizing that the Vietnam War was *our* war—all of ours. In the words of Sen. Chuck Hagel, himself a combat veteran, "[The Wall] has allowed those who opposed the war to honor the warrior without honoring the war. It has allowed those of us fortunate enough to return to pay our respects to our fallen comrades. It truly has become The Wall That Heals for millions of Americans."

The only limitation placed on the writers for this anthology was that their contribution should have some "fantastical" or "magic realism" element, with the Vietnam Veterans Memorial playing some role in the story, and that it should not dishonor any person whose name is on the Wall. Some of the authors are veterans. Others are not. Some stories are vehemently antiwar. Most are not. Many are somber, while a few are funny (at least in parts). All the stories are the result of the writers looking at a blank piece of paper and asking themselves what kind of story do they want to tell about the Wall. What can they add to the understanding of the most divisive event of our time? That is the power of fiction.

The authors were asked to write an afterword so that they could, in part, answer the age-old question: "Where do you get your ideas?"; or if they so chose, to add their personal feelings about the Vietnam War and the Vietnam Veterans Memorial. Writers are a passionate lot, and this group is no exception.

▨ ▨ ▨

There is a "new" Wall. The family and friends of the firefighters, policemen, and rescue workers who died in the September 11 terrorist attacks have created their own memorial, which has been likened to the Vietnam Veterans Memorial—not because of any design (that is yet to come), and not because it has become a place of public tribute to those who died in the service of others, but because, like the Wall, it is where the families can share their grief. They bring pictures, flowers, letters . . . many of the same things that veterans have been placing at the Wall for almost twenty years. This method of communing with the dead is a legacy of the Vietnam Memorial. The Wall has taught Americans for two decades that whether it is 5,000 lives or 55,000 lives, each individual is unique and precious.

Whatever type of monument our country and the people of New York City decide upon, one hopes that it, too, heals and unites.

50 WPM

Orson Scott Card

"You know a lot of these guys?"

"No. We didn't fight the same war."

"I thought you went to Vietnam."

"Oh, sure, yeah. But I never fired a rifle at anybody, and nobody ever fired one at me. I never even left Saigon."

"But I always thought . . ."

"What?"

"You know."

"What?"

"Your hand. Your fingers. The missing ones. I thought that happened in Vietnam."

"It did. . . . There he is."

"Who?"

"My guardian angel."

"Man, if I got a guardian angel, I hope mine ain't *dead*."

"Yeah, well, he was joking, too, I think. Got in country, he saw I was kind of green. You know. I was young, I'd never been out of Hickory, I didn't know a thing, so he says to me, 'I'm your guardian angel. I'll not only keep you alive in this hellhole, I'll even keep you sane.'"

"Well, one out of two ain't bad."

"I know you don't mean anything by it, son, and there's nothing wrong with joking, but I got my fingers resting on the name of a friend who died saving my life."

"Sorry, Dad. You know I didn't mean . . ."

"Funny thing is, your grandpa had it all figured out so my life wouldn't need saving. See these hands? All seven fingers? Would you believe I used to be a typist?"

"That before or after you were front man for the Beatles? No, sorry, I want to hear. Dad, I do. Really."

⊠ ⊠ ⊠

Your grandpa was a grunt in World War II. Volunteered the day after Pearl Harbor, and when they saw how that country boy could shoot, he was infantry all the way. He wasn't stupid; he didn't volunteer for anything, didn't get himself into Airborne or the Marines, turned down sergeant's stripes three times. He just knew how to shoot, so they had him on the front lines in North Africa, Sicily, and in slow motion all the way up the boot of Italy.

He told me it got so he didn't even bother learning the name of a new guy till he'd been there for a week, so many guys got blown away just cause they were new and didn't know enough to keep their heads down. Dad and the other guys'd tell 'em, but they just didn't have survivor instinct, that's what Dad called it. The sense to know just how far you had to bend over to keep from giving them a target.

Helmets don't stop bullets, son. You got a helmet so you don't get killed when a bullet knocks a chip out of a stone wall and the chip comes and hits you in the head. But somebody aims right at you, that helmet just adds a little more metal to get slammed into your skull.

Anyway, Pop comes to me when I'm thirteen years old, summer before eighth grade, and he says, "No, I'm not going to teach you how to shoot. Knowin' how to shoot got me three and a half years on the front lines killin' guys and having guys get killed all around me. What you're going to do this summer, boy, you're going to learn how to *type*."

Now, I didn't even hardly know what typing was. Something girls took in high school, something you saw secretaries doing when my mom took me with her to pay, like, the water bill or something. Pop had to drag me there—I ain't kidding, kid—had to drag me up to the high school and sign me up for summer school typing. Bought me a typewriter, too, and he didn't have a lot of money. That was a big deal. We had to be the only people we knew had a typewriter on their kitchen table; it sat there during meals and everything. At least an hour a day, he set the kitchen timer on me, and it was worth half the skin on my butt to fiddle with it and cheat. So I sat there and typed, and a lot of the time he was watching me, saying stuff like, "Don't look at the keys!" and "Spell it like it's written, you moron!"

No, he actually called me shit-for-brains, but your mother doesn't like me talking to you the way my Pop talked to me. And yes, this is about how Samuel I. Keizer saved my life. Look, forget it, let's go find your mother and your sisters.

It's not like I tell this story a lot, son. So I don't know which parts to take out so it's entertaining.

It's about my father trying to save my life. That's why he made me take typing class. He says to me, "Bobby, there's gonna be a war. There's always gonna be a war. First thing they do, they find out what you can do. Me, I could shoot the shit off a squirrel's ass so clean he'd think he wiped himself, so they put me in the dust and the mud and had people tryin' to kill me. And all I got in exchange was the G.I. Bill, but I never got me a single one of my buddies back; they stayed just as dead as they were when I left 'em behind in Italy. Well, that ain't gonna happen to you, Bobby. You go into that recruiting office and where they say 'skills,' you put down 'typing, fifty words per minute.' That's the magic number, boy. You type fifty words a minute—and that's fifty words without a single mistake, every minute, page after page—and they never put you near a rifle. After basic, you just sit at a desk and type and type and type, and when the war's over you go home and you ain't dead and nobody you knew in the army is dead because they were all typing, too, or giving orders from some nice safe place ten or twenty miles back, or five thousand miles even. That's where I want you in the war."

So I says to him, "Pop, what if I want to fight?" And he says, "Bobby, you volunteer for infantry, I'll kill you myself so I don't have to worry about you getting killed by somebody else. Better me than a stranger. Your mother and me, we'll cry over your grave, but we sure as hell never gonna sit there waiting for some letter or some telegram from the government to find out whether you made it through another day of people shooting at you. You get me?"

Didn't matter whether I got it or not, I was going to learn to type. And that first summer I kept telling him to go ahead and kill me, because hell couldn't be worse than breaking my fingers on that damn machine.

But by the end of that summer I was typing thirty words a minute, and that's after you take off ten words a minute for each typo.

All through eighth grade he makes me type all my homework—and that was before computers, hardly anybody typed their stuff, not in Hickory anyway—and I had to practice an hour a day. And then every Saturday morning first thing, he'd time me and correct my paper, and if I ever did worse than the week before—lower speed or more typos— then I couldn't go anywhere with my friends that whole weekend.

By the end of eighth grade I was typing fifty words a minute, just like he wanted. He let me off then, no more hour-a-day practices, but those weekly tests kept right on, and any week I didn't stay over fifty words per minute, I was back to the practicing.

So I graduate high school and Johnson's escalating the war in Vietnam and everybody who went to college got to sit it out and I could've, too. You can bet I got accepted at college—I mean, hell, kid, I could spell, I could type, that made me an intellectual in the hills of western Carolina. But, see, I figured I'd get drafted, put in my two years, and then come out with the government paying all my college bills cause I'd be a veteran. I wasn't worried about no war, kid, cause Pop took care of that: I could *type*.

No, it worked just like Pop said. I come in there looking and talking like a hillbilly and I put down on my form that I can type fifty WPM, and the recruiter looks at me and says, "It's a federal offense to lie on this form," and I says to him, "I ain't lyin', man." And so he sets me down at his own desk and opens a book and puts a paper in the machine and looks at his watch and says, "Go."

Well, I made that thing sound faster than a machine gun. A minute later he says to stop, and what I got on that page isn't fifty words, it's ninety words, all spelled right and pretty as you please. And then he says, "Do it again," and this time he doesn't say stop after a minute, he just has me keep typing and typing. I blew through three sheets of paper and the other recruiters are standing around laughing and he looks over my typing and I didn't make a single damn mistake and even including changing sheets, I was over ninety words per minute.

I don't know what he wrote in my file, but even in basic I kept getting called out of my company to go type stuff for the base commander, and when I got to Vietnam I think I'd fired a rifle exactly once. My pop, he knew what he was talking about. I was going to live through that war.

Course it wasn't really as easy as all that. Cause I kept thinking about how other guys were going to go out into the jungle and lay down their lives and the worst that was going to happen to me was getting my fingers smudgy when I changed ribbons. But when I wrote that to my mom in a letter, my pop read it, too, and he wrote back to me cussing a blue streak right there on the paper and he says, "It's just as much part of the war to type up orders and reports. Somebody's gonna sit in that chair in that nice clean office, and usually it's some lily-assed faggot son of a congressman but this damn war it's gonna be a hillbilly from Hickory, North Carolina." In those days you could still say faggot, son; it was a different world. Wasn't better, just different.

So I get to Nam, my orders put me right in the typing pool in an office building in downtown Saigon, and that's where Sammy Keizer spotted me.

Sammy wasn't in the typing pool. He was the guy in charge of all the guys who typed up orders every day. You know, sending this regiment to that place and telling where supplies had to go. And it was pretty high level; I mean, the stuff he typed got sent to other offices where other guys had to type up fifty more orders just to carry out the orders Sammy's office sent them. And Sammy comes into the typing pool and there I am, showing off, typing as fast as I can, and he says, "What're you typin' there, ass-face, 'Now is the time for all good men' or 'When in the course of human events'?" And he comes over and looks at my paper and he gives this low whistle and twenty minutes later some guy comes over and lays a paper on top my machine and it says I'm assigned to the office of sit-and-dick-around-with-Sammy effective immediately.

No, that wasn't the real name, but that was the job description whenever we weren't actually working. I mean, Sammy kept that office humming. He did his job and made sure we did ours, but as soon as we were done for the day, all he wanted to do was have fun, and he'd take along whoever wanted to go.

Which wasn't me.

I had fun, it just wasn't the same fun. Come on, you know your Gran, she's Baptist through and through, and that means I never even *danced* when I was growin' up and I sure as hell never smoked or drank. And as for women, well, there wasn't no double standard in my parents' house; they said a boy should be just as virgin as a girl till he was married, and my pop let it be known that if I wanted to keep my dick, it was going to stay inside my pants and not go gettin' anybody pregnant. And I wasn't one of those kids, the second he's away from home, he goes wild. I may not be as die-hard Baptist as my folks were, but I was then, and no way was I going to go out whoring and drinking with Sammy I. Keizer and his cronies.

So Sammy sees I'm not going, of course, and he asks why and I tell him, not judgmental or nothing but still, you know, how it was against my Christian upbringing. The other guys just groan and I figure I'm gonna get a hard time, but Sammy, he just puts a hand on my shoulder and says, "Good for you. Got more brains than all the rest of us put together." They still go out, mind you, and I stay in, but he didn't let 'em give me any crap about it. They just went and I just didn't and after a while they kind of liked it that way; it meant they had somebody sober when they got back to, you know, help get the booze and the vomit off 'em and get 'em to bed. And believe me, there was nothing I saw about their condition when they came back that made me want to take up drinkin' or whorin' or smokin' dope.

But one day Sammy says to me—and it wasn't that long after I got there, either—he says, "Let's go to a place I know and have lunch." So we go to this canteen about three blocks away. They served pretty good food, and there were reporters there, too, so you knew it was a place where you wouldn't puke or get the runs from eating the food. Always crowded. And Sammy sat me down and I said, "I can't afford to eat in no restaurants," and he says, "I can afford to buy this restaurant because my father is a car dealer in Minnesota and he makes so damn much money he can give thousands of dollars to politicians, which is why I'm here."

And I says, "Your pop got his politician friends to send you to Nam?"

And for a second he didn't know I was joking, but then he did and he says, "Very funny, Deacon."

I hated it when they called me that, and I says to him, "My pop is a deacon and I'm not."

And he says, "I'm sorry, man. I guess I just keep saying the wrong thing, is that it?" And then he tells me about how he had his college deferment, but he was such a screw-up he ended up getting kicked out of college and about fourteen seconds later he was drafted, because his dad was a Democrat but the local draft board was mostly Republican and they hated him big time. His dad didn't even try to get him out; he just pulled some strings—and Sammy said it was Hubert Humphrey who pulled 'em, and maybe his dad even said it was, but I mean, come on, Hubert Humphrey was Vice President of the United States. Who the hell would listen to him? Anyway, Sammy only typed, like, negative-twenty words a minute because he made so many typos, but they assigned him to the typing pool anyway, and the way he tells it—the way he told it—the guys in charge of the typing pool kept trying to get him kicked out and the orders kept coming back that Sammy was a *permanent* member of the typing pool. So finally the only way they could keep things going smooth was to put him in charge of the typing pool himself. Or anyway, that's how he told it. But I also think it had something to do with him being just, you know, a likeable guy. The officers around him, they liked working with him, so they promoted him. That simple.

I liked him, too. Couldn't help it and I didn't try not to. Even though I knew he was a hard drinker, and I figure half those half-American Vietnamese kids they talk about must look like Sammy; he never talked about that kind of thing with me. Never even swore— hell, I swore more than he did. My pop used to say he came from a long line of Swearin' Baptists, and he didn't care if I swore, too, as long as I never did it in front of my mother, which I never did. Though they said a lot worse things than just swearing that I never could bring myself to say. Anyway, he never talked rough around me at all, never even swore. Just talked about . . . everything else. Everything except the war.

He asked about my family, how I grew up, and finally I says to him, "Am I, like, a sociology project or something?" and he says to me, "What I hope is that you're a friend." And then he made a face so I'd know that he meant it but he wasn't queer or anything, but after that he told me everything about his own life and his family and everything. Every lunch, or almost every lunch—every lunch that some officer didn't take him along to lunch with him—Sammy would take me down to lunch with him and he always paid, even though I tried to pay my share. He just laughed and said, "Somebody stateside bought a Chevy from my dad today for five hundred bucks more than he should've paid, so lunch is on him."

And all the time we were talking, he kept giving me advice. On the streets of Saigon, he'd say, "Don't ever go in there, you get V.D. just from window shopping." And he'd say, "Look out for little kids with their shirts buttoned up, cause the V.C. like to strap grenades to them and send them over to G.I.s to blow them up." He told me the parts of town never to go into, and he especially told me all kinds of stuff about what it was like in combat. What the booby traps looked like, how walking point is the safest place because the V.C. always wait till you're past their ambush so they can kill the main bunch of guys in the middle, how if you hate your lieutenant all you got to do is salute him and he's a dead man, some V.C. sniper'll get him. And all the time I'm thinkin', *how the hell do you know about combat, Mr. Sammy I. Son-of-a-Guy-Who-Owns-Politicians?*

And I guess he knew I was skeptical because he says to me, "Bobby, this isn't like other wars. Desk jobs aren't safe here. Just cause you don't take a rifle to work doesn't mean the other guy isn't trying to kill you. They love nothing better than killing G.I.s walking around Saigon thinking they're safe. You're never safe. We're all combat troops, and the guys who don't realize it are the ones who're gonna die. That's why I ask every guy I know who's been in combat, I ask 'em how to stay alive, and they tell me because anything can happen. One day they're gonna come into our office and hand out weapons and say, 'Congratulations, boys, you're all infantry now,' and they'll take us out and get us killed *unless* we got some idea what we're doing."

That's when he told me he was my guardian angel. "You're going to amount to something, Bobby," he says to me. "You need to stay alive."

And I just laughed, cause what does it matter what happens to a boy from Hickory, except to my mother and daddy? But he says, "No sir, it's the way you type. Maybe at first your pop made you learn, maybe you hated it then"—cause, see, I already told him about that—"but the way you type now, that's ambition. You got to be the best. That's in you, to be the best. So that means you're worth keeping alive. So I'm your guardian angel. My job is to teach you what you got to know to stay alive in this war."

I says to him, "My daddy already saw to it I know what I need to know," but he says, "Every soldier needs a guardian angel; it's the only way you get through the war, I promise you." And I says, "Who's your guardian angel, Hubert Horatio Humphrey?" And he says to me, "I got no guardian angel; God doesn't waste time on screw-ups like me." And I says, "If you believe in Jesus he'll forgive all your sins," and he says, "I like Jesus too much to ever repent of my sins, cause as long as I don't repent, he doesn't have to pay for them," and that was pretty much the end of our discussion of religion.

He never took advice from me, though. Like when he typed, he was fast, but he wasn't very accurate. Typos on every order he ever sent out. I tried to tell him to slow down so he wouldn't make mistakes, and he just said, "Faster I type, faster they're out of here." And when I told him I thought that stunk cause a mistake on those orders could get somebody killed, he just looks at me like I'm crazy and he says, "Bobby, even when the orders are exactly right they get somebody killed." Afterwards I thought of all kinds of things to say to that, like how maybe if the orders were right the guys who died might accomplish something first, but I never said it to him cause I knew with him it was all the same. He didn't want my advice, cause he didn't want anybody's advice cause he didn't care enough to want to get better at anything. Except staying alive.

So he'd come back to that guardian angel thing now and then. "Don't do that," he'd say. "This is your guardian angel speaking." And then I'd laugh and sometimes I'd do it anyway and sometimes I wouldn't—you know, just stuff like going out in a jeep with a guy when we had a pass, or going up to a kid and giving him a candy bar. "Listen to me, Bobby, and someday I'll save your life."

So we were sitting in that very restaurant, the first one he ever took me to, and there's the usual crowd, all kinds of soldiers and reporters and Vietnamese businessmen and officers and whatever, and I see this kid come in, little beggar kid. They come in, you know, to beg cause the doors are open, with ceiling fans, the place wasn't air-conditioned. I mean this was Vietnam; we didn't even have air-conditioning in Hickory in those days. So I see this little beggar kid, and I've seen a hundred just like him—five hundred—only there's something wrong. He's going from table to table just like they did, only I keep watching him, not even thinking about why. I'm listening to Sammy, only I can't take my eyes off the kid.

And Sammy says, "What're you looking at?" and he turns and sees the kid and he waves the kid over to our table and he pulls out a candy bar to give him, and all of a sudden I know.

"His shirt's buttoned up," I says to Sammy, and without even thinking about it, I'm standing up. I stood up so fast I knocked my chair over, and I remember somebody cussing cause my chair fell against him, and I says, "Sammy, no, his *shirt's buttoned up.*" But it's like Sammy doesn't even hear me; he's holding out the candy bar to the kid and the kid's right there in front of him and I'm around the table, reaching for him, grabbing to pull him away, and at the exact moment that Sammy is between me and the kid, the kid blows up.

Wasn't even grenades, they said, it was high-tech explosives. It was a big enough deal it made the papers back in the States. Mostly I think because reporters got killed. Hell, everybody in the place got killed or so blown up they were in the hospital for months. They strapped enough explosives on the kid that people were killed on the street outside, that's how bad it was.

Except me. They told me it was a miracle that all that happened to me was getting three fingers blown off.

Only it wasn't a miracle, it was Sammy. He was right between me and the kid. He took the whole blast that was meant for me. I mean, I got knocked back fifteen feet and I blacked out. It's not like *nothing* hit me; my head hit the floor so hard I had a concussion and it took a month for my ears to heal, but I was no more than six feet from the kid, and I should have been dead, blown to bits like those other guys. But there I was, lying on the floor, and when I came to—and I was only out for, like, a couple of minutes—when I came to, everything was silent, cause of my ears, you know, and when I tried to get up, my head hurt, but I had to see if Sammy was OK, you know? I had to see about Sammy. And I sit up and I got stuff smeared all over my eyes, but I wipe them off and I look and the whole place looks like a tornado hit a meat locker. It's all bloody and pieces of people are everywhere and I'm thinking, "This is combat. Sammy was right, the war is everywhere and this is combat."

Only the one thing I don't see is Sammy. And I start to get up to see if maybe he got thrown over me, you know, right over my head so he's behind me, only as I get up my clothes move wrong and I think my legs are cut off inside my pants. I mean, that's what it looked like: I was getting up, only my clothes didn't move right, and then I realize those aren't my clothes. I pull at them and I've got another whole uniform spread out on my body like somebody had held it up against me to see if it fit. Only it was torn open in front—it was really only just the back half of a uniform—and then I recognize the shirt, the stripes on the sleeve, the way they were rolled up. It was Sammy's uniform. It got blown clean off him. Or he got blown clean out of it. And the stuff I wiped off my face, that was probably . . . that was . . .

Oh God. Oh God. This is why I don't tell the story. He saved my life, see? I had got around behind him to pull him away from the kid, and it just happened that he was exactly—he was so perfectly between me and the kid that he took it all for me. Everything. Except where I was reaching my right hand around to grab him. What happened to my hand, that's what would have happened to my whole body except for Sammy. He was my guardian angel.

No, not just because he took it all for me. Think about it. Lord knows I had plenty of time to think about it. A month in the hospital, and then coming home with my damn Purple Heart and Pop calling it my million-dollar wound till I got so sick of it I moved out and went to college just to get away from home. And the whole time I was thinking about Sammy, and he really *was* my guardian angel, because if he hadn't told me to watch out for kids with their shirts buttoned up, if he hadn't pounded it into me that when you see something like that you just get out, you don't talk about it, you just *go*—I mean, I would've still been sitting at that table. Maybe getting something out of my pockets to give the kid. The only reason I was exactly behind Sammy was because I was on my feet getting the hell out of there the second I realized that kid had his shirt buttoned up.

Only it wasn't just that, either. Cause if Sammy had listened to me, if he'd headed for the door like me, we'd both be dead. Everybody in that place was dead, or had pieces blown off them a lot worse than fingers, you know. I'm the only guy walked out of that place. And if Sammy hadn't bent over to give that kid a candy bar, if he'd run for it like I was running for it, you wouldn't be here and neither would I. It was just like he fell on a grenade to save his buddy in a foxhole. And sometimes I even think that he *knew* he was doing it. I mean, he's the one who taught *me* to look for a kid like that, he taught me to get out of there, only when the time comes he doesn't even see it? Come on. I think he knew. I think he chose between me and him, or anyway he knew that the only way I'd live is if I had protection, and he decided my life mattered.

And when I get to thinking that way, for a long time I thought, "Wrong, Sammy I. Keizer. Wrong. My life wasn't worth saving. I haven't done one thing important enough to be worth you or anybody else dying for." That's why I never came to the Wall before. I couldn't face him.

And then they blow up the World Trade Center and you come home and you start talking about volunteering so you can fight the way Pop did in World War II and the way I did in Vietnam and I realized for the first time. I looked at you and I thought, no way are those bastards going to take you away from me, but then I looked at your sisters and your mother and I thought, "What if they blew up the school where one of my girls was? Or the grocery store when your mom was shopping?" And I knew you had to go, cause you thought it was right, and if you went, I knew you might die because that happens, guys die. There's a wall full of guys here who died.

No, hell no, I didn't bring you here so you'd change your mind. I brought you here because I finally knew I could face Sammy. Because I had done something with my life. I really was worth saving.

You. You're the thing I did. You and your sisters. Your mom and I had you all, and I worked all my life paying the bills and I also tried to raise you decent, we both did. And whether it was because of us or in spite of us, you're a great kid, you're a good man, and your sisters, they're terrific, too, and I knew I could face Sammy cause I had you here with me.

See, I taught you how to type, but I also taught you how to shoot, because it isn't my choice. It's your choice. But right here at this wall, here's my guardian angel. I wanted him to meet you. I don't know where you'll go or what you'll do, but I'd like to think you got somebody with you like I did, watching over you. Because I know you'll do right, but when it's all over, I don't want your name on a wall somewhere. I want you to come home to me, just as bad as Pop ever wanted me to come home. You do whatever you think is right, but let Sammy watch over you, and if he sometime whispers in your ear, then by God you listen, you hear me?

Afterword: I didn't serve in Vietnam. Born in 1951, I wasn't eligible until the lottery came along, and my number was above the cutoff. By then— 1969—the war had already been declared pointless by a government that was now sending soldiers to Vietnam to die just to save face for America, the sort of cause I have never thought worth the expenditure of more than six bucks and a hangnail. So I spent those years of my life either as a theatre student at Brigham Young University or as a missionary in São Paulo, Brazil, reading everything about the war but experiencing nothing. Yet I am a lifelong student of matters military and was not an opponent of the war as originally sold to the American people; I cared and care about what happened in Vietnam and have shed my share of tears at the Wall.

So how could I write about Vietnam and the Wall when I had no personal experience there and did not pay any price myself, though I was of that generation? I struggled with that issue for months, wanting to contribute a story but not knowing what sort of story I had a right to tell. And then I realized—I should write, not about the kind of war that most of the guys whose names are on that Wall were fighting, but the kind of war that I would inevitably have fought, had I been drafted. Physically soft and not particularly skilled at anything the infantry needs, and highly unlikely to be tagged as having the leadership that makes one an officer, the only thing that stood out was my typing. I was fast. No, let me get technical here, I was damn fast, and accurate, too. There's not a chance that I would have seen action. Even if I had gone to Vietnam, I would have been in an office somewhere. This story, then, is about the kind of war I might have fought, though none of the characters in it are in any way like me.

LONG TIME COMING HOME

Elizabeth Ann Scarborough
and Rick Reaser

*For those still missing in action, whose names have not
been inscribed with those of their comrades on the Wall.*

THEY FOUGHT ALL THE way to the Vietnam Memorial, which wasn't surprising since they'd been fighting about one thing and another for the last thirty years. Their fights weren't noisy, they were the low, nasty kind, full of sharp hisses and angry looks like poison darts. It hadn't always been that way. You'd think after all those years and raising three kids everything would have been ironed out by now, smooth and sweet as one of the well-blended milkshakes they used to share at the soda fountain before Woody got drafted. Sometimes it was almost like that for them, but always there was a distance, however slight, like the edge of a sock caught in a drawer that kept it from closing. In the Johansons' marriage, the thing between them wasn't a sock. It was a ghost.

Had Woody Johanson never gone to Vietnam, or been in the firefight that killed his buddy, Nick Amato, maybe Woody and his high school sweetheart, Becky, would have been happy. But Nam was always there, like the scar Johanson carried as a permanent souvenir from the firefight that got him a three day R&R at a field hospital. The scar was a tangible reminder, as was Amato's lighter, the deluxe metal Zippo with the 1st Cav insignia, which Johanson had borrowed just before all hell broke loose. The lighter had been in his pocket when Amato hit a trip wire at the beginning of the firefight.

27

The last tactile physical sensation Amato remembered was the intense, searing pain as he was blown to pieces that sank into the monsoon muck of the forest floor without a trace. The pain had lasted only a moment, and then what he supposed he would call his spirit—the core of himself, anyway—was free. But he didn't want to be free to wander Vietnam forever. He wanted to stay himself, stay with his friends, and go home to the States. The only thing left of him and his was the lighter Johanson carried. No sooner had the idea of attaching himself to the lighter and to Johanson occurred to him than it was done.

Maybe it had been made easier because Johanson got hit, too, and was out of it long enough for Amato to join him. Johanson's wound wasn't mortal, but it was bad enough to get him a free helicopter ride to the nearest hospital. It didn't take much from an AK-47. Like the rounds in the M-16s, the bullets tumbled once they hit something, smashing more flesh and destroying more tissue as they went, so there was no such thing as a clean wound.

Johanson's wound gave Amato the weirdest sensation. He was aware that the body he was in hurt, but his friend's pain couldn't touch him.

However, poor old Woody was spouting blood like a fountain and too out of it to do anything about it. Amato knew then that if he couldn't do something to help, he would be out of body a second time—this time with the company of his friend, who, from everything he'd told Nick, had a lot to live for.

Unlike Nick, Woody Johanson had a home to return to, parents who had been together his whole life, a piece of land to inherit, a high school sweetheart waiting for him. He was a calm, stable sort of guy, no drugs, no booze, faithful to his girl, from what he said. He even blamed Nick for starting him smoking and said he should get to keep the flashy lighter Nick had bought himself at the PX for his birthday. Woody said he deserved some compensation for the money he was going to end up spending on smokes because of Nick's bad influence. It was a joke between them. Woody was stubborn as hell and hung onto the lighter until Nick snuck it away from him again, then borrowed it back and the same thing happened all over again. But he was a square in the best sense of the word, a squared-away guy who knew who he was and where he was going. Nick, on the other hand, had considered himself something of a free spirit even before he literally became one.

His mother was dead, his dad, a musician, reborn as a melancholy alcoholic who disappeared when Nick turned fourteen, leaving his son on his own. His mom's relatives lived out of state and his dad's were all dead, but Nick didn't want to go into a foster home, so he got by staying with the family of one school friend after another, making up stories and elaborate schemes to cover for his dad's absence while he finished high school. Maybe his friends' folks suspected that he was lying, but they went along with it. Most of them had big families anyway, and he made himself useful and got part-time jobs to help out. He was half Italian, by nature quick to get upset over stuff and just as quick to calm down, and pretty smart, and he went out of his way to fit in, to make nice, to be agreeable. He didn't want them regretting that they helped him. And if every once in a while one of them patted his cheek or ruffled his hair or called him by a pet name like his folks used to do before his mom died, that made him want to try harder. The last family he lived with was pretty upset with him when he joined the army. They said he'd get killed and they'd never see him again. But he was old enough to be on his own and he wanted to travel and he wanted to go to college someday, too, and get to be somebody who knew about the interesting things he saw when he visited museums and galleries, the things he read about in books. He figured all he had to do was make it through Nam alive and he could get a free education. Meanwhile, he'd see what the world was like outside of New York City. He'd meet different people.

And he did. Like Woody. He admired Woody's cool, and Woody was impressed by his edgier, let's-see-what-happens approach to life.

Dying together was not what they had in mind when they became buddies. And dying twice in one day was not the kind of unique experience Amato favored. He reached automatically to staunch the flow of blood from Woody's arm. To Nick's relief and surprise, when *he* reached, *Woody's* arm moved and Woody's hand applied the necessary pressure until the medevac chopper landed, and the medics applied the pressure dressing. That was when Nick realized that by attaching himself to the lighter Woody carried, he could, at least temporarily, take charge of parts of Woody's body.

So Amato stopped the bleeding, but the damned thing still got infected, as they learned once Johanson was bunked down at the hospital, safe except for the swollen red arm and a raging fever.

Nick surfaced in time to see a girl—not a Vietnamese girl but an American with red pigtails and big round hazel eyes—bending over him.

"Jeez," he said. "Dying ain't so bad. You're one of the angels right?"

She smiled at him, "Cool it, G.I., you are way too hot as it is. Besides, you think I haven't heard that line before?"

"I bet you hear it all the time," he said. He noticed the olive drab fatigues then, and the lieutenant's bars. Her voice was low-pitched and soft when she talked to him. She smelled like perfume—not a lot, maybe some just left over on her skin after a night out and a morning shower. A hint of vanilla and gardenias. Her nametag said "Ryan."

"Shhhhh," she said as she took his blood pressure. He noticed there was a needle in his arm with an IV drip. She had a basin of cool water on the bedside stand and dipped a white washcloth in it and laid it on his—Johanson's—head. He anticipated the touch from the time she lifted it dripping from the basin and wrung it out until she smoothed it over his forehead, but he didn't feel a thing. He couldn't feel it when she brushed Johanson's hair back from his forehead to make room for the cloth either. Then she moved on to the next patient, and a corpsman put ice-filled plastic gloves against Johanson's groin and armpits, to finish bringing the fever down.

As the fever cooled, Amato watched her moving around the ward, sitting at the station, charting. A tall, curvy girl, the kind he'd always been attracted to. He was short and wiry himself and had to try a little harder to impress tall girls, who always wanted someone to look up to. She wasn't taller than he—had been—he guessed, and was quite a lot shorter than Woody.

Johanson kept tossing and turning, though, which gave Nick a chance to talk to the nurse again. "Can he—I—have something for pain?"

She came right away with a pill but took his temperature again first. "Hey, way to go. You're cooling off," she said before she gave him the pill. She had to put it in his mouth. It took more concentration than he seemed to have to move anything but Johanson's mouth and eyes.

"Can I have a smoke?"

It was night time by then and everybody else seemed to be asleep. She cranked the bed up and handed him an ashtray, but he couldn't manage it, so she stood there by him and helped him light the cigarette with her own lighter.

"Want one?"

"No, I don't smoke," she said. "But we all carry lighters for the patients."

"There's one in my—was one in my pocket."

She checked the drawer of the stand. "It's still there."

"Good," he said, and he told her it belonged to his friend.

"Did he get medevaced, too?" she asked.

"I don't know. I didn't see him after I got hit," he said, which was sort of true. He changed the subject and told her about the joke he and Woody had with the lighter.

The mortar attack happened the second night they were there, and Lt. Ryan and the corpsman ordered everybody who could to move under their bed. Amato couldn't get Johanson's body to move for him. Lt. Ryan—he had heard the other nurses call her Shari—trotted briskly down the ward, her flashlight and the corpsman's the only lights. They covered all the guys who couldn't get out of bed with extra mattresses. When she came to Johanson, she clucked her tongue and said, "Can you get up? You seem to be pretty weak still from your fever. Here, I'll help you." The truth was, Johanson was whacked out on pain meds and weak from the wound infection and fever. The IV he was hooked up to with its hose and pole confused Amato too much to make the kind of basic moves he was able to negotiate with Johanson's body.

Steadying him with a hand on the IV pole, Shari Ryan pulled him out of bed, lowered him to the floor, and then, with a worried frown, lay facedown beside him.

A mortar *crumped* so close by, the windows in the Quonset huts rattled. The IV bottle clanged against the metal pole, and the lieutenant held onto it so it didn't tip over and break the bottle. He stretched Johanson's uninjured arm protectively toward her and she made a funny sound. It took him a minute to realize it was a giggle. "Don't worry, Johanson," she told him with a reassuring smile that was as excited as it was nervous, "the V.C. use the hospital, too. They're not going to hit us on purpose. They couldn't get treated afterward if they did. Besides, they're lousy shots."

"Not always," he told her.

"I'm sorry. I guess they got you, didn't they?" she asked as another mortar crumped. Her eyes glittered in the dark like a wild animal's, but there was something in her attitude of a kid playing hide-and-seek.

"And my friend," he said.

So then she asked where he was from and he told her—all the standard stuff about growing up in the City and some of the funny stuff that happened before his Mom died. She'd never been to the City and asked him what it was like, about the museums and galleries and all of the places he liked the best. He told her some of the stories behind some of the things he'd seen, some of the artists he'd met, about the band his dad used to play in.

She said, "You are so lucky. I would love to see those places."

"Hey, I'll take you there when we get out of here. Really," he said, perfectly sincerely. "So where you from?"

"Colorado," she said, and told him about growing up with horses, cows, dogs, and a small army of cats.

"So you're a cowgirl?"

"Not me. My sister was. I'm the throwback. I always made friends with the cats who were better lapsitters than mousers, and I'd go find someplace to sit and read."

"Animals are great," he said. "Some of the people I stayed with had cats and dogs, and there was the zoo . . ." And he told her a funny story about one of the sea lions that had been in the newspaper when he was a kid.

He wished for the first time since coming to Nam that the enemy would never stop shooting. Lying there in the dark, with the mortars thundering and the rockets whistling, it was very cozy, and he felt very close to her, even though when he did manage to get Johanson's hand to touch her shoulder, he, Amato, couldn't feel anything. He just lay beside her, smelling that sweet scent and listening to her voice, and her muffled giggle when he said something she thought was cute. She told him he was going to get to go home and he asked for her address, which she wrote down on a little piece of paper she took from her pocket and tucked into his hand.

But he still couldn't feel it or really touch her. And when she left after finally getting him back into bed, it started to hit him what had happened to him.

As Johanson regained his senses a little, Amato found he wasn't able to say anything or even get Woody to say something for him. He could only watch while Woody acted baffled when Shari Ryan asked him about some of the things she'd talked about with Nick while they were under the bed. Johanson was flattered by the attention from the pretty nurse but puzzled by the references to conversations he didn't remember. He said no, he wasn't from New York City; the lieutenant must have him confused with someone else. His friend Amato had been, though. Maybe he'd been talking about Amato when he was delirious and the lieutenant misunderstood. Did she know if a Spec 4 Nick Amato had been admitted? Shari looked hurt and sounded a little more professional.

But ol' Woody wasn't stupid and he wasn't completely immune to a pretty face. He spent more time in the hospital stateside, and he wrote to Shari a couple of times, even got up the nerve to send her a Christmas present. Amato knew this, but he didn't really instigate it. He felt as if he and Woody were together inside a long tunnel and Woody was at the mouth of it, where he could talk to everybody and see the sun and move around, while Amato was trapped in the back in a dark narrow part, trying to come to terms with the fact that he was dead. He didn't notice a lot of what Johanson did, and if he influenced his friend's behavior at all, he wasn't aware of it or much of anything else.

He started reviving when Johanson got a note back from Shari, a really sweet thank-you note saying how touched she was by his gift and that she hoped he was doing well and she wouldn't mind hearing from him again. So he, Johanson, that is, sent her a Valentine—the biggest, fanciest velvet heart full of Russell Stover's chocolates he could find, and a funny card, which Amato got him to pick out instead of the mushy one Woody reached for first. If Nick was going to have a second-hand life, he wanted the guy representing him to show a little class, at least.

Woody covered his bets by sending his Becky the mushy card and a box of chocolates, too, but he could have saved his money on the second box—the first one came back, the package unopened. She must have rotated out—gone home maybe. But she'd told them that she still had time left to serve after she left Nam—funny they hadn't forwarded the package to her new duty station.

Johanson didn't pursue it then because he was on his way home, and the lighter and Amato with him. Becky was waiting.

At first, Amato was simply glad they had somewhere to go. He was starting to reconcile himself to his situation as part of Johanson's life.

Johanson's parents had moved from the farm to Florida while he was gone, but he went back to Ohio first and found Becky at the bank where she worked. The folks came back up from Florida briefly when the Johansons got married a couple of weeks later.

Amato watched Johanson's dad, who never touched his son and barely tolerated Becky's brush on the cheek. His mother fluttered and talked a little too much as if to make up for the father's silence. Nick was glad when they left. He had idolized his own dad when he was a kid, learned to play guitar like him, remembered all of his stories, all of his expressions of speech and face, learned from him how to get around the City. He thought having his own father half his life was maybe better than what Woody had after all.

Woody deserved better than that. With all this good stuff around him—his new wife, his folks, the nice house and land he inherited from them—Woody was still worried about what had happened to Nick. He'd light up, using the Zippo, and stare at it. He made a few phone calls and got quietly, stolidly pissed off when nobody seemed to know anything or be very interested. Most of the other guys in their unit were dead or still in Nam now. Everybody had been real busy keeping alive when Amato got hit and none of them saw what happened to him. Amato knew this, from the eyeblink between the time he died and the time he joined Johanson. Not one other guy had any idea that he was gone. Amato wished he could tell Woody what the deal was, but somehow or other, it didn't seem to work that way.

The only time Amato was able to come out was when Woody slept, or got drunk or sick. Then it was easier to take control. The first time Becky and Johanson made love, Woody checked out, mentally, for a short time and Amato moaned Shari's name, wondering what it might have been like with her. He knew in that moment that the lovemaking which seemed to Johanson too trivial to talk about in view of all the death he'd seen was about the most important thing a person could do. It would be worth dying all over again if he could feel this, do it with someone he cared for.

The profundity of the moment was interrupted by Becky smacking poor old Woody silly and rolling out from under him. She'd heard the moan, of course, since it had been made with her husband's vocal equipment. She left him for a couple of weeks, but then she found out she was pregnant and returned.

Amato knew he was causing trouble for his buddy but he couldn't seem to help it.

After that, whenever Woody tried to talk to Becky about Nick, which wasn't all that often, she shut him down.

"Yeah, sure. You say it's your old buddy but it's really that nurse you met, isn't it? You fell for her and now you want her and you're sorry you married me. We promised each other before you left that we'd be faithful—I kept my promise, Woody. Did you?"

And Johanson swore he did, of course, and felt annoyed with Becky for dwelling on some imaginary love thing when he was trying to tell her about life and death. He couldn't talk to her about the important stuff. Not back then. So he didn't talk to her very much.

He started to drink heavily after his first kid was born.

Instead of letting him lapse into one of his brooding silences, Amato came out during a blackout and made Becky listen to what he had to say about the last firefight and about himself. He made her believe him, too. He was a better talker than Woody, even when he was pretending to be him, and Becky wasn't used to that, so she listened, if grudgingly.

Maybe interfering wasn't the best thing to do, but if he was going to still be part of life, even by proxy, he didn't want to spend it on the streets someplace when "he" had a wife and a kid and a home. He didn't want Woody's kid to go through what he'd gone through. Maybe if he had felt everything Woody felt and had the chance to enjoy the drinking, it would have been different. Maybe he wouldn't have cared about the consequences if he could have just got drunk, too. But Woody's life was all he had, and while he wasn't mad that he was dead and Woody was alive, it seemed like *Woody* was. There were times over the next thirty years when Amato had to wonder who was haunting whom.

Becky was as stubborn as Woody and stuck it out. Both of them were hard workers and the kids turned out OK, though all of them moved away from home. Amato didn't blame them. His own parents used to argue, before his Mom died, but they did it out loud, got over it, kissed, and made up. Woody and Becky didn't say much when they fought, but the house filled with tension way more tangible than Amato could ever hope to be again.

After a long time Amato realized that, in spite of all the fighting and all of her bitching, Becky actually loved Woody, actually saw him as something more than a paycheck, even if the marriage seemed more like a battlefield sometimes than anything in Nam. Becky wasn't trying to be a pain in the butt. She was a desperate woman who had been using every weapon in her arsenal over all those years to try to get Woody back.

Finally, she bought them both tickets to D.C.

"I'm not going there," Woody protested. "Nothing there but damn politicians. Why do you want to go there now? We could take the grandkids to Disneyland cheaper."

"Why would the grandkids want you spoiling Disneyland for them?" Becky asked, not sounding mad, though she was. "Come on, Woody, you're not in the rice paddies anymore. I want you to go see the Wall. That's where they put the guys who died there. Look. If your name is on there, I'll leave you alone. If it isn't, you come back and come home with me. You got to put this behind you sometime."

"That's easy for you to say." He brandished the lighter and held it in front of him like she was a vampire and it was a cross.

"What are you hanging on to that thing for? You stopped smoking ten years ago."

"Amato gave it to me," he mumbled. That was a lie. Amato had loaned it to him and he, cheap SOB that he was, still hadn't given it back when they were hit. Woody crammed the lighter deep in his pants pocket, like Becky would try to take it away from him.

"Come on," she said, "Maybe you'll find his name on the Wall. You can give that damn thing back to him."

So he got on the plane. They *all* got on the plane in Columbus and got off in D.C.

And here they were. And there it was, like a giant tombstone or the half-buried wing of some black marble airplane, sticking up out of the ground. There was a hill behind it so you could only really see most of it from the front side.

Becky herded Woody down the hill toward it. The sun had set an hour ago, but the place was lit up with floodlights and there was a guard on duty.

"Twenty-four-hour service, huh?" Woody said.

Becky ignored the cynicism in his question and said, "They say a lot of the men who most need to see this won't come during the day, with tourists here. They wait until it's dark. Nobody will bother you. Come on."

Woody strolled up to it nonchalantly, pretending disinterest as he read a few names. Amato was struck by how many people were here, even at night. Everybody but them seemed to be guys, most of them in jungle fatigues. A reunion maybe? It was nearly Veteran's Day. There was one other couple in civvies, just leaving, and a guy in a dress uniform standing by a book. Becky walked up to him and he explained to her how to find names. While he was talking, Woody walked up and asked, "I got a buddy who went MIA at the same time I got hit. Where would he be?"

"MIAs aren't on here, sir," the guy told him. Young guy. Maybe twenty. Still, he looked older than all the guys in the jungle fatigues. Now that Amato looked at some of them more closely, he decided they were way too young to be vets having a reunion. Maybe they were one of those historical re-enactment groups. Or maybe there were some guys on active duty who were training to go some place like Nam, God help them.

"Why not?" Woody asked belligerently.

"Because the memorial is for those killed in Vietnam, sir. Missing personnel are not classified as killed."

Woody glared and fidgeted, as if he were ready to leave. Becky was examining the panels, name by name.

Amato took in the scene before Woody could haul them both away. He wanted to remember this. Remember people remembering, if not him by name, then at least remembering people who went through the same thing he did. He found himself tuning in to the conversations going on around him.

"Damn, these guys look *old*, don't they?" one jungle-fatigued kid was saying to another.

"Yeah, well, man, time has passed out there in the world," the other replied.

"No shit," yet another said. "And it just goes to show you, long life ain't all it's cracked up to be. Look at that bald dude and know that there but for the grace of Charley go all of us—gray hairs, gravity, hemorrhoids, heart problems, and all."

Woody moved toward them and they parted. Becky was kneeling, still scanning names.

Amato looked at his friend and his wife with Woody's eyes but without his viewpoint. Other than being dead, Amato felt just as he ever had. Woody, on the other hand, did have all of the afflictions the guy had mentioned, including high blood pressure, high cholesterol, reflux that woke him up at night feeling like he was going to puke, and a bad back and knees. Arthritis, the doctor said. He also lost most of his hair.

Becky was no spring chicken either. Her fair skin, after fifty-two years, was wrinkled around the mouth and eyes and her chin sagged a little, as did other parts. She'd packed on a little weight, hard as she tried to watch it. She was still a pretty woman, though.

"Woody?" Becky said suddenly.

"Yeah?"

"She's here. Oh, Woody, I'm sorry. I know I've been jealous of her because of the way you used to talk about her when you were drunk or asleep. You didn't tell me she'd been killed."

"Killed? Who got killed?" Woody asked, but he knelt beside his wife and looked where she pointed.

The engraved letters were silvery shadows in the black. "Sharyl P. Ryan," it said.

"Shari?" Amato and Woody said in one voice. Woody said, "Well, I'll be damned. Guess that's why she never wrote again. I just figured she rotated or got married or something. That's too bad."

"Too bad?" Becky demanded indignantly. "Is that all you have to say? I thought you were in love with this girl! I thought all these years you were still wishing you were with her instead of me, which is why I never seem to be able to get your full attention, no matter what. And you find out she's dead and you say 'too bad'? What the hell is the matter with you, Woody? Did you get replaced with some sort of pod person when you went to Vietnam?"

Woody scratched the back of his head and then tucked his hands under the opposite armpits, standing with his legs straddled. This was his serious-thinking posture. For once he wasn't clamming up and turning away. "It *has* felt like that sometimes," he said slowly. "But whatever you think, it had nothing to do with Shari."

It seemed to Amato that the people in uniform had all stopped talking to listen, though their backs were still turned to Woody and Becky.

The Wall curved around them all like the ironically sheltering wing of an overfed carrion crow.

"It didn't?" Becky for a change seemed ready to believe Woody instead of just believe in him. She stood up. "Is it *really* more because of the firefight? The one where your friend died? I mean disappeared?"

"Yeah, I guess so." He took the lighter out of his pocket, and Amato watched, fascinated, as Woody rolled it over and over in his hand as he had done a hundred times until the insignia was almost entirely worn level with the rest of the metal surface. "But you were right the first time, hon. I just didn't want to admit it. He probably got hit when I did and they never found him."

Before Amato knew exactly what was happening, Woody knelt and propped the lighter up against the section of wall under Shari Ryan's name, then stood and took Becky's hand.

"Honey, are you sure?" Becky asked.

"It's time," Woody said, and they strolled back up the hill again.

Which was all very well for them, but there was Amato, alone for the first time in thirty years, his disembodied ass sitting by the big black wall that didn't have his name on it. Abandoned. Soon to be forgotten for good. After all they'd been to each other—the three of them.

"Hey, bro," a voice said, and Amato looked up to see one of the fatigue-clad guys standing over him, extending a hand. "Welcome home, buddy. What kept you?"

"Can you believe that? I've given those people the best thirty years of my—well, thirty years. I kept him from becoming a drunk and her from divorcing him. I—I—" The guy nodded slowly, grinning. "I guess I got too good and now they don't need me any more."

"Guess so. That's OK. You gotta be tired of all that hitchhikin' anyway."

Amato reached out a hand that was not Woody's hand but a younger hand, more deeply tanned and slimmer in shape—his own hand—and grabbed the one extended to him. He rose to feet that wore jungle boots, like the ones the other guys wore. He was wearing fatigues, too. He almost didn't recognize his own—well, not body, exactly, but his appearance. It had been a long time since he'd been just himself. "You can see me?"

"Sure I can. You can see me, can't you?"

"Yeah."

"Same difference. Look, Amato, you've had a long detour on the way home but you're OK now."

"Who *are* you guys?" Amato asked as the two of them walked over to the group. "Are you all haunting this place or what?"

"You could say that."

"I bet all of you have your names there, though, right?" Amato said, jerking a thumb—his thumb—back toward the Wall.

"Most of us, yeah. But look, man, if they knew you were dead, you'd be here, too. Don't make no nevermind to us. We don't stand on formality."

"So isn't there a heaven or a hell after all?" Amato asked. He hadn't thought about any of that since the split second before he attached himself to his lighter but now found the subject vitally interesting.

"Oh yeah, sure, but you're not stuck there, you know. You can come and go. Most of us were ready for a war when we died. Eternal peace is a little hard to take when you're jazzed for action. So we hang out here a lot, look at the presents, read the poems, wait and see if any of our folks or our old buddies are visiting."

"So you can go on leave from heaven? That's a new one."

"Yeah, and some of the brothers have been to hell and back, too."

"Sounds complicated."

"That's why we're here. We're sort of the pathfinders for any new recruits. We've lost a lot of guys *since* Nam, too, because of it. Died from wounds, physical or otherwise, or got cancer from Agent Orange and died that way. Not too many of you dudes who were missing show up like this, though. We're glad you're here. Even if you're not so sure."

"Oh, I am. I mean, I thought that I had to stay with Woody to stay—well, me. But—" he looked back toward the lighter, feeling a little insecure without it. Kind of like a genie without his bottle might feel, he guessed.

Someone was there, reaching for the lighter.

Amato freaked. "'Scuse me," he said to his guide and headed back to the intruder, "Hey, my buddy left that for a friend of ours. It's very special to us and—"

The intruder looked up, the boonie hat falling back to reveal wild red curls corralled into pigtails, and wide, round hazel eyes. "Sorry," she said. "But I think it was left for me. I had a patient once who carried a lighter like this. It belonged to his friend who disappeared during a firefight."

"Shari?"

She stood up. The boonie hat was the only piece of military attire she wore now. Otherwise she was in sandals and one of those Mexican dresses in bright turquoise embroidered around the neck and hem with flowers in hot pink, purple, red, lime green, and bright blue.

"Do I know you?"

"Well, we didn't meet while I was alive exactly, but I'm Woody's friend—Johanson's friend. I died in the same firefight where he got wounded. That was my lighter. And, uh—my ride home and my connection with life for the last thirty years."

"I can see why you might be a little possessive of it," she said. "I wasn't going to take it anywhere. I just wanted to see it, kind of as a reminder . . ."

"Oh, hey, no, that's OK. I haven't smoked in years—I mean, Woody hasn't. He left it with you. I guess he left *me* with you. Only—what's a nice girl like you doing in a place like this?"

"I was on my way to a party with some other nurses and the chopper was shot down," she said, after all these years still looking as bewildered and hurt beyond death as he had felt himself. Life had dumped her out so early.

He reached out, awed and exhilarated by how easy it was this time, and gathered her into a hug. "Oh, baby, I'm so sorry. I didn't know. Woody didn't know."

She returned the hug for a moment but then backed off a little way. She still didn't really know him.

So he used the charm that had got him through his teens and said, "Well, a party, huh? That explains the dress. Very nice, by the way."

"Thanks."

"You weren't here when I got here," he said, when she remained silent.

"No. I stayed here for a while right after they put my name up. At first I met a lot of my former patients who crossed over after Nam in one way or another—and a couple of other nurses I served with. But, I don't know. I just feel like something didn't go right in life, you know? That something was interrupted, or left undone."

She looked back at the lighter and sighed, her golden eyes bright and teary.

"I really liked your friend," she said. "He was a little strange and had a pretty short memory, but—did you know he sent me a Christmas present?"

"Yeah, I knew. We sent you a Valentine, too . . ."

The dress was sleeveless, her crossed arms bare. She shrugged, as if she was suddenly cold. "I wish he'd left that here, too," she said in a small voice. "My folks didn't want me to join the service. They put a stone with my name on it in the veterans' cemetery. " She smiled up at him but her smile was a little quivery.

He quickly began telling her about life with the Johansons, the irritating funny stuff he knew she'd appreciate.

But instead of laughing, as he hoped she'd do, she said wistfully, "It must have been great living with Woody all these years, being close to people."

He thought about it for a minute then dropped the act and said seriously, "Better than staying in Nam, I guess. But I was sort of eavesdropping on their lives. If was OK when Woody was younger, back when we first got home from Nam. But he should have got rid of the lighter—rid of me—sooner."

"But you helped him and his wife."

"Maybe if I hadn't been in the way, he wouldn't have needed so much help. The only time I was really glad I was there—all the way glad—was that night we were in your hospital and taking cover with you under the bed."

"*You* remember that?" she asked. "Your friend didn't. He promised he'd take me to see New York when we got out, then he said he didn't remember anything about it."

Amato said, "Of course he didn't. He was out of it. But I wasn't going to let him waste time being delirious when we could be talking to you. When I could be talking to you. And that was *me*, by the way."

"All that time I was talking to a ghost and I didn't even know it?" she asked. "You sure fooled me."

"I didn't mean to. I didn't—well, I didn't feel like a ghost."

"No, you didn't. You felt more like a person than your friend did, to tell you the truth." She bit her lower lip and those big gold-green eyes searched his face. At last she grinned.

"Sounds like you remember an awful lot about it after all these years."

"I do."

"Me, too. I've never forgotten your face."

She laughed and moved closer to him. "You're way ahead of me. I never saw yours before now. But it's very familiar—you're very familiar."

"I ought to be," he said. "I was living through Woody and Becky, and you know what? Becky is a terrific woman, and Woody is so damned lucky to have her. But I was really disappointed when we didn't hear back from you at Valentine's Day, and he just turned around and married her. I always wished he'd married you, because I wanted to."

She reached up and touched his face, and he was thrilled all over again that now he could feel her fingers, light and strong and cool as he had imagined they had been touching Woody back in Nam.

"I doubt I ever stood a chance with him," she said. "I was surprised to get that bracelet for Christmas. I just knew that in spite of the feelings that I thought were between us, he'd forget all about me."

Amato looked down at her left wrist and saw that just above the big, sturdy nurses' watch she wore, there was an MIA bracelet, a simple thin silver-colored cuff. He suddenly felt a lightness that had nothing to do with being disembodied.

She followed his glance and held up her hand. He took it in his own, supporting her wrist with his fingers as he read the name engraved on the bracelet.

"Sp 4th Class Nicholas Xavier Amato," it said.

"Of course he wanted to forget about you," Nick said, slipping his arm around her. "He knew, somehow or other, that you're my girl."

"Yeah?" she asked, and snuggled against him a little. He could even feel warmth, just as if they were still alive.

"Yeah. That's *my* name you're wearing, lady."

"No kidding," she said. She hooked the wrist with the bracelet around his neck and said, "Well, then. I guess I can date enlisted men if I want to now."

"Damn right," he said, eyeing the group of guys still laughing and talking at the far end of the Wall. "But this place is a little crowded with people who can eavesdrop on our private conversation."

"We don't have to stay here," she said. "We can go anywhere we want."

"So I hear. OK, that being the case, tell you what. You want to see the City? I know a nice little Italian place in my old neighborhood. We won't be able to taste the food but the atmosphere is great."

Afterword: Although I actually did the writing on the story, I asked my friend Rick for an idea for a story he would like to see written. As he often can do, he told me a story with a plot line and a complete first scene, which I used pretty much as he narrated it, though I added a few details. I checked with him to make sure my changes jibed with his concept. His original idea would have been pretty much a guy kind of story—all of the characters being buddies who served together. He liked the idea I had come up with in an earlier draft of the spirits who hang out at the Wall being Pathfinders for their comrades who come later, as an elite group in Nam had been Pathfinders in a different sense, so that concept remained.

Because I am a female vet and I was writing it, I felt like there needed to be strong feminine component in it, too, and the nurse was a natural under the circumstances. Finally, as I turned Rick's ideas and my own over and over in my mind, I realized that this was a love story, and the MIA was the soulmate of the nurse, whose name was on the Wall. One symptom of Post Traumatic Stress Disorder is a failure in the ability to bond and have a lasting relationship—especially with the opposite sex. Woody Johanson is obviously having that kind of problem with his marriage. My own romantic fantasy about those of us vets who do not find someone to share our lives with is that for us, our personal Mr. or Ms. Right died in country before we met them. It's nice to think everything could still work out in the afterlife.

THE PILOTS

L. E. Modesitt, Jr.

*T*HE SOBAK REVOLT WAS *a long time ago, but I remember my part in it as though it were yesterday. I don't talk about it, Brother Estafen. At least, until now I didn't, and I won't now. It won't change anything. What happened after the second war with the Sobaks is something else. You're young for recalling that, for it was little more than ten years after the Revolt. My younger brother Waltar . . . he was a pilot, too, almost as good as I'd been . . . but Vergenya would never have recognized what he did . . . except for the spirits of the Wall . . . except I never told anyone, not even Sereh . . . it's better that way, sometimes, when you really can't explain . . .*

※ ※ ※

The summer sun came up like always—above the trees on the east side of the river, rising over the swamps and ruined temples of the ancients, all of them wreathed in the steamy mist that meant the day would be one of those where the sun scorched everything, even subduing the river into a sullen flat expanse of warm water by mid-afternoon.

Two gunboats were docked at the end of the Navy pier, the canvas on the schooners' masts tied down tight. A smallish Nenglan square-rigger hogged the other pier, and figures began to move across the exposed decks soon after the six bells sounded from the cathedral.

I didn't want to go where I had to, but there was no help for it, and I needed to go before the ferry or the packet docked, and I might be called to work, such as it was then.

Waltar had had three rooms to the west, before the War, but Sereh was living in a room smaller than a closet in her sister's cot. Sereh might have been working in the kitchen, but by the time I climbed the low hill and the steps, she was waiting for me, standing in the hot morning on the narrow porch. Holding Syreena in her left arm, Sereh thrust the gray sheet of paper at me with her right. Her eyes were red and puffy.

I couldn't reach it without taking a step forward. In my haste, I was less than careful, and the crutch slipped on the gravel of the path. I staggered but caught myself, then took the broadsheet from her. It had been folded in thirds and held the stamp of the Council on the outside, along with the bold cursive that bore Sereh's name.

The words blurred as I read them.

". . . the pilot Waltar Emmson was not of the Vergen Navy, and his death did not result from enemy fire or attack. Regrettable as it may be, his heirs may not receive death annuities but only the lump sum payment already received for death by accident . . ."

I didn't need to read more, but I finished the short document.

"Those cables snapped because they were weakened by Sobak cannon . . . you told me that," Sereh said. "I told him not to go. I told him we didn't need the risk bonus." She took a deep breath, looking at me.

A man has to do what he believes he should, or before long he has nothing to believe in. I was like that, and Waltar had been that way, too, but I couldn't tell Sereh that, not then, not with Syreena in her arms and another on the way. Not then. "I didn't tell him to go."

She just looked at me with those deep, red-rimmed eyes. "They gave us nothing, except a few duhlars. At least they gave you a position, Arlen."

Position? They had—greeter at the Strangers' House opposite the ferry, and a duhlar a week from the Council. Then, I had no wife. Few wanted to wed a man with but one eye and one good leg, and I'd certainly not wanted to be a burden on anyone.

"Aye, and it's better than begging or working in the almshouse."

"You're alive, Arlen. Waltar isn't." Her words were sharp, but I understood.

"I know. He was a good man, and he was my brother."

"Can't you do something? Can't you make them understand?"

Make them understand what? "We petitioned the Council, Sereh."

"And the Council said no." Her eyes flashed, and even in her anger, I could see why Waltar had asked for her hand. "Can't you do something?"

"I'm not a counselor, and I'm not fancy with my words, Sereh. I was a pilot."

"I'm not mad at you, Arlen. You've stood by me, as well as you can, and . . ." She shook her head.

In time, I had no more words, and I left Sereh, wordless, for what could I say? I made my way back down toward the Strangers' House.

There, under the overhang of the front porch, for a time, I leaned on the crutch and looked out across the river toward the ruins I knew were on the east shore and could not see through the trees and the mist, though the mist would be gone in the heat of the day when everything simmered under the summer sun.

"Arlen . . ." The voice was that of Ryssah.

I didn't turn.

"I heard."

"So has all of Zandra," I replied, still without looking at her. "So have the Brothers and the Council. A few duhlars, a fancy gilt paper, and they think they've done right by Waltar. Half that fleet would have gone down under the Sobak batteries if it hadn't been for him."

"Times are hard now, Arlen."

"Times have always been hard."

"She's young. She can wed again."

"She'll have to, won't she?" My voice was hard. "Or go to the streets or the cribs and lie with strangers. Unless she'll settle for a man with one eye and a single room."

Ryssah didn't answer for a time. When she finally spoke, her voice was both soft and tired. "Arlen . . . I can handle the greeting today. You wouldn't do it well."

I didn't protest. Instead, I hurried, as well as I could, down to the ferry pier. There I waited. Because I'd been a pilot, Tomas always let me ride as a courtesy.

The ferry runs north of Zandra and docks at Gorgton. From there, I made my way off and down the pier and along the stone road that flanks the east side of the river. Storm clouds were rising into the midday of summer before I reached the flats that bordered the swamps—and the ruined temples where the ancients practiced their necromancy.

The black wall has been there, half-rising out of the earth, for longer than any can remember. It sits to the north and east of the ancient temple of the seated god. The seated god has long been dead, for never do the ravens flock to the time-smoothed white stone, and the pigeons despoil the almost tottering columns. Still, the tree-shaded steps would be a pleasant place from which one could watch the schooners coming up the river to port at Zandra. A pleasant place, were it not for the warnings of the Brothers about the evil buried there. A pleasant place, if one did not have to look westward across the river at the cathedral—and the mass of stone that was the Council Seat.

I hadn't come through the heat and steam for the view. I'd come, as I had years before, because it was said that sometimes the black wall offered answers. It hadn't the last time, when I'd first been able to hobble there on a crutch, but, again, there was nowhere else to turn, and I owed Waltar—and Sereh—that much.

The ancients invested that stretch of polished black stone—with its endless runes cut so precisely into the surface—they invested it with the manna of sadness. The power is so great that even after all the centuries, a man who believes not in ghosts, nor in the necromancy about which the Brothers prate, nor in that which he cannot see nor feel . . . that man—me—hoped for answers that black stone had never given him.

I'd thought that the ancient stretch of polished stone—or the manna within it—might offer some answers. Then, I thought that once before but had gotten none.

Still . . . I looked at the black stone, and kept looking from one end of the long line of blackness to the other. In the afternoon stillness, not even a pigeon fluttered, so alone was I.

The wall said nothing, offered nothing. Walls don't, even ancient black walls raised for necromancy on the power of the dead.

"Why?" I poured all the anguish into the cry and the plea, feeling foolish as I did.

Nothing happened.

I eased myself forward, and my fingers brushed the time-worn runes, each set gathered in groups, usually of three or four, and cut precisely into the stone so that each group was level with the group flanking it, seemingly for as far as the black stone stretched before it finally sank into the mossy ground.

"Why?" I asked again.

"The Wall doesn't offer explanations," came a voice. "It never does."

I knew I was alone. No one could have crept up on me. But I turned.

A man stood there, with silver hair cut shorter than even a recruit's. His clean-shaven face was smooth, but he wasn't young. He was no ghost. Above the lines in his face, I could see the dampness of sweat on his forehead. He wore a black waistcoat with a cotton-linen shirt beneath—but such a linen shirt!—so tightly woven that I could not even see any trace of an individual thread, and with fine black stripes against a brilliant white. His trousers were coal black, as were the shimmering boots he wore. For a moment, I just stared.

He blinked, as if looking into a bright sun, though we stood in the shade of the green oaks that towered to the east. Finally, he spoke again, thoughtfully. "We have to find the explanations. You shouldn't be here . . . or I shouldn't."

"Why are you here?" I finally asked.

"The same reason as you, I'd guess. Still seeking reasons, explanations, after all these years."

"Are you a Brother of some sort?"

"I'm just a pilot."

He didn't look like any pilot I'd ever seen but more like a dandy. His eyes narrowed as he looked at me.

"What are the runes for?" I asked quickly.

"Runes?"

I pointed to those etched into the stone before me.

"Each one is someone who died in the war." He laughed bitterly. "Except they're not all there."

For the first time, he looked beyond me, taking in the tall oaks and then the part of the temple of the seated god that was visible through the scrub and swamp grass. He shook his head. "I'll bet you don't even know why the Wall is here."

"No," I admitted. "The Brothers claim it holds evil manna of the ancients, worse than that of the seated god. They say that it was raised in evil by necromancers."

His eyes remained on the white stones of the temple of the seated god. "Poor Abe. No one knows you, either." His lips curled. "Vanity of vanities . . ." He shook his head again and turned those deep eyes toward me, but I don't think he was looking at me but somewhere else. When he spoke, his words were low, as if only for himself, but my ears have always been sharp. "You've really gone round the bend this time, Pete, and without a single beer."

"What war?" I asked. "How did it get all the manna?"

For a long time, he looked at me, standing in the shadows.

I looked back, and when I squinted, it was almost as though I could see through him, see the black stone and mossy ground and scrub bushes behind him.

"The Vietnam War. The one that killed fifty-five thousand men . . . and some women . . . and lots of others."

The name meant nothing to me, and I couldn't believe he'd said fifty-five thousand. That was as many people as lived within Zandra and all the towns within three days or more of travel. "You were a pilot?"

"Search and rescue. Flew H2s, mostly. That was thirty years ago, but you never quite forget. And you never forget the ones who didn't make it. Or the ones who aren't on the Wall . . . the ones who died testing the birds, or in the wrong places, or outside the magic lines drawn by the bureaucrats."

I heard the words, but not all of them made sense, but perhaps the Brothers were right about the black stone. The spirit pilot—if that was what he happened to be—was talking about magic lines and pilots who flew strange birds, rather than vessels upon the sea.

"Like Waltar," I murmured.

He waited for me to continue, an expression between amusement and disbelief on his clean-shaven face. His eyes held something I didn't want to see.

So I talked, since no one else except Sereh would listen, or care. "He was a pilot on the *Wariner*. He was the lead pilot on the Savnah expedition because he knew the channels, but he wasn't Navy. The Council promised that they'd take care of his family if anything happened during the attack. The Sobaks were waiting, and they'd even mined the side channels. Waltar was better, though, and got the *Wariner* and most of the invasion fleet back to sea, even through the bombardment from the shore batteries and a running attack from fast gunboats. Once they were clear, they hit heavy seas. They didn't know that the Sobak batteries had almost cut the rudder cables. In the storm, one snapped. It broke through the housings and snapped Waltar's neck." I shrugged.

"Your Council said that it didn't happen during the attack," suggested the spirit pilot in the waistcoat, a bemused expression on his face, as if he'd heard the story already.

"How did you know?" I demanded.

"Because nothing changes." He gestured toward the black stone. "They say that all those who died are here, but they're not." He laughed sardonically. "They never are. There are always those who sacrificed, who didn't fit the definitions, who didn't die with the right ceremonies, or who sacrificed themselves for the wrong reason in the wrong season. . . . That was true when they built the Wall, and apparently it was true for your brother."

"Waltar didn't sacrifice himself. It wasn't like that."

"We all make sacrifices, if we're really alive."

Then, as suddenly as he had come, he vanished.

I shivered.

Even hurrying, a man with a crutch has trouble going long distances, and I barely made the twilight ferry back from Gorgton to Zandra—back to ready myself to appear before the Council with the words of the spirit pilot that I held within my heart and soul . . . and back to Sereh.

☒ ☒ ☒

The ancients were powerful . . . and that we no longer have such power, for such I am supposed to be grateful, according to Brother Diere.

Yet . . . on many twilights, I have seen the figure of that silver-haired ancient, and not just near the wall but on my own portico, the portico Sereh and I built here when we left Zandra. Far older than I was then, older than I am now even, and yet his face was that of a man in his prime. But his eyes . . . and his words . . .

"They're not all there, you know. They never are. There are always those who sacrificed, who didn't fit the definitions, who didn't die with the right ceremonies, or who sacrificed themselves for the wrong reason in the wrong season. . . . We all make sacrifices, if we're really alive."

Perhaps the only thing I ever learned, truly learned, was from a spirit, and the only answer I ever got was because I didn't ask for myself.

You won't be telling anyone, now, Brother Estafen. Who would believe you? They didn't believe me. The Ecclesiarches wouldn't believe that the old idols have power, or that the ancients held the skies . . . or that the runes on the wall are names, names of more dead men than all those who live in Zandra, and that even the magics of the old ones couldn't hold all those who died in a war so long ago that we don't even know what it was about—except so many died and created such sadness that their spirits and those who mourn them still cross the times between us.

———

Afterword: I wasn't one of the heroes. While I flew SAR (Search and Rescue) and off carriers during the 1967-69 period, and while I had two very abbreviated tours in Southeast Asia, so far as I know, no one even fired a shot at me. The war still had its effect, and it was more than twenty years after I left the Navy in 1970 before I went to see the Wall. What upset me the most then, and still does, wasn't the names on the Wall, though that sadness permeated me, as I suspect it does all veterans. What upset me the most was the names that weren't on the Wall, the names of those who died supporting the war in the places that didn't qualify them for inclusion on the Wall for one reason or another. Like those who died because there weren't enough funds to re-engineer the H-2 helicopters correctly, or those who died in ORIs (Operational Readiness Inspections) getting ready to go to Vietnam, or . . . the list is long, and those who were there will know what I mean. For those who weren't, this story was about the only way I could think to put it.

WALLGATE

Laura Resnick

THE DAY THAT CHANGED my life forever was the day that I, Barclay Biddlegate-Kermode, was called upon to serve my country in its hour of need. That was the day that fate snatched me from the jaws of bureaucratic obscurity, only to thrust me into the voracious maw of international scandal and interdimensional intrigue.

It was late on a Tuesday afternoon in early January when I got the phone call from destiny. The shrill ringing startled me out of the somnolent state which I only later recognized as incipient hypothermia; my office was in the basement of an old and neglected building several blocks away from the White House, and the current mean temperature at my desk would have been perfect for chilling vodka. I flexed my cold-stiffened fingers a few times, then reached for the phone.

"B-B-Barclay B-B-Biddlegate-Kermode," I said, my teeth chattering a little. "Special Sub-Deputy Assistant to the Under-Deputy Counsel to the—"

"Please hold for Caden Jarvis," a woman coolly instructed me.

My heart, functioning in a state of near-hibernation, suddenly leapt with hot excitement and began pounding hard. Caden "Mad Dog" Jarvis was the President's most trusted political advisor, with a suite of offices right next to the Commander in Chief himself. Jarvis had never even phoned this department before, let alone me personally!

He came on the line a moment later, his thick-as-molasses down-home accent sounding just as improbable as it always did on TV. "Mr. Biddlegate-Commode, this is—"

"Kermode," I corrected, my breath frosting the receiver.

"Whatever. Son, I won't beat around the huckleberry bush, we are facing a national crisis of monumental importance, if you'll pardon the pun —"

"Did you make a pun, sir?"

"Don't interrupt."

"Sorry, sir."

"And it has come to my attention that you are the right man to solve our problems."

I rose from my chair. "*Me*, sir?" My circulation-deprived legs wobbled, and I sat back down rather suddenly.

"Berkley, are you—"

"Barclay, sir."

"Don't interrupt. Are you ready to serve your country in her hour of need?"

"Am I ready?" I cried. "Sir, I've dreamed of this moment my whole life! This is the moment I've studied and prepared and waited and prayed for! I believe in the unique supremacy of the Constitution as an enduring—"

"Good, good."

"And I'm so thrilled that you've singled me out in this way!'

"Yes, well—"

"I promise you, sir, I will not let you down! You can count on me! I will—"

"Stop prattling, son," Caden Jarvis said, "and get your ass out to the street."

"The street?"

"There'll be a special car waiting for you right outside the building in five minutes."

"Where am I going, sir? The White House? FBI headquarters? The Capitol?"

"The Mall."

"The Mall?" I shivered. "But, sir, if you'll pardon me for saying so, it's sixteen degrees Fahrenheit out there today, with winds gusting from the northwest at up to twenty miles per—"

"Don't be a pansy-ass, boy."

"Um, no, sir."

"You gonna let a little frostbite stand between you and your country's national security?"

National security? I frowned. "What's on the Mall, sir?"

"You'll see, son," he said ominously. "You'll see."

"And after I've, um, seen?"

"You'll get your ass over to the Oval Office to make a preliminary report."

The Oval Office!

"Yes, sir!"

⊠ ⊠ ⊠

The National Mall, that exceptional stretch of monuments, museums, and open greenery in the heart of our great nation's capital, was a deserted tundra today. Snow fell intermittently out of a dull gray sky. My driver, a silent and unsmiling black man roughly the size of the Lincoln Memorial, pulled to a stop at the corner of Constitution Avenue and Bacon Drive.

"Here?" I asked.

Arturo (according to his nametag) met my gaze in his rearview mirror. The slight dipping of his chin was evidently an affirmative nod. I pulled on my wool cap and got out of the limo. The ruthless cold slapped me in the face, and the wind whistled around me as eerily as if I were lost in the pages of a gothic novel.

I looked around. Apart from being cold and deserted, everything looked normal on the Mall. I tapped on Arturo's window. He rolled it down a crack and gazed at me with unblinking eyes.

"What am I supposed to do?" I asked him.

"The boss said: Look at the Wall."

"Look at the Wall," I repeated, puzzled. I gazed over my shoulder at the somber, looming, black granite monument honoring the missing and the dead of the Vietnam War. I turned back to Arturo. "I don't underst—" But he had already rolled up the window and was now engrossed in reading *The Economist*.

I pulled up my collar against the vicious wind and trudged through the ankle-deep snow to the Wall.

The dull light and falling snow made for poor visibility. So I was within a few yards of the Wall before I saw what had made Jarvis use the words "national crisis of monumental importance." Some pun.

"My God," I murmured, staring at the Wall in shocked bewilderment. "How is this possible?"

⁑ ⁑ ⁑

"Mr. President," I said, standing before him in the Oval Office less than an hour later, "I regret to inform you that someone has removed all of the names from the Vietnam Memorial Wall."

He was taller than he looked on TV, and well-groomed, with distinguished gray sideburns and black hair. Excellent dental work, a fine tailor, and a well-practiced handshake. He glanced briefly at Caden Jarvis, then said, "Tell me, Mr. Biddlegate-Commode—"

"Kermode."

"Tell me, Kermode—"

"No, sir, it's Biddlegate-Kermode."

Caden advised the President, "Call him Berkley."

"Barclay," I corrected.

"Son," said the President, "are you telling me the Vietnam Wall has been defaced?"

"Not exactly, sir. There's no evidence of sanding, scratching, chiseling, gouging, or anything of that nature. The names are simply . . . *gone*. All of them!" I spread my hands in helpless confusion. "More than fifty-eight thousand names were inscribed on the Wall, and not a single one of them is left, nor any other writing or inscriptions which were there."

The President raised his brows. "So you're saying . . ."

"You've got about one hundred fifty meters of beautifully polished, smooth-as-glass, absolutely blank, black granite out on the Mall now, Mr. President."

"Incredible."

"That would be an understatement, sir."

"How do you propose to investigate this?" Jarvis asked me.

"Me, sir?" My mouth worked stupidly for a moment. "Sir, with all due respect, I really don't think I'm the right person to lead this investigation."

"Hell, you're a lawyer, ain't you, son?" Jarvis said.

"Yes, sir. Graduated second in my class from Harvard."

"Second? Well, don't feel too bad about that." Jarvis slapped me on the back. "After all, you've been doing a fine job ever since you came to work for this administration."

"Um. Thank you, sir. I didn't think anyone noticed."

"Now it's time to dig in and prove what you're made of, son."

"But, sir, don't you think this is a job for, oh, the FBI? Or the—"

"Good God, no!" said the President. "We've got to keep this quiet. Surely you can see that?"

"Um . . ."

"Just think of the panic that will spread when word of this gets out! Think of the chaos!"

"Just think," said Jarvis, "of the *polls*."

"So I'm supposed to . . . conduct a secret investigation?"

"Exactly! I knew you were a fast study!"

"But—"

"If you can solve this thing before the weather improves, the world might never even find out it happened."

"But—"

"So get your ass back out there to that Wall and figure out where the hell all those names went!"

"How am I—"

"I'm afraid I have to cut this meeting short," said the President, glancing at his watch. "I've got to get ready for a state dinner with the Hollywood film community. I wish I could cancel, considering the current top-secret crisis, but this dinner is too crucial an event. I'm sure you understand."

"Well, I—"

"Good lad. Jarvis?"

"If you need any help," Jarvis said, hustling me toward the door, "just give me a call."

"But, sir," I said as he was shoving me out into the hall, "I don't have your phone num—" The door shut in my face. "—ber."

Out there in the hallway, two Secret Service agents looked at me as if I were the embodiment of evil.

"Spread 'em," one of them said.

"What?" I protested, "You already searched me!" And I really, really didn't want these guys searching my groin twice in one day. I was already pretty sure I'd have disturbingly ambivalent nightmares about it tonight.

"Standard procedure. Spread 'em."

"Standard procedure? But that's absurd! You searched me *before* I went into the Oval Office. You don't need to search me again now that I'm *leaving* it."

"Spread 'em!"

"But I'm coming *out* of the Oval Office. I'm going *away* from the President's presence. I can't possibly be a danger to—"

They simultaneously pulled out their guns and pointed them straight at me. *"Spread 'em!"*

"But, of course," I said, turning my face to the wall and assuming the position, "I naturally want to cooperate with standard procedure."

When they were done with a process I'd rather not describe, I retrieved my coat, hat, and gloves, then went outside and got into the limo, where I interrupted Arturo's perusal of the *Atlantic Monthly.* "Take me back to the Wall," I instructed him. "I've got to look for evidence."

When we returned to the Mall, however, the Vietnam Wall was gone.

                     ▧ ▧ ▧

"You were supposed to keep this secret!" the President raged at me during a top-level emergency conference at the White House three days later.

Caden Jarvis shook his head sadly. "You've let us down, son."

"CNN is all over this thing now!" the President said.

"There are already pages of articles about the Wall and its disappearance on MSNBC.com," Jarvis added.

The Attorney General said, "Barbara Walters has already set up half a dozen teary-eyed interviews with Hollywood stars who've appeared in movies about Vietnam who are going to talk about what a terrible thing it is that the government has let this happen."

Jarvis winced. "That'll kill us in the polls."

The Joint Chiefs of Staff were present, too, as was the Secretary of Defense. "We'll bomb them from the air! We'll bomb them from the sea! We will reclaim that Wall if it's the last thing we do!"

Jarvis looked at the Secretary. "Reclaim it from *who*, Seymour?"

"That's what your brilliant expert here is supposed to figure out!" the Secretary snapped, gesturing dismissively to me.

"Now, now. The boy's only been on the job for seventy-two hours, Seymour," Jarvis admonished. "Give him a chance."

"Yes," replied the Secretary, "and on his very first day, he managed to lose the whole goddamn Wall! By this time next week, the entire Mall could be gone! I *demand*—"

"If I may, gentlemen?" I said, a little stung by the criticism. After all, I hadn't leaked any of this to the press, nor had I actually lost the Wall. I just happened to be the first one to notice it was missing. All of it.

"What?" snapped the President.

"Well, sir, I've discovered an interesting corollary."

"We will bomb that corollary back into the Stone Age!" shouted one of the Joint Chiefs.

Jarvis sighed. "What's your corollary, son?"

"The Berlin Wall is missing," I announced.

The Attorney General frowned. "The Berlin Wall has been missing for years. I mean . . . it's been a heap of rubble for years."

"True, sir. But several days ago, the heap of rubble which was once the Berlin Wall . . . disappeared. Completely. *All* of it."

"Disappeared?"

"Just like the Vietnam Wall?"

I nodded. "So," I continued, "with the assistance of the FBI, whom the Secretary of Defense authorized to help me after I discovered the Vietnam Wall was missing—"

"*Discovered*, he says," the Secretary grumbled with a noticeable sneer.

"I've run a worldwide search on similar events."

"And?"

"Hadrian's Wall has been missing from Great Britain for weeks."

"We will pledge air support to Hadrian!" vowed one of the Joint Chiefs.

"Why haven't we heard about this before?" the President asked.

"The British are trying to keep it quiet," I said. "Apparently, it's causing a tremendous breakdown in domestic relations. The English claim the Scots took it, the Scots claim the English took it, and so on."

"Hmmm. In-ter-est-ing," said the Secretary of State, who had been silent until now.

The Attorney General asked, "Is anything disappearing besides walls?"

"No, sir."

The President was frowning at me. "Your analysis, Commode?"

"That's Biddlegate-Kermode, sir."

"Whatever."

"Clearly someone with extraordinary technology is, er, collecting walls for some reason, sir."

"Terrorists?" the President asked.

"It seems unlikely," I replied. "No one has died or been hurt. No industry or military capability has been affected. In fact, due to the time of year, not even tourism is hurt by this."

One of the Joint Chiefs said, "It's the Russians! This is their revenge for the collapse of the Iron Curtain!"

We all just looked silently at him.

After a moment, he shrugged. "Just putting forward a theory."

"What puzzles me," I said, "is the obvious omission."

They all looked blank.

"You know," I prodded. "The biggest wall ever built, the wall which is visible even from outer space."

They all continued to look blank.

"The Great Wall of China!" I said. "It's still there. Right where it's supposed to be. I checked."

"Ah-hah!" cried one of the Joint Chiefs. "It's those Godless Communists!"

"Unlikely, sir," I said. "When I told the Chinese foreign minister about Hadrian's Wall, the Chinese government panicked. They're mobilizing one hundred thousand troops to guard the Great Wall. They seem to be afraid it'll be next."

"It sounds like we should petition the UN to form an international committee to look into this," said the President slowly.

"The UN? It'll take them years just to definitively determine that the walls are missing," protested the Attorney General.

"I'm with the boss on this one," said Jarvis.

"You're always with him, Mad Dog," said the Secretary of Defense with open disdain.

"Perhaps we could negotiate a return of the Wall," said the Secretary of State.

Jarvis sighed. "Negotiate with *who*, Jessica?"

"Approaching the UN may be the globalist solution," said the Attorney General, "but let's keep in mind that the theft of the Wall has occurred on American soil and is an American problem."

"For once, I agree with you," said the Secretary of Defense. "The theft of some moldy heap of Roman ruins that used to divide Scotland and England is a British problem, and the Berlin Wall stopped being our problem years ago." He thumped his fist on the conference table. "But this is an American war memorial honoring those who gave their lives in service to this country! We've got to get it back!"

"I agree, sir," I said.

"Do you have anything resembling, oh, a *plan*?" the Secretary asked me.

"I'm working on it," I assured him. "I think I may be onto a way to find the Wall."

Jarvis and the President exchanged a look. Something about it made me uneasy.

"Gentlemen," said the President, "I've listened to your views and have now made my decision. The military will close all access to the site where the Wall stood. In view of the international nature of this phenomenon, I will instruct our Ambassador to the United Nations to place the matter before the General Assembly first thing Monday morning."

"Now wait a minute!"

"This is a terrible decision!"

"Even Commode here could do a better job than that!"

"Sir," I protested, "you entrusted this job to me only three days ago. Won't you at least give me—"

"I'm sorry, Commode, that's my final decision. Thank you for a job well done, but it's time you returned to your normal duties . . . whatever they are." He glanced at his watch. "Now if you'll all excuse me, I've got to attend a star-studded concert being given in my honor. I wish I could cancel it, given the nature of the current crisis, but it's too crucial an event for that. I'm sure you understand."

▧ ▧ ▧

At midnight that night, I talked my way past the soldiers guarding the site where the Wall had previously stood. They thought I was still in charge of the investigation and so let me and my companion wander around the cold, empty, dark landscape by ourselves.

My companion, Morwenna Blumenthal, was the crux of the plan which the President's decision had nipped in the bud. I didn't understand why he and Jarvis had lost faith in me so quickly, but I intended to restore it by resolving this crisis before Monday morning, when they would turn things over to the UN. Now that I had been given a chance to make a difference in the world, I couldn't bear the thought of going back to my obscure basement office to produce piles of obscure legal paperwork that no one ever used for any truly productive purpose.

So I was going to continue this investigation despite the President's orders.

"Ohhhh, ohhhh, ohhhh," Morwenna Blumenthal moaned, swaying in the cruel January wind.

"Are you getting something?" I asked.

"Yes," she replied through clenched teeth. "Pneumonia."

"I meant—"

"I know what you meant." She inhaled deeply, then made a loud gurgling sound. "Oh, yes! The vibrations are very strong here."

Morwenna was a psychic who, upon learning of the crisis, had e-mailed me that morning (right after CNN aired nearly every single detail about my entire life, including contact information) to suggest a theory which, while bizarre and fantastic, nonetheless seemed to me the only reasonable theory which I'd heard so far: The Vietnam Wall, like the other missing walls, was still here but had been encompassed by another dimension and therefore gave every semblance of being completely gone.

Not even Morwenna Blumenthal, however, had a theory for why the names had been removed from the wall before it had been transported out of our dimension.

"Can you contact someone in the other dimension?" I asked Morwenna.

"Yes, but I need your coat."

"Why do you need my coat?" I demanded.

"Because I have to sit on the ground, and it's *freezing*."

"And what am I supposed to do while you're sitting on my coat?"

"Grin and bear it."

"I'm really starting to hate my life." I unsnapped, unzipped, and shrugged out of my coat, then gave it to Morwenna. By the time she sat down on it and starting chanting, my teeth were already chattering. I started jumping around to keep my blood from coagulating in my veins while Morwenna kept chanting.

After a period of time roughly equivalent to the director's cut of *Titanic*, Morwenna shrieked, "Someone is here! Someone is here!"

I stopped leaping around long enough to ask, "*Who's* here?"

Morwenna slumped over like a rag doll and didn't respond.

"Morwenna?"

"Well, no, actually. I go by the name of Smith," said a cultivated male voice coming from Morwenna's slumped and motionless body.

"Yagh!" I leapt back, suddenly realizing I hadn't *really* expected this to work.

"It doesn't *have* to be Smith," said the voice, "if it bothers you that much. If there's a name which you'd prefer—"

"No! Er, no. . . . Thank you. Smith is fine." I started shivering as I stared at Morwenna's slumped body.

"Is there a particular reason you summoned me on such a ghastly night?"

"I, uh . . ." I started trying to stamp some feeling into my feet. "Who are you?"

"I'm Smith. I thought we'd covered that."

"Right. Smith." I searched my mind and could only think of one thing to say. "Where's our Wall?"

"It's in my dimension now, of course," Smith said.

"What do you mean, 'of course'?" I demanded in outrage.

"Look, you people were *paid* fair and square for the thing, so don't start making trouble now."

"Paid?" I was shivering violently, so I started jumping around again to warm up my muscles. "Are you telling me you *paid* for the Wall?"

"Well, of course. What do you take me for, a thief?" Smith sounded insulted. "Oh, wait a brief-span-of-relativistic-time. You're not the individual I dealt with before, are you?"

"No, I'm not," I confirmed as I leapt around. "So you're saying someone in this dimension *sold* you the Vietnam Wall?"

"Of course! I'd have brought the contract with me if I'd known there were going to be questions asked now."

"What do you want with the Wall?"

"I'm a wall dealer, of course."

"A what?"

"A wall dealer. You know. I deal in walls."

"I've never heard of such a thing!"

"Well, every dimension's different, you know. Here you've got art dealers, arms dealers, antiques dealers, drug dealers. . . . Back home, walls are all the rage."

"Why don't they just build their own instead of stealing ours?"

"Buy! I do not steal! I *buy* walls. I am a licensed interdimensional wall dealer."

"Why *walls*, for God's sake?"

"Oh, once people found out about them . . . well, you know how it goes. Suddenly *everyone* wanted one. Understandable, really. Walls separate competing wizards, warring clans, incompatible magical elements, past and present, present and future. Really, they're quite amazing! I'm very impressed by your technology. You people have so many walls! Business is booming, and I'm making a fortune back home. I'm even saving up for a little wall of my own."

"This is incredible."

"Oh, not really. You should travel more."

"Between dimensions?" I asked incredulously.

"Yes. I was just like you, back when I was green. The first time I met an interdimensional poodle dealer, I was almost speechless with surprise."

"Interdimensional poodle—no, I don't even want to know about this."

"Do you always jump around like that? It must be exhausting."

"I'm freezing to death."

"Perhaps it's time to finish our chat, then? I've got a huge amount of work to do. Interdimensional wall-dealing is profitable, but you wouldn't believe the paperwork involved."

"Oh, no you don't. We're not nearly done here. For one thing, are you aware that every wall you've 'bought' is actually stolen property?"

"Impossible! I've got contracts! I've got transport permits! I've done everything legally!"

"Oh, yeah, buddy? Then tell me who the hell 'sold' you Hadrian's Wall."

"An organization in Belfast."

"Belfast? Northern Ireland?" I nearly fell over with surprise. "Oh, my God! Of course!"

"Oh, so *now* you believe me?"

"The English and the Scots are at each other's throats since the disappearance of Hadrian's Wall," I said excitedly, starting to understand.

"Oh, dear. Are you sure?"

"And who would want to sow domestic chaos in Britain?"

"Now you're losing me."

"Extremists in Northern Ireland!"

"If you say so."

"Who sold you the Berlin Wall?"

"That heap of rubble! I had to unload it for a pittance."

"Who sold it to you?"

"He was Russian. They seem to be selling everything, have you noticed? Tried to foist some nuclear warheads on me—but good grief, where could I possibly sell such useless detritus?"

My head was spinning by now. "And who sold you the Vietnam Wall?"

"Quite a colorful gentleman. Very quaint accent. Told me to call him Mad Dog."

"Oh, no."

⊞ ⊞ ⊞

Once I explained, while hopping up and down the whole time and hoping I wouldn't lose my extremities to frostbite, that the Vietnam Wall was more than just a wall, Smith was very cooperative. Even in his dimension, it turned out, they built monuments to honor warriors who died in battle. So once Smith understood what our Wall really was, he agreed to give it back in exchange for my promise to return his payment in full.

Smith had paid the President in gold. Apparently they manufacture the stuff in his dimension the way we make French fries over here.

By dawn, Morwenna had recovered from hypothermia, the Vietnam Wall had reappeared, and the Attorney General had advised the President that a sudden, unexplained resignation would be better than a trial for high treason—which, if he *didn't* immediately resign, was the very least that would happen to him for selling the Vietnam Veterans Memorial in order to finance his re-election campaign. (Apparently those polls that Jarvis was always worrying about showed that the President would have trouble beating even a poodle in the next election.) ·

Jarvis had been in on the plot, of course, and had acted as the President's bagman. And that's why Jarvis chose me, an obscure functionary in the Executive Branch bureaucracy, to lead the investigation. Jarvis and the President knew there would have to *be* an investigation, and they wanted to make sure that it would fail spectacularly and that there would be someone to blame when that happened. They hadn't counted on me coming so close to realizing the truth within just a few days, which was why they'd subsequently tried to kick me *off* the case.

The two of them left the White House together, under far less disgrace than they actually deserved. The true explanation just seemed too outlandish even for the credulous media, so I helped the Cabinet concoct a cover story about light refraction making it *appear* as if the Wall had disappeared for several days. (The British and the Germans would have to come up with their own explanations for *their* missing walls.)

❂ ❂ ❂

"Got my gold back, thanks," Smith said from the depths of Morwenna's slumped body a few nights later at the Wall. "How have things worked out at your end?"

"Very well. Jarvis and the President are going on an interminable goodwill tour of Siberia. Morwenna will use the reward money from the Defense Department to open a psychic studies center someplace where they never have winter. And the Attorney General has promoted me to a prominent position in the Justice Department with paid holidays and an annual six-figure salary."

"I don't know what most of that means, but it sounds as if I should congratulate you."

"Thanks." After a brief, shivering pause, I said, "I'm curious about something, Smith. Why haven't you ever acquired the mother of all walls, the Great Wall of China?"

"Profit-and-loss margin," Smith said. "Have you ever seen that thing? It's *HUGE*. The cost of moving it would eliminate any profit I could make on the deal."

"Ah."

"So . . . I take it we're done here?"

"No, there's one more thing, Smith."

"If you need an interdimensional poodle, I can't help."

"I don't need a poodle, I need the names."

"The names?"

"The names that were on this wall when the President first started bargaining with you to sell a war memorial that he didn't even own. The names of more than fifty-eight thousand Americans who gave their lives in Vietnam. This Wall is nothing but a big hunk of granite if their names aren't on it."

"The names!" Morwenna's slumped body quivered briefly, and I had the impression that Smith was trying to slap his own forehead. "Of course!"

"Where are they? Why were they removed?"

"I *had* to remove them. Interdimensional law. You can't transport magical symbols between dimensional planes. Too dangerous."

"They're not magical symbols," I said, puzzled.

"But you just *said* those names are what make your Wall a memorial to fallen warriors instead of just a big hunk of shiny black rock."

"Oh. Yes. I see your point." I smiled.

"I run a strictly legal and well-respected operation, after all."

"Of course."

"Well, all right, I admit, I did perhaps bend a few interdimensional trans-substantiation laws when I purchased the Iron Curtain—"

"The Iron Curtain? But that was a *figurative* curtain."

"Not when it reached *my* dimension, dear boy."

"Wow." I looked at the Wall again. "So where are the names? I have to get them back."

"I've got them in storage. I'll get them back to you before dawn tomorrow—I'm referring to *this* space-time continuum, of course."

"Of course." I frowned. "If you couldn't transport them across dimensions, where are they in storage?"

"Poughkeepsie."

"You're kidding."

"There's a very reasonably priced ethereal storage facility there. I can give you the name, if you're ever in need of such services."

"Thanks, Smith, but if you'll just get the names back by dawn, that's all I need."

"Count on it."

As CNN reported the next day, the peculiar panic over the Vietnam Wall's "disappearance" was eliminated when it was re-opened to the public, who found it right where it always was, with the names of the honored dead glowing in the winter sunlight.

Afterword: As soon as I was asked to write a fantasy story about the Vietnam Wall, the thought instantly came to me that the Wall would disappear. I was taken with the notion of something that big simply vanishing into thin air. This seemed to me the basis of a comedy, rather than a drama. I wanted to make sure that the true purpose of the Wall—to honor those who gave their lives in service to their country—wouldn't be obscured by humor; but I also hope that you've smiled (maybe even laughed) while reading it.

WHAT'S IN A NAME

Michael P. Belfiore

Zack walked along listlessly with the crowd of tourists, the sweaty masses, the elderly, the people lugging their cameras, and the ghosty-eyed vets. He hated coming here, and yet he was compelled to, some-how, maybe by the culmination of all the years of being dragged here by his mother. "Your father would have wanted you to," was all she would say in answer to his question, "Why?"

Why? Why this black slab of granite rising from a gash in the ground, the midsummer sun blazing on it, and himself reflected in it along with all the others, the trees, and the lawn behind them. He hated this reflective surface. Hated it because it told him nothing. Nothing of all those thousands of names etched upon it. Sixty thou-sand faceless names, all of them dead and gone twenty years and more. Zack stepped closer to the Wall and ran his fingers along it. Each set of nicks in the polished granite was a lost life, gone and probably not even buried, as cold and anonymous as the granite itself. This wall wasn't here for the people inscribed on it; it was here for the gawking tourists. See how many died? See how many deaths the war machine turned out, like little plastic widgets from a Taiwan factory?

"Know someone here?"

Zack had unconsciously stopped before the one name that should have meant anything to him. He never knew why he did that; the name was just as faceless as any other. The vet beside him was typical: scruffy gray beard, baseball cap pulled down low, the wide stance, as though to brace himself from an enemy's charge. His eyes held the haunted look Zack associated with vets: the slightly too-wide stare, a bit unfocused, as though he were looking through and beyond Zack rather than directly at him.

"Nope," said Zack. "Not a one."

"Looks like you do, the way you're staring like that."

"I said no."

"Didn't know him but would like to maybe?"

Zack turned away from him, but he could still see him reflected in the black granite; the vet watched him intently. It made Zack uncomfortable. He wished the guy would go away and leave him alone. But he didn't. And Zack's pride wouldn't let him walk away. So he just stared at the Wall and the vet's reflection within it.

"How old are you, kid?" said the vet.

"Nineteen," said Zack.

The vet nodded, as if this explained everything. "I remember it. Couldn't forget it if I tried. I'll always remember it."

Zack turned again, losing his patience. "Listen, old man. No, I wasn't there, and no, I can never know what it was like for you, but I don't really care."

"Don't really care? Then why are you here?"

"My mother dragged me," said Zack. "She drags me here every year."

The vet looked around in mock surprise. "You're mom's not here now."

"Just a bunch of stupid names," Zack mumbled, looking away.

"But you're not here for just a bunch of stupid names, are you, kid?"

"Don't call me that," said Zack, temper flaring. "I'm not a kid."

"No, you're not," said the vet. He nodded toward the black slab before them. "And he wasn't either, was he?"

Almost involuntarily, Zack glanced back at the marble, at the name etched there that was just like the tens of thousands of others that marched off into the distance on either side of him. Its only distinguishing mark was the small diamond beside it that showed that the man named had been killed rather than gone missing in action.

"Funny what a man's name can mean, isn't it?" said the vet behind him. "Nothing's more precious to a man than his name. Nothing more personal. And yet, looked at another way, nothing so anonymous."

Zack didn't trust himself to say anything. He just looked at that name, still hoping that the vet would go away, and yet, somehow, suddenly hoping that he wouldn't.

"Would you like to say a word or two?" said the vet quietly. "To him?"

"Sure," said Zack, shrugging. "Who wouldn't?"

The vet grasped him by the shoulders. "Look in there," he said. "Look in close."

"Yeah? So?"

"Just look at the name. But take in the blackness all around it, too."

Zack's gaze wandered into the field of black, and the vet's hands tightened in response. "Don't *look* at the blackness. Take it in. Look at the name."

Zack returned his gaze to the name and let the blackness crowd in around the periphery of his vision.

The voices of the tourists and the other vets around them seemed to fade away then to a dull buzzing in the back of his head, and at the same time their footsteps grew very loud, becoming a pounding to match the beating of his heart.

The vet shoved him, hard, sending Zack's face into the Wall.

Impact.

Bright white light.

Pain.

And then nothing.

Blackness.

Hands braced on the Wall, he tried to right himself, to pull his head back, but the vet's strong hands held him there, with his head caught in the blackness on the other side of the Wall.

Outside, his fingers felt the heat of the sun on the smooth granite surface, the notches and grooves of all those names. Inside, his head felt muffled, as though wrapped in black cloth. He couldn't find his breath, and he panicked, pushing harder with his hands, kicking at the unyielding surface with his knees.

The vet shoved him again, and this time, he tumbled through, arms pinwheeling.

He slowed. His body slowed. His thoughts slowed.

He couldn't see until his eyes slowly adjusted, and the roaring silence was interrupted by faint murmurings.

There were bodies all around him. They hung upright in space, turning slowly toward him like flowers to the sun.

They closed in around him, touching him with their whispers, seeking him, seeking the warmth of him.

Faintly, through the press, Zack saw a light, and he pushed toward it. The bodies gave reluctantly, turning aside, murmuring as he shoved past them.

And, abruptly, he was through to the other side.

The blood pounded in his veins.

Blast furnace of heat.

Smothering humidity.

The sweat dripping from his face felt like his flesh melting away.

The straps of his pack bit hard into his shoulders, and his feet were raw and bleeding in his boots. Still he climbed with the others. They were lined up along the path, scrabbling over rocks when they had to, leaving the cover of the trees. He didn't know whether that was good or bad; Charlie could be hiding in any decent ground cover. And yet, being caught out in the open didn't appeal much to him either.

He stood at the base of the ridge. A climb into clouds. The seat of the gods up there, and they were way the hell down here. How long would it take them to make the top? How many more blisters would he open in his feet?

The platoon toiled up the wall, the sergeant up top, clawing for handholds where one misstep could mean a tumble to his death. Those heavy packs could easily pitch them backwards, and any one of them falling could take out a couple of guys below them.

No, thanks. He wasn't having any of it.

He shrugged his pack off one shoulder, then the other, and let it fall to the path, where it kicked up a little puff of that goddamn red dust that was everywhere in Nam.

Then he sat down on the pack and fished in his pocket for his smokes. He squinted up the line at the Sarge leading the way, the others struggling up behind him.

The Sarge looked down, saw Zack sitting there, just as Zack knew he would, the son of a bitch. Still, Zack wasn't going to budge.

The Sarge scrambled sideways, off the path, and with a slap on the next man's pack, sent the rest of the men up without him.

He worked his way down, taking his time, Zack thought, not taking any chances, placing his feet and hands carefully.

"You hurt?" the Sarge asked him when he reached him.

"Nope," said Zack, blowing smoke.

"Then get your ass up that hill."

"Nope," said Zack. "I ain't moving. This is a bullshit detail. No fucking way I'm getting up that hill, not with all this gear, in this heat. Someone wants to carry it for me, that's fine with me, maybe then I'll think about it."

"You'll *think* about it."

"Yup."

The Sarge tilted his gaze back up the trail. "Doc!" he called.

The medic looked down, breathing hard from the climb. "Yeah, Sarge."

"Come down here and take a look at this man."

"Yeah, Sarge."

The medic climbed down and, still panting, knelt beside Zack, felt his forehead, told him to stick his tongue out, looked at his pupils. "How you feeling?"

"I feel like hell, that's how," said Zack. "I plain just had it with this shit. I just can't go no more."

The medic turned to Sarge. "He doesn't have heatstroke."

"All right, Doc, get going."

"Yeah, Sarge."

Zack watched the medic hump up that hill for the second time. No way Zack was doing that. The rest of the platoon was already disappearing behind the next pile of rock.

"Get your ass moving," the Sarge repeated to Zack.

"No way," said Zack. *And what are you going to do about it?* he thought but did not say. He just didn't give a shit any more. It felt good to call his own shots for once.

The Sarge reached down and lifted Zack's M-16 from where Zack had dropped it. "Suit yourself." He slung the weapon over his shoulder with his own and began humping back up the hill behind his platoon.

"Hey!" said Zack. "Where are you going with that?"

"You can die if you want to," said the Sarge without looking back. "But I'm not going to let Charlie waste any grunts with your weapon."

Zack stood and watched the Sarge disappear around the rock pile after the others. And then he was alone.

The heat, the heavy moist air closed in on him.

A distant waterfall sounded loud in sudden stillness.

Jesus, Jesus. Those assholes just left him here. All he wanted was just a little rest. Did he have to die for that?

A branch snapped somewhere in the trees.

Zack grabbed his pack, shouldered it, and reached for handholds in the rock wall. Heart pounding, he scrambled up it, finding toeholds where he needed them, reaching for crevices to hold him. *Keep your weight forward*, he told himself, *and move, move move!*

They were just behind him, he was certain of it. He felt them back there, felt the crosshairs of their AK-47s on his back.

He reached the top of the wall, where there was a relatively level path and that rock pile. Zack scrambled forward on his belly, his only thought to get it between him and *them*.

The Sarge was waiting for him there, sitting behind the rock. "Thought so," he said. "You're damn lucky I judged you right."

He stood before Zack could say "Don't!" But nothing happened, and Zack felt some of the tension leave his shoulders.

"Let's get going," said the Sarge.

Zack stood, too, warily.

Time froze.

The sky turned black.

The light faded to gray, as though a curtain had been drawn across the world.

The Sarge frowned. "What happened?"

Zack tried to move from his spot. Found that he couldn't. He shook his head. "I dunno. I think this is where I came in."

The Sarge looked at him as if for the first time. "Who are you?"

Zack swallowed. "Your son, I think. Wearing the body of one of your men."

"Jesus." The Sarge turned his head slowly and saw that a single 7.62 mm round hung in the air just before his left eye. "I'm dead, aren't I?"

"Yeah. I think so, now." Zack turned, too, saw two more rounds in midflight toward his own head. "Your man, too, I think."

"Stupid goldbricker got us both killed. I knew it had to come to this, though. Knew it. Knew it was coming. Stupid son of a bitch.

Stupid goddamn green son of a bitch." He looked again at Zack, squinted at him. "You're really my son?"

"Yeah," said Zack. "I think so." He looked at the man before him more closely. Nodded. "Yeah. You're him. You're my dad. Like twenty years ago. Mom had me when you were gone. I never met you."

"No shit. Goddamn. I would have liked to know you."

"Really?"

"Oh yeah. Always wanted a son." He managed a smile.

"Why'd you do it? Why'd you go away? Mom said you re-upped. She never could forgive you for that."

The smile vanished. "That's just wistful thinking. I *should've* re-upped, goddamn it. They let you go home if you sign on for another four years. Pull you right out of combat. But I didn't do it. Couldn't stand the thought of another four years in the goddamn army. Thought maybe I could live through this, get home to my . . . family." he swallowed.

"She says you stayed here on purpose, got yourself killed so you wouldn't have to come home to responsibility. So you wouldn't have to come home to me."

"Jesus Christ. She said that?"

"Yeah."

"That's bullshit."

"That's what she said."

"Would I lie to you at a time like this?" He jerked his head at the rifle round now only an inch from his eye. "Ah, shit. It's getting closer. I don't have much time left, do I?"

"No," said Zack.

"Listen," said the other man. "Listen to me. Are you listening?"

"Yeah, I'm listening."

"Stop blaming me for your problems. Get on with your life. Stop blaming your mother, too. She did the best she could for you. And remember how goddamn lucky you are."

Zack didn't know what to say to that. The other man didn't seem to know what to say either. So they stood there in roaring silence, looking at each other across a gap of five feet and twenty years until the rifle round punched into Zack's father's brain and Zack fell into the blackness that was the sky, and the murmuring dead turned toward him like flowers to the sun.

They clutched at him, seeking his warmth, his life.

Zack tried to cry out, but he found he had no breath.

A shout.

A clap of hands.

Light in the distance.

Someone stood at the edge of the blackness, legs braced, hands now extended toward Zack.

Zack took a step forward. Then another.

Rough hands gripped his, pulled him through and out to the other side, and he was back in sunlight and air and gasping like a drowner.

Heart pounding, shaky, he stood with his back against a black granite slab, panting, feeling cool air on his face, feeling the sweat drying on his skin. The vet held his hands tight.

"You all right?"

"Yeah," said Zack weakly. Then, louder, "Yeah, I'm all right." He pulled his hands free.

"Did you see him?" asked the vet.

"Yeah. I saw him."

"What did he tell you?"

"Nothing," said Zack, but his eyes had begun to sting.

The vet placed a hand on Zack's chest, and Zack felt that the bone there was fragile and that in another second the vet would have his fist clenched around his heart. "Remember it. Keep it close to you. These memories can fade quickly."

"Yeah," said Zack as the vet took his hand away. He looked at the man more closely now, searching his eyes, the lines of his face for something familiar. "Do I know you?" he said.

The vet watched him a moment. Then, "What do you think?"

For the first time, Zack thought maybe he could begin to understand the slightly absent gaze that afflicted veterans. "Yeah," said Zack. "Maybe a little."

The vet nodded. He pulled off his baseball cap and with a quick, sudden motion pitched it at the Wall. It struck and vanished, leaving a pale afterimage that faded quickly. "See, Zack, when all of our names were committed to this Wall, it gave us some power to act in the world, to help people to remember, maybe just one name at a time." He took a deep breath and faced Zack again. "It's all we can do."

"It's enough," said Zack. He swallowed. "Thank you."

The vet nodded. "So now move on. Don't stay stuck in what might have been if only. It's too late for me but not you. You really can still make something of your life. Do it. Do it for me. Do it for *him*."

Zack didn't trust himself to speak. He nodded instead.

"Good man," said the vet, and he turned and walked away down the line, alongside this wall covered with rows upon rows, columns upon columns of name after anonymous name. Zack watched him go until he faded into the crowd of vets and tourists and schoolkids and was gone.

Afterword: I initially struggled with the invitation to write for this anthology. On the one hand, it was an opportunity not to be missed—the chance to appear alongside some of the best writers in science fiction. On the other hand, I would be writing about a subject I felt very much less than qualified to address, and I would be held to a very high standard. Joe Haldeman, for instance, is considered to have written the definitive science-fiction work dealing with soldiers in war.

I finally concluded that the only way I could pull off this challenge was to come at it from the only perspective I had that people like Byron Tetrick and Joe Haldeman didn't have—namely, from the perspective of the next generation that struggles to understand the effects of war on its parents. I chose to set my story a decade or so in the past because that would make my protagonist roughly the age I was when I myself began to try to understand.

That was when I and a friend, fresh out of college, picked up a hitchhiker named Don on Highway 5 in central California. Don had been forever changed by the Vietnam War, and over the next few days he tried to show us exactly how. He brought us to the memorial wall in Sacramento, where he traced the name of his childhood best friend, and he took us to his home, an encampment of fellow vets on the shore of the American River, all the while giving us a view of a world I had never before seen up close.

And I'm still trying to understand.

BLACK REFLECTION

Robert J. Sawyer

*It is an odd thing—as far back as we can go in history
we find that the two signs of Man are a capacity to Kill
and a belief in God.*
—William Golding

"THERE'S SO MUCH FOR me to show you here in Washington," said Mary Vaughan to the man from another world, "but I wanted to start with this. Nothing else says more about this country, and about what it means to be human—my kind of human."

Ponter Boddit looked at the strange vista in front of him, not understanding. There was a scar in the grass-covered landscape, a deep welt that ran for eighty paces then met, at an obtuse angle, another similar scar.

The scars were black and reflective—a . . . what was that word these humans had? An *oxymoron*, that was it; a contradiction in terms. Black, meaning it absorbed all light; reflective, meaning it bounced light back.

And yet that's precisely what it was, a black mirror, reflecting Ponter's face, and Mary's, too. Two kinds of humanity, not just female and male but two separate species, two different iterations of the human theme. Her reflection showed what she called a *Homo sapiens* and he called a Gliksin: her strange upright forehead, minuscule nose, and—there was no word in Ponter's language for it—her *chin*. She was an exemplar of the kind of human that had become dominant on this version of Earth.

And his reflection showed what she called a *Homo neanderthalensis* and he called a Barast, the word for "human" in his language: a Neanderthal's broad countenance, with a doubly arched browridge and a proper-sized nose extending across a third of his face. Ponter was the first of his kind to slip between the worldlines and visit this reality. And Mary, the Canadian geneticist who had proved to her skeptical people that he was indeed what they knew as a Neanderthal, from a world in which Neanderthals had survived and developed a technological culture, was accompanying him on his tour of this Earth.

"What is it?" asked Ponter, staring at the oblong blackness, at their reflections.

"It's a memorial," said Mary. She looked away from the black wall and waved her hand at objects in the distance. "This whole mall is filled with memorials. The pair of walls here point at two of the most important ones. That spire is the Washington Monument, a memorial to the first U.S. President. Over there, that's the Lincoln Memorial, commemorating the President who freed the slaves."

Ponter's translator bleeped. "The slaves?"

Mary let out a sigh. Evidently there was still more complexity, more—what had she called it?—more dirty linen to be aired.

"We'll visit both those memorials later," said Mary. "But, as I said, I wanted to start here. This is the Vietnam Veterans Memorial."

"Vietnam is one of your nations, is it not?" said Ponter.

Mary nodded. "In Southeast Asia—Southeast Galasoy. Just north of the equator. An S-shaped bit of land on the Pacific seaboard."

"We call the same place Holtanatan. But on my version of Earth it is very hot, very humid, rainy, full of swamps, and overrun by insects. No one lives there."

Mary lifted her eyebrows. Ponter was always surprised that she had two distinct ones, instead of a continuous swath of hairs, and that they could slide so far up her perpendicular forehead. "Over eighty million people live there in this reality."

Ponter shook his head. The humans of this version of Earth were so . . . so *unrestrained*; in his timeline, there were only 185 million people on the entire planet.

"And," continued Mary, "a war was fought there."

"Over what? Over swamps?"

Mary closed her eyes. "Over ideology. Remember I told you about the Cold War? This was part of that—but this part was hot."

"Hot?" Ponter shook his head. "You are not referring to temperature, are you?"

"No. *Hot.* As in a shooting war. As in people died."

Ponter frowned. "How many people?"

"In total, from all sides? No one really knows. Over a million of the local South Vietnamese. Somewhere between half a million and a million North Vietnamese. Plus . . ." She gestured at the wall.

"Yes?" said Ponter, still baffled by the reflecting blackness.

"Plus fifty-eight thousand, two hundred and nine Americans. These two walls commemorate them."

"Commemorate them how?"

"See the writing engraved in the black granite?"

Ponter nodded.

"Those are names—names of the confirmed dead and of those missing in action who never came home." Mary paused. "The war ended in 1975."

"And this is—as you reckon the years?"

Mary told him.

Ponter looked down. "I do not think the missing are coming home." He moved closer to the wall. "How are the names arrayed?"

"Chronologically. By date of death."

Ponter looked at the names, all in what he'd learned were known as capital letters, a small dot—a bullet, isn't that what they called it, one of their words that served doubled duty?—separating each name from the next.

Of course, Ponter couldn't read English characters; he'd only begun to grasp the notion of a phonetic alphabet. Mary knew that. She moved in beside him and, in a soft voice, read some of the names to him. "Mike A. Maksin. Bruce J. Moran. Bobbie Joe Mounts. Raymond D. McGlothin." She pointed at another line, apparently chosen at random. "Samuel F. Hollifield, Jr. Rufus Hood. James M. Inman. David L. Johnson. Arnoldo L. Carrillo."

And another line, farther down: "Donney L. Jackson. Bobby W. Jobe. Bobby Ray Jones. Halcott P. Jones, Jr."

"Fifty-eight thousand of them," said Ponter, his voice as soft as Mary's.

"Yes."

"But—but you said these are dead Americans?"

Mary nodded.

"What were they doing fighting a war half a world away?"

"They were helping the South Vietnamese. See, in 1954 Vietnam had been divided into two halves, North Vietnam and South Vietnam, as part of a peace agreement, each with its own kind of government. Two years later, in 1956, there were to be free elections throughout both halves, supervised by an international committee, to unify Vietnam under a single, popularly elected government. But when 1956 rolled around, the leader of South Vietnam refused to hold the scheduled elections."

"I learned much about this country, the United States, when we visited Philadelphia," said Ponter. "I know how highly Americans value democracy. Let me guess: The United States sent troops to force South Vietnam to participate in the promised democratic election."

But Mary shook her head. "No, no, the United States supported the South's desire *not* to hold the election."

"But why? Was the government in the North corrupt?"

"No," said Mary. "No, it was reasonably honest and kind—at least up until when the promised election, which it wanted, was canceled. But there *was* a corrupt government—the one in the South."

Ponter shook his head, baffled. "But you said that the South was the one the Americans were supporting."

"That's right. See, the government in the South was corrupt—but capitalist; it shared the American economic system. The one in the north was Communist; it used the economic system of the Soviet Union and China. But the northern government was much more popular than the corrupt southern one. The United States feared that if free elections were held, the Communists would win and control all of Vietnam."

"And so Americans soldiers were sent there?"

"Yes."

"And died?"

"Many did, yes." Mary paused. "That's what I wanted you to understand: how important our principles are to us. We will die to defend an ideology, die to support a cause." She pointed at the wall. "These people here, these fifty-eight thousand people, fought for what they believed in. They were told to go to war, told to save a weaker people from what was held to be the great Communist threat, and they did so. Most of them were young—eighteen, nineteen, twenty, twenty-one. For many, it was their first time away from home."

"And now they are dead."

Mary nodded. "But not forgotten. We remember them here." She pointed discreetly. Ponter's guards—here, in Washington, members of the FBI—were keeping people away from him, but the walls were long, so incredibly long, and farther down someone was leaning up against the black surface. "See that man there?" asked Mary. "He's using a pencil and a piece of paper to make a rubbing of the name of someone he knew. He's—well, he looks in his mid-fifties, no? He might have been in Vietnam himself. The name he's copying might be that of a buddy he lost over there."

Ponter and Mary watched silently as the man finished what he was doing. And then the man folded the piece of paper, placed it in his breast pocket, and began to speak.

Ponter shook his head slightly in confusion. He gestured at the Companion embedded in his own left forearm. "I thought you people did not have telecommunications implants."

"We don't," said Mary.

"But I do not see any external receiver, any—what do you call it?— any cell phone."

"That's right," said Mary gently.

"Then who is he talking to?"

Mary lifted her shoulders slightly. "His lost comrade."

"But that person is dead."

"Yes."

"One cannot talk to the dead," said Ponter.

Mary gestured at the wall again, its obsidian surface pantomiming the sweep of her arm. "People think they can. They say they feel closest to them here."

"Is this where the remains of the dead are stored?"

"What? No, no, no."

"Then I—"

"It's the *names*," said Mary, sounding somewhat exasperated. "The names. The names are here, and we connect with people through their names."

Ponter frowned. "I—forgive me, I do not mean to be stupid. Surely that cannot be right, though. We—my people—connect through faces. There are countless people whose faces I know but whose names I have never learned. And, well, I connect with you, and although I know your name, I cannot articulate it or even think it clearly. Mare—that is the best I can do." Although his translator had been modified to produce the sound when needed, his Neanderthal mouth couldn't manage the *ee* phoneme that made up the second half of Mary's name.

"We think names are . . ." Mary lifted her shoulders, apparently acknowledging how ridiculous what she was saying must sound, ". . . are *magical*."

"But," said Ponter again, "you cannot communicate with the dead." He wasn't trying to be stubborn; really, he wasn't.

Mary closed her eyes for a moment, as if summoning inner strength—or, thought Ponter, as if communicating with someone somewhere else. "I know your people do not believe in an afterlife," said Mary, at last.

"'Afterlife,'" said Ponter, serving up the word as though it were a choice gobbet of meat. "An oxymoron."

"Not to us," said Mary. And then, more emphatically, "Not to me." She looked around. At first Ponter thought it was simply an externalization of her thoughts; he presumed she was seeking some way to explain what she was feeling. But then her eyes lighted on something, and she started walking. Ponter followed her.

"Do you see these flowers?" said Mary.

He nodded. "Of course."

"They were left here by one of the living for one of the dead. Somebody whose name is on this panel." She pointed at the section of polished granite in front of her.

Mary bent low. The flowers—red roses—still had long stems and were bundled together by string. A small card was attached to the bundle with a ribbon. "'For Willie,'" said Mary, evidently reading from the card, "'from his loving sister.'"

"Ah," said Ponter, having no better response at hand.

Mary walked farther. She came to a fawn-colored envelope leaning against the wall, and she picked it up. It was unsealed, and she gingerly removed the single sheet within. "'Dear Carl,'" she read. She paused and searched the panel in front of her. "This must be him," she said, reaching forward and lightly touching a name. "Carl Bowen." She continued to look at the incised name. "This one is for you, Carl," she said—apparently her own words, since she wasn't looking down at the sheet. She then lowered her eyes and read aloud, starting over at the beginning:

Dear Carl—

I know I should have come here earlier. I wanted to. Honest, I did. But I didn't know how you would take the news. I know I was your first love, and you were mine, and no summer has been as wonderful for me as that summer of '66. I thought of you every day you were gone, and when word came that you had died, I cried and cried, and I'm crying again now as I write these words.

I don't want you to think I ever stopped mourning you, because I didn't. But I did go on with life. I married Bucky Samuels. Remember him? From Eastside? We've got two kids, both older now than you were when you died.

You wouldn't recognize me, I don't think. My hair has got some gray in it, which I try to hide, and I lost all my freckles long ago, but I still think of you. I love Buck very much, but I love you, too . . . and I know someday, we'll see each other again.

Love forever,
Jane

"'See each other again'?" repeated Ponter. "But he is dead."

Mary nodded. "She means, she'll see him when she dies, too."

Ponter frowned. Mary walked a few steps farther along. Another letter was leaning against the wall, this one laminated in clear plastic. She picked it up. "'Dear Frankie,'" she began. She scanned the wall in front of her. "Here he is," she said. "Franklin T. Mullens III." She read the letter aloud:

Dear Frankie,

They say a parent shouldn't outlive a child, but who expects a child to be taken when he's only 19? I miss you

*every day, and so does your pa. You know him—he tries to
be strong in front of me, but I hear him crying softly to this
day when he thinks I'm asleep.*

*A mother's job is to look after her son, and I did the best
I could. But now God Himself is looking after you, and I
know you are safe in his loving arms.*

We will be together again, my darling son.

Love,

Ma

Ponter didn't know what to say. The sentiments were so obviously
sincere, but . . . but they were *irrational*. Couldn't Mary see that?
Couldn't the people who wrote these letters see that?

Mary continued to read to him from letters and cards and plaques
and scrolls that had been left leaning against the wall. Phrases stuck in
Ponter's mind.

"We know God is taking care of you. . . ."

"I long for that day when we will all be together again. . . ."

"Keep well, till we meet again. . . ."

"Your sister and I know that you are at peace now. . . ."

"I know you are not lonely because you have Barney there and the
58,207 others whose names are on the wall with you. . . ."

"Rest well, my friend."

"So much forgotten / So much unsaid / But I promise to tell you all /
When we meet among the dead."

"Sleep now, beloved. . . ."

"Just thought you should know that everyone's doing fine. . . ."

"I know you're watching over me. . . ."

"I look forward to when we are reunited."

". . . on that wonderful day when the Lord will reunite us in heaven . . ."

"God will keep you in his loving care. . . ."

"Good-bye—God be with ye!— until we meet again."

"Joy and peace are yours."

"Take care, bro. I'll visit you again next time I'm in D.C. . . ."

"Rest in peace, my friend, rest in peace. . . ."

Mary had to pause several times to wipe away tears. Ponter felt sad,
too, and his eyes were likewise moist, but not, he suspected, for the
same reason. "It is always hard to have a loved one die," said Ponter.

Mary nodded. She knew that Ponter had lost his own woman, Klast, to cancer not that long ago—and at an unfairly young age.

"But . . ." he continued, then fell silent.

"Yes?" Mary prodded.

"This memorial," said Ponter, sweeping his arm, taking in its two great walls. "What is its purpose?"

Mary's eyebrows climbed again. "To honor the dead."

"Not *all* the dead," said Ponter, softly. "These are only the Americans. . . ."

"Well, yes," said Mary. "It's a monument to the sacrifice made by American soldiers, a way for the people of the United States to show that they appreciate them."

"Appreciated," said Ponter.

Mary looked confused.

"Is my translator malfunctioning?" asked Ponter. "You can appreciate—present tense—what still exists; you can only have appreciated—past tense—that which is no more."

Mary sighed, clearly not wishing to debate the point.

"But you have not answered my question," said Ponter, gently. "What is this memorial *for*?"

"I told you. To honor the dead."

"No, no," said Ponter. "That may be an incidental effect, I grant you. But surely the purpose of the designer—"

"Maya Ying Lin," said Mary.

"Pardon?"

"Maya Ying Lin. That's the name of the woman who designed this."

"Ah," said Ponter. "Well, surely her purpose—the purpose of anyone who designs a memorial—is to make sure people never forget."

"Yes?" said Mary, sounding irritated by whatever picayune distinction she felt Ponter was making.

"And the reason to not forget the past," said Ponter, "is so that the same mistakes can be avoided."

"Well, yes, of course," said Mary.

"So has this memorial served its purpose? Has the same mistake—the mistake that led to all these young people dying—been avoided since?"

Mary thought for a time, then shook her head. "I suppose not. Wars are still fought, and—"

"By America? By the people who built this monument?"

"Yes," said Mary. "Right now, they are fighting a war on terrorism. Remember when we were in New York, you saw where the World Trade Center used to be? The United States has declared war on those who would use terrorist tactics."

"Where was the war declared?"

"Well, it's not an *official* war," said Mary. "I mean, no specific nation has been named as the enemy. But President Bush called it a war, said he was declaring war. . . ."

"Where did he do that?"

"Umm, in New York. Manhattan. You know: at the site of the destroyed towers."

Ponter shook his head. Couldn't she see? Couldn't *he*—the President—see? "Are not his home and office in this city?" asked Ponter.

"Yes," said Mary, pointing. "We'll take a tour of the public parts this afternoon."

"Can the President see this memorial from there?"

"This one? No. I'm sure he can see the Washington Monument, but . . ."

"He should have done it here," said Ponter, flatly. "He should have declared war right here, standing in front of these fifty-eight thousand, two hundred and nine names. Surely *that* should be the purpose of such a memorial. If a leader can stand and look at the names of all those who died a previous time a President declared war and still call for young people to go off and be killed in another war, then perhaps the war is worth fighting."

Mary tilted her head to one side but said nothing.

"After all, you said you fight to preserve your most fundamental values."

"That's the ideal, yes," said Mary.

"But this war—this war in Vietnam. You said it was to support a corrupt government, to prevent elections from being held."

"Well, yes, in a way."

"But in Philadelphia you showed me where and how this country began. Is not the United States' most cherished belief that of democracy, of the will of the people being heard and done?"

Mary nodded.

"But then surely they should have fought a war to ensure that that ideal was upheld. To have gone to Vietnam to make sure the people there had a chance to vote would have been an American ideal—and if the Vietnam people . . ."

"Vietnamese."

"If the Vietnamese had chosen the Communist system by vote, then surely the American ideal of democracy would have been served. Surely you cannot hold democracy dear only when the vote goes the way you wish it would."

"Maybe you're right," said Mary. "A great many people thought the American involvement in Vietnam was wrong. They called it a profane war."

"Profane?"

"Umm, an insult to God."

Ponter rolled his own eyebrow up his browridge. "From what I have seen, this God of yours must have a thick skin."

Mary nodded, conceding the point.

"What about this new war?" asked Ponter. "This war on terrorism?"

"Yes?"

"What is the reason for it?"

"Well, I suppose there are two," said Mary. "First, of course, to put an end to the ability of others to perform terrorist acts."

"And the second?"

Mary lifted her shoulders again. "Revenge." She paused. "Retribution. Punishment."

"But you have told me that the majority of people in this country are Christians, like you, is that not so?"

"Yes."

"How big a majority?"

"Big," said Mary. "Let me think . . . the U.S. has a population of about 270 million." Ponter had heard this figure before, so its vastness didn't startle him this time. "About a million are atheists—they don't believe in God at all. Another twenty-five million are non-religious; that is, they don't adhere to any particular faith. All the other faith groups combined—Jews, Buddhists, Muslims, Hindus—add up to about fifteen million. Everyone else—almost 240 million—say they are Christians."

"So this is a Christian country," said Ponter.

"Welllll, like my own country of Canada," said Mary, "the U.S. prides itself on its tolerance of a variety of beliefs."

Ponter waved a hand dismissively. "Two hundred and forty million out of 270 million is almost ninety percent; it *is* a Christian country. And you have told me the core beliefs of Christians. What did Christ say about those who would attack you?"

"The Sermon on the Mount," said Mary. She closed her eyes, presumably to aid her remembering. "'Ye have heard that it hath been said, An eye for an eye, and a tooth for a tooth: But I say unto you, That ye resist not evil: but whosoever shall smite thee on thy right cheek, turn to him the other also.'"

"So revenge has no place in the policies of a Christian nation," said Ponter. "And yet you say it has declared a war of revenge. Likewise, impeding the free choice of a foreign country should have had no place in the policies of a democratic nation, and yet it fought this war in Vietnam."

Mary said nothing.

"Do you not see?" said Ponter. "*That* is what this memorial, this Vietnam Veterans wall, should serve as a reminder of: the pointlessness of death, the error—the *grave* error, if I may attempt a play on words in your language—of declaring a war in contravention of your most dearly held principles."

Mary was still silent.

"That is the reason why future American wars should be declared here—*right here*. Only if the cause stands the test of supporting the most dearly held fundamental principles, then perhaps it is a war that *should* be declared." Ponter let his eyes run over the wall again, over the black reflection. "These two walls should remind those clamoring for revenge of the vast, pointless loss of life that goes with fighting a war that is against one's principles."

"I'm no lover of war," said Mary. "And I don't dispute what you're saying. 'Vengeance is mine; I will repay, saith the Lord.' But what you suggest makes no room for emotion."

"The decision to kill, or to put others in a position in which they might be killed, should never be made emotionally."

Mary frowned, apparently having no answer for that.

"Still," said Ponter, "let me make a simpler proposition. Those letters you read—they are, I presume, typical?"

Mary nodded. "Ones like it are left here every day."

"But do you not see the problem? There is an underlying belief in those letters that the dead are not really dead. '"God is taking care of you.' 'We will all be together again.' 'I know you are watching over me.' 'Someday I will see you again.'"

"We've talked about this before," said Mary. "My kind of human-ity—not just Christians, but just about all *Homo sapiens*, no matter what their particular religion—believe that the essence of a person does not end with the death of the body. The soul lives on."

"And that belief," said Ponter firmly, "is the problem. I have thought this since you first told me of it, but it is—what do you say?—it is driven home for me here, at this memorial, this wall of names."

"Yes?" said Mary.

"They are *dead*. They are eliminated. They no longer exist." He reached forward and touched a name he could not read. "The person who was named this." He touched another. "And the person who was named this." And he touched a third. "And the person who had this name. They are *no more*. Surely facing that is the real lesson of this wall. One cannot come here to speak with the dead, for the dead are *dead*. One cannot come here to beg forgiveness from the dead, for the dead are *dead*. One cannot come here to be touched by the dead, for the dead are *dead*.

"These names, these characters carved in stone—that is *all* that is left of them. Surely that is the message of this wall, the lesson to be learned. As long as your people keep thinking that this life is pro-logue, that more is to come after it, that those wronged here will be rewarded in some *there* yet to come, you will continue to undervalue life, and you will continue to send young people off to die in swamps and jungles."

Mary took a deep breath and let it out slowly, apparently com-posing herself. She gestured with a movement of her head. Ponter turned to look. Another person—a gray-haired man—was placing a letter of his own in front of the wall. "Could you tell him?" asked Mary. "Tell him that he's wasting his time? Or that woman, over there—the one on her knees, praying? Could you tell her? Disabuse her of her delusion? The belief that somewhere their loved ones still exist gives them comfort."

Ponter shook his head. "That belief is what *caused* this to happen.

The only way to honor the dead is by ensuring that no more enter that state prematurely."

Mary sounded angry. "All right, then. Go tell them."

Ponter turned and looked at the people and their ebony reflections in the wall. Was he upset with them, he wondered, or with himself? When his own woman-mate had died, he had had no comforting thought of her continuing in some form; such a notion never even occurred to him. But still, his people, the Barast, almost never took human lives, and Mary's people, the Gliksins, did it on such large scales, with such frequency. Surely this belief in God and an afterlife had to be linked to this readiness to kill.

He looked at the people by wall, kept away from him, from the visitor from another world, by armed agents. No, he would not tell these mourners that their loved ones were truly gone. After all, it wasn't these sad people who had sent them off to die.

Ponter turned back to face Mary. "Perhaps I will tell my thoughts to the President. It is he, after all, who declares war."

"It's actually only the Congress who can officially declare war," said Mary, "but the President is the Commander in Chief."

"Then let us go see him," said Ponter.

"What? Now?"

"Will he not accept visitors?"

"Well, no—I mean, not usually."

"I am a representative of a foreign government, of another world. Perhaps he will make an exception."

Mary's eyes were wide. "Perhaps."

Ponter looked once more at the people taking comfort, standing in front of and kneeling before and touching the wall.

"Let us try," said Ponter. "You said his house is this way?"

"Yes, but—"

"He must be made to know the truth," said Ponter. "He must learn that no comfort can ever be taken in death."

Mary looked dubious, but she started walking. "You'd better pray that he'll see you," she said.

Ponter walked beside her, hands clasped behind his back. "That," he said softly, "is the one thing I cannot do."

Afterword: So what the hell is a Canadian doing writing about Vietnam?

Actually, I'm a dual citizen; my mother is an American, and although I was born in Ottawa, I have a U.S. passport and Social Security number. For a long, long time, I downplayed my American heritage—growing up during the Vietnam War made it very hard for me to come to grips with that part of who I am.

The Vietnam draft ended in 1973, the year I turned thirteen. But seven years later, Jimmy Carter reactivated selective service, in case more troops were needed to respond to the Soviet invasion of Afghanistan. And so, to keep my dual citizenship, I had to go to the American embassy in Toronto and register for the new draft. Still, had my name been chosen, I could have renounced my U.S. citizenship, kept my Canadian one, and stayed safely at home in Canada. And, to be honest, that's probably what I would have done.

I had a choice—a choice very few young men had during Vietnam. If the U.S. Commander in Chief had called for me, I could have thumbed my nose and not suffered any real inconvenience. Still, it astonished me that Carter was preparing again to draft young American men, so soon after the end of the Vietnam War.

In 1992, I went to Washington D.C., and saw the Vietnam Veterans Wall for the first of several times. It was one of the most devastating emotional experiences of my life: all those names, all those people, all those lives cut short.

It occurred to me that you couldn't see the Wall from the White House; indeed, it was just about as far removed from the President's home as you could get on the Mall. Out of sight, out of mind?

Perhaps there are times when war is necessary. If so, it seems to me that the President should have to tell the American people that they—that we—are going to war not from the opulent confines of the Oval Office but rather there, standing in front of the Wall, with those fifty-eight thousand ghosts looking on. If he (or perhaps someday she) could in good conscience do that, maybe even someone like me would feel compelled to answer the call.

GETTING THERE

Barry N. Malzberg

"WE'RE DEAD, YOU KNOW," Gerald Hollers said. "We're going to wind up with our names on some fucking wall somewhere, long after everyone has forgotten us and forgotten what the hell was going on here. We're just gone."

Tracer fire, incoming. Pinned by the fire in a bunker, staring into the darkness, the little flower flashes, the cold, wet, useless steel of the M-16s. "Maybe not," I said. "Maybe we'll get out of this."

"We may get out of this," Hollers said, "but we won't get out of the next one. Or the one after that. You poor son of a bitch, you don't even know how dead we are."

This was in December of 1967, a month before Tet, while we were grab-assing in country waiting out an election. The election was our only hope, Hollers had said. He was nineteen, a college dropout, a little bit of a philosopher, he said, with a belief in current events. "Lucky Lyndon goes," he said, "we might get out of this. Otherwise our little nephews are going to be going after the coonskin twenty years from now. You know it's the truth."

Maybe it was the truth. Who the hell knew? Who could tell truth in country when there was nothing but the fire and the fear we wouldn't show to one another? "A wall," I said, "a fucking wall? No way. A cemetery. Maybe a nice headstone in Arlington with my name spelled wrong. A little plot of grass outside First Presbyterian in Mobile, Alabama, still with my name spelled wrong. No wall. No fucking wall."

A piece of hot slag came in, clouted Hollers on the helmet and then, in the stink of gas, the bunker went total.

"This is it," Hollers said, "we're going over." The heat was intense; I felt that my body had turned into fluid, was running in the fatigues. "Over," Hollers said, "over."

Not fucking quite, though. Hang on a couple of months.

※ ※ ※

This was 1969. McCarthy had made his run and RFK had settled with a bullet in his head. Hubert, he wanted the politics of joy. The politics of joy weren't working too well just about then, not anywhere near Haiphong Harbor, and now it was our boy Dick. Dick had a secret plan. Just vote for me and watch my secret plan work, he had said. So now he was President and we pretty well knew the secret plan. He would take the war home. Who needed battle dispatches when the Guard could be mobilized to kill you in your own living room. Every place was a hootch now.

"We'll never see this end," I said to the First Lieutenant. I didn't even know his name; names were only a way of getting you too close to the situation. The less damned names you knew the better. "Dick likes it too much. He's turned the country into a combat zone."

This was at Fort Benning after I had been cycled out. I had lived though Hollers hadn't, and now I was a clerk, typing days and drinking nights to make those last five months a blur.

"That's not true," the First Lieutenant said. "It's ending for you. You're five months from discharge and you're safe. Me," he said looking me in the eye, "I'm a different case. I've got a real good chance of buying it. The next training company finishes and goes out: I'm attached. I'm going to wind up with my name on a wall. But you can still call me sir."

I knew this guy there who said the same thing, I said. "Gerry Hollers. He said that we'd be names on a wall someday. I was thinking more like Arlington."

"Oh, a wall is definitely the deal," the First Lieutenant said. "You can get more names, not take up space with embarrassments like coffins and burial plots. Your guy was pretty smart. Did he get out of there?"

"Not so you'd notice," I said.

※ ※ ※

On the television I watched the exit, the helicopters beating and throbbing, the helpless Vietnamese staff at the Embassy clinging and then losing their grip, the bodies falling away. "There you go," I said to my wife. "That's the coonskin on the wall. That's the secret plan. That's the great triumph." This was 1975, of course, a few weeks after Phnom Penh had fallen next door and as the troops were making their way toward Saigon. All we knew was that we had to get the hell out of there. "A year in country," I said to her. "A year not knowing from one minute to the next if I'd be alive, breathing the breath that could have been my last every time. That's what I did it for, for this."

"Hush," she said, coming to sit next to me. She was twenty years old, my wife, twelve when I had been in country, although not my wife, of course. I had met her in 1974, and marrying her had seemed as good an idea as fucking her and not marrying her. One thing after Vietnam: One thing really looked pretty much like the other. "It's over," she said. "You're out, you survived, you're OK."

"I knew this guy in country," I said, "Hollers. He bought it when he was twenty days short. He said we'd wind up names on a fucking wall, that was all we'd be."

"Well, you're not," she said. "You're alive and you're not on any wall. You're right here."

I watched the Vietnamese scream: Close-up. Good camera work by people who were themselves hanging on the edge of the helicopters. "I'm not so sure of that," I said. "It could have been me just as easy as him. We were only ten yards apart when the land mine went cold zero. Maybe we both died. Maybe I was the one who died, and I'm just dreaming this in the last seconds of my life."

"No, you're not," she said, "you're not dreaming. This is real life and you're right here."

"Hollers," I said. I hadn't remembered the name for years until then. "He said that the fucking war was just an expedition to the wall, just a way of losing life and getting on there. What do you think of that?"

"I think you should shut that off and we should fuck," my wife said. Sensible girl, too sensible. It didn't last, couldn't have lasted; she was gone by 1977.

I don't know where she is. I barely know where I am.

※ ※ ※

At the wall, after the book and the pacing, I find the name GERALD I HOLLERS. February 4, 1968. He was nineteen years old. "You know, I didn't even remember his name for years," I said to my son. This was 1993, March, the earliest time that I felt I could look at it. "Then it came to me during the final retreat. He believed that there was nothing to believe in. It could as easily have been him as me."

"But where would that have left me, Dad?" my son said. Twelve years old and knew all the hockey and basketball lineups. Vietnam was just a word to him, which is why I had insisted that he come there with me. Now he was tugging at me. "I've seen it," he said. "Let's go somewhere else. I don't want to look at it anymore."

Sensible kid. As sensible as my first wife, who was not his mother. My second wife was his mother, and I wasn't married to her by this time either. "Just a minute," I said. "Just a minute more."

I stood there, my son beside me, crouching to read the lower names, and looked at GERALD I HOLLERS. For a moment, a strange conversion of light, it felt as if my name was on the wall, as if I was in the wall looking out, and Gerry Hollers, concerned and sad, was looking at me. "He was my friend," Gerald Hollers is saying about me. "Either or both of us could have died. I told him that we'd wind up on a wall. Now here he is. And why isn't it me?"

This is a good question. Why isn't it him? Why is he looking at a dead spot, my dead name, and I long extinguished? Why am I not the one with his son crouched beside him, looking at the name GERALD I HOLLERS? Looking and thinking and then not thinking at all, shuffling away then, shuffle with the crowd all the way down the long mall to the Capitol. The buildings shining like napalm in the thin and urgent light.

Afterword: A long time ago, Jack Dann's Fields of Fire, *a great Vietnam anthology, gave me an opportunity to write "The Queen of Lower Saigon," about Vietnam's embrace. Here is another view of that embrace, this time masked as an expulsion. Same thing. This goddamned war will never end, and like generals fighting the last battle, I will hate it until I die. "I will oppose this war as long as I draw breath," said Wayne Morse to Dick Cavett in 1967. Me, too. Don't tell me it is over.*

OBSESSIONS

Leah R. Cutter

"It's a huge wall, full of names. They died in a war or something. It's some kind of memorial," Green said.

I ignored him, as well as everyone else that had gathered around the fire under the rail bridge that night. As usual, I had all my attention focused on my obsession—my world of make-believe men. A particularly rugged one gripped me currently. He was tall, good-looking, good-smelling. He had moles on his face, one below his right eye, the other on the side of his nose. They tasted like that popcorn you find in the gutters after a street fair, salty and sweet. He was oral as hell, lapping at my neck, my breasts, my thighs. I only wanted to feel his mouth on me, my own imagined crooning drowning out Green's rants. However, a line sometimes slipped through.

"It's nothing more than government-sponsored tagging. Signing their names, all over that wall," said Leon, the other tagger in the group.

Come on my man, my dreamboat. Take me all the way home.

"—yeah, our names should go up on some kind of wall. We've all been struck down in the war of commerce." That had to be Randi, who claimed to have had a real job once—window cleaner—before they invented the Nans that ate shit and grime for power and kept everything pristine.

"War heroes, every one of us! We should add our names to that wall." Paulo? Trace? Rob-Dog? It didn't matter. They all felt that way.

Tease me, my love. Yeah, like that.

"This time my tag won't fade. I got special paint."

That sucked me out. Nan paint—semi-fixed nanites—could be dangerous. My dream man faded. Oh, what the hell. We were all going to die anyway. I willed myself back into my obsession, drawing my imaginary friend back down on me.

"A battle of the Nans!"

"All right, Green. Way to go!"

"This is going to be great! Can't you just see it?"

"No," I said, startling everyone. I wasn't sure at first if I talked to the fading image or to Green. Then my eyes cleared and I saw the crouched assembly drawn to the fire, its flickering light hiding the dirt ground into their hands, around their eyes.

I cleared my throat. "No," I repeated. The way my voice cracked made me wonder how many days it'd been since I'd spoken. "Don't be stupid. Putting up a normal tag, even with special Nan paint, well, the guards'll see it." I wasn't going to mention the danger. Tell a kid the fire's hot and the first thing she'll do is go and stick her hand in it. At least I would.

People looked at me like I'd been doing some good drugs while I was in nah-nah land, ones that had sucked away all the knowledge in my famous brain.

"Of course they'll see it, Skull. That's the point," Randi said.

"No. *You* don't get it. They'll see it and remove it. Now, what if we could coax the paint into reproducing the same kind of tagging already on the wall? Leave your name forever and for real?" I didn't tell them that if it was indeed Nan paint, it was probably dead: living Nans needed to eat. They had a very short shelf life. Just something more to shove up the price.

Leon chimed in. "Yeah, something to show your kids." Guttural laughter followed that. Like me, Green took johns now and again. But like me, he preferred men, even though he was a guy.

The talk dissipated and I eased back into the arms of my sweet obsession.

⊠ ⊠ ⊠

Green didn't forget what I'd said. He came to find me the next day. I was sitting on K Street, outside the VR sex shop, supposedly panhandling, but I was actually in the grips of another of my favorite obsessions: watching the clouds, imagining their inner workings. The patterns of droplets fascinated me, and, of course, whatever companions I'd conjured that day. I'd gaze for hours at the sky or Nan walls, watching photons shoot from stars or Nans protect the surface they covered. I couldn't really see the minutia of our world. However, I'd had enough schooling to understand the principles. My imagination did the rest.

"Hey, Skull," Green said, sitting down. He handed me a cigarette, the universal bribe. A real black-market one, too, from Uzbekistan, full of tar and sweet nicotine, not one of those made from genetically engineered tobacco plants, supposedly good for you. "Could we change what the Nans make? Instead of, say, red paint, make 'em white? And maybe look like carving?"

I literally pulled my head out of the clouds. I only had two imaginary friends sitting at my feet, neither clamoring for my attention, so I took Green's bribe and answered.

"Theoretically. I mean, they're paint Nans, right? They're made to cover something. Changing the color isn't changing their nature, just what they look like." It sounded good to me. I didn't know if it was bullshit or not. A big part of being the acknowledged egghead in the group—hence my nickname, Skull—had to do with my conviction, not knowing actual facts. My imaginary audience nodded sagely, admiring my wisdom.

"How would you do it?" Green asked.

I wondered if I should negotiate something more from him. I decided not to, not until I found out if I was right.

"Get an imager," I said, as if it would be as simple as that.

"Don't computers program Nans?" Green asked.

"Yes, but who programs the computers? Humans do, using tricky software, not straightforward voice stuff. It calls for images, metaphors."

Green looked confused. My friends also wanted me to go on, to hear more of my brilliance.

"Nans have to work together, in a group, like a beehive or a city, where everything's connected. You have to come up with its food, how it processes its waste, energy that enters the system, energy that leaves the system, like that. Nan programming is complex."

"And to change the Nans I have, I'd need an imager?"

"And someone to work it."

"You could do that, Skull, couldn't you?"

I shrugged. I didn't know. I'd once had a john who'd bragged about working in one of those plants. He'd also said that only special people worked the software, and that I seemed as weird as them. Whatever. My abilities weren't going to be tested anytime soon. That only happened in proper schools, and all I had was the school of life.

As Green hadn't heard of any of this, he didn't react to the impossibility of the proposal. He simply asked, "So where do we find an imager?"

I sighed. I'd already accepted Green's first bribe. I was going to have to continue helping him, stop my brain from obsessing, and focus more attention on the real world.

I knew they didn't have such equipment at the library. However, the library might have a list of public imagers, if there were such things.

So we took the Metro to the library. Lots of slow terminals that used keyboards. Ancient software that didn't respond to voice commands. That sour smell that comes from the homeless who shelter there but don't take care of themselves. The musty book smell, though most everything was electronic. My imaginary companions crowded close to me, like henchmen worried about their boss.

I made sure I knew Green's plan before I started. "You want to change the paint you have, to make it work with the Nans in that wall you were talking about, right?"

Green nodded. "I need to make a mark. Something permanent. On one of those Nan walls. I don't intend to live and die as just a statistic."

I didn't feel the same way, but I could empathize. I'd watched Green paint a garden once. It had been after midnight, in that little square on M Street. I still remember the colors, the textures, the vitality he brought to that cold concrete. For the first time I sort of understood him. I mean, just tagging—signing your name everywhere—is pretty dumb. Changing the environment, bringing some warmth to the streets, that was something. We had different world views: I'd chosen to float, in the grips of one obsession or another, while he fought to bring life to the stones.

First I checked if my theory was right. To my surprise, it was. You could alter the nature of some Nans, like make paint Nans look like carving Nans. Next I checked on our quarry, finding close-ups of the Vietnam Veterans Memorial. If I understood the imaging process right,

I'd have to memorize the fancy typeset on that wall, be able to carve every letter in my dreams, then pass my dreams to the Nans. Then I searched for public, that is, free, imagers. No luck there. None were listed for rent either. However, I figured if you had the right connections, you could gain access to one.

Maybe we could find one and sneak into it. I told Green we could try.

That was the moment my obsessive world changed.

It wasn't gradual at all. It was like a switch had been flicked.

My two imaginary guys disappeared. That didn't bother me too much; it happened when I let the real world intrude too far.

However, a new guy appeared, and not my type at all. My taste in men runs to the Latin or darker. I like black hair and dark eyes, that five-o'clock shadow pressed against my chin when they kiss me. Blond hair and blue eyes have never done it for me. Maybe that's 'cause my dad looked like Thor after a couple years of too much feasting. Or maybe it's always been my preference.

Yet, there he was.

This guy was shorter than I was, with carrot-colored hair cropped in a jar-head haircut, sickly white skin, thin and ghostly. You could see his collarbones. Two wiry arms stuck out from under his vest, a shapeless green jacket with the sleeves torn off, really. No padding or muscles to hold onto. He wore his matching pants so loose you couldn't see his butt. He wasn't as solid as my usual imagining either. He was more transparent, an afterthought.

I almost believed I hadn't seen him when my other companions reappeared. However, when I peered beyond them, he was still standing there.

Green was used to my continual entourage and had never commented when I talked to the air. However, he must have seen something in my face.

"Hey, Skull, you OK?" he asked.

I was tempted to ask if he could see the guy. Of course he couldn't. I was still tempted, just the same.

"Come on," I said. "Let's get out of here." We were going to check with our compatriots to see if they knew where an imaging complex was.

All the way back to the rail bridge I kept looking behind me. The two men from my regular entourage walked shoulder to shoulder, protecting me. I caught glimpses of the stranger, the one who didn't belong, staring at me. I didn't stare back. I hadn't invited this image into my obsession. I wanted it to go away.

Of course it didn't.

I found myself a fat john that night, one who wasn't too particular about my lack of personal hygiene, got him worked up and swallowed it all down. It was a shade more horrible than usual. I couldn't stay focused, so I didn't have any of my own men distracting me during the job. Instead, that skinny redhead stared at me the whole time.

I walked away richer, enough to buy a bed for the night if I decided to not sleep under the bridge. After I did my usual upchuck I went looking for some real comfort. Maybe a warm sandwich or some soup.

That's when the redhead stopped me.

"You don't have to do that," he said. His voice—whisper thin—barely registered above the sounds of the whining electric cars jockeying for position.

"What would you know about it?" I muttered under my breath. This guy was obviously clueless. He'd never had a john. He didn't understand how the upchuck helped me separate the job from my life. I may have been vile, unclean, unworthy, or at least that's what my father had tried to beat into me. Whatever. Upchucking after a john was my way of pretending I was better than I was, that I could force the vileness from me. I needed to do it.

I invented a few companions and started walking again. I could have jumped onto the Metro—maybe even paid for it—but I didn't want the hassle. The bridge was only a couple of miles away.

I gathered my people around me, like a rich woman pulling her fur collar tighter, and settled into my long stride, the kind I can keep up forever, when I've had enough to eat.

The damn redhead pushed his way through the man on my left.

I've never seen that happen. My men co-exist. Sure, they get jealous of each other sometimes. I let it happen, encourage it even. It's good for my ego. However, one can't dismiss another. I was the only one with that power.

Until now.

Mr. White Guy dismissed the rest of my cohorts with a wave of his hand.

Now I was angry. How dare he? What did he want? Why didn't he just leave me the hell alone?

"You're the only one who can see me," he said, by way of an answer. I didn't realize I'd spoken out loud.

No. This wasn't happening to me. My obsessions weren't real. Everyone thought I was loony because I talked and responded to men who weren't there. Yet, I always knew they weren't there. I just wanted—needed—to escape. I refused to go fully mad, unable to distinguish who did and didn't exist.

I closed my eyes and wished the redhead away. I willed that when I opened my eyes, I'd only see the orange streetlight spotlighting shiny bits of garbage in the gutter, the sharp neon escaping between the shop window bars to my right, the scarlet graffiti creeping up from the sidewalk like a tropical blossom. I willed myself back into the freezing wind blowing through my clothes, the bitter leftover vomit taste in my mouth, the way the dirt encrusted in my joints ground together when I closed my hands into fists.

Of course he hadn't disappeared when I opened my eyes. He hadn't grown more solid either. He still had that translucent quality to him that none of my other men had. I could see lights through him.

The night grew colder as he approached.

My breath came short and harsh from my lungs. Sweat broke out on my forehead and instantly froze. I knew my mouth was open by the way the icy air froze my teeth.

Gathering all the courage I'd built up since I'd left home, I punched him. My hand passed through his belly, like I suspected it would. I didn't expect the cold and heat and disemboweled feelings that came with it. I gagged again.

He stood with arms crossed in front of his chest, disgust mingled with impatience on his face.

"What?" I asked, defiant now. If he were a ghost, as I now suspected he was, what could he do to me? Besides dismiss my men, make me lonely and honestly crazy?

"Why don't you make something of yourself?"

I snorted. That didn't even deserve a response. I was where I wanted to be. I'd chosen my obsession a long time ago, when I'd left home. I had to believe that if I wanted to survive.

"You could be more," he insisted.

His words triggered a memory. I realized he was wearing fatigues, that green cheap army crap shown in movies about the "good" old days. Vets dumped on the streets these days wore self-repairing Sali-suits coated with Nans and micro-cameras that turned them half invisible.

"Like you? Be all I could be? Where the hell did that get you?"

It was his turn to snort. He looked away, studied the wall, the tag-ger's desperate attempts to make a mark, then he looked back at me.

"Dead," he said. He paused for a moment, his eyes boring into me. "And forgotten. But not forever. With your help."

He needed my help? I nearly laughed. Being insane didn't seem as bad, if my non-made-up companions were all this funny.

We talked as we walked. He, too, wanted me to change the Nans paint to permanently sign the wall, but not with Green's name. He wanted his name up there. He said he deserved it. He'd died in that war. He'd been captured, his dog tags stolen, sold to the highest bidder.

I told him that didn't make sense. How could a Vietnamese have passed for this skinny white kid?

Then he told me he'd been listed as MIA, but his state's senator hadn't been popular, so his name had been lost. He had other paranoid theories, too, but none of them made any sense. I wondered if he'd done something bad and had gotten a dishonorable discharge, which is why they didn't want his name on their wall. Madness lurked in the corners of his eyes, but that might have come from being a ghost for too many years.

"Look, I'm not sure what you heard, me talking with Green. I might have been making that stuff up, about the Nans."

We'd gone past the rail bridge by that time, this shadow and I. The night air had the crisp edges of diamonds, hard enough to choke a man. The light pollution was too dense to make out any stars, but the half-moon valiantly battled to be seen. The hill we sat on overlooked the channel: a black band of rolling sludge.

"No, you have it exactly right. I've been studying that colony for years, trying to make friends with it. It only likes its own kind—the cover Nans only accept other cover Nans; the carving Nans, only other carving Nans. Each one knows its place, its turf, and it eats any invaders. You're going to have to convince the cover Nans that the carving you add has always been there and get them to defend it."

"And how would I do this?"

"Use an imager," he said.

I laughed, a dry hollow sound in the cold night. "So I was right? That's how you'd do it? And where am I going to find one of those?"

The ghost shook his head and laughed, a sound like thin ice breaking. "You already have one," he said, pointing to my head.

Now I knew I'd gone mad. I couldn't change paint at an atomic level by thinking at it. I needed a machine, probably a big one that would dim the lights in the city when I switched it on and was worked on by lovely scientist boys with intense eyes and white coats.

"Just supposing you're right. Why would I do this for you?"

"I'll show you," the ghost said. He held his hand out to me.

I hesitated, remembering the gut-wrenching nausea I'd had when I'd punched him.

"No matter," he said, withdrawing his hand. "Close your eyes."

I did. A cold wind caressed my skin, making me shiver. I drew my knees up to my chest and wrapped my arms around them, trying to preserve what little body heat I had.

No music came, no pictures either. Just feelings. Here I was, alone, not even an imaginary companion around. Drifting through the night, through life, no one to remember me, say my name in a prayer. The hopelessness seeped through every pore. I clung to this half-life without belief of respite. Others had been helped, thousands of others stood with their names for all to see, but I was excluded. I could never force my way into their ranks, though I longed with all the heart of a beaten dog to be accepted.

It took me a while to dig myself out of the morass the ghost had blown into me. They were, but weren't, my feelings. This was his life, how he saw the world. He wanted to join, however symbolically, his buddies. This was why I had to help him. It didn't matter to me how I floated in my obsessions. I'd chosen my life. He hadn't.

The ghost told me I should sleep, that he'd show me how to proceed the next day.

Sleep. Right. Even the crazed sleep, I suppose. I made my slow way back to the bridge, to huddle under blankets and thick plastic news sheets Green had saved for me. I didn't sleep. I conjured my own men to comfort me, but I couldn't bring myself to satisfaction. I felt that damn redhead's eyes staring at the back of my head, raising my hackles, bringing a freezing touch to the choices I'd made so long ago.

▨ ▧ ▨

I asked Green the next day to see the paint he'd scored. All this was moot if the Nans were dead. The bottle glowed with a blue light, like a designer drink, the ones that make you smart, or healthy, or something. It felt warm to the touch.

The "dead-by" date glowed, too, powered by a strip battery. Once it faded, the Nans would starve to death. I didn't know that day's date. Neither did Green. The ghost wasn't certain, but he thought the Nans would be dead in a day or so. We didn't have much time.

I read the instructions out loud, pretending I was doing it for my benefit, but I don't think Green could read. Also, now that we were getting closer to the deed, I wanted to make sure he knew the danger.

According to the label, these Nans would react only to other Nans of a certain brand. However, we'd all seen adverts for horror flicks where Nans mutated and invaded people's bodies. Besides, if they were so safe, why did they need to be applied with an "inert spreader," something specifically manufactured that the Nans wouldn't react to?

I raised these fears to my companions, both seen and unseen, but neither seemed to care.

I never found out who Green rolled to get this paint. It wasn't something you could buy at the local market. This was the real thing here, industrial-strength Nan.

The ghost told me we needed to do an experiment, to make sure we could work it. Green asked about using an imager. I told him I'd found a way around it. I hoped. The ghost shrugged.

We needed to find someplace with active Nan walls but not downtown or an office park, where we'd be conspicuous. We hit on the telephone center, close to the bus lines but not too upscale.

One of us had to be made presentable to go buy the inert spreader. I didn't want to embarrass Green by asking if he could read or not, so I volunteered. Green stood guard while I used the water in the toilet at the park to clean up. You never went into one of those stalls alone. Too easily trapped, and though I had nothing, that wouldn't stop someone from trying to take it. I stripped down and then only put back on my middle layer. It was cleaner than the clothes laying either next to my skin or exposed to the polluted air.

I tried dragging my fingers through my dreadlocks, rearranging them in an orderly fashion. Wasn't going to happen. So we borrowed Randi's straight edge, and I chopped my hair short. When I finished, Green evened it all out, made it look stylish, and me, almost respectable. Let me stress: Almost. Even in that dinged piece of metal they called a mirror I could see layers of street-armor that a little water and a new hairdo wouldn't wash away.

I still had the john's money from the night before. No one glanced twice at me when I walked into the block-long hardware store. I looked more like the next-door neighbor after a weekend binge than a kid from the streets. The ghost pointed the spreader out to me before I got lost in that labyrinth of aisles. The aged female cashier even tried to be nice to me. I knew better than to say more than three words. I'd wrapped myself in a tight ball: anyone got too close, and something nasty would spring loose.

All the way to the telephone center I studied Green's tag: the angular way the *G* set the name off; how the *R* resembled a five-pointed star; how both *E*'s looped and swirled, like seawater flowing over rocks; and how the *N* dripped off the page. I had to know it well enough that my imaginary men could reproduce it if they had to. Those letters formed my marching orders; how harsh every life started, followed all too soon by that slippery slope into death. Only by truly knowing that tag could I reproduce it.

We located a remote corner when we arrived, out of the flow of pedestrians. I sat for a while communing with the Nans. I saw them as spinning balls in the primary colors of children's toys, dancing. I imagined how they worked together, how they bred and ate and defended their turf from all invaders.

When the flow was right, I motioned for Green to use the spreader—just a long, dull-looking flat stick, like a plastic putty knife. He tagged his name on the wall.

Then the ghost stepped in. He put his hands on my shoulders. I'd never felt ice so cold. He pushed me forward, made me get close to the wall, and told me to breathe on it. I hesitated. He pushed down on my shoulders, forcing the breath from my body, like a musician squeezing an accordion. I breathed as hard as I could, from deep in my belly, like I was trying to fog a window.

Suddenly I could see, really see, the Nans in the wall. The ghost had lent me its sight. My simple globes disappeared, their uncomplicated country dance unfinished. A silver fractal pattern of twelve-sided stars blossomed ahead of me, then kept growing like crystal. I concentrated on each part, adapting the shapes to form Green's tag. Each curve had its own specially shaped Nans, which only knew that minute segment of space. So did each line. The area between them was a continent. However, I forced myself from one place to the next, breathing form and shape and meaning. I struggled through every nanometer, like hacking through a rain forest with a plastic sword.

Finally I reached the end. I pulled back and found myself on the cold concrete, shivering, drained, my legs numb.

There was Green's name—a silver talisman against the black building. The phrase that went through my mind was "the breath of life." The ghost had willed it from me and given it to the Nans.

Green was ecstatic. Finally, a permanent mark on a Nan wall, the holy grail of all taggers. It didn't dissolve in two minutes, like normal paint. He patted me on the shoulder. The warmth from his touch shocked me almost as much as the cold from the ghost had.

We stared at the wall like a couple of catatonics. Green told me we had to get going, but I didn't want to. I begged the ghost for another look, at the Nan level. I knew that it was only an illusion spun by the ghost, but it was more satisfying than any of the men I'd ever dreamed up.

He finally acquiesced. At first, it was beautiful. The fractal edges continued to sprout, only much more slowly. As one tiny silver thread disappeared, a new one appeared next to it, joined with its black twin. The inner core of stars had stabilized and changed more gradually, each shifting against the other, like flowers seeking better light.

Then the black Nans started moving faster, like they were agitated. They butted against the silver Nans, nuzzling them, like an overly friendly john looking for a breast to suckle. They were hungry. Some kind of food wasn't getting passed through to them. Thorny black Nans started being manufactured. They threaded together and forced their way across the silver path. They swirled against the stars, broke them apart, then devoured them.

The glimmer faded, curve and angle alike, the paint Nans providing fuel for their black brethren.

"What happened, Skull?" Green asked.

The ghost told me. "Not enough energy."

I repeated his words and waited for more.

"The Nans, they need to feed. The paint Nans couldn't exchange enough, well, food, with the inner layer, to keep their colony alive. They were marked as different, killed, eaten."

Green shook his head. "I'll never be able to leave a permanent mark."

"Don't worry Green," I said, still the human parrot. "I didn't give them all the energy I could have. When we go against the wall, the Nans'll have more than enough to keep them going."

Green helped me stand. I'd taken half a dozen steps before I realized exactly what I'd said. Was this crazy ghost thinking I was sacrificing my life for him? Just so he could put his stupid name on a wall?

When I turned around, I realized no, that wasn't the case at all. The ghost was putting *himself* into the wall, to maintain his Nans. Going to die all the way, if he could.

Somehow, it didn't make me feel any better.

🖾 🖾 🖾

We walked by the wall that afternoon, part of the continual parade of people. I pretended to help Green find a name. I was the clean-cut one after all. We were actually scoping our hit, finding where to make our mark. On half of the wall, the names are all right-justified. On the other half, they're all left-justified. We needed to find a space big enough to fit the ghost's name.

Green moaned as we walked past slab after slab. "I haven't gone to war," he said. He reached out to touch one of the carved names. "I haven't died. But I want to leave something behind. Like them. Gone but not forgotten. You can understand that, can't you, Skull?"

I nodded. I hadn't had the heart to tell Green that I wasn't helping him leave the mark he'd intended, that the spirit who traveled with us wasn't going to preserve Green's name. He still knew something was going on, that my hot air wouldn't change the Nans, that I hadn't turned into an imager overnight.

Once we found our spot (and I convinced the ghost that putting his name up was more important than getting it on the right slab, since the names are chronologically ordered by date of death), I sat down to study.

That damn typeface was much more difficult than Green's tag. All the letters were regular, identical. I couldn't fake a single curve or line. The name had to be perfect, or it wouldn't be accepted by the Nans.

When I finally stood up, unsure if my knees remembered how to unbend or support my weight, night had fallen. Green led me to a bench some distance from the wall. He'd scored a neo-protein burger, complete with vitamin-enriched tomatoes on fiber bread. It tasted like cardboard—healthy junk food always did.

I nodded my thanks and started eating my half. However, I got distracted, forming the ghost's name out of the seeds on the top of the bun. I must have been more out of it than usual. Green broke my stare by moving my hand to my mouth, making me eat. I didn't notice I was shivering, but Green did. He made me sit on his lap. When I protested, he looked around, forcing me to do the same.

The wall formed a long, low line in the distance, its middle humped, like a dead slug. The trees were planted well apart from each other, no space to hide. Most people hurried by, rushing to get out of the cold. The ones that were left were couples. So Green and I snuggled together, trying to blend in. It helped keep away the chill of the night.

The wall memorial is open until midnight, lit with bright lights and the occasional patrolling guard. Green hadn't discovered any other security measures: they didn't need them, not with the Nans. So we settled in to wait for our witching hour, until after the grass was covered with crunchy dew.

Green and I didn't talk. I did start obsessing. It worked for a while. The man I conjured was Asian, hard and sweet. Long hair in a ponytail, rough little beard, bunched muscles across his chest, down his arms. His eyes never left mine as he went down, his hands and lips working magic.

However, something was missing. I pulled up short of completion. I couldn't help but see my machinations in his actions. The magician had been spotted behind the curtain. My dream man was based too much on me. I desired that other obsessive world, the one of fractals and twining strings of atoms.

After the last patrol, when the lights dimmed, we swooped in like vultures after prey. I thought our target would be harder to see, but it wasn't. That wall reflects all that is held next to it: sometimes shiny with flowers, ribbons, medals, and poems, and sometimes black with the night. Its darkness drew us.

As I was setting up, Green leaned over to whisper in my ear. "You see why I have to do this? I have to make a dent in this mass of tags. Please," he said.

What could I say? He and I weren't part of some kind of Hollywood gang, one for all and all that crap. But I needed to try something, so Green's mark could stay as well.

I pulled the Nan paint out of the bag. The dead-by date flashed at me like a police strobe. Hopefully the Nans still had enough life to do their job. I put the paint bottle on my left side and the spreader on my right. Then I closed my eyes, put my head next to the wall, and pushed myself into that other view.

My childish version of the Nans had altered a little: the balls were now multi-colored, and the dance they did had a touch of sophistication. I couldn't recreate the ghost's view on my own though.

The Nans instantly formed ranks to face me, growing spikes. They seemed more active than the wall Nans I'd seen that morning. I don't want to say that other spirits fed these Nans. That's getting too metaphysical. However, they had more life than I expected.

They couldn't see me, but they sensed the coming attack. With one hand, I waved at Green. He grabbed his spray paint from the bag and started to do his thing. The plan was for him to draw the cops away from me by tagging the wall with regular paint so I had time to do my thing.

The attention of the wall Nans shifted away from me. Green tagged his name, looping marks in his signature emerald-green spray paint, over and over again. The internal defenses of the wall were good: the paint was absorbed as soon as he applied it. He kept moving away from me, going down the wall.

I spread the other paint, the Nan paint, over the spot we'd selected. I took the tip of the inert spreader and carved marks in it. It didn't have to be precisely the name that was going to go up there, that came later, with the imaging. Just some strokes and curves, to start with.

I heard the sirens. Didn't stop. Braced myself.

The ghost didn't just put his hands on my shoulders this time. He threw himself into me. The cold choked off my breath. I couldn't move. The darkness of the wall threatened to invade me, suck me into a whirlpool. I'd never escape that night. I'd float in nothingness, never knowing if I was alive or dead, locked in an obsession not of my choosing. I couldn't push back, couldn't look away, could only wait for the inevitable swallowing.

The ghost came to my rescue: warm images of summer at a lake cabin, diving into lime-colored water from an inner-tube swing. The taste of the Midwest filled my mouth, humid nights and the sound of combines.

Then the cold returned, but I could handle it now. I saw winters with snow, skating on black ice, patterns of leaves and twigs frozen underneath it.

The ice, that was bad. That was the killer. The unexpected patch of it, the jackknifed truck taking out his parents and his grandparents at the same time. The move to the state orphanage. No more lake cabin. Concrete walls, rusted iron beds, and hissing showers. He'd only spent a couple of years there, long enough to lose his old friends, not long enough to make new ones. He had nowhere else to go, nothing else to do, so he'd volunteered. Then he'd been killed.

He really had died over there, still a member of his company. The taste of the jungle, hot, humid, damp, the end of his life, and the metallic taste of blood filled my mouth.

The ghost blew out of my body, mingled with the breath of my life, making changes to the Nans, filling them, making their circuit complete. I asked him for a favor as he passed through me, using me as so many other men had. I fell over, cold, sore, gagging as he withdrew. The infamous upchuck.

The cops grabbed me before I could see my work. I heard Green screaming obscenities while they brought him down. He'd tried so hard. I heard later he tagged the face of the arresting officer. They had to stun him before they could wrap his wrists in those damn plastic strips. I passed out—too much life drained from me.

I gave in to my latest obsession fully while I was in the slammer, staring at the walls, imagining the atoms there. It worried one of the cops enough to take me to the infirmary. A doc actually listened to my conversations, called in a favor, and got me tested. Maybe it was because I had that clean look about me, no longer just a street kid. Or maybe the ghost had nudged someone, made an atom change its orbit. They found what I could do, that I had the kind of discipline mixed with imagination that they needed to help them run their Nan factories.

They brought me out. And raised me up. It's easier working with the machines, the software, the chemicals. Easier than working with spirits. It doesn't drain my life from me. Well, not as much.

So I made it. I left the neighborhood, the rail bridge, the cold outdoor nights, the panhandling, the johns. Green never made it out of prison. He was liked too much by another inmate, who killed him in jealousy.

Work is now my obsession. My nights are warmer, yet at the same time colder and more lonely without imaginary men. I think about taking a john sometimes. If I actually went ahead and did it, I wouldn't do the upchuck when they were through. The whole world is real, and I can't push away the parts I don't like.

I've gone back to see my handiwork. I was afraid to go at first, afraid I'd see my ghost again, but I never have. I don't think he's a ghost anymore: his name's still on that wall.

Though I wonder. He never told me he had a middle name. Yet a *G* stands between his first and last name.

I like to think it stands for Green.

Afterword: For me, a story isn't just a single idea. It also doesn't come from a single inspiration. The formulaic idea for this story actually came from my husband, who suggested that in the future the Wall might be protected by nanotechnology.

Another background element: I attended a seminar once, taught by the police, about graffiti. (This was when I worked for a business consortium—the Dinkytown Business Association—ninety-five businesses in a small, five-block region, mostly ma-and-pa types of stores.) The police were primarily interested in teaching us how to recognize the difference between tagging (name signing) and gang markings. I've used that knowledge often when in strange cities, noting which neighborhoods were safer than others.

Another element was a memory of my first trip to New York. I remember walking for blocks without seeing a single tree. Then seeing some amazing graffiti art in a little square—literally, a garden growing in the middle of the concrete jungle.

I mixed these all together, along with talks with my friend Leon (who spent many years on the street) and this story came out.

names in marble

Joe Haldeman

stuck in Washington for seven hours,
holiday Sunday, nothing open
try to walk twenty miles
get the kinks out

mile upon mile of manicured grass
putting green of the gods   Japanese tourists
takes a lot of fertilizer   taking pictures of each other
                                    before these alien shrines

          the air heavy   with vapor   with history

and weirdos everywhere

                   I mean   every where

do this do that for me an
my friends or the whole   (one balding hippy
fuckin thing's comin down   scraggly beard   clean rags
aroun yer ears man   quiet smile
                  and blue policeman's eyes)

whales   lesbians   farmers   veterans   supply-side economists

on a raised platform
a man with a microphone
and no legs   screaming
praising God   standing on his stumps
    for the gift of tongues   in the wheelchair
                                      praising God for the gift

        three women down below
        shout amen   periodically

    beer bellies sucked into the fourth dimension
        as nylon jogging shorts whisper by
            caressing the lean flanks
            of determined women

    people looking at each other looking at each other

  the air heavy with curiosity   with humidity   with expectation

and then you have the slabs of marble   names in marble
                                          names to conjure with

                Looking down on it all
                the colossal joke: a tenth of a mile
                                      of marble spike
                                      erect
                                      for the Father
                                      of his Country

            but then

    Jefferson   invisible behind the columns
    hidden   from the children of his slaves

Lincoln   still brooding in the shadows
perhaps for the children of his slaves

the air heavy with sadness   with history   with rain withheld
the air heavy

asked a uniform where you could find the Wall
surprisingly, she pointed:

so close you could have hit it with a grenade.

In and out of town ten times
since the Wall went up
but never sought it out

if you pick at the scab the wound stays open

besides it wouldn't work
fifty-seven thousand names   like some small town city square:
engraved in marble   The World Will Never Forget
                                  The Names Of These Fallen Brave
we didn't know each other's names Who Gave Their Lives That We
no law against it   but   Might Enjoy The Fruits Of Liberty
for radio security
we were Professor Hot Rod Farmer Frosty

so that's what we answered to anyhow
and forgot the other names

now on this sacred wall
they can't put Goofball Jewboy Tex

so you stand there in front of the names of strangers
the children of strangers
laughing and playing

you stand in front of the names
and do the arithmetic on 1968

somehow
the ones who were nineteen then
are dead a lifetime now

a short lifetime

their names endure

Afterword: I have in-laws in the Washington area, and after the Wall went up I must have gone within a few miles of it twenty times before I got the nerve to go there. I wrote this poem, naturally enough, as a reaction to the first time I went to the Wall. I was taking the train down from Boston to Florida and had a half-day layover in Washington, so I walked to the Mall and found my way to the Wall. There I had a disturbing experience of see- ing dead friends' names but not knowing which names they were. We knew each other only by code names (for radio security). We had always been encouraged to use our radio code names in everyday conversation. So I was Professor; and the other guys had monikers like Hot Rod, Jew Boy, and Frosty. They didn't put those on the Wall. I knew the two dates when everybody died. I looked in the register and had the strange, helpless feel- ing that I was looking at their names without knowing which they were.

Of course I cried, not being made of marble myself. People gave me space, but I needed more space and walked for miles and miles. I wound up in a fancy French restaurant in Georgetown and had a martini and half a bottle of wine more expensive than I could afford. Then I walked back to Union Station and, on the train, started writing this poem. I finished it later, banging on a manual typewriter in my office at MIT.

Second Chance

Ralph Roberts

Given the same amount of intelligence, timidity will do a thousand times more damage in war than audacity.
—Clausewitz, *On War*

THE WALL STRETCHES TO my right and left, it looms before me. Polished, black, the names of men I knew—comrades—march forever silently in place, column after stately column.

In the dark surface I see, reflected, Frederick Hart's Vietnam Veterans statue, *The Three Soldiers.*

In the dark surface also I see, reflected, William E. "Billy" Bumpers. He's fifty-five, an insurance salesman from Waynesville, North Carolina. Three kids, all grown and moved away—one grandkid, one on the way. A Vietnam vet. A little overweight. A little bald. Me. That's what I see: me in jeans and a yellow shirt, camera hanging from a strap around my neck.

Damn tourist. Damn teary-eyed tourist looking at the Wall. Remembering. Recalling.

I came back alive in 1970, a little guilty but selling insurance like crazy ever since. My own agency now, Bumpers Everystate Auto and Life, right there on Main, downtown—largest in the county, three agents working for me—all vets like me, aggressive and always closing the deal, just like I've done for years. We take no prisoners, we just write policies. Lots of policies. We play board and computer war games to hone our skills, we strategize, we plan attacks resulting in our agency being top seller in its region for the last eight years straight. I should have been a general. Yes, we write policies like crazy.

I'm taking a little time out from a boring seminar on the new insurance regulations for 2003, being held here in Washington, to visit the Wall for the first time. Should have come sooner . . . I owe it to them. Should have come sooner.

I expected to be moved but . . .

"If you had it to do over again," says a voice in my head, *"what would you do? How would you fix it?"*

Suddenly it's dark and I'm falling. I hit with a thump, forced to my knees by the impact. Dirt, a dirt trail in jungle, a little moonlight now as eyes adjust and I take this in. Automatic weapon firing somewhere in the distance—sharp *cracks*. I *know* this jungle; I *know* that sound— it's AK-47s, North Vietnamese army weapon of choice! There are answering shots; tight groups of three. M-16s? Yeah!

Something never forgotten—those sounds of a firefight—and old instincts take over. I drop the rest of the way to the ground and roll my fat ass off the trail. You *don't* stay in the open on a trail you know nothing about. Off in the distance I see some kind of glow—a fire!— dimly reflected off the vegetation.

"Where the hell did you come from?" a voice, not *the voice*, whispers, the man I had landed against startled.

Rough hands grab me and quickly pat me down.

"Some damn civilian, Sarge! No weapons. Just a camera."

I hear slithering sounds as someone else crawls over to us. My night vision is coming in now; I see two faces looming out of the night, camouflage grease paint. Jungle fatigues. I know jungle fatigues. I know that smell of men out in the field for days. Thirty years drop away like I wish thirty pounds would.

"What's a friggin' reporter doing out here?" the sergeant whispers in growl. "Friggin' up my friggin' ambush site!" He pauses and a sudden thought seems to come. "Were you on that chopper shot down a few minutes ago?"

Now I understand the distant light of flames and the sound of weapons.

He turns my head to better see my face in what little light there is.

"Ah, shit," he says, "sorry, General. Damn glad to see you, sir! We though you had bought it when they got your chopper." He turns and hisses a whisper back into the trees: "Garcia, get on the horn and get me the friggin' reaction platoon out here ASAP. Tell 'em we found the general!"

※ ※ ※

"If you had it to do over again," says a voice in my head, *"what would you do? How would you fix it?"*

I come fully awake and open my eyes. I'm in a bunker, lying on one of those brick-hard army cots. Harsh yellow light, a far-off drone of a generator. A short Vietnamese man stands over me, dressed in fatigues, grinning, with a razor, shaving brush, and soap in one hand and a bowl of steaming water in the other. A towel is draped over his shoulder. His broad face shows what appears to be genuine affection born of long association.

"Wakey, wakey, General, sir," he says. "You must be shaved and in numbah-one condition today to save all our butts. We are most thankful you survived crash that burned up everyone else. Most thankful."

The hand holding the razor shook a little.

"Er . . ." I say, watching the hand warily, "thanks . . . er . . . Tranh."

Now . . . *how the hell* did I know his name?

I swing my legs over the bed and sit up. I am still wearing my civilian clothes—the jeans and yellow shirt. My camera hangs from the back of a chair near the army cot.

He nods, pleased, steps forward, places the water carefully on the chair, and gently lathers up my face. He squints in concentration as he smoothly shaves me.

"May I ask General where he got camera? Very nice. Did you buy it in Saigon while meeting with big boss General Fat End?"

"That's General *Falence*," I say, smiling at the private joke between us.

How do I know all this?

Yet, I also know I bought the camera at Wal-Mart in Waynesville day before yesterday, just before driving to Asheville for my flight to the insurance seminar in Washington.

He finishes the shave, cleans up my face with the towel. "Uniform spicky-span. I go hide from rockets now," he says, and leaves.

I hear the thunderous *thumps* of rockets hitting somewhere nearby.

Another sound never forgotten, 122 millimeter rockets—incoming! The ceiling shakes and a little dust drifts down from the beams up there. I'm in a bunker. I'm safe.

I stand and look at the uniform draped neatly over another chair. Two black stars embroidered on the collar. The nametag reads "Bumpers." I'm a major general. Funny. In that other life, I was just a sergeant when I returned stateside and left the army.

I take off my civvies and put on the uniform. It fits! It fits like the proverbial glove. Well . . . OK, it's maybe a little tight—I've been eating at McDonald's and Sagebrush a lot lately for lunch. And my wife's one fine cook. No army rations for me.

Tranh pokes his head back in. "Good. General is dressed. Ham and eggs for breakfast. Now, most illustrious one. Staff meeting in fifteen minutes."

I grin at Tranh and walk into the next room. A single setting is laid on a folding olive-drab table. Piles of ham, bacon, sausages, hotcakes, coffee. I make straight for the coffee. It's good. This General Bumpers, he eats well. I guess all generals did. Should have been one sooner.

"Hurry, hurry," Tranh says, his tone more like that of a mother than a servant.

"How long have you been with me now, Tranh?" I ask, buttering a stack of hotcakes. I was remembering an old military axiom to the effect that if you have a chance to eat, EAT. There may not be another anytime soon.

Tranh shakes his head fondly. "You know well. Since your third tour here, way back when you were nothing, just lowly major. Twenty years."

"Right," I say, smiling.

Inside I try to make sense of conflicting memories. Pat, my wife in Waynesville, I recall her well. But . . . there's a Megan back in the States; we're divorced now. Something about me spending too much time in the war zone. She couldn't take it anymore.

I keep shoveling in the food, Pat always says I think better while I'm eating.

Why? Why am I here? In someone else's place. Even if it's me I'm replacing?

A colonel stomps in, that's the only way to describe it. Neumann—built squat and strong as a fireplug. Yeah, Gregg Neumann—my Chief of Staff and second in command now that the XO, Brigadier Thomas, was killed two days ago, just before my trip to Saigon for a quick briefing and good old-fashioned ass-chewing by General Falence.

"Get off your damn rear end and do something!" he'd yelled at me.

"We've got to do something . . . sir," Colonel Neumann begins without preamble.

I finish eating and wipe my mouth with the white napkin there. Real linen. Generals live well, even in the middle of a war. I look at Neumann. We don't like each other. He thinks I'm too hesitant, that our position being surrounded and our present dire straits reflect my military incompetence. It's been reported to me that he tells other officers my whole career has been like that, me advancing only through longevity and doing things exactly by the book.

I'm not sure I like the general I am.

"They broke through in three sectors, last night," Neumann is saying, disgust barely disguised in his voice. "We had to fall back to the backup bunkers. Once they get through those, they'll be right in our midst here and we're all dead! . . . Sir!"

I know Neumann is not one of the ones happy I "survived" the chopper shootdown last night. He wants to take command, to save the situation as he sees it. I also know, however it is that I know these things, that while I've been complacent and gotten us into a horrible military predicament, I am really competent and have earned my two stars. Neumann is ill-suited to lead this force. He has neither the experience nor the temperament. Everyone might die here through my inactivity, but Neumann would find a quicker, more stupid way to waste lives.

I stand. "Let's get the staff meeting underway, Colonel."

We walk into the next room of the bunker—a large, dusty space with maps tacked to the wall and rickety chairs full of waiting officers. Battalion commanders; my staff officers for operations, intelligence, personal, psyops, supply; and all the rest that make up a two-star general's headquarters, a division HQ.

The officers come to their feet, slowly, not with the usual military snap; obviously they dislike me as well. Before I came, evidently the other General Bumpers had spent a lot of time making a bad thing worse. Mostly, I seem to remember, through his inaction.

"Be seated, gentlemen," I say. "Who's first this morning?"

I take my seat, and the tall, almost cadaverous Lieutenant Colonel Meacham, the G-2, or intel officer, places himself before a large map.

"General Bumpers, gentlemen," he says, "the intelligence situation is this: basically, we're screwed." He taps a pointer on the map. "The division has been emplaced here so long," he says, not quite looking in my direction, "that the North Vietnamese have managed to scrape together five divisions and a number of independent battalions. We're completely surrounded now. Any day they'll make a major push and overrun us."

Behind my back, there is a murmur among the officers. I hear the words *Dien Bien Phu* more than once.

In both lives—as a general and selling insurance—I know my military history. The French were in Vietnam before us. After a near-decade of protracted war and several billion dollars of U.S. aid to the French, they gambled everything militarily and got their forces trapped in a place called *Dien Bien Phu* in 1954. It was like Custer at the Little Big Horn only bigger. The French suffered a huge defeat and left Vietnam, and our involvement began. Almost fifty years later, here we were still.

Meacham taps the map more vigorously. "We've been bombing North Vietnam for more than thirty years now. They're on their knees. But we remain here in the south, in static positions, and we've given them a chance to turn the war around! If they defeat us here . . ." He pauses and says out loud what the others have been whispering: "Well, it's just like Dien Bien Phu was for the French. We lose here and the politicians will cave in. Vietnam will be gone." He lets it sink in that this all could have been prevented by a little action on the part of a certain commanding general.

He taps the map again. I'm ready to stand up, grab his little pointer, and wrap it around his neck.

"We know what a stretch it is for the NVA, the North Vietnamese Army, to put together the force currently besieging us. Gentlemen, they've got all their eggs in this basket. But if they win here, they've won, period."

He lets the pointer drop to his side. "They're about out of ammo and food. . . . But . . . then . . . so are we. And they outnumber us five to one."

He throws the pointer on a table and morosely takes his chair again.

Others follow, painting the picture blacker and blacker. I know—but how, again, I do not—that there has been mutinous talk of Colonel Neumann relieving, a truly drastic action for any military officer to take. I recall, from that royal ass-chewing General Falence launched on me yesterday, that he would replace me if he did not already think it was too late and that he was simply sending me back to die with my men . . . to pull at least a little honor out of the mess I'd made.

One more person reports before it is my turn to take charge of the meeting. It's the chaplain, Major Resnick, as stocky and bereft of hair as I, sadly reporting on the many killed and wounded in just the last day, leading us in a moment of silence for the hundreds that we have lost over the two months of this siege.

Colonel Neumann finally has had enough. He stands and stomps to the front. I know what he's about to do.

"General Bumpers," he says, "This cannot continue. It's likely the NVA will make their final ground assault today. I would in their place!" He looks to his fellow officers, now grumbling, some out loud, that the Colonel was right—meaning, of course, that I am wrong. I see Neumann steeling himself to relieve me and assume command.

I rise and glare him silent. "Just a minute, Colonel, I have a few words."

The force of habit stays his mutiny, at least temporarily, and he sits down. I see he's on the edge of his seat and others are casting him encouraging glances. I don't have but a moment to turn this around.

I pick up Meacham's discarded pointer and turn to the maps to give myself a brief instant of thought. I remember the decades of fighting in Vietnam . . . the events that silenced the war protests in the '70s and allowed Nixon to finish his second full term and drive us toward military victory. Yet, the North Vietnamese, bolstered by stronger Chinese and Soviet support, drove back. Like two boxers in late rounds, we both kept slugging, hoping to win on points.

It had come down to this: the North Vietnamese finally on the ropes, but my alter ego's inactivity was about to let them, as the old cliché goes, snatch victory from the jaws of defeat. The protesters were on the march back home again. Any loss here by American forces—such as the tasty potential massacre I dropped into the NVA's slimy rice bowls—and their victory appears assured. No wonder they were gambling everything they had on it.

In my head surges both General Bumpers' years of training and experience and my own many hours of war gaming back in Waynesville. I turn to face my officers.

In my head, I hear the voice:

"If you had it to do over again, what would you do? How would you fix it?"

Colonel Neumann is getting up again, face determined.

"Siddown!" I say, in my best command voice. He does.

The plan is full blown in my head now. Inspired!

"Audacity," I say, "is the order of the day. It's like that brave American army medic said during the Battle of the Bulge in World War II, 'They've got us surrounded—the poor bastards!'"

Officers sit up straight and begin to pay attention. This was a General Bumpers they had not heard before, but one they had dreamed of hearing.

I spend fifteen minutes laying out my simple plan to use the forces we have, breaking through the NVA lines, then rolling their lines around us up like a fuse burning from both ends.

I fired up the officers, they fired up their troops. And by 1500 that afternoon, we had won.

With no effective opposition, I roll north toward Hanoi, our division doing a George Patton imitation, just as he had roared through France and Germany in that earlier war.

A week later, General Falence radios me an order. "Do not take Hanoi yet. Hold up. We want to bring our allies in on this. Let the Aussies and Koreans march in there first."

"Should I give it back?" I say, echoing Patton again, from where I sit comfortably with my feet up on the desk that used to be Ho Chi Minh's, smoking a victory cigar. I don't know where Tranh got the Havanas, but they're damn good.

An hour later, I am looking at myself in a restroom mirror when that voice is again in my head:

"Yes, this is the way it should be."

I am in bright sunlight and falling, seeing myself topple in the black, polished face of the Wall.

"Hey, the old dude fell," says a young voice.

Two kids in baggy jeans carrying skateboards come over and help me up.

"You OK, old dude?" one of the kids asks.

"Yeah . . . thanks," I say. "I was over there." I gesture toward the Wall.

"Where's that? Some old war," the kid says. "You like a general or somethin', dude?"

They smile and leave in good spirits. I vaguely wave my thanks again. I look at myself in the Wall. I have on jungle fatigues. There are two stars on my collar. My nametag says "Bumpers."

Afterword: I saw a T-shirt years ago; it read: "Southeast Asia War Games, Second Place." Rightly or wrongly, we lost that war. Yes, we came close to winning it, but as the old military saying goes, Close only counts in horse-shoes and hand grenades.

Could we have won? Yes, in my opinion, if there had been a little more resolve on the home front, a few less protests.

Should we have won? The politics of it aside, you should not go to war unless you plan on winning.

Would those millions of Vietnam veterans, myself included (First Cav, 1968-70) have liked a different outcome? Damn right! After all, I invested three years of my life in that endeavor.

This story comes from years of frustration and thought. I feel no guilt over losing; it was beyond my control and I certainly did my part, but still, defeat rankles.

I address in this piece not "how" we could have triumphed but rather the feeling that we should have triumphed and would have, if only we got a second chance. It made me feel good . . . and that's what a story should do. Please enjoy, and if it makes you think, well that's the risk we writers take.

BLOOD BONE TENDON STONE

Michael Brotherton

Getting out of the taxi in front of the Hotel Washington, Duke's pull reached me even though the Wall was a mile away. I felt an urge to head there immediately, but the ancient doorman had started for my wheelie and I didn't have the heart to deny him. I tipped him a dollar and felt guilty for being thirty-three.

"Scott Crenshaw," I told the woman at the desk. "I have a reservation for two nights."

Waiting for the computer to bring up the files, the pull developed into a faint voice. I couldn't make out words yet, but it was a voice nonetheless and conveyed the character of my father—such as it was.

I endured the glacial check-in, packed myself into the tiny elevator, and dumped my things in a sixth-floor room. I thought about changing out of my running shoes, but I'd spent all day on an airplane and I was tired. I wasn't going to risk a blister.

I did remember to put the paper and charcoal pencil in my jacket pocket.

I hiked to the Mall, past the T-shirt vendors, past the Bush cardboard photo-op, and hung a right at the Washington Monument. It was a brisk Friday evening in late February, but the walk warmed me. Winded me, too. I was out of shape. I promised myself I'd go running in the morning.

"Enough diddy-bopping," Duke said. "Step it up!"

Sometimes words did make it through clearly. All right, I was on my way. I stepped through the mud and scattered seagulls hanging around the reflecting pool. A nice sunset was taking shape beyond the Lincoln Memorial, but Duke would bitch more if I dawdled.

I veered right, toward the Vietnam Veterans Memorial. The V-shaped wall of black granite had a good share of visitors. Adults helped children make rubbings of the names of relatives they had never known. A couple speaking French took flash photographs. A teenage girl complained to a friend, "Why didn't they put the names in alphabetical order!"

They'd put them in a more natural order: time of death. Alphabetical order would have been a nightmare for me. I made a beeline for Duke's spot on the Wall. I could find it in the dark with my eyes squeezed shut under a blindfold.

I waited for an overweight girl in a Harvard sweatshirt to shuffle clear of my dad's panel. She deserved her turn. Duke wouldn't see it that way. His unearthly mumblings bordered on the frenetic. I took out the paper, pressed it against his name, and made a rubbing with the pencil. I had to squat for the second name; Craig "Alton" Dover was Duke's buddy and I always woke him up, too. I picked a third soldier at random. It introduced an element of surprise to these outings. I'd awakened as many as five at once, but I found that confusing, so I kept the parties smaller now.

My rubbings complete, Duke quieted. He knew what was coming. I stepped back and regarded the names on the Wall. They deserved a moment of sober consideration, no matter how many times I had made the visit. They'd had to make a sacrifice I'd never been asked to make.

My stomach gurgled. I hadn't eaten since the plane, and that had been no culinary holiday. I rushed toward the Ebbits Grill, at my own urging this time. I needed to hurry to avoid a long wait.

While I walked, I twisted the rubbings into three tight rolls. I slowed my steps enough to light each. The wind of my walk made them flare like sparklers on the Fourth of July. As they burned down against my pinched fingertips, I watched the smoke curl up to catch the golden rays of sunset and open a bridge to the other side.

⬚ ⬚ ⬚

The cigarette smoke was irritating, even in the non-smoking section, as in most East Coast restaurants, but the crab cakes were excellent. I'd also downed a Sam Adams. Alcohol usually made the connection better.

Duke was coming through clearly before the dessert menu arrived, not just grumblings and the occasional outburst. Complete sentences hinted at rational thought. Mom said he never did much better when he was alive, so I was satisfied.

"I want to taste the chocolate cake!" Duke advised.

"How about some port?" I thought at Duke and the other two, whom I could also sense. I hoped they'd be satisfied with port. I was full, and even without dessert I'd really need to run in the morning.

Alton took Duke's side like usual. "CHOC-O-LATE!"

I sighed. I tended to indulge them. They were dead and gone most of the year.

"What about the FNG?" Duke asked. "What you want?"

I fished for him. I couldn't think of him as the "fucking new guy." College and graduate school had given me different sensibilities than the average Vietnam-era soldier. For most purposes these guys were still only nineteen.

"How about both?" responded a deep voice.

"I *like* this man!" crowed Duke.

I ordered both and the guys introduced themselves. Duke told him how his real name was Earl, but the guys in his platoon said maybe he was a Duke but he was no Earl. Alton got his moniker because they'd asked him where he was from and he'd told them "Alton," as if everyone knew it was a town in Illinois. Nicknames were one way the guys bonded. The FNG was a LURP—a member of the long-range reconnaissance patrols—and went by Dragon. Sounded cold and tough to me.

That was OK. Vietnam did that to some people, and I wasn't going to judge. I hadn't been there.

❖ ❖ ❖

A strange thing happened when the cake arrived. An older bald man sat down opposite me as the waiter departed. He wore a gray suit that hung so naturally it had to be expensive. His crystal-blue eyes made me feel like a deer in headlights.

"Dr. Crenshaw, we must talk of the dead."

I was flummoxed. "Excuse me?"

"Don't play coy," the man said. He had a touch of an accent, German maybe. "I appreciate what you can do."

"What I can do?" I was really sounding like I had a Ph.D. I had a flashback to my dissertation defense when I had nearly vomited.

"You converse with spirits. This is a valuable abilty."

Well, shit. When I'd come to Washington in a high school program and discovered my "ability," I'd hidden it. I didn't want a TV show, or to be challenged by the Amazing Randi to prove my abilities. Hounded the rest of my life. I enjoyed the chance to talk with my dad and hang out with him and his friends. I didn't want my ability to make life choices for me.

On TV, it's dumb when someone obviously knows something and the other guy denies it. What I could do was something no one should know about, or believe even if they did. This man's knowledge made me curious, so I went with it.

"Can you do it, too?" I began. "Did one of the guys tell you about me?"

My questions gave the bald man pause. Maybe he'd expected denials. "Something of the sort, yes."

"Does the mechanism derive from forces undiscovered by science? What's the energy source? What are the religious implications? Aside from the obvious, that there is a consciousness that can be roused after death. I know that, but none of the vets knows anything about God or which religion is right, if any. Christians, black Muslims, Jews, I've talked to them all. Do you—"

Baldy raised a long-fingered hand and gestured at me to stop. Hands of a pianist, or a puppeteer, those. "There is time for this later, Dr. Crenshaw. These questions are not the first order of business. My information concerning you is incomplete. You mentioned 'vets.' What did you mean?"

"Name, rank, and serial number," Duke told me.

"We didn't do it," Alton chimed.

"Ask the man for his name," Dragon said. "Man hasn't given you anything yet."

I'd been so excited to talk to someone who knew about what I did I'd forgotten to ask who he was. I rectified my error.

"Karl Mannheim," he said. "I am a necromancer, although a

different stripe than yourself. I wish to understand better exactly what stripe you are. Tell me again about these 'vets.'"

I told Mannheim how I'd stumbled across my ability and first connected with my dad, how I could do it with other veterans memorialized on the wall, but only the ones who had died after I had been born.

"Remarkable. All these years you have been doing this unnoticed. And you truly have a career as a laser scientist?"

He made it sound like something I ought to be ashamed of. "Electro-optical physicist. Lasers are cool."

He shook his head, smirking. "What a tremendous find you are!"

"Psst," Dragon whispered. It wasn't like anyone was going to overhear him talking, but a lifetime of habits carry over. "Three tables over is a man you ought to check out. He ain't right."

My port arrived and I took the opportunity to look while I sniffed the alcohol. Big guy sitting stiffly, overcoat and hat, a single glass in front of filled with red liquid and celery stalk: a Bloody Mary. Dragon was correct. The guy just sat there, staring at nothing, ignoring his drink. He sat like a stone.

"Is your port unagreeable?" Mannheim asked.

I quickly took a drink, more of a gulp than the sip I'd intended. The strong cherry-tinted alcohol went down the wrong pipe and made me cough.

"Are you all right?" Mannheim asked, half rising.

I set down the port and waved him off, still coughing. "It's OK," I managed. I'd make a poor James Bond.

"Smooth one!" Duke snorted.

"Look," I said, trying to regain some control, "I promised the guys a night out. Can we continue tomorrow?"

"Damn straight," said Alton.

Mannheim stared at me for a long moment, a hunter looking through a sniper scope, wondering if he should take the shot or let his prey walk and wait for a better opportunity.

I didn't like how I kept seizing on hunting metaphors with this guy. I blamed the vets. Their perspective biased mine, which was one reason I only did this once a year. When you'd never been in war, let alone the military, and worked for a national laboratory and had a small sort of security clearance, you couldn't afford to be twitchy on a regular basis.

"Very well. Perhaps we could meet at the memorial for a demonstration?"

I was fine walking with three ghosts but didn't care to add many more to that total. Still, if I gave him a show maybe he would answer the rest of my questions. "OK, what time?"

"Say, dusk?"

"Sure."

Mannheim said good-bye, rose, and left.

I looked for the goon in the trenchcoat. He was gone. On his table sat a glass empty save for a piece of celery.

"The man poured the entire drink down his throat like it was a funnel, then got up and left just before Mannheim," Dragon told me.

Duke added, "You should look at his seat on the way out."

I finished the cake and the port and did as Duke advised. There was a damp red stain on the chair. Someone was going to be pissed about it.

I wasn't pissed. I was deeply unsettled.

▨ ▨ ▨

We walked south. It was early, and still safe. Doubly safe, since the vets would warn me of trouble. I'd get a cab back later—no sense pushing things. But I needed the walk now, both to work off dinner and to think.

"I want to see some pussy that ain't gook pussy!" Dragon said.

"Amen," agreed Duke.

It's hard to think when your head is crowded with that sort of talk.

What the guys always wanted when they woke up was the same thing they wanted when they were living, horny nineteen-year-olds: women. Now, they received sensations through me, but I was *not* going to have sex for their entertainment. I mean, I couldn't do it with *anyone* around watching, let alone my dad! Not a chance. Oh, he'd once kept me awake all night trying to talk me into it, but I was adamant. We compromised. I usually took them to a high-class strip club filled with tens, and they could look all they wanted.

I'm not a priest. I'd look, too. These weren't bad nights by any means, but I was the one spending the money. At least the lab paid more than academia.

The Nexus Gold Club wasn't a long walk. I figured they did great business with all the politicians. D.C. is a funny place, governed directly by the Feds. Not many states let you have alcohol and nude dancers in the same place. I understand Congress sets its own salary, too.

The place was upscale. Seated in the darkness were more suits than I ever saw in one place in California. No suits onstage, just beautiful women: petite red-heads, buxom blonde bombshells, athletic black girls who could shake their booty faster than eyes could follow.

I sat away from the main stage and ordered an overpriced Sam Adams when the waitress came by. No need to sit by the stage and tip every dance; the vets could roam, invisibly, any place they wanted. I supposed there was some range from me, or the Wall, that they might have to remain within, but I'd never found it. Their sensory perspectives were probably inches away from the gyrating young ladies.

I was still full, so I nursed my drink and turned away the dancers soliciting me for table dances. There would be time later, and I did want to think about Mannheim, and moreso about the goon in the trenchcoat.

Knowing my own ability, and knowing Mannheim could do something similar, I realized that there were new things to consider. How many were there like us? What could others do? Mannheim implied that my career choice was unusual. There were implications there: secret jobs for necromancers, who knew what else? What had I gotten into?

I took my keychain out of my pocket. I had a laser pointer on the ring, and I spun a melancholy pattern on the table. Usually the magic of the ruby light perked me up, how it zipped around in its monochromatic perfection, but not tonight.

I took a draw on the beer. It was the big weekend out with the boys and I should be having fun. Nothing to worry about until tomorrow, at the earliest. I'd be careful with Mannheim, I promised myself.

"Hey, Scotty!" Alton said. "Found a guy who can score you some smoke!"

"No thanks," I replied. A lot of the vets had smoked pot regularly, and wanted me to do it, too. Given their era, and where they were and what they'd had to do, I didn't blame them. I didn't do drugs, though, and didn't dare to with my job. One more lab scandal and Congress would have us peeing in cups before touching the lasers.

The song changed and suddenly standing before me was a platinum-blonde goddess in an ice-blue bikini. "I'm Kennedy. Would you like a dance?"

Even if she hadn't looked like a dead ringer for the captain of the Swedish volleyball team that had been playing in my head since puberty, I realized I was ready. Mannheim was for tomorrow, and tonight was for treating Duke and the guys, myself included. I fished out a twenty and nodded.

The club had low tables that the women danced on. No contact, which was fine by me. I didn't want my ghost dad floating around while some naked girl ground her bottom into my lap.

Kennedy wasn't a great dancer and was slow to remove her bikini. Maybe she looked so good she had never developed any skill. She did, on the other hand, make a lot of eye contact. Her eyes drew mine even though I would have preferred to be looking elsewhere.

"Scott," my dad said. "Something is up."

Not now, Duke.

"Listen up," Dragon ordered.

Duke went on. "None of the other dancers know the girl dancing for you. She doesn't work here."

That was odd. Why would a beautiful woman come into a strip club and pretend to be a dancer? Could it have something to do with me?

"Bouncer's coming," Alton said.

Kennedy must have seen something in my eyes. She spotted the approaching man. She slowly winked at me and stepped down from the table.

"What's going on?" I asked her.

"Sorry, sir. Excuse me, miss," the bouncer said. He was a short black man built like a fire hydrant. "I don't think you belong here."

He reached out to take her arm, then suddenly grimaced and fell to his knees, groaning.

Kennedy calmly reached for a fur coat slung over the back of a nearby chair. I hadn't noticed it before. She headed for the exit.

I felt like I ought to do something. She hadn't tried to hurt me, at least in no way I could perceive, but she didn't seem like a friend. And she had hurt the bouncer, somehow.

I dashed after her. "Wait a second!"

Another bouncer near the door had been watching and moved to block Kennedy. He crumpled like the first bouncer had, but this slowed her enough for me to catch up.

"Hey!" I called.

I reached out, and as my hand neared her shoulder all my joints flared with sharp pain. *Excruciating* pain. I wanted to curl up into a little ball, and that's exactly what I started to do.

"Scott!" Duke cried.

"I got him," Dragon said.

An amazing thing happened. The pain remained excruciating but receded nonetheless. It was like a hypnotic state (I'd taken a hypnosis class in college), where you are aware of your surroundings but completely compliant. Dragon was helping my body do what I wanted to do.

My fingers touched Kennedy's bare shoulder and spun her around like she was hanging on a string. I immediately let go, for her skin was literally ice cold. We made eye contact again. No wink from her beautiful blue eyes this time—she was surprised.

She stepped over the fallen bouncer and ran out the exit. I stood there and let her go, profoundly confused.

"What the hell just happened?" Alton wondered.

No one knew, but the owner of the club apologized profusely. He thought I'd been the victim of some psycho dancer with a grudge against the club, a notion the bouncers were happy to agree with. I wound up with a complimentary bottle of champagne, free entrance to the VIP room, and coupons for three free dances.

I just wanted to get out of there, hole up in the hotel until tomorrow.

"Kick back for a while," Duke urged. "We're not ready to go yet."

Something this weird happens and the vets didn't think it was a big deal? Typical. When you're dead you just have no perspective.

※ ※ ※

Dragon was telling a dirty joke when I woke up, something about a priest, a rabbi, and a drill sergeant. I rolled over and groaned when I saw the red digital letters that said it was past ten. "Shit."

"The prince is awake," Duke said.

"And in an excellent mood," Alton added.

It was too late to run. I crawled out of bed, into the bathroom, and showered. I tolerated the guys teasing me about my tiny penis. I had learned not to protest. They already knew I was shy about the bathroom, and their time in the military had hardened them in a way I'd never know. They were ruthless.

In a strange way, it made me feel good to give them a good time, even at my own expense. What else could you give dead people on holiday?

⊠ ⊠ ⊠

We spent the day at the Smithsonian. I reasoned that all the walking could replace my morning jog, and besides, I loved the museums. They're so good that the vets even took some time away from peeking up skirts. We touched a piece of the moon, gazed into the jaws of a *T. Rex*, and waxed nostalgic over the ruby slippers from *The Wizard of Oz*.

"I remember wanting those in Nam," Duke said. "Wound up jerking off thinking about Dorothy."

In the normal course of events, fathers mature ahead of their sons. This is not a terrible thing.

The afternoon drew to a close. I felt like I should be coming up with a plan or something, but I didn't understand Mannheim's agenda. Should I be impressive, or tank this demonstration? My ability was a fascinating extra in life, a bonus that let me spend time with Duke, not something that controlled me. Still, I was a scientist; I hadn't learned much on my own despite many experiments. Mannheim could teach me plenty.

We strolled west on the grass, past the Washington Monument, and beside the reflecting pool. Not much of a sunset tonight. I noticed the seagull crap and dead seagulls littered along the pool's edge.

A steady crowd filed along the Wall, a few standing or squatting before a name of particular personal significance. My gaze danced over the people, wondering what was in their heads, able to talk to the dead but not able to have them talk back.

One of the stationary figures wasn't facing the Wall. She was watching me. A tall blonde in a long fur coat: Kennedy, from the club.

"Go for it, man," Alton urged. "Maybe you'll get lucky!"

I was trying to decide what to do, *if* I should do anything, when Dragon gave me a nudge and a hand touched my shoulder. Despite the warning I still jumped.

"Excuse me, Dr. Crenshaw," Mannheim said, withdrawing his strong-fingered hand.

"It's OK," I said, shaking my head. "I was just looking at something."

Mannheim smiled, more calculating than spontaneous. "Somebody, I think. She is my backup and will be maintaining security. She wanted to get a close look at you last night."

I thought I had been the one who had gotten the close look. Then I thought of that intense, cramping pain. "What is it that she does?"

"We will talk of that later, and of your surprising resistance, but for now it should suffice that she describes herself as 'mistress of tendon.'" Mannheim smiled again.

Duke suggested a crude revision to her title and I told him to hush. "Let us now talk of you."

He already knew the basic outline, and I hoped he'd be just as forthcoming when it was his turn. "OK," I agreed. I pulled some paper out of my jacket pocket. I started toward the nearest panel.

Mannheim stopped me. "Over there," he pointed to a spot near the right end. "At the bottom. Charles P. Grobmeyer."

I shrugged again. "Fine."

I guessed that Mannheim knew some details about this man and wanted to test me. No problem. I'd gone to school for a long, long time and excelled at tests.

My cold fingers had warmed by the time I had rolled and burned the paper.

"How long now?" Mannheim asked.

"It varies," I said. "It should be quicker if we stay near the Wall. Ten minutes, maybe less."

We waited.

I scanned the visitors for Kennedy.

"She bugged out," said Dragon. "Down the way leaning against a tree now, watching us."

I started to pick up Grobmeyer quickly. The presence of the other vets helped. In just a few minutes he was talking to everyone, opening up. He preferred to be called "Rat." Apparently his first week in country a rat bit him on the face and it had left a scar.

"I got him," I told Mannheim.

He quizzed me about Grobmeyer's birthplace and -date, where he went to high school, his mother's maiden name. He was a veritable credit card company. It bored the vets.

Finally Mannheim asked, "Where is Grobmeyer's father buried?"

"I was a kid," Rat said. "I didn't understand what was going on. When I got older it seemed odd. Men wearing black ski masks lowered Pa into a sinkhole on the west edge of Uncle Shiner's farm, wrapped in sheets that smelled of cinnamon."

That *was* odd. "Why do you want to know?" I asked Mannheim.

He smiled again. "This is information you could not fake."

So I got more details, enough to prove myself, and passed them on.

"Excellent," he said. "Now that we know his place and method of concealment, Calistrago's secrets will not vanish from this plane."

"Calistrago?"

"Later," Mannheim said. "I am satisfied with this aspect of your ability. Under proper tutelage, you will be able to compel spirits from times before your birth and spirits from other foci of attention. I am also curious about the temporal abilities of your minions."

"What's he saying?" Duke asked.

"Sounds like my math teacher, Mr. Sand," said Alton. "Couldn't understand him either."

Mannheim drew himself up and grasped his lapels tightly. "What do I have in my jacket?" he challenged.

"Shit!" Dragon exclaimed. "He's packing. Shoulder holster. I should've seen that."

"Forget the heat," Duke said. "Look at that bottle!"

"What is it, Dad?"

"Small orange-brown bottle, smoked glass, twisted neck with an ivory stopper. But it's the thing inside that's so freaky. It's a *head*. A complete human head, shrunk to a couple of inches. And that's not the worst thing. That head is *alive*, whispering and shit."

"A head?" I said aloud. I was a scientist to my core. I always figured my ability depended on some branch of undiscovered natural laws. But a talking head in a bottle? That smacked of supernatural forces. I thought again of the goon with the Bloody Mary.

"Excellent!" Mannheim declared. "What an asset you will be!"

I was in over my head, drowning in a sea of weirdness, not knowing where this would lead. All I wanted to do was play with lasers and visit Dad once a year. I never asked for this.

"Mr. Mannheim," I began, "I'm not an asset. I mean, I fly back to California Sunday. I'm eager to learn more . . ."

Mannheim's smile twisted into a scowl.

". . . but this is a bit fast."

"You will adjust, and thrive, within the organization. Money, women, power, all will be yours. Everything you might desire." Mannheim had remanufactured his smile during his pitch.

"Sounds cool," Alton said.

I wasn't sure. I didn't have everything I desired, but I was happily in pursuit. My lab job was permanent and I was dating some. Still, here was an opportunity to learn things I'd wanted to understand for years. "Just what's involved?"

"We move you here. Give you expert training with a facilitator, maximize your abilities. Move you beyond the need for rituals. Then we pump every dreg of information from these Wall people while you train. Get them to eavesdrop around Washington."

The night was deepening. Mannheim's face had shifted into shadow as we'd spoken. I still didn't know what all this meant, but it seemed as if a gulf yawned before me and things would never be the same.

"Who's he calling Wall people?" Dragon asked. "This guy sounds like a bad spook I had to kill once."

"Hey," said Duke. "He's got an envelope in his pocket with a note from someone named 'Nikita.' Got a picture of you, Scott, your bad side, and says to secure you or eliminate you."

Eliminate me? Sweat beaded on my forehead, amplifying the chill. This was a massive disaster. I'd have to do whatever Mannheim wanted.

"The veteran exploitation can be completed in a year," Mannheim continued.

I didn't like this. I'd gone to grad school to follow my passions, to have control over my life. Without an advanced degree you got ordered around—I'd seen first hand as an intern. My dad had been ordered around by the politicians and military, and it had cost him everything. I'd lost control.

"No, you haven't, son," Duke told me. "You *always* have control over your own actions. I could've run for Canada, but I chose to go overseas. I don't regret it."

"I regret it," said Alton.

"Shut up," Dragon said.

"I have to think," I said.

"Don't think too long, Dr. Crenshaw," Mannheim said.

"Who's Nikita?" I asked.

"Excellent!" Mannheim pronounced. "You will be quite valuable. Come now. We'll check you out of your hotel and set you up in nice quarters. We'll have people move your things from California."

"I'm still thinking!" I said.

"That's telling him!" Duke encouraged.

"You'd better not be." No smile from Mannheim.

Emboldened, I continued, "I'm going to sleep on it."

"I can't allow that, Dr. Crenshaw. You know too much, and with what you can do, you might know ten times as much tomorrow. The organization cannot permit you such freedom." He rested his hand on the concealed gun.

"He's an amateur," said Dragon. "Don't be intimidated."

Alton agreed. "Yeah, tough titties for him if you don't want to. But I think it's a sweet deal."

"Shut up, Alton. My son can make up his own mind."

Could I? I was being pressured, with incomplete information, forced to make a choice that could get me killed. I did know I didn't want to be involved with any group that used these kinds of tactics.

"You make the choices you have to make, Scott. You *have* to. I did and I don't regret it." Duke—my dad—wasn't just repeating himself. He was reminding me about how he'd died. It wasn't anything like a booby trap or an enemy sniper. It was one of the guys in his squad. They'd caught a papa-san and his daughter with a case of canned peaches. For a week straight, they'd been eating 'eggs and mother-fuckers,' a vile sort of c-rations, and it pissed them off that this old man had peaches. To make a painful story short, my Dad stopped them from killing the old guy and raping the girl. He knew his actions could have consequences. Next time they faced live fire, one of his so-called buddies plugged him in the face.

Integrity like that kept me coming back even though it was tedious hanging out with perpetual teenagers. Duke was worth it.

Was I?

"Mr. Mannheim, I'm no threat to your organization, I assure you.

I'm leaving now." I clenched my jaw shut, turned, and began walking away as steadily as I could. He wouldn't, couldn't, just shoot me here in the Mall within a few hundred yards of the White House and its swarm of agents.

"That's it, Scotty," Duke said. "The chickenshit is letting you walk."

"Goon squad, one o'clock and three o'clock," Dragon countered.

I broke into a run. Two big men in trench coats flew at me, running quickly, but they didn't swing their arms. Strange how things slow down and become clearer when you're running for your life.

"Help! Help!" I yelled. I was proud, but not that proud. There had to be law enforcement nearby. I spotted a uniformed cop and ran toward him.

And collapsed.

Everyone did. We all fell, me, the cop, the scattered tourists, all twisted in agony. It was the same pain from the club the night before: Kennedy. She was Mannheim's trump. There would be a story about a terrorist attack, gas or something, and no one would notice that I'd gone missing.

I said we all fell, but that wasn't true. The goons kept running and piled on top of me. They raised their fists and brought them down, over and over. They were killing me.

"We can't have this," Alton said.

"Shit no," agreed Dragon.

"Let us in, Scott," Rat said.

"And we'll do the rest," said Duke.

It was easy to let them in—I was fleeing the pain. I stepped back into the dissociated, hypnotic state. I could watch, direct, but they did the work and I was safe. Sort of.

Dragon was a bad ass. Within two seconds he'd struck back, and I learned what it was like to break bones with my bare hands.

"I'm bad but not that bad," Dragon said.

Rat said, "Look at them."

They had anonymous gray faces, the life washed out of them. Smelled of formaldehyde, too. My fist broke one of their noses—I heard the crunch—but there was no blood, and no reaction. They were just bodies acting on the commands of their master. Mannheim was some kind of animator.

It was worse than fighting for my life. I was in a damn monster movie!

Then the scene was over. The goons lay at my feet, squirming, their broken bodies unable to rise.

I directed and my squad executed. I looked around. I'd run south past the Lincoln monument. I was the only one in sight standing; Mannheim and Kennedy were not visible. What to do now?

"Get cover, call help," Dragon said.

Great idea. I dashed for a tree and squatted against the trunk's far side. Mannheim would be somewhere near the Wall. His goons had failed, Kennedy couldn't stop me, so he'd have to let me go now, right?

"No, he's got eyes out and he's coming," Alton said. "Look up."

Tattered, dirty gulls circled overhead. Undoubtedly as dead as the goons and similarly under Mannheim's control. He knew where I was.

"Time to get help," Dragon said. "I know some guys."

"We all do," said Duke.

The seas parted, the doors of perception blew open, and the abyss looked into me. A chorus of voices rose from an infinite distance to crashing crescendo, drowning me. That sensation flashed by and the voices fell into rank and file. These were veterans, thousands of them, coming to my aid. Trigger, Sal, Butch, Moochie, Pistol, Beaster, Tank, Easy Rider, and a legion more, each with his own experiences and skills, each ready to help.

I should have been paralyzed, but they all fit, filled a role, communicating in an orderly way with a speed and efficiency the living can't achieve.

"Mannheim is in the Lincoln Memorial. Time to stop him," they said.

I agreed, committed. I strode forward, my body an army. The stairs moved under my feet as if I were floating, and I found myself between the pillars facing a giant stone President and a small bald man standing between his legs.

"I am impressed," Mannheim said. "Most novices would be dead by now. Still, you have made a mistake. You might have been able to survive several hours if you had kept running."

I wasn't here to talk to him, or listen to speeches. I had to stop him. I wouldn't kill him. I wasn't like that.

"Maybe you'd better be," said Duke.

Dragon said, "This isn't Nam, but it ain't far from it."

If we incapacitated him somehow, left him for the police . . .

"They couldn't hold him, and he'd be after you," Duke said.

Mannheim drew his gun and aimed at me.

He drew eleven criticisms from the vets, ranging from his choice of caliber to his stance to his one-handed grip.

I wasn't listening. My body was rolling, my whole world tumbling over the cold stone, finishing behind a pillar. My hands were taking off my belt, knotting it in a fashion I'd never seen. I was standing, swinging my belt overhead like a bolo. I was extending my other hand, holding my laser pointer. I couldn't see what I was doing, but the vets could. Without giving him a target, my laser shone in his eyes. Stepping away from the pillar, my hand released the belt.

A loud clang, a groan, and Mannheim lay sprawled, grabbing his empty hand, blinking and grimacing. The belt and gun were ten feet away from him.

"I may be a novice, but my friends aren't," I said as my body moved toward him.

He scuttled back like a startled crawdad. As I approached, he started gesticulating. His fingers darted around with the speed and precision of a hundred-word-a-minute typist.

A loud bang deafened me. White dust billowed around. Was the building collapsing?

Mannheim's fingers kept moving.

"I don't fucking believe this," said Duke.

My head turned and I saw.

President Lincoln stood up.

Then I was moving, rolling, dodging, keeping just ahead of giant stone hands and feet that struck after me. On and on, and seconds turned to minutes. It was chaos and I didn't know what was happening. From my distanced vantage I was less aware of pain, but not completely unaware. They were pushing my out-of-shape body past its limits.

"We've got to escape," I urged.

"We're trying, but he keeps cutting us off," they replied.

"Then cut the puppet's strings!"

"Working on it."

It was another thirty seconds before we were in position. My body cartwheeled toward Mannheim and my foot caught him in the head.

I knew his neck was broken before he hit the ground. Then Lincoln was falling and the vets kept me out of the way of the pieces.

I expected to feel more. A man was dead, a national treasure destroyed. Maybe it was the distance of my hypnotic state, but I didn't feel guilty about what I had done. It wasn't my fault, and I had done what had been necessary. Was this what war was like? Surviving, doing what you had to do moment by moment without hesitation?

I was sure it would be a hard thing, later.

Eventually the dust settled. I would have collapsed, too, if I hadn't had so much help holding me up. The chorus faded, not completely, but receded.

"You ought to get his Ruger, his papers, his wallet, and that head in the bottle," Dragon said. "You might need them."

"I don't want any of it," I complained aloud.

"Of course you don't," said a feminine voice.

"Sorry—I was about to tell you," Alton said.

I turned to see Kennedy. Under other circumstances she would have made a fantastic picture standing there, the Washington Monument as backdrop. "Are you going to try to kill me, too?"

"No," she said. "I'm not an arrogant fool like Karl. I'm also not sure I could."

She walked toward me, then past. She rifled through Mannheim's pockets. I let her.

She said, "This hasn't been a good day. We'll be busy cleaning up this mess for some time. I'll encourage Nikita to try to recruit you again, rather than kill you."

"Why?"

"Because you're powerful, and you're cute." She stood up and winked at me. "I enjoyed dancing for you."

I didn't know how to respond to that, although the vets provided suggestions.

She walked by, her heels loud on the stone. "I advise you to run. I'll be releasing my grip momentarily." Then she was gone.

"I didn't choose this power, or any of this. I don't want it. I just want my old life back," I whispered.

"Sometimes you get drafted," Duke said. "You still make your own choices. Live your own life. It's all anyone can do. And whatever happens, we'll be here to help you."

"Thanks. I know you will."

"And we'll be there if you get killed, too."

"Shut up, Alton," I said.

I ran down the steps and into the rest of my life. However long it was going to last, I was going to do it my way and I was going to do it right. I was my father's son after all.

Afterword: I was born in 1968 while my father was serving in the Air Force overseas. He had enlisted after he'd been kicked out of college for cutting ROTC classes and lost his deferment. Call him "Irony." He spent a year in Thailand and came home safely. My only personal memory of the Vietnam War was seeing our last POWs get off the airplane. I'm the next generation, the son of a veteran. The Wall is for people like me. The people who were there don't need help remembering.

I wanted to write a story from the perspective of my generation, of a son whose father's name was on the Wall. I wanted to be respectful but honest. I wanted to have some action but also comedy to lighten the load.

I was fortunate enough to have an astronomy meeting in Washington when I started thinking about the story and was able to visit the Wall again. I was also spending too much time playing a computer game, Diablo II, which features necromancers. I outlined the story while sitting in the emergency room after a strange bout of temporary blindness that turned out to be an "ophthalmological migraine," which is a kind of headache that doesn't hurt, but it does blind you. I'd had no idea such things even existed. My father laughed when I called him the next day; he told me he'd been getting them for years.

Fathers and sons should talk more often, about their family medical history and everything else in the world. Not everyone's father comes home.

REFLECTIONS IN BLACK GRANITE

Mike Resnick and Michael A. Burstein

*F*or a moment, the Wall seems to flicker in the late afternoon fog. Eustace Horatio Nolan stops a short distance away along the Mall. He squints his eyes and pulls his overcoat tighter against the cold, humid wind.

Must be my imagination, he thinks, as the Vietnam Veterans Memorial Wall clearly stands where it always has, off to the right of the Lincoln Memorial. He clears his throat and continues trudging along the path to the Wall. In his pocket, he fingers the small envelope that contains the quarter he intends to leave for his friend, the quarter he has left every year on this date since the Wall was built in 1982.

He arrives at the Wall and enters the pathway from the west side, slowly descending into the rift as the designer had intended. As he walks, he traces his hand along the Wall. He has to pull away a few times and walk around other people staring at the names. At one point, he softly treads around a kneeling man who quietly weeps.

Eustace fingers his quarter again and takes note of some of the other offerings left at the Wall: a small American flag; a fuzzy white teddy bear wearing a red bow; a bouquet of flowers; a photograph of men his age, in their early fifties—

"It swallows you up," Eustace hears. He stops short, and turns to look at the man who just spoke.

"Say that again?"

The man has dark hair, and he fiddles with his glasses. He appears to be in his late twenties. "I was just talking to my wife about the Wall." He points toward one end, where the Wall begins, built into the earth low to the ground. "It starts low and by the time you get here—" He points upward, indicating the height of the Wall at the center, more than ten feet above the walkway. "It swallows you up."

"I like it," says the man's wife. "It's quiet, serene."

"Calm," Eustace suggests, although he doesn't feel that way. He can't shake the image of the Wall swallowing people up. It disturbs him.

"Yeah," the woman says. "Calm." She offers her hand. "I'm Shari Ledowitz. This is my husband, Andy."

Eustace shakes their hands in turn. "Eustace Nolan," he says, as other people walk slowly past. "I didn't mean to spy on you."

"No, it's OK," Andy says. "I imagine people tend to pay more attention to others here."

A moment of awkward silence passes, with Eustace and the Ledowitzes looking around them at other people passing by. Then Shari asks, "Were you in Nam?"

Eustace nods. "I'm here to pay my respects to a friend. From a long time ago."

Andy and Shari exchange a glance. "We're sorry," Andy says. "I mean—we don't know anyone who was in the war."

"But you came here anyway," Eustace notes.

Andy shrugs, as if shielding embarrassment. "It just seemed important to us. What with all the recent talk of memorials . . ." His voice trails off, and Eustace nods.

A silent moment passes, and then Shari softly asks, "What happened to your friend?"

The two strangers seem honestly interested, although the husband keeps facing away from Eustace and toward the list of names. For a moment, Eustace considers telling them the full story. Instead, he simply says, "We were in the Army Press Corps."

"Like Al Gore," Andy says.

Eustace nods, although after the 2000 election debacle he doesn't like being compared to Gore. "Right. Anyway, my friend went out on a routine, safe assignment and got himself killed." Eustace looks into the distance, away from the Wall, and he feels as if he is looking back in time.

He remembers being drafted out of college into the army; he remembers his father pulling strings to get him out of any sort of combat unit; he remembers meeting the other members of the press corps . . .

Another question from Shari brings him out of his reverie. "What was your friend's name?"

"Craig," he says, and he sees his breath condense as he speaks. "Craig Crichton."

"When did he die?" Shari asks.

"February 27, 1970. A Friday."

Andy jerks his head away from the Wall. "February 27—that's today."

Eustace nods. "I know. That's why I'm here." He pauses. "When Craig died, I owed him two bits. So every year, I leave him a quarter."

"Can we help you find his name?" Shari asks.

"I know where it is," Eustace says, but then realizes that these two fellow Americans thirst for some emotional connection to the Wall and to the war in which he fought. So he adds, "But it's been a while. Sure, help me find his name."

The three of them scan the portion of the Wall in front of them.

"It would be easier to find if the names were alphabetical," Andy says.

"The names are on the Wall in the order of date of death," Eustace replies. "It's better that way." He pauses, running his eyes across the seemingly endless list of names. Suddenly, he gets worried. "Craig's name is around here somewhere," he says aloud. He knows it must be; he remembers its location vividly—and yet he can't find it. He starts running his hands up and down the smooth, polished stone.

"You don't know exactly where?" Shari asks.

"I haven't been here in a year."

She nods. "We'll keep looking."

For another minute, the three of them scour the Wall. The husband studies the names to Eustace's left while the wife goes to the right. Eustace himself scans the panel in front of him repeatedly, never seeing Craig's name.

Finally, Eustace stops searching, genuinely confused. "The name's not here," he says aloud.

By this time, the Ledowitzes have converged onto his panel again. "Maybe we're spelling it wrong," Andy suggests.

Eustace spells Craig's name for them, and they shake their heads. "That's what I looked for," Shari says. She turns her gaze back to the Wall.

"I guess I'll go check the Directory—" Eustace begins, but then Shari tugs at the sleeve of his overcoat.

"Um, Mr. Nolan?" Shari points at the panel. Eustace follows the crook of her finger to one of the names on the Wall. For a moment, he stares in disbelief, and then he moves in closer and traces his fingers along the name.

There, overlaid by the reflection of his craggy dark eyes and wispy white hair, Eustace reads his own name: EUSTACE H NOLAN.

※ ※ ※

For the next few hours, Eustace confronts the rangers working at the Vietnam Veterans Memorial. He insists they check one of the copies of the Vietnam Veterans Memorial Directory of Names, located at both ends of the Wall. Sure enough, Craig's name appears in the alphabetical list and Eustace's does not. It becomes clear to them that someone has made a ghastly mistake, or even perpetrated an elaborate practical joke. They apologize profusely to Eustace and assure him that the Park Service will clear up the mistake as soon as possible.

Eustace walks home, slightly mollified but still with a nagging feeling of unease. At least it has nothing to do with the neighborhood. A few years ago, he and Alissa moved from their suburban Maryland home to something smaller and closer in. With Samantha pursuing her dot-com career in California, it didn't seem necessary for them to hold onto the house anymore. And fortunately, they found a very nice apartment in Georgetown.

Eustace finally arrives home. The first-floor brownstone feels welcoming after the bizarre shock of the afternoon.

"Hi, Alissa," he says as he enters the apartment and removes his coat. From the kitchen, Alissa calls back a greeting, and tells him that she is still in the middle of making dinner.

After hanging his coat in the closet, he walks into the kitchen and greets his wife with a kiss, briefly interrupting her stirring.

"How are you?" she asks.

"Just fine," he replies. "But you're not going to believe what happened today."

Eustace takes a seat at the kitchen table and tells Alissa the story of

Craig's missing name, and of his own being on the Wall. When he finishes, she shakes her head.

"Creepy," she says.

He smiles. "Yeah. I figure they must have crossed wires somewhere." He sighs. "I think I'll call Stephanie and tell her about it."

Alissa stops stirring whatever sits in the pot, and she places the wooden spoon in the sink. "Stephanie?" she asks.

"Yeah. I'll call her tonight once I'm sure she's home from work."

Alissa presses his lips together, then asks: "Who's Stephanie?"

Her question, so casually asked, surprises Eustace.

"'Who's Stephanie?'" he echoes. "Our daughter."

Alissa looks puzzled. "Daughter?"

"Yes," he says, looking for her punch line and not finding it. "Ours. The one we raised together."

She shakes her head. "I don't know what you're talking about."

Eustace stands up. As he speaks, he cuts the air with his hand. "Enough already. Stephanie. Our daughter. Born in 1975."

Alissa turns the water on at the sink, removes her apron, and sits down at the table. "Eustace, is this some kind of joke? Because I don't think it's very funny."

"I'm talking about Stephanie, damn it!" Eustace shouts, and as he leans over his wife, he sees genuine fear in her eyes. She pulls back.

"Eustace, why are you shouting about Stephanie?"

He blinks rapidly. "What?"

"Stephanie—how is she? Did she call you at work today? Is something wrong with her?"

Sudden dizziness overwhelms Eustace, and he sits down at the table again. "No, Stephanie didn't call me," he says. "I was talking about calling her tonight."

Alissa nods. "Well, you don't have to shout."

Eustace shakes his head and rubs his eyes. "Alissa, do you feel OK?"

"Of course I do," she says. "Do you?"

Eustace considers a few things to say, then simply nods. "Yeah. I'm fine."

They watch the news on television while eating the stew, and shortly before going to bed they call Stephanie out in Silicon Valley. Eustace makes one change in his plan, however; he decides not to tell her about seeing his name on the Wall.

⊠ ⊠ ⊠

When Eustace wakes up the next morning, Alissa already has the coffee going, as usual. He showers and dresses and joins her in the kitchen. Then, as casually as possible, he asks her about their conversation from the night before.

"What do you mean, I didn't remember Stephanie? That's the silliest thing I ever heard."

He wonders for a moment if Alissa might be showing the starting signs of Alzheimer's, then grimaces. That might explain why he saw his name on the Wall, as well.

"I'll be late tonight, honey," he says.

"Something at work?" she asks.

"No. I'm going to go check the Wall."

She puts her coffee cup down. "But you went there yesterday. For Craig."

"Yes, but I couldn't find his name, because someone erased it. I want to make sure they restore it."

Alissa nods, but Eustace chooses not to ask her if she recalls that part of their conversation. Instead, he eats breakfast quickly and quietly, kisses her good-bye, leaves the apartment, and takes the Metro to his job at *The Washington Post*. After Vietnam, he never managed to finish college, but his father got him a job at the paper. He's worked at the city desk ever since, as a copy editor. He's aware that he missed the glory days of Woodward and Bernstein, but it doesn't really matter to him.

He takes the elevator to his floor and settles into his torn vinyl chair. As usual, he finds himself the first copy editor to arrive at the huge city desk bullpen. He turns on his terminal and finds a few articles already on his plate for checking.

By the time ten o'clock rolls around, Eustace's fellow editors have joined him in the circle of desks. The noise of a dozen conversations fills the room.

Eustace has been so busy editing that it only comes to him slowly that no one has greeted him as they came in this morning. He looks up from his computer to see the senior editor, Carl Grabowski, passing by.

"Carl?" he says. Carl stops in his tracks and turns around.

"Yes, Eustace? What can I do for you?"

"Um. Nothing." He pauses. "I've just felt invisible this morning, that's all."

Carl laughs; it reassures Eustace. "Busy day." Carl turns to another copy editor. "Jack, can I have the edits on the school committee piece?"

Eustace frowns. He glances at his computer, and sure enough, there's the school committee piece. "Um . . . Carl, Jack? I seem to be working on that one."

Jack gives him a quizzical glance. "No, you're not, Eustace. I just finished it."

"But—" Eustace begins, and then he takes another look at his terminal. Where the article had been displayed, he sees a blank screen.

⊠ ⊠ ⊠

After work, Eustace returns to the Wall. This time, not only does he read his name on the Wall, but he finds it in the Directory of Names as well.

There is no mention of Craig Crichton anywhere.

⊠ ⊠ ⊠

For the rest of the week, nothing out of the ordinary happens. Then, on Sunday afternoon, the doorbell rings. Eustace calls to Alissa to answer it, then remembers that she has gone out on a walk. He folds up the newspaper and walks to the front door of the brownstone, as the speaker system is broken and he hasn't yet had a chance to repair it.

The man standing at the door looks almost exactly like Craig Crichton. For a moment, Eustace believes he is seeing a ghost. Then he starts spotting little differences here and there, and his heartbeat goes back to normal.

"Eustace Nolan?" the man asks.

Eustace nods slowly.

The man smiles and extends his hand. "Peter Crichton. My father has told me about you so many times."

Carefully, Eustace puts out his own hand for the handshake. Peter's grip feels real.

Eustace finds his voice. "Peter, you say?"

Peter nods. "That's right." He pauses awkwardly. "This is really a fluke of luck. Dad told me you died in Vietnam, but he must have had the wrong man. I just took a chance—I mean, how many Eustace Horatio Nolans can there be, right? Dad'll be thrilled to know you're alive after all these years."

"Your dad's alive?"

"Of course he is."

He hears Alissa call to him. "Eustace? Who is that?"

Confused—didn't she go out today? Eustace looks away for a moment. When he turns his head again, there is no trace of Peter Crichton anywhere.

※ ※ ※

That night, Eustace dreams.

He's back in Vietnam with the press corps on that fateful day. The posted list of routine assignments curls up in the humidity that permeates their makeshift buildings. Eustace glances at it. Amazing, but almost a decade after her husband was overthrown, Madame Nhu is still news. Someone's arranged an interview with one of the Dragon Lady's former bodyguards at a little cantina a mile north of town.

Eustace's name is atop the duty roster, but he figures the interview can wait; after all, who cares about Madame Nhu anymore? So he heads off to the local whorehouse like the carefree bachelor he is, and he drinks a little too much, and suddenly he's sick as a dog and has to be carried back to the barracks in a litter.

He doesn't hear about what happened until the next morning. Craig decided to cover for him, went off to get the interview, and got himself killed when the Viet Cong blew up the cantina.

The guilt is intolerable. Eustace jumps up in bed, covered with cold sweat.

※ ※ ※

Monday. As a copy editor on the city desk, Eustace is used to calling down to the morgue for old files. He requests everything they have on Craig Crichton. Within an hour, he signs for a thin manila envelope.

As the courier departs, Eustace reaches into the envelope and finds one lone article. Not even an article, actually, but simply a report of another casulty in Vietnam. Name, date of death, hometown, and the letters KIA stare back at Eustace.

The pain is almost palpable. Eustace sighs, and opens the envelope to slip the article back in. But as he does so, his hand brushes against another yellowing piece of paper.

Funny, he thinks. *I must have missed that one.*

And suddenly there is more than one.

He keeps reaching into the empty envelope, and keeps pulling out more and more articles about his dead friend. Craig Crichton graduating from college, Craig Crichton marrying his high school sweetheart, siring a future All-American linebacker named Peter, running for local office in Massachusetts, then for a Congressional seat—

The final article, dated a few weeks ago, details Crichton's current campaign for the Senate.

Eustace goes back, studies Craig's record. Craig's done a lot as a congressman. Funding for NASA, recompense for victims of crimes, a tax cut and a debt paydown, a bailout for farmers—it's an impressive record, even for a ghost. For a moment Eustace discounts the impossibility of these articles and believes them.

Until he reaches for the other articles again and can't find them. He knows they sat on his desk just a moment ago, but now the envelope holds just the KIA notice. Eustace flicks through the rest of the papers on his desk but finds nothing. Even the article he last held in his hands has suddenly vanished. He descends to his hands and knees; panting, he searches the floor around his desk, to the left, to the right, in front, and underneath. Nothing there.

Suddenly, Eustace sees a pair of brown loafers in front of his face. He follows them up a pair of khaki slacks, a blue button-down shirt, and finally to the face of Carl Grabowski. "Eustace, you OK?" Carl asks.

Eustace feels his face flush, and he quickly stands back up. "Yeah, I'm fine. I'm just looking for some articles I thought I'd lost."

Carl nods, and looks down at the floor for a moment. When he looks back up at Eustace, his face displays no sign of recognition. "Excuse me, sir," he says, "but can I help you?"

"Carl? It's me, Eustace. Don't you recognize me?"

"Of course I recognize you, Eustace," Carl says with a surprised look. Then, his expression puzzled again, he says, "Who are you?"

⬛ ⬛ ⬛

What is happening? wonders Eustace as he walks the last two blocks to his apartment after getting off the bus. *He went on my mission and died in my place, and it's tragic, and I've felt guilty ever since—but it's like the universe is trying to change things, to right a wrong. I can't even blame it for trying, but it's crazy. Or, more likely, I'm crazy . . . or going crazy. Much more of this and I'll have to see a shrink.*

He's read about guilt complexes, heard about them, but could guilt do this many things to his mind all at once? He doubts it—but he also doubts that Alissa would forget their daughter, or that Carl can't recognize him.

Ah, well—he'll take his shoes off, sit in his recliner, watch some TV, get a good ten hours (he hasn't been sleeping all that well), and maybe things will improve.

He reaches the front door and tries to push all such thoughts from his mind. He'll hug Alissa, she'll reassure him that he's not going crazy, that it's just some long-delayed post-war symptom, and everything will be all right again.

He tries to put the key in the lock. It won't fit.

He frowns, tries again. It still doesn't fit.

He goes through his key chain. He must be using the wrong key—but he's not.

He tries a third time. No luck.

Suddenly the door opens, and a slender, twentyish woman with short blonde hair and dark brown eyes confronts him.

"May I help you?"

"Where's Alissa?" demands Eustace.

She looks puzzled. "Who's Alissa?"

"My wife, damn it!"

"How should I know?"

"Goddamnit, I live here!" yells Eustace.

She looks at him as if he might start foaming at the mouth any minute. "I've lived here for the past three years."

He looks at her much the same way. "Right here?" he repeats. "On the ground floor?"

"Yes."

"And you've never seen me before?"

"Never."

He peeks past her into the living room. Not a single piece of furniture or artwork is familiar.

He blinks very rapidly. His world seems to be spinning uncontrollably. "I'm sorry," he says. "I must have made a mistake."

She stares at him, then closes the door without a word. He hears her snap the deadbolt into place. He doesn't blame her.

He goes to the drugstore on the next block and asks for the phone book. He looks for "Eustace H. Nolan." There is no listing. He tries "E. H. Nolan" and "E. Nolan" and even "Alissa Nolan." No luck.

He cashes a five-dollar bill, gets twenty quarters, and goes to a phone booth. He closes the door behind him and dials Alissa's parents in Butte, Montana.

"Hello?" says his mother-in-law's voice.

"Hello," he says, trying to disguise his own voice. "I know this seems strange, but I'm an old schoolmate of your daughter's. I've misplaced her phone number. I wonder if you have it?"

His mother-in-law seems hesitant but finally rattles off the number. The area code is in Chicago.

"Is she still married?" he asks.

"Oh, yes," says his mother-in-law. "She and Eddie just celebrated their twenty-fifth anniversary. And she's a grandmother now."

"You don't say," says Eustace, his hands starting to tremble. "Tell me—does she ever mention Eustace Nolan?"

"Now there's a name I haven't heard in ages. They were engaged, you know—before the poor boy was killed in Vietnam. Why do you ask?"

But Eustace has already hung up the phone. Now his entire body is shaking.

He waits until he's finally calm again. Crazy things are coming and going. Maybe this is just another of them. He calls home. A recorded voice tells him the number doesn't exist.

His face ashen, Eustace emerges from the phone booth, walks out of the drugstore, and heads back toward his apartment—except that he takes a quick look in the window and realizes that it's not his apartment anymore.

Stop, he tells himself. *Just stop for a minute and think this through. Let's look at this logically. Either history is adjusting itself, which means that there's no such thing as cause and effect, or else I am hallucinating.*

But if I am, it's one hell of an hallucination. That's my apartment, but there's a stranger living there.

OK, then it isn't my apartment. He pulls out his wallet, checks his credit cards. *I'm still Eustace Nolan. So that much I know. And I don't live here. Maybe I never did. I was engaged to Alissa when I was drafted and went to Nam. Something happened to me there. I'm not sure what, but it's affected my memory. I thought Craig Crichton died in my place, that I was dead drunk in a whorehouse when he took a hit meant for me—but I just met his son, so he can't have died. I don't know what's going on, but I know that much. Craig and I are both alive. As for Alissa—God, she seems as real as everything else in my life, but maybe I'm wrong.*

On a hunch, he summons a cab and has it drive him to the Wall. He goes right to the spot where he imagines he's been going for years, looks for Craig's name, and feels a certain satisfaction that he can't find it.

All right, we're both alive.

But are they? He reads down the list a bit, and comes to it: *Eustace Horatio Nolan.*

It's disconcerting, but it's a mistake. It has to be. If there's one thing he knows, it's that he's alive.

Well, that's got to be it. I'm alive, and I'm crazy. Or, rather, I've been crazy, and I've finally come back to my senses. I don't know what caused it—maybe it was in Nam, maybe afterward—but I'm finally me again.

But can I really have dreamed Alissa and Stephanie? They seemed so . . . so real. How can they be figments of my imagination?

He's been ill. Very ill. He's hallucinated a whole life. Where can he find out what's really happened all these years since he's returned home?

The paper.

He summons a cab, goes to the *Post*, walks to his desk, sits at his terminal, orders it to search for everything it has on Eustace Horatio Nolan.

It hums and chatters to itself for a moment, then throws the following up on the screen:

EUSTACE HORATIO NOLAN. BORN APRIL 14, 1948, IN PITTSBURGH, PENNSYLVANIA. ATTENDED SOUTH CENTRAL HIGH SCHOOL. WON SCHOLARSHIP TO UNIVERSITY OF MONTANA. DEAN'S LIST, 1967. DRAFTED, 1968. DIED IN SAIGON, VIETNAM, MARCH 6, 1970.

And that's it. No wife, no daughter. Not even a photograph.

He gets up, walks to the kitchenette in the back, pours himself a cup of coffee, then returns to his terminal.

He decides to have it bring up whatever it can find on Alissa.

It won't respond.

He frowns, then asks it for what it has on Craig Crichton.

No response.

He reboots the machine.

PASSWORD, PLEASE.

He types in his password: STEPHANIE.

INCORRECT. PLEASE TRY AGAIN.

But it is Stephanie. Maybe he misspelled it. He types STEPHANIE.

The machine shuts down.

"Hey, Carl!" he shouts across the room. "Give me a hand here. I'm having trouble with the computer."

Carl Grabowski walks over. "Who are you?" he demands.

"Cut the crap," says Eustace. "I don't have any time for it today. My computer won't recognize my password."

"Why should it?" says Carl. "I don't recognize you."

"Then take a good look. I'm Eustace Nolan."

But unlike the last time, there's no recognition whatsoever on Carl's face.

"I don't know who the hell Eustace Nolan is," says Carl, "but I'm going to give you thirty seconds to get your ass out of this building, and if I ever see you in here again, I won't hesitate to call the cops."

"But I *am* Eustace Nolan, damn it!"

"I don't doubt it," says Carl, looking at his wristwatch. "Ben Bradlee had it easy," he mutters. "All *he* had to worry about were crooks and killers, not nut cases."

Eustace gets up and walks to the door. "You'll remember in ten minutes, or an hour, or tomorrow," he says bitterly.

Then he's outside, trying to think of his next move.

Who creates these databases? Who is telling the goddamned computer that I'm dead? That's the man to see!

But of course he has no idea how the database is compiled. All he knows is how to access it.

He cashes another five and calls Stephanie's room at college. A young man's voice answers.

"May I speak to Stephanie, please?" says Eustace.

"Yeah, hang on a minute."

Thank God!

"Hi," says another masculine voice. "This is Steve."

"There's been a mistake," says Eustace. "I want Stephanie."

"I want Catherine Zeta-Jones," says the voice. "We all have to live with disappointment."

"Damn it!" snaps Eustace. "I want to speak to Stephanie Nolan!"

"Then next time don't call the Phi Delta Theta frat house," says the voice, breaking the connection.

What now what now what now what now?

He decides to try his apartment one last time. He summons a cab.

"Where to, buddie?" asks the driver.

He is about to give the cabbie the address when he realizes that he can't remember it. He mumbles an apology, backs out of the vehicle, and starts walking aimlessly.

Where the hell does he live?

Georgetown, somewhere. Or maybe Pittsburgh. No, definitely Georgetown. That's what he's doing here. He lives here. He works for . . . for a newspaper. The *Post*, the *Times*, the *Trib*? One of them, anyway.

An address pops into his mind. He's almost sure it's his apartment. He's about to summon another cab when he realizes he's only got three dollars in his pocket.

He spots an ATM on the corner, walks over to it, inserts his Visa card.

The machine rejects it.

He looks at the card. It's a perfectly smooth piece of plastic. No name. No raised numbers. Just the Visa emblem.

He checks his driver's license. It still has his name—but the face . . . the face is difficult to recognize. It seems familiar, yet somehow different. Could this be the face he's shaved every morning for decades? If it is, why does he feel so uncomfortable when he stares at it?

All this started at the Wall. Whatever the answer is, it must be there. And somehow, though bits and pieces of his life are leaving him, though he can't remember where he lives or works, he knows exactly how to reach the Wall.

It's a long walk. After a mile his leg begins throbbing.

Damn! That old war wound! The one I got the day Eustace bought it.

He walks to an ATM, inserts his card, withdraws fifty dollars. *Funny*, he thinks; *the card didn't work before. Must have been a faulty machine.* He looks at it, looking for flaws. The name's right: It's made out to Craig Crichton. He turns it over. There doesn't seem to be any damage to the magnetic strip on the back.

He flags down a cab and has it take him to the Wall, gives the driver a nice tip, and then descends into the rift as he has done so many times in the past. Two middle-aged men are staring at a name from 1966 and weeping quietly. He walks around them. He's looking for 1970.

"Hello!" says a familiar voice.

He turns and finds himself facing Shari Ledowitz.

"You know me?" he says.

"We met just the other day," she replies. "Don't you remember?"

"*I* remember," he says. "I just wasn't sure *you* did."

"How could I forget a man who leaves a quarter for his friend every year?" she replies with a smile. She turns to her husband, who is standing about twenty yards away, staring at the wall. "Hey, Andy! Look who's here!"

Andy Ledowitz walks over and extends his hand. "It's good to see you again."

"Thanks."

"I saw you last night . . ." begins Andy.

"No, we met during the afternoon, and I'm almost certain it was more than a week ago."

"I mean on television," says Andy awkwardly. "After we met you here, I felt like I knew you, so when I saw you were going to be on the tube, I decided to listen to your speech."

"How did you like it?"

"You've got my vote." He smiles. "Shari is still making up here mind."

He turns to Shari. "Well, I hope you'll consider me when the time comes."

"Of course I will," she assures him.

He glances at the Wall. It seems like the name of Crichton has vanished right in front of his eyes. *Funny how the mind plays tricks like that. Why would my name be on the Wall?*

"Eustace Nolan," he says, tears welling up in his eyes as he reads the name on the Wall. "Friends don't get any better then that. I think

I told you: he gave his life to save mine. That was when I knew that I'd spend my life in public service, helping others as he'd helped me, as a way of paying him back."

He stares briefly at his reflection on the polished Wall. *Amazing how my driver's license captured my likeness so much better than any of the election posters. I'll have to speak to my staff about that.*

Craig Crichton touches Eustace Nolan's name, as he does every time he leaves the Wall. *Good-bye, old friend.*

Then, his spirit renewed, he heads off to the Capitol for this afternoon's vote.

And, the poison finally removed from their system, Cause and Effect once again take up their accustomed places on History's endless timeline.

Afterword: When I agreed to write a story for this anthology, I was initially at a loss for subject matter. I've never fought in a war, in Vietnam or anywhere else—and I was reasonably sure that if I invited a collaborator to join the project (as I eventually did), that he wouldn't have fought in Vietnam either. Except for Joe Haldeman, very few combat veterans embark upon careers as science-fiction writers.

The more I thought about the Wall, the more I was taken by the fact that there were no heroic statues, no representations of soldiers, nothing but names—and finally a Twilight Zone kind of idea hit me: What if a man who had survived the war saw his own name on the Wall? And what if, from that point on, his life began fragmenting, as if the universe were trying to overcome the blunder of having allowed him to live? One day his wife loves him, the next day she doesn't recognize him, and the day after that she's been married to someone else for thirty years . . . what would it mean, and how would he react?

I mentioned it to Michael Burstein at the Philadelphia Worldcon, he brought a number of suggestions to the notion (including the ending), and we agreed to collaborate. He wrote the first half, I wrote the second half, and the rest is history.

WHILE THE BAND PLAYED

Paul Allen

Ricky took slow, careful steps. Twenty-four . . . twenty-five . . . twenty-six. He stopped and looked past his paunch to the scuffed tips of his boots to make sure that they lined up evenly. Smiling, he stood as tall as the effects of poor posture would allow. The morning sun glinted off the black monument just another fifty feet away. Head high, dressed in his faded camouflage shirt and pants, he continued counting his steps as he approached the wall of writing. He didn't need to watch his feet taking strides as he kept count. He was twenty-six years old, retarded, couldn't read, but he could count to at least twenty-six. He held his pudgy arms out for extra balance as he lengthened each stride. It was very important to have his last step bring him exactly to the beginning of the monument. This was his Sunday morning outing, and each step that brought him to the names on the wall was important.

The band members were assembling on the grass in the center of the memorial. They formed rows on the edge of the walkway opposite the monument. A crowd had been gathering since dawn—the faithful wearing old uniforms from every military service, older women in black, some holding American flags. A tired-looking woman held a placard—*Remember the Missing In Action*. Everyone came to hear the band while they remembered.

Washington, D.C., police units were stationed at both ends of the wall. They maintained a respectful distance while keeping an eye on the crowds. Two patrols of U.S. Marines in dress uniform were deployed at attention, one on either side of the musicians.

Ricky noticed that he was about three feet from the monument's end . . . twenty-two . . . twenty-three. He reduced each stride to less than one foot in length. The twenty-sixth step brought him standing at attention exactly at the monument's end. Ricky clumsily saluted the wall then wiped his nose on the sleeve of his shirt.

A military policewoman broke from her unit and headed toward Ricky. Holding her riot shield casually at her side, she smiled when their eyes met.

"Happy morning, Emily," Ricky called out brightly.

She stopped at his side, turned and smartly saluted the same spot on the wall. "Good morning to you, Ricky. Did you remember that a band is going to play this morning?"

Ricky beamed and nodded his head fiercely. Emily slipped an arm protectively behind his shoulders as the overweight man began teetering off balance.

"I remembered, Emily . . . yes, I did." Catching his balance, he stood back at attention.

"Come on, Ricky, let's go find you a good place to sit so you can see and hear the band."

"You'll help me find another name, another family . . . right, Emily?" His brow furrowed.

"Of course, Ricky. We'll find you a seat after you find a name."

"I found one so far . . . maybe I can find another one today . . . because the band is here today and that makes it special. I found one and now they're a happy family."

She navigated them carefully through the growing crowds. "Yes, you did. And I was happy to take the information you got to the MPs. Have you eaten breakfast yet?"

"I had two donuts and a glass of milk at the workshop before I came." Leaning closer he said in a loud whisper, "They were old donuts. Old donuts don't taste the same as new donuts, but don't say I told you, OK? The man from the donut shop thinks retarded people can't tell old donuts from new ones!" He grinned at her.

"I promise I won't say a word."

"Old donuts are better than no donuts!" Ricky wobbled to a stop. "Right here, Emily. Right here!"

"OK, Ricky." She took his hand in hers. "On your mark, get set, go."

Ricky held his free hand out with his palm a foot from the wall. He closed his eyes, began counting his steps, and let his mind melt into the feeling of flying as Emily guided him slowly along the monument.

When he reached the twenty-sixth step, he sighed loudly and began counting from the beginning. At the seventh step he halted, released Emily's hand and squeezed his eyelids together tightly.

"Here it is, Emily. I can feel a family looking for this one. Read it to me, please?"

At first, Emily had a hard time believing in his gift, but when Ricky located her father's unknown resting place in Nam and the Army made a positive ID when they returned the remains to her . . .

Stepping in front of him, Emily grasped Ricky's outstretched wrist and gently drew his hand away from the wall. His hand was glowing white, and the faint light made the black granite sparkle. Her fingers began tingling the instant she touched his skin.

"Christopher Patrick Masnick."

He whispered the name a few times. His memory for names was always better when he flew. "My hand feels real hot. I want to go see my dad now." Tears brimmed and fell down the stubble of his upper lip and chin as he thought about seeing his dad. "He tells me stories about the war he died in. . . . I still have a dad when I come here and fly. But it makes me happier than happy when I can find someone who's lost from their family. . . . I used to feel lost . . . before I found my dad."

Emily nodded as she held back her tears—remembering the last time as a small girl she saw her soldier father alive. She brought them both to an empty bench near the band.

The band began playing "The Star Spangled Banner." Emily and Ricky stood still and watched the sunlight dance on the polished brass instruments. When the song was finished, he joined her salute to the flag held by the color guard.

"Here's the best spot . . . just right for a very special man," said Emily motioning for him to sit down.

"And it's a very special day, Emily . . . because the band will play . . . and maybe . . ." He sat on the bench and sighed deeply. "I'll come and tell you if I find him, Emily. Then you can tell the story to the military police, OK?"

"Yes, Ricky. That's what the police are for. They help people when they're lost."

"OK, 'bye now," said Ricky closing his eyes and leaning back. As the band struck up a rousing version of "From the Halls of Montezuma," Ricky felt his body tingle, then go completely numb. His eyes twitched beneath his closed lids as lightness filled him. Embracing the sensation, he flew down the dark tunnel that took him to a far-off land.

When Ricky's mind emerged from the tunnel he was a little boy of six, running down the cracked asphalt alley. He smelled the overripe vegetables and rotting fish guts mingling with the smell of diesel fumes as he ran to the back door of the brothel.

He saw himself pass through the locked steel door and into the musty corridor. He looked up into the dark eyes of the old Vietnamese woman standing before him.

She was very old, wore a beautiful long emerald satin gown with puffy silk sleeves, her long silver hair coiled high on her head.

"Happy morning," she said, and bowed to the little boy.

"Can I see my mom?" He held his breath, hoping she would say something different today.

The old woman's dark eyes flickered and the faintest smile reshaped her thin lips. "You must not keep your father waiting. Are you searching for bones today?"

Ricky shook his head. "No, someone living."

The old woman turned and hobbled down the hallway, leading Ricky to the familiar staircase that led to the rooms on the second floor. The staircase was dark, smelled like toilets in the shelter work-shop before the janitor cleaned them, and the steps creaked and shifted a little as he made his way to the landing.

This was the part Ricky hated most. He walked down the poorly lit corridor, bringing his head close to each of the closed doors. Sometimes he heard grunting noises, sometimes laughter, sometimes he heard people crying. Ricky never opened any of those doors.

Ricky's father was always behind the door where there were two voices, a man's and a woman's. They were always talking happily together, and when he would float through their closed door he would see the young woman, her long black hair fanned out over a pillow, lying next to his father, her naked Asian body beautiful in the sunlight that came through the open window above the main street. Her emerald gown lay folded neatly at the bottom of the bed near her small feet.

Ricky thought he could remember an image of a most beautiful golden-skinned woman; something about her felt like mother. But that was before he was three. She didn't come with the missionaries who brought him to America the Beautiful.

When Ricky was thirteen and living in San Francisco, the other Amerasian kids told him that probably his mother was a whore who got pregnant by an American G.I. That was OK with Ricky. He could see, in his mind's eye, his mother and father lying together, holding one another, talking about everything and telling each other wonderful stories. A whore was a good thing to be.

Today, he heard the voices behind the door that had a large cardboard patch over a hole where someone's shoe had broken through the wood. He felt a little sad each time he entered his parents' room because the woman never stayed. But then his father would rush to him, lift him high into the air by holding him under his armpits, and fly him in a single circle around the room.

Ricky snuggled into his father's lap once the burly Marine had seated himself on the edge of the torn, stained mattress.

"Tell me a story, Daddy," Ricky pleaded.

"Sure thing, kiddo. Which story do you want to hear about today?"

"Tell me the story of Christopher Patrick Masnick. Do you know that one?"

"The world is full of stories, and I can learn about them all," said his father, kissing his son's neck and tickling him lightly around the ribs.

"No tickling!" squealed Ricky. "Tell me about this Christopher; he's not just bones, right? He's lost from his family?"

Ricky's father closed his eyes and grew still. "He is not bones . . . and he is with his family."

"He is? How can he be lost, then? He and his family called to me when I came to his name on the wall."

"Sometimes," his father began while stroking the boy's hair, "sometimes people can't remember that they are lost. They can't remember important things about themselves from before the war. Chris has a new family now. You felt an old connection at the wall."

"But what about the first family? Don't Christopher's children remember and want to be with their dad?"

His father held him close. "Children can get a new dad . . . they were babies when Christopher went to war, and now they only know their new dad."

"Maybe, both families could live together . . . and the children, all the children would have extra moms and dads . . . like in case there are more wars?"

"What matters, son . . . is that everyone finds someone who loves them. Love belongs to anyone who is willing to receive it."

Ricky nodded and rested his head against his father's shoulder.

❖ ❖ ❖

Ricky returned to his everyday body somewhere near the end of "Anchors Away." He sat up, looked around, and, not seeing Emily, got awkwardly to his feet and started making his way through the crowd.

Emily waved to Ricky as soon as she saw him up and moving. She could not discern his feelings that lay behind his calm features.

"How'd it go? Any news?" Emily let her riot shield drop to the ground. She took a notebook and pen from her inner jacket pocket.

"Dad says, 'What matters most is that everyone finds someone who loves them.' I love you, Emily." Ricky whispered the words so that only she could hear. "You are good to me. We are friends. We can try and find someone else next Sunday."

Afterword: I lost many high school and college friends in the Vietnam Conflict. Most died in action, but some lived and have endured great mental torment. I have witnessed the suffering of family and loved ones left behind to cope with their losses. It has taken all of us considerable time and effort to heal these wounds.

During and after group experiences of suffering there are the shamans who tend to the losses—of an amputated limb, a bruised mind, and the loss of life within a family. It has always been the role of a shaman to bring together all of the broken and shattered pieces to begin the the process of reconstructing a new wholeness. I wanted to tell the tale of one shaman— one considered to be a most unlikely agent—who reached through the losses to recapture any bright moment that gives hope and renewal. Loss can never be fully restored, but the gratitude for those gifts that remain is more than enough to inspire us to create a better world.

It is the shaman, the healer, who reminds us of the simplest and most profound gifts that remain ours.

THE ONE-HALF BOY

Nick DiChario

I've heard grown men say there's magic on this mountain. I've seen them shrug and motion toward the hills without looking me in the eyes. I've seen the magic blow cold, dead leaves at their feet when there was no wind, almost as a warning to remain silent. The One-Half Boy is a secret for plenty of reasons, most of them good, but I've decided to tell my story anyway, or as much of it as I can without betraying the trust of the people who live here. I think it's important that somebody say something, even if it's me, a man who has learned wisdom only through failure.

🙟 🙟 🙟

"Are you sure you want to know?" asked a man I'll call Smith. He had a lazy eye, and the left side of his face sagged as if he'd suffered a stroke, although he couldn't have been more than fifty years old at the time. He was a heavy smoker; you could hear it in his lungs when he spoke.

Someone had introduced us at a tavern that lay in the shadow of a jagged northern peak, on a ridge hundreds of feet above a pine valley that stretched for miles. The tavern was as roughly hewn as the wilderness that surrounded it. I won't tell you the name of the place, but I guess it's all right to say that you couldn't reach it by car. You had to hike there. Someone who lived in the area had to trust you

173

enough to mention its general whereabouts, giving you, for all intents and purposes, the OK to find it.

It took me a year of living among these people to gain that trust. I wasn't trying to fool anyone. I had made it known to as many people as possible that I had come to the mountain looking for the One-Half Boy.

"I want to know. I need to know," I told Smith.

"That's what they all say till they find him."

"It's true, then?" I still wasn't sure I believed it, although I'd spent years hoping and praying.

"What do you think?" Smith scratched at his rust-colored beard.

I'd heard talk, rumors. Hang around enough support groups and Vietnam vets, you'll hear all kinds of stories. I'd fallen into the habit of showing my son's dog tags around and asking if anyone knew him. No one ever did. I can't remember the first time I'd heard mention of the One-Half Boy, but it went something like this:

"Even if you find somebody who remembers your son, ain't nobody gonna know what happened to him, 'cept maybe the One-Half Boy."

After that, my questions became less about my son and more about the boy. Who was he? Where did he live? What did he know? And how did he know it? Why was he called the One-Half Boy?

"He has a gift. . . . He's blessed. . . . He has the magic. . . . All he has to do is touch you. . . . Lives somewhere in the hill country. . . . Some people find him, some don't. . . ."

No one knew why he was called the One-Half Boy, but that didn't matter to me as long as he had answers and I could track him down. It took me years to gather all the bits and pieces of information that led me to this small town in the mountains.

"I don't know if the boy's real or not," I finally told Smith. "But I aim to find out. Can you help me?"

I'm not sure why I got an answer from Smith. I had asked the same question many times before of many others. So many times and so many others, in fact, I'd given up hope. Maybe Smith understood that I wasn't leaving, not ever, until I found what I'd come looking for, even long after hope had failed me. But I'm sure it hadn't been left entirely up to Smith. The townspeople had decided it was all right for me to know. Otherwise I would have died an old man here in these hills, none the wiser.

"There's a trail north side of the lake," Smith said matter-of-factly. "It's lit by a strange kinda light even when everything else is in shadows. Lookin' for light in the dark is the only way you'll find it. Follow that trail up the north hill and you'll come to the cabin where the One-Half Boy lives. Go by yourself, and bring food."

"Food?"

"Food for the boy. It doesn't matter what you bring. Just don't bring too much. Too much'll look like you're trying to buy him. Only an outsider would do something like that."

So I was no longer an outsider. I'd earned my way in. These people I'd come to see as the boy's loyal guardians had allowed me access to their child king. I thanked Smith and bought a round of beer for everyone in the tavern; I should have paid more attention to why Smith wouldn't drink his. "What's wrong?" I asked him, smiling stupidly. "Why so dismal?"

He frowned and nudged his beer. "If you still got reason to thank me after you see the One-Half Boy, then you can buy me a drink."

Smith turned away to roll a cigarette, leaving me alone with a mug in my hand and a question on the tip of my tongue that I couldn't quite put into words.

⊠ ⊠ ⊠

I had always been a careful planner, so I loaded up my canoe with enough supplies to last me several days. Canoeing to the north side of the lake would be far faster and easier than hiking. I'd lived most of my life in a big city, but a childhood of Boy Scouts—first for me and then for my son—had left me no stranger to the woods, or the dangers that might occur there.

I didn't expect to find the trail right away, but as two days stretched into four, I began to think that my new friend Smith might have played me for a fool. *"Let's send the old man into the woods and see how long it takes him to come out. Maybe he'll get lost, and we'll be rid of him once and for all."* I spent a good part of my time cursing Smith and the entire tight-lipped town.

By the fifth morning I had run through all my food, except for the three cans of beans I'd put aside for the One-Half Boy. So I decided to pack up and head for home, maybe confront Smith and see if we'd had a friendly misunderstanding, or just restock and come out on my own for one last expedition before winter. I can probably tell you without giving away too much that here in the mountains the winters are fierce. The leaves had fully turned by the time I'd ventured out, and there was already a frosty nip in the air. If I didn't find the trail soon it would be a long winter for me.

I circled my canoe around and decided to follow the opposite shoreline home. That's when I spotted a glow in the woods near the base of the mountain. The sun hadn't fully risen yet, and even if it had, it wouldn't have naturally fallen in that secluded place. It was so near my camp, I was sure I'd been by there at least a dozen times. How could I have missed it? I thought it might be a trick of the shadows, an illusion of some sort, but I wasn't about to take any chances.

I fixed my gaze on the spot, paddled hard for the water's edge, and drove my canoe straight up shore. Leaping out, I twisted my ankle on a branch and practically fell into the water, but I didn't let that slow me. I followed the light through the tangles of underbrush and there—there—I found the trail—a narrow pass, barely visible at its starting point except for the light itself.

By then I was panting. My legs trembled. I took a moment to gather my wind and stare at the trail, my reasoning powers desperately taking control even then. Where could that light be coming from? I was under a canopy of mountains and foothills and trees. A reflection, perhaps? Some kind of rare crystalline stone wedged in the side of a mountain? A geologist or scientist might have offered a thousand explanations, but I had none. To me it was an inexplicable radiance—call it magic if you will—just as Smith had described it. Smith, God bless his dismal soul.

I don't mind saying that I fell to my knees and cried. I was emotionally drained. How long had I searched? How long had I been tortured by insomnia and, when the insomnia subsided, nightmares of my son? He was my only child, and eventually my marriage disintegrated because I could think of nothing but my loss. After the Wall was built, I sold my business and moved to Washington so that I could spend whatever time I wanted with his name. That had been my great comfort. I felt so close to him there. I would ask him the same questions day in and day out: "*What happened to you, my son? What happened? When did you die? Where did you die? Did you suffer?*

Did you think of your parents and wonder why we brought you into this world, just as I have so often wondered?"

The One-Half Boy was my only lead, so I'd followed it like a ravenous wolf. And here it was, at last, not just myth or legend or rumor or mystery, but reality. So I let go of all those pent-up emotions, and I cried because I knew even as the tears fell that I would not cry again. From here on out, it was me, the mountain, and the One-Half Boy. Purpose, focus, and objective.

⊠ ⊠ ⊠

Purpose. Focus. Objective.

Here was my situation: The trail that led up the mountain was a steep one. Although I was a fair hiker, I was by no means an experienced mountain climber, and I wasn't a young man anymore. I had twisted my ankle during my moment of blind enthusiasm, and the ankle had begun to throb. I was out of food, except for the three cans of beans. Winter had an annoying habit of coming fast and furious in the mountains, sometimes before the trees shed all their leaves. I wasn't prepared for what the locals called an "ice snap."

On the other hand, I had found the trail. I didn't know for sure that if I returned to town to restock food and supplies and allow my ankle to mend, that I would be able to find the trail again even if I marked it. If an early winter storm hit, I wouldn't get back until next season. I even tried to think logically about the magic. If it was magic that illuminated the trail, and magic that had pointed me in the right direction, who's to say the magic would be so kind as to give me another shot at finding it? Maybe the supernatural radiance was a momentary beacon of light. Take it, and unearth the buried treasure. Turn my back on it, and never get a second chance.

As I'm sure you've guessed by now, I decided that I had come too far to turn away. I would find the One-Half Boy, or die trying.

⊠ ⊠ ⊠

I would need plenty of strength for the climb, so before I began I opened one of the cans of beans, mixed it with some chestnuts, and made a meal of it. Smith had told me to hike the trail until I came to the cabin, but he'd failed to mention how long of a hike it would be, and I had failed to ask. I knotted my boot tightly around my injured ankle and swallowed some ibuprofen in hopes of keeping a lid on the swelling. I had packed a couple of ski poles to help me with the climb, so I hauled my canoe ashore, unpacked the poles, and began my ascent.

I'm not sure how high I climbed, but I was probably at a few thousand feet when I started. The exertion and altitude left me breathless at times, so I took it slow, with plenty of stops to catch my wind.

Eventually the incline lessened and I reached a broad, flat ridge where I saw a cabin tucked neatly among a shoehorn of ancient oak trees. Thick smoke curled out of the cabin's stone chimney. A large woman with the shoulders of a prize bull, dressed in what amounted to filthy rags, stopped chopping wood to stare at me. She leaned on her long-handled ax and wiped the sweat off her face with a soiled bandanna.

I stood frozen until I noticed the children, half a dozen of them at least, running and playing among the trees beside the cabin. The sight of those children reminded me of my purpose. I moved forward and said in my friendliest voice, "Hi, there. How are you? I was just on the trail here. . . . I mean I was hiking the trail, looking for someone. Maybe you can help. . . ."

She kept staring at me. I stopped at what I hoped was a safe distance from the ax. "Actually," I said, "I'm looking for the One-Half Boy. I suppose I could make lots of small talk and try to win you over. The fact is, I've come looking for the boy and I've brought some beans. I've lost my son, you see, lost him in Vietnam, and people say the One-Half Boy has the power to show me what happened. They say he has magic in his hands, and if he touches me, he can make me see. That's all I want. I just want to see. I want to know what happened to my son. Does any of this make sense?"

I'm not sure why the whole thing suddenly sounded so ridiculous, but it did. The woman stared at me without changing expression. She looked younger than I'd originally thought. I didn't know what to do next, so I took the beans out of my backpack and held them out to her.

She lifted the ax and stuck its blade in a chunk of wood, then started walking toward the cabin. I took that as an indication to follow. The children watched us from the woods but didn't seem very interested in what was going on. I wondered if one of them might be the One-Half Boy, but I didn't think so. I had a feeling the boy was in the cabin.

The cabin was a small, rugged construction built of gigantic logs that had a worn and muscular look about them. It gave the impression of a fortress more than a home, maybe because there were no windows in front, no porch or entranceway to make guests feel welcome, just three steps and a broken railing. It was far too small for a clan to live in. I looked around for another cabin and spotted one through the trees deeper in the woods.

The woman led me through the front door. The cabin was so sweltering I broke into a sweat as soon as I crossed the threshold. The fireplace was an inferno of smoke and billowing flames and snapping wood, barely contained by the hearth and stone chimney. I felt as if I'd slid down the belly of a dragon.

My eyes slowly adjusted to the dull, orange flickering firelight. A small bed sat in the corner of the room, atop it a heap of blankets, and beneath that a slight movement that looked frighteningly like that of a shivering body. I wanted to run for no logical reason I can think of now, except that maybe I'd had a premonition of what was in store for me, but I won the battle against my nerves by finding the woman in the shadows and asking her what I should do with the beans.

She motioned toward a spot in the darkness that turned out to be a wooden table. I set the beans down and saw her move a chair beside the bed. She sat down and peeled back some of the blankets. I could not see around her, but I was certain the One-Half Boy was there. I wanted to step closer for a better view, but I was afraid to move.

In a motion so genuinely kind I wouldn't have thought the woman capable of it, she reached over the bed, cradled the boy in her arms, and helped him sit up. I could see a form in the darkness now, hidden among the blankets. She whispered something to the boy while I waited dumbly in the wings.

Finally she turned to me and said, "You can come over here now."

Sweat stung my eyes, and a stench that I thought might be sickness grew stronger as I stepped forward. The boy, I saw immediately, was not a boy at all, but a thin, frail, cadaverous man with stringy brown hair and dark circles under his eyes. He had no expression to speak of, or perhaps no expression worth reading. He looked as dry and brittle as the wood stacked beside the fireplace, and just as ready to perish.

"He's not a boy," I said.

The woman looked at me as if I were too stupid to tie my own shoes. "He's grown."

"Yes . . . but . . . yes . . . of course. I guess I was expecting a boy. What's wrong with him?"

"Sick," she said. "Because of folks like you. You come up here and want this and want that and he's too good to say no. The more he gives, the more you take. My father wants to help everybody. That's just the way he is. Too good for his own good is what I say."

"He's your father?"

"That's what I said, isn't it?"

"Will he speak to me, then?" I was suddenly afraid that I had come so far only to be turned away. It was a possibility I hadn't allowed myself to consider until that moment.

"He's never said no to anybody, mister. He won't say no to you."

"Thank you, thank you."

The woman rose from the chair and nodded for me to take her place. A man of more honor and sensitivity might have left then, but I decided to ignore what she'd been trying to tell me, so I walked to the side of the bed and sat next to the One-Half Boy. His lips were pale blue, his skin jaundiced. I thought that maybe he'd been called the One-Half Boy because he had no legs, but I could see his knees under the blanket, with just enough of his flesh exposed to prove they weren't artificial limbs. I looked at the woman because I could not bear to look at her father. "What do I do?"

"Came here to talk, didn't you? Ask him what you come to ask."

I found it hard to believe that this bag of bones would understand anything I had to say, let alone give a coherent answer, but what choice did I have? This is what I had come for, after all. "I want to know about my son. I know he's dead. He died in Vietnam. I just don't know when, or how, or why. I've been told that you can show me, that you have some kind of magic that will help me see it. That's why I've come."

The One-Half Boy didn't answer. He made no indication that he'd so much as understood a word I'd said. I looked at the woman for some sign of encouragement.

"He wants more," she said. "He wants to know why you want to know."

"Isn't it obvious? He was my son."

The woman shrugged. "Don't tell me, tell him."

I turned toward the bed, but I couldn't bring myself to look at him. "He was my son. He was my son and I lost him and I . . . I . . . if I know what happened to him, I can let him go. I can say good-bye. We can both rest in peace. I guess that's what it comes down to. I want to put it all to rest. The war, my loss, my son. I just have to know."

Again, nothing from the One-Half Boy.

"He wants to know more," the woman suggested.

I turned to her. "What the hell else does he want to know? I told him why I've come. He'll either help me or he won't."

"That the way you see it?"

"Is there another way?"

"Come awful far, mister. Maybe you can think of something else to say if you try real hard."

I turned to the One-Half Boy again. "What do you want to hear? He was my son. I brought him into this world. I gave him life only to send him off to war so he could die before he was twenty years old. I wish he were never born. Do you understand that? I mean it with all my heart. I wish he were never born. I remember . . . I remember the day I first made that wish. It was a year or so after my son's death. I was out in the yard raking leaves. There was nothing special about the day. I was just raking in the backyard and thinking about how my son and I used to rake the leaves into a big pile and how he would jump in and mess them all up again. I was thinking about that, and I sat down on a rock in our garden, and I watched the wind blow the leaves in circles, around and around. I watched for hours. My wife came out to see what I was doing but I wouldn't talk to her. I guess I was crying. That's what she told me later, although I don't remember it. So I sat there watching the leaves until nightfall, wishing my son had never been born. My wife eventually called the police. They came and told me I could go inside my house or spend a couple of days in a psychiatric facility. It was up to me. So I went inside. But I was never the same after that. The world had changed somehow, someway, there in the leaves. The world had changed."

I can't say that he reacted any differently, but something about him shifted, and something shifted about the room. The bark in the fireplace cracked like a cannon. The cabin itself breathed hotly. And the One-Half Boy came suddenly alive. He reached up with his claw-like hand and held his palm out to me. I felt no need to look to the woman for approval. Something in my story, or perhaps in my tone of voice, had earned me his acceptance.

I clasped his hand.

Something bright black flashed behind my eyes.

Then a deeper darkness collapsed around me, and I experienced a moment of blind calm.

I'm sure I'll never be able to explain how I knew I'd fallen inside my son's body. It's not the sort of thing a man can describe and sound reasonably sane after saying it. But I'll do my best.

I felt my heart pound—but I also felt my son's heart pound in union with my own. Our muscles tightened together like tungsten screws. A cold shock of panic and pain ripped through the intricate pattern of nerves that somehow linked us through space and time. In all my years, I've never felt a connection to someone in body and mind and spirit even remotely like it. I knew, on some primitive level, that the One-Half Boy had not only put me inside my son's physical form, he'd put me inside my son's soul. The fact that I saw nothing there but white-hot terror was more horrifying than anything I could have seen with my own eyes or in my worst nightmares. I knew immediately that no man had a right to feel what I'd just felt, unless it was his own time to die.

The experience was mercifully short. When I opened my eyes, I lay on the floor of the cabin, looking up at the One-Half Boy. I thought I was looking at a skeleton mocking me. I felt sick and disgusted. I had gotten exactly what I'd asked for, but not in the way that I'd hoped. I'd seen nothing—not my son or where he was or what had happened to him when he died—nothing to put the mystery of his death behind me. I'd seen only my son's blind terror, a terror that would forever be my own from this day forward. I was so furious I think I actually growled. I wanted to get up and break the One-Half Boy into a thousand pieces, but first I had to find my strength. I leaned against the bed, pushed myself up, and reached for his miserable excuse of a body that lay helplessly in bed.

Before I could get my hands on him, the woman yanked me back and shoved me up against the wall.

"What the hell do you think you're doing?" she said. "You come here wanting to know, and when you find out you take it out on him, is that it?"

"No, you don't understand. He didn't show me anything. All I did was feel it."

"Of course you felt it. What did you think was going to happen?"

She pressed her hands against my chest. The flickering firelight allowed me to see a slight resemblance between her and the One-Half Boy, a similarity in the way their eyes carried the remote despair of captivity. I understood her then, at least I believed I did, for the pain she must have felt for her father.

"I thought I would see a vision, a picture in my mind. I thought if I saw it, if I saw what happened to my son, I could . . . I could . . . put it behind me . . . end it. . . ."

"You were there inside him, weren't you?"

I nodded.

"Isn't that enough? Haven't you learned enough, now, to put it behind you? To end it? Because of my father, you were with your son when he died. Tell me, isn't that enough?"

She'd put it into such simple words that it didn't seem possible. Wasn't the concept more complicated than that? No, no, I don't think so. What's more elegant than the simple truth? It's only when we lie that life becomes ugly. "My son . . . did he feel it, too? Is that the way the magic works? Did my son know I was with him when he died?"

"I don't know. Nobody knows."

"Not even him?" I glanced at the One-Half Boy.

"If he knows, he's not saying."

I reached up and rested my hand on the woman's arm. She was pressing even harder now against my chest. I was drenched in sweat, suffocating in the overheated cabin. "I'm just an old man. I'm not going to hurt your father. Maybe you could let up on me."

She hesitated, but finally let go.

"Thank you."

"Don't thank me, thank him."

She was right, of course. I went to the One-Half Boy and kneeled beside the bed and thanked him. I don't remember much of what I said, except that my words were awkward and clumsily spoken. What I recall is the way he looked, even more distant and physically depleted than when I'd first arrived, although I wouldn't have thought it possible.

I stood and saw the woman holding the door open for me, so I stepped outside the cabin and felt the cool mountain air breathe life back into my legs. She followed me out and handed me the cans of beans.

"No, please, keep them. I brought those for your father."

She shook her head. "Not really. That's what the people say, but they're really for you. The magic steals your strength. If you didn't have any food to eat afterwards, you'd never make it down the mountain."

"The magic. It's stealing his strength, too, isn't it? It's killing him."

She didn't answer, but I knew it was true. It was the reason why he was so hard to find, why the people protected him. How much longer could he go on like this? How many more hands would he grasp, in hopes of showing people like me a simple truth we did not want to see?

"I'm sorry," I said to the woman.

"That's what they all say."

"I'll see to it that I'm the last."

"How will you do that? Talk people out of coming? Could somebody have talked you out of it?"

I heard the children laughing and playing in the woods very near the cabin, but I could not see them. The wind kicked up. I felt suddenly cold. The mountain air carried a bitter chill that spoke of winter.

"You best be leaving," she said. "We'll get an early snow this year. It's in the air already."

"Yes, yes, I think you're right."

I was ready to go, but there was one last question I had to ask. "Maybe you could tell me . . . why do people call him the One-Half Boy?"

She leaned against the log cabin, crossed her arms in front of her, and gazed out at the woods. I thought she might not answer, but I had learned patience over the years, if nothing else, patience.

"It's a name that came to him after the Wall," she said. "The Vietnam Veterans Memorial in Washington, D.C."

"The Wall? What does that have to do with it?"

"The people who came to see my father and then later went to the

Wall, when they touched the names . . . when they went back and touched the names . . . the magic did something . . . something they didn't expect. Those people saw what happened. They saw the pictures in their minds, just like what you wanted to see."

I almost couldn't believe what I was hearing. "You mean if I go to the Wall now, if I go to my son's name and touch it, I'll see?"

"Yes. You'll see his death, and you'll feel it, too. Both those things together. That's how my father got the name. He's one half the magic; the Wall is the other half."

"Dear God, I'll be able to see."

"Don't do it, mister. Take it from me, no man is meant to see another man's death, not from the inside like that, especially his own son's. It'll be every bit as terrible as what you just went through in the cabin—times ten—times twenty. I'm only telling you because you're sure to find out sooner or later. At least this way I can give you a warning. You won't ever recover from it. That I can promise. Let it go, before it kills you."

"But I'll be able to see," I whispered, more to myself than to her.

I reached out with my left hand then, imagining that I was at the Wall touching my son's name, considering the possibility of going through with it—yes, even after all I'd just experienced—wondering if seeing and feeling his death really would be ten or twenty times worse than the One-Half Boy's magic—when a leaf landed on my hand, fallen from one of the gigantic oak trees. Another leaf fell on top of that one. Then another beside me, and another and another.

I looked up, and in the time it took me to raise my arms overhead, all the leaves on all the trees in the field fell at once. Thousands and thousands of leaves rained down on me. In a matter of moments I was buried to the waist. The leaves felt as clean and light as dew. It was such a stunning impossibility that my spirit soared with an irrepressible joy.

The woman laughed, I laughed, and we turned about in the leaves, throwing armfuls of orange and auburn and golden-brown foliage into the air.

And then . . . and then . . . I saw him.

My son.

My son.

There he was, running through the piles of newly fallen leaves, his arms widespread, his small face red with delight, running and laughing and spinning like a top. In that moment, in that one precious moment, my son and I were together again, in the backyard, raking and playing just the way we used to when he was a boy and I was a young father. In that one glorious moment, thirty years had disappeared, and life stood still, and I was healed.

Was it really my son dancing through those heaping piles, or was it one of the children who'd been playing in the woods? Does it matter? I don't think so. I knew that I'd seen the true magic. The One-Half Boy had given me the gift of the fallen leaves. He'd given me one perfect moment of eternal hope, raining down from the heavens. I no longer wished that my son had never been born. Instead I understood finally, finally, that he was at peace, and so was I.

❈ ❈ ❈

I live among the hill people now. I'll never return to the Wall. I still miss my son, and I grieve in my own way, but life has gone on for me. I'm told that I'm the only person who's ever returned from the mountain a better man. I'll never know why I was blessed with this distinction, but I cherish it.

To this day I'm not sure when my obsession with learning the truth about my son turned me into something less than human and started to live and breathe for me. These things happen, or we let them happen, without knowing the how or why of them. But I do know when it ended. It ended on the mountain, in that field, outside the One-Half Boy's cabin.

I won't tell you who I am. I won't say my son's name. I'll give you no specific information other than what I've already told you, which perhaps is too much. I don't want to make it easy for anyone to track me down or find the One-Half Boy. Whenever people come to town searching for him, I try to talk them out of it, telling them my story—this story—all of it, thinking that it will make a difference. It never does. I see so much of myself in them that it pains me to look.

Each time someone heads out for the north side of the lake—it doesn't happen often these days, less and less as the years go by—I pray for the One-Half Boy. I keep thinking I'll hear word of his death echo down the mountainside. But maybe not. Maybe he will outlive all of us who are victims of Vietnam in one way or another. Perhaps the One-Half Boy will finally rest when there are no more suffering survivors to beg him for his gift. I hope so, for that would truly be magic.

Afterword: When I was a boy, Vietnam was the war I was unlucky enough to fear for many years, and lucky enough to miss by a few. A good friend of mine spent plenty of time there and came out alive. He tells a story of sitting down to eat his lunch on the side of the road one sunny and pleasant afternoon, and realizing after a time that, although he hadn't noticed it at first, he was sitting on a dead body—that of a Vietnamese soldier killed and left to rot on the side of the road with nothing more than a thin veil of dirt and a few branches to cover him. My short story is for all the names on the Wall, for all the men and women who fought in Vietnam and made it back to tell their stories, and for my pal, who does not know how special he is.

DIRTY LITTLE WAR

Michael Swanwick

*T*he daiquiris were made with crushed ice and poured into cut-glass tumblers from a pitcher that sat on a towel on the hunt cabinet. The men wore jackets without ties, and the women wore cocktail dresses. Herb Alpert's latest album was on the hi-fi, turned down low so it wouldn't disrupt conversation. The hostess had timed the roast so they could linger over their drinks.

Nobody acknowledged the patrol, smaller than mice, that was fearfully making its way across the room.

"Did you hear?" the hostess said eagerly. "Did you hear what Diana Vreeland said? She wants women to wear belts like rings. Four, five, six at a time—the woman's perfectly mad!"

"But who could *wear* them?" Annie Halpern asked. "I'm not exactly Twiggy, you know."

"And thank God for that," her husband threw in.

She patted his cheek. "Isn't he sweet? He always knows the right thing to say."

"Then he's the only man in the world who does," Andy Wexler said belligerently. His wife reached swiftly for his drink, but he held it out of her reach. "None of that, now. I'm wise to your little tricks."

Cindy Wexler laughed with embarrassment. "Why, dear, I don't know what you're talking about."

"I'm sure you don't."

❧ ❧ ❧

The mission was completely fucked. It had been fucked from its inception, and probably for a long time before that. You didn't get this bollixed up without lots and lots of planning. There'd been seventeen men in the platoon when they'd started out but only eight had made it this far, and still they were still supposed to go on. The Lieutenant didn't even understand what the point of this operation was supposed to be. The orders made fuck-all sense, as far as he was concerned.

Fuck it. That's all you could say. Just fuck it.

Out on the deck, several of the men were smoking cigarettes and holding forth on greens fees and the economy. "Freezing prices!" one of them said. "It doesn't do any good—it's just political grandstanding. You'll notice that the price of a membership at the club has just doubled and yet, oddly enough, nobody's been arrested for it."

"This isn't Russia," the host agreed. "That's for sure."

"I just don't know what's happening to this country," Lionel Wallace said. "Riots and draft-dodgers and bra-burners and I-don't-know-what."

The host stubbed out his cigarette in an overflowing glass ashtray perched precariously atop the railing. "I blame Nixon."

His wife materialized at his side and scooped up the ashtray. "We won't mention that name tonight," she said firmly. "Let me empty this for you."

Lionel batted irritably at a hornet and gazed out over the yard. The Japanese maples were beginning to turn. "You're going to have to drain your pool soon," he commented.

"Don't I know it."

It was Joe Martinez who bought it first. He'd been walking point, and he'd tripped the mine, and then he was dead, and Red Walker was lying on the ground beside him clutching his stomach and howling, and then Howie Simms was shot right in the head.

It happened as fast as that.

They'd returned fire, of course, even though they were in deep bush and couldn't even figure out where the enemy *was*. They'd just blasted the hell out of everything and called for air support, and then air support came and blasted hell out of everything, too.

When the jungle was quiet again, the dead were coptered out in body bags. Red was among them. Also Jimmy O'Brien, their medic, who'd tried to crawl over to Red and drag him back to cover, even though that was exactly what the snipers waited for you to do.

Then, because they had a mission to fulfill and it didn't matter to anyone back at HQ whether it made any sense or not, the platoon proceeded on its way.

▨ ▨ ▨

The Falkners arrived, and a tension, light and bracing as the first touch of autumn, raced through the women. The Falkners' marriage was like a loose tooth, hanging by a thread, that might go at any instant. Genevieve had responded with peroxide and tennis lessons. She and Daniel fled each other the moment they entered the room. It pained the hostess to see how little care they took to hide their antipathy.

"Seat?" Andy Wexler said, popping out of a leather armchair. Genevieve smiled widely, graciously accepted, and sat down carefully. She *had* to sit down carefully, in a dress as short as that.

Cindy Wexler turned her back and marched out onto the deck. "This is so bad of me," she said brightly. "But I would *kill* for a cigarette."

Lionel gave her one of his, then lit it for her. When he bowed his head over the match, the sun caught on his fine, thinning hair and on the pink scalp underneath.

▨ ▨ ▨

It was a nightmare. It was like being run down a gauntlet. They couldn't run the one way because the river was there and the land got boggy. To the other side, the land rose and there weren't any trails. There was mortar fire behind them. Were those fuckers sadists, or just incompetent? The Lieutenant couldn't tell. But so long as they kept moving ahead, changing position, the V.C. couldn't seem to get any kind of accurate fire on them. So they ran, straight down the trail.

The Lieutenant flashed back to the gauntlet he'd had to run down, blindfolded and in his briefs, when he pledged for a fraternity in college. That was before he'd flunked out. He'd been shoved through a doorway, blind, and forced to run between two howling lines of fists and sticks.

He wished they'd try that on him now.

Suddenly, the V.C. had their range, and the mortar fire swept over the rear of the line, like a rainstorm.

Then, mysteriously, it stopped.

They burst into a village. Right through some fields and into a village. It was so unexpected that for a second they could only stand and gawk. It was like suddenly finding yourself in Disneyland. Then the Lieutenant fired his rifle into the air, and they were all running again and shouting at the top of their lungs. Villagers came boiling out of the huts and scattered like pigeons. He figured it would distract Charlie. Maybe they'd be lost in the confusion.

When the barrage started again, it fell upon the soldiers and the villagers with terrifying impartiality.

※ ※ ※

"I'll have you know, my dear, that we saw Woody Allen in New York, back when he was a stand-up . . ." The hostess heard Dorothea Dunletz make a high-pitched kind of an *eep* noise. "Excuse me."

She hurried over to see what was wrong. To her horror, she discovered that Dorothea had stepped on one of the soldiers.

"Don't give it a thought, dear," she said soothingly. "These things happen. I'll take care of it. No, really, you wouldn't know where anything is."

She got the sports section of yesterday's *Times-Dispatch* and some paper towels. Then, crouching and averting her eyes, she managed to brush the little body onto the newspaper with a few anxious jabs of the bunched-up towels. Hurrying into the kitchen, she hastily dumped the body into the trash can in the cabinet under the sink.

Then she returned with seltzer and more towels, to scrub the stain out of the carpet.

At last, with relief and a certain sense of accomplishment, she was able to rejoin the party.

※ ※ ※

The Lieutenant wasn't sure when he'd started seeing the hallucinations. But there they were: People eighty, a hundred, a thousand feet high, with legs like sequoia trees, dwindling away from you, and faces so distant you couldn't make out their expressions when they thought you weren't looking and glanced downward. It must've been the bennies he was popping to keep going. Sometimes he was in the bush and other times in a room so vast it seemed they would never cross it. At its end was the wall that, for no reason he could understand, they were supposed, at any cost, to reach.

Not that he believed there were any of them going to make it that far. There were only Sammy and Larry and Crazy Bill and himself left out of all who had started the mission. It seemed impossible that so many had died. It seemed impossible that so few could survive.

※ ※ ※

The roast was ready.

The hostess stuck a fork in it to make sure, then called her husband into the kitchen and told him it was time to start bringing the men inside. "And stop talking about MacNamara!" she whispered fiercely. "We're not mentioning *that* name either."

"You're the boss, dear." Her husband patted her on the fanny, smiling that tolerant smile she found so infuriating, and turned away.

In the living room, Andy was still hanging over Genevieve's chair, and Genevieve in her turn was laughing far too loudly at his jokes. The only saving grace that the hostess could see was that it was keeping Andy away from the daiquiris. Twice he'd asked her to bring him another, and twice she'd gotten conveniently waylaid by other obligations.

"Everybody—everybody, it's time to sit down. Everyone? Dinner is served. Sweetheart, would you carve? You're so good at it."

As the guests came drifting into the dining room in twos and threes, she guided them to their chairs. She was careful to place the Falkners and the Wexlers as far apart as possible.

※ ※ ※

Sammy died.

Larry died.

Crazy Bill lasted a little longer than the others, but he died, too.

The Lieutenant felt like he'd somehow outlived the end of the world. Everyone he cared about—everyone he *loved* was dead. He had family back home, and he supposed that in a sense he loved them, too. But it wasn't that kind of intense feeling you had here for the guys you relied on to keep you alive. It didn't grab you in the gut and make you ready to lay down your life for somebody.

The guilt he felt was a living thing. These men had relied on him to keep them alive, and he'd failed them, failed them utterly.

It almost made him grateful that he'd been shot as well.

⊠ ⊠ ⊠

The host rapped a water glass with a fork to get everybody's attention. He cleared his throat. "I'd like to propose a toast." He raised his wine glass and said, "To good friends—" There was a rumble of approval. "—both present and far away. And, if I might add a personal note, to family as well. Some of whom are close at hand, and others of whom are far away. Some of whom are—"

His wife caught his eye, and he coughed again. "All of whom are missed."

He sat down.

⊠ ⊠ ⊠

The Lieutenant hurt like a sonofabitch. He'd dropped his pack and his rifle, and was just running now, stumbling really, through the bush. Leaves and branches whipped against him. They hurt pretty bad, but not as bad as this fucking wound in his side. It hurt like fuck. He was afraid even to look at it.

He smashed full-tilt into something hard.

Dazed, he staggered back a step or two. Then he pulled himself together. The jungle was entirely gone now. There was nothing in front of him but featureless, colorless nothingness.

He reached out a wondering hand. It touched plaster, smooth and cool.

Somehow, he'd reached the wall.

For a second, he couldn't find his pencil. He slapped at his clothing in a panic and on the third attempt found it, right where it should be, in his shirt pocket. It was a little stub of a thing but functional.

Carefully, ignoring the pain, he wrote the names of all the men in his platoon on the wall. Joseph Martinez. Johnny Walker. Howard Simms. James O'Brien. Paul S. Holloway III. Pedro Swenson. Francis Parks. Ulysses S. Brown. Garry Liones. Robert Starbuck. Kent Johnstone. Barry Moyer. Kenneth Fletcher. Samuel Brown. Larry E. Lee. William Daugherty. Last of all, he wrote his own name.

"We were here, damn it," he muttered. *"We were here!"*

But then all the strength left him, and he slid to the carpet. Away in the distance, he could hear the doorbell chime. It had nothing to do with him anymore. He was busy at the business of dying.

Death was a smooth and featureless black wall. It stretched to infinity in all directions. He felt himself moving toward it. It was so close now, he could almost touch it. On this side were warmth and light, trees and grass and bumblebees, filing cabinets, the Miss America pageant, rebuilt carburetors, Saturday morning cartoons . . . everything he had ever known or thought or experienced. And on the other? He had no way of knowing. He was going to find out.

In the dinner party far above, the doorbell rang, and somebody got up and went to the door. A courier stood there, envelope in hand. He said the hostess's name, with a little rise in his voice at the end, like a question mark. The soldier looked up, vaguely curious. Then the wall was upon him. For an instant it filled the universe. He took a last gasping breath. Then he passed through.

He didn't hear his mother scream when she read the telegram.

Afterword: I was one of many of my generation fortunate enough not to have served in Vietnam. I had a student deferment and then a high number, and with my lungs the military probably wouldn't have taken me anyway. But I was constantly aware—everyone was—of the terrible price so many were paying. Friends shipped off overseas, and strangers returned. If you got them drunk, they told you stories you didn't want to hear. Sometimes they cried.

I tried writing about the war while it was going on and couldn't.

Whenever I tried, a feeling of inchoate rage against the wicked old men who sent so many to die in a war that could not be won (and which, it turned out later, they knew could not be won!) would rise up so strongly within me as to render me incapable of writing a rational sentence. Later, when the war was over, it seemed to me that I did not have the moral right to write about it. Like most people in this country, I came to the conclusion that the only Americans who had anything worth saying about the Vietnam War were those who had been there—the vets.

So this story isn't really about the war. It's about the strange peace we had while the war was going on. We never went on a wartime economy. Things were booming. We didn't have rationing, or travel restrictions, or any inconveniences at all that I can think of. Disney World, for Pete's sake, opened in 1971! Somehow, we were able to have a war without sacrificing anything but fifty thousand American lives.

I couldn't understand it then, and I can't understand it now.

THE ANGEL OF THE WALL

Byron R. Tetrick

A miracle happened one day at the Wall. I wasn't there, nor was anyone I know, but I heard about it from a friend who had a friend—you know how it goes. Anyway, when I first hear about this "miracle," it makes me . . . well . . . shiver. That may not be the best description: It's kind of a ripple that goes up both shoulder blades, meets at the base of my neck, and shoots up the back of my head. Sure, out loud I scoff and tell Jack, my buddy, that it is bullshit; in fact, I get a little mad, and Jack knows me well enough that he lets it drop. But all the rest of that day, although I try to put it out of my mind, I can't think of anything else. What if it is true?

It seems that there is this blind woman—a street person who sometimes shows up at the Wall. She walks up to a friend of Jack's who's at the Vietnam Veterans Memorial—none of us vets call it that though . . . it's the Wall. She walks up or taps up or however the hell you'd describe a blind person walkin' and tells him to put her hand on the name of his friend who died. She traces her fingers over the etched name like she's reading braille, and then she gives a message to this guy from his friend who died in Nam. Jack's friend swore it was his buddy, that she said things in the message that only his friend would know. So this guy is really shook, you know. Before he realizes it, she's gone.

Pretty eerie.

So all that day it haunts me, and later, when I see Jack again during a break—we both work at the docks here in Baltimore—I apologize for getting short and ask him if he wants to meet at Birdy's for a few beers.

⬚ ⬚ ⬚

By the time Jack shows up, I've already had a couple. I'm at my usual table by the jukebox and nod to Jack as he walks in and spots me. He makes a drinking motion with his arm and I nod again, and he gets a couple of beers from Jabba behind the bar, sits down and raises his bottle in a toast.

"To cold beer and hot women," he says, even though we both know that he loves his tiny little wife so much that he wouldn't recognize a hot woman if she walked up and rested her tits on his forehead.

"Fuck Communism," I answer, and drain the last of my beer and reach for the fresh one.

We both take another swallow and listen to the music on the juke-box. "I can only stay for a couple," Jack informs me as he glances at his watch.

"No problem. I'll probably just have one or two more myself," I say, knowing already that I'd be drinking dinner.

"Goin' to the Ravens' game Sunday?" Jack is looking at the sched-ule taped to the mirror behind the bar. The unbroken row of "W's" has even got us diehard Colts—I should say ex-Colts—fans excited and thinking another Super Bowl.

"Yeah, I might," I answer. "It's supposed to rain, so I should be able to get a ticket cheap."

We talk some more football, laugh a little about the hapless Bengals in Cincinnati, switching to college basketball as we finish our beers. I get Princess Leia's attention and order another two beers. Actually, the barmaid's name is Chrissy, but we named her Leia mainly because of naming Augie, the bartender, Jabba the Hutt—not that Chrissy's not pretty, but she's no Carrie Fisher either. Birdy's really ought to be called the "Star Wars Bar"—full of the dregs of the universe. I guess in keeping with that theme, Jack would be Lando. Did I mention that Jack is black? Probably not. I would definitely be Chewbacca—kinda big, and come to think of it, with my full beard, hairy, too. Leia brings the beer and Jack says to me, "I'm going to the Wall tomorrow."

I just look at him, take a pull from my beer, shake my head and say, "You really believe that shit about the blind woman, don't you?"

"I gotta check it out, man. This friend of mine that it happened to is not 100 percent, but he's no dope-head either."

I can see the old pain in Jack's eyes. We first met at the Vietnam Vets Center and became friends. It was Jack who got me the job at the docks. Apparently, he had been even more fucked up than most of us, but then he met Julia, fell in love, and got his shit together. The demons were still there; he just had something and someone to live for, so he did his best to ignore it and seemed to be doing a good job until this guy puts this crazy idea in his head.

I know I shouldn't say it, but I do anyway. "I suppose your friend is black."

"What the *fuck* does that got to do with anything!" He says fuck by pushing his lower lip past his top teeth so hard that he sprays me with a mixture of spittle and beer.

"It's just that you guys are too spiritual. You look for your answers from smooth-talkin' preachers or some crazy woman who's hallucinating at the Wall." Jack is religious, and I should know better than to pick at it, but this blind woman's thing smacks of con to me. I put my hand on top of his, and he tries to jerk it away, but I'm stronger and I press down. "I just don't want to see you get your hopes up on something like this. I didn't mean anything bad."

"I was gonna see if you wanted to go with, but I guess you answered that." Jack's anger is now gone and he looks at me like *he* feels sorry for *me*.

"You're right, I don't want to go," I say as I get the Princess's eye and signal for another beer.

Jack gets up, lays a buck on the table for Leia, and tells me to have a good weekend. We do a honky version of a black handshake so I know we're still friends, and he waves to me again from outside as he walks past the big window at the front of the bar. The Miller Lite neon paints red and yellow streaks across his face as he gives me his big smile and passes out of sight.

The Princess brings my beer, and I ask her to bring me a Cuervo shooter. I also hand her a five and ask her to bring me some quarters. A few minutes pass and Jabba waddles up to the table and delivers the quarters. He clicks the shot glass down on the Formica and puts his hand out with his huge palm up. I reach in my jacket and pull out my car keys and drop them into his hand. Jabba and I have this understanding: He lets me drink—I don't argue. I tried it the other way once, and he pounded the crap out of me and threw me out the door. I'm big . . . Jabba's gigantic, a Sumo wrestler disguised as a bartender.

I suck down the tequila, grab some quarters, take my beer along for company, and go over to the jukebox. It's an old Seeburg that Jabba keeps stocked mostly with oldies, some country, and a little bit of rock. Checking to see that Jabba's not watching, I reach behind the jukebox and twist the volume control up a notch. I vary my selections, even play a couple that I know Princess Leia likes, make a piss stop, and return to my table. Leia had apparently made another pass by the table, for the empties are gone. My solitary beer beckons to me. My first selection starts playing: Elton John's "Candle in the Wind."

⊠ ⊠ ⊠

I'm mellow.

⊠ ⊠ ⊠

I kinda wish Jack could have stayed a little longer. I smile at the memory of his big grin and easy friendship . . . and quick forgiveness. I'd be a hurtin' puppy if I lost the only friend I've got left. I probably shouldn't have hassled him about going to the Wall. It's just that both of us had some very bad years after returning from Nam. Both of us continue to walk a ledge that we've fallen off before, and neither of us may have the strength to get back up again. What if there really is a woman who is some sort of psychic who can communicate with dead soldiers? Why does Jack think the dead will say something that will bring him peace?

⊠ ⊠ ⊠

What would Danny say to me?

⊠ ⊠ ⊠

I wish Jack would let it go. I wish I could let it go.

⊠ ⊠ ⊠

Randy Newman is singing "I Love L.A.," and Leia gives me a wink—that's her favorite song. Maybe that's what I should do, move to L.A. and get away from this city, the bureaucrats, and the politicians that sent us to a war they wouldn't let us win.

⊠ ⊠ ⊠

I went there—once—shortly after they dedicated it. It pissed me off. It's made of black granite and is nothing but vertical slabs with the names of all the soldiers killed or missing etched into the stone. Some Marine called it the Vietnam Dead Memorial—appropriate name.

I went on a sunny, weekend day, and it had been crowded with lots of civilians; it just made me angry. Where were the crowds of people supporting the soldiers when we were alive and fighting? These same people had probably been burning our flag and demonstrating against us. A few men were wearing suits, probably corporate types who dodged the war, were making big bucks, and wouldn't give a veteran a job if it meant it might cost them a nickel more an hour. Jane Fonda had married a gazillionaire, and together they owned more land than Vietnam and Laos put together—or at least they had until they divorced. She should have been shot as a traitor. They were saying that the Wall was healing our country. America didn't deserve forgiveness.

⊠ ⊠ ⊠

I wanted them to hurt.

⊠ ⊠ ⊠

The only reason I went to the Wall was to see Danny's name. I didn't make it that far. I couldn't face Danny. I thought it was my anger at the people swarming at the Wall. Now I don't know.

⊠ ⊠ ⊠

Jabba's system works. I wake up late the next morning in my own bed, feeling like shit but in one piece. My last memory of the night was playing my phantom acoustic guitar to Dire Straits' "Money for Nothing," wishing I could play like that, and thinking that Mark Knopfler sure didn't get money for nothing!

I hike down to Birdy's later, intending to pick up my Chevy, end up surrendering my keys to Jabba again, and waking up the next morning with absolutely no memory of the night before. Sunday I manage to pick up my car, toy with the idea of driving over to the stadium, but wind up watching the Ravens lose to the Bengals on TV.

⊠ ⊠ ⊠

Jack and I don't cross paths Monday, and it is almost quitting time when I see him on Tuesday.

"So, did you see the oracle?" I say with a cynical grin.

"No, but it was a nice visit to the Wall. There was a bus there from the VA hospital. I felt like I helped some other guys. It was the first time for some of them. What'd ya do? Go to the game?" Jack asks.

"Nah, just hung out." Jack knows well enough how I spend my weekends. I give him a wave and start to walk away.

Jack grabs my arm. "I talked to someone else who had the same experience. He described the same street person that my friend had seen. He called her an angel." He waits for me to laugh or snort or something; when I don't, he continues, "He told me that it was like she had chosen him. It was just like my buddy described it. She told him to put her hand on the name, and she gave him a message."

"What was the message?" I ask.

"I asked him that; he didn't say. He just said it was good. It was good. He kept repeating that, and then he said it healed him." Jack was looking through me now, eyes glazed, as if wondering what it would be like to be healed.

"Well it sounds like a crock to me. Don't believe everything you hear. Gotta run—see ya," I say as I start walking toward the time clock.

"I'm goin' back," Jack hollers after me.

"Fool," I whisper under my breath.

⊞ ⊞ ⊞

Fall gives way to winter. The Ravens lose three straight games, and we're all worried that they may not make the playoffs. I have a run-in with Jabba, say some things to him that I'm ashamed of now; I even say things to the Princess that I know will hurt her. Jabba tells me not to come back. I've walked this road before . . . many times. I'm scared.

⊞ ⊞ ⊞

Jack goes to the Wall every weekend. He's obsessed with seeing the "Angel"—he calls her that now. I knew this would happen. I only see Jack at work now. I want to go to the Wall and kick that old bitch for what she's doing to Jack . . . for what she's doing to all the vets who believe in this shit.

Oh yeah, lots of guys have fallen for this con artist. I still go to the Vietnam Veterans Center and that's all everyone talks about. Last week at the Center, I walk up to a large group that has gathered around Johnny Reb—he's a mean and crazy son of a bitch from Richmond who is usually in jail or prison. Johnny's telling the guys about the "angel" and his visit to the Wall. You might figure, the only first-person version I hear is from a wacko. He pretty much tells a story like all the rest. Everyone is oohing and aahing, and I can't stand it.

"You're so full of shit, Johnny," I say. I tense, anticipating him to pull a blade. It wouldn't be the first time we've been at it.

Johnny turns in my direction. I fully expect to see the usual Charles Manson craziness in his eyes. Instead, they crinkle at the edges and he laughs. "Well, I won't argue with that," he says. Then his face turns thoughtful, almost pensive, and he adds, "but not about this. The Angel spoke to me."

I say something crude and walk away in disgust.

⊞ ⊞ ⊞

Late in January, I get a call from Julia inviting me to their house for Sunday dinner. I try to make some excuses, but Julia insists, and when I finally agree, I'm glad, because Jack and I had been drifting apart and his friendship is the only thing of value in my life. It's just that Jack is obsessed with his "angel"—and the Wall—and I want only to forget I ever heard of either one.

I show up with the best bottle of wine that I can afford, and I'm surprised to find Jack already tipsy. Jack is my drinking buddy, but I had never seen him drunk at home.

"How 'bout a beer?" is the first thing he says to me.

"Jack, let him get his coat off, at least," Julia says as she walks up and gives me a big hug.

We sit down in the living room and start watching the late afternoon NFL games. Julia says that dinner will be ready in about an hour and brings in some snacks.

The Bears are playing the Eagles, and it's a real defensive game. Jeremy, their oldest, and a running back for his high school team, is quizzing me about my college ball—before I flunked out and got drafted. Rowena, nearly ten and already looking the young lady, sits at my side on the big, overstuffed couch. She sneaks glances at me that are half bashful and half adoring, making no secret of the crush she's always had on me. Jack once told me that he liked having me over because I was the only white person his kids were around. He'd seen enough racism on both sides and didn't want them to grow up hating whites. I'm probably a bad example, but I sure do love his kids.

Julia walks in carrying Jack's coat. "Here," she says. "Walk down to the corner and get some milk."

Jack moans but gets out of the lounger. "Wanna go with?" he says, turning to me.

"Sure." I get up, but Julia puts her hand on my arm.

She squeezes my arm and says, "You stay right here. You've been out in that cold already. Jack can get it." She scoots Jack out the door and yells out, "And don't drive!"

Julia takes me by the hand and pulls me into the kitchen. "Come here and help me with the cooking," she says.

She walks over and stirs something on the stove. She turns around and faces me, big tears filling her eyes. "Help me, Andy. I'm scared. I'm gonna lose him." Julia holds out her arms, and I walk to her and wrap her up like a mother bear hugging her cub. She sobs against my chest and tries to tell me more, but she can't catch her breath.

My cheek is laying on her head. Her hair smells like some kind of flower, and for the first time in a long time, I feel the bleakness of my life. I think of my two-room apartment, now suddenly sterile and cold.

I pull the sleeve of my flannel shirt over my hand and wipe the tears from her cheek. "What's wrong?" I say, but I've got a good idea.

"It's the war. His nightmares are back, worse than ever. I feel so helpless." Julia starts crying again.

I say some simpleton thing, like: He'll get over it; or it'll pass; or something like that, that neither of us believes.

She tells me some more details, including how he won't talk to her about it. How they argue about it. Finally, she shocks me with the kicker. "He hit me, Andy. He hit me." She starts crying again.

I'm stunned. Jack loves her more than life itself—I *know* that. At that moment, I want to go strangle that witch at the Wall. Jack had been happy. She had done this to him!

Julia composes herself. We both know that Jack will be back shortly.

"I'll talk to him, Julia. We'll straighten him out, you'll see," I say to her and give her another hug.

Julia smiles, and then says something to me that I thought I'd never hear again: "You're his best friend."

Where moments ago I had felt desolate about my life, I now feel reborn. Jack was my only friend, but to be someone else's *best* friend, that had never entered my mind. I always assumed that Jack had better, black friends. A familiar ripple of unworthiness courses through me like the memory of a childhood sin, and I feel shame for the way I had ridiculed Jack's desire to find his "Angel." This had been his cry for help, and I thought him a fool. I was the fool.

"I'll help him, Julia," I say with a passion that was deeper felt than any I had experienced since returning from Nam.

🐟 🐟 🐟

Dinner is great. The kids cut up for me at the table, and I revel in the feeling of family; I feel like I belong. As we clear the dishes, I tell Julia that I want to borrow her husband for a while, and Jack winks at me, thinking that we are going out just to drink some more. I promise Julia that I'll have Jack home early and, on the sly, press her hand and tell her I'll do whatever it takes.

▩ ▩ ▩

We go to a place that Jack knows is open on Sundays—I'm the only white guy there—and take a booth in the back. I let Jack move the conversation because I know it won't take long for him to start talking about his "Angel" or the Wall.

We talk sports all of ten minutes and then Jack says, "I just missed seeing the Angel yesterday. The Wall was crowded. It was twenty degrees outside and still there were hundreds of people there."

"How much did you miss her by?" I ask, choking back my rage at this charlatan that was playing God with my fellow veterans . . . and my friend.

"No more than half an hour," he says. "You should have heard what the people were saying. Hundreds of people saw her touch the Wall and trace the name. Andy, everyone says it's true. She's an Angel that heals."

Jack's eyes take on that same far-away look they did the day he first started calling her an angel. It's time to bring him down to the real world.

"Julia tells me that you're having nightmares again, bad ones. She also said things weren't going very well between the two of you." I look hard into his dark eyes.

"What else did she say?" Jack is suddenly angry, and I realize too late that I had taken the wrong approach.

"That's all, Jack . . . really. She's worried about you." I need to keep talking. I know he cools off quickly, but I can't let his anger—and his guilt—build. "Tell me about your nightmares. I know how bad they can get. I have them, too."

Like every night.

"There's nuthin' to tell. They're back, and they're not going away until I see the Angel." He means it. I know that now.

I guess in the back of my mind I knew all along what it was going to take. Part of me holds back, and if Julia hadn't said what she said to me tonight about me being his best friend, I never could have done it.

But best friends have responsibilities.

"I'll make you a deal." I pause to let him think about what kind of deal I might propose. "If you tell me why you think your angel can help you, I'll go to the Wall with you."

I expect him to turn the deal down initially, so it's a surprise when he says OK.

"So, speak," I say.

"I need forgiveness. Only she can give it to me." He looks at me as if that's going to satisfy me.

"Why . . . do . . . you . . . need . . . forgiveness?" I space my words, telling him by doing so that it's no deal unless he answers without holding back.

Jack struggles. He fidgets, shakes his head, looks me in the eyes, but can't hold it and looks away. He notices the beers we had forgotten about and gratefully picks his up and takes a large gulp. Finally, he says, "I can't. I can't tell anyone . . . ever."

"I've been there . . . remember? We all have shit we want to forget, want never to talk about." As I speak, my demon raises its head.

🀰 🀰 🀰

What about Danny? Who's going to forgive you, and who can you tell . . . and will you?

🀰 🀰 🀰

"I'm sorry, Andy, I just can't. We could never be friends again." He does look at me now, unblinking, wanting reassurance.

"I'll always be your friend. You hurt . . . I hurt. Tell me. I know it's got to be bad or you wouldn't struggle so, but I promise you'll always be my friend." And I'm surprised at how much I really do feel my friend's pain.

Jack takes another deep drink of beer. "It's bad, real bad. You'd never think the same of me again. I don't think I can do it."

"Give it a try," I urge. "Tell me what you can, bud, and if you just can't finish it, at least you tried."

Jack lowers his eyes, and his body sags into what I assume is reluctant acceptance. A long moment passes—long enough that I start to doubt again that he's going to tell me—but finally he raises his head and straightens himself in his chair. In a voice that is almost a whisper he says, "OK . . . I'll try."

🀰 🀰 🀰

Jack looks at me and his lids lower. "Did you ever hate us niggers?"

"Come on, Jack. You know me better than that. I may have grown up in Baltimore, and yeah, I still got some prejudices, but I fight 'em, and I've never hated blacks. I don't even like hearing you call *yourself* a nigger."

"You're the only white friend I've ever had," he says.

"Shit, you're the only black friend *I've* ever had," I respond, smile, and tip my "long-neck" Bud on the lip of his beer bottle.

He smiles at that, but then says, "Well, I used to hate whitey. I hated him with a burning, wild-eyed passion that twisted my gut so bad that sometimes I couldn't keep food down." For a second, I saw a trace of that hatred cross his face. "You remember what it was like in the sixties: race riots in all the big cities, church bombings, Klan marches, Black power?"

I don't think he expects me to respond. But yeah, I remember.

Jack signals the bartender. "I got my draft notice the Monday after Martin Luther King was shot. My mother was still alive then, otherwise I wouldn't have gone. I didn't give a shit about Vietnam—I didn't give a shit about anything . . . 'cept my mom."

The bartender stops by our table, and we order a couple more beers.

"So I go to basic training," Jack continues. "Barely make it through without a court martial and get shipped off to Nam. Nineteen-sixty-eight—Tet. It was a bad year to go off to a bad-ass war."

"Sixty-eight sucked," I agree, thinking that seventy hadn't been much fun either.

Jack nervously starts pulling strips of the beer label off the bottle and wadding them up. "The brothers didn't associate with whitey . . . at all—at least not in my platoon and not in any of the platoons that I ever saw. The officers kept us busy hating the gooks more than each other, and that was what passed for *esprit de corps*. I was the worst. If one of the brothers would show any sign of friendship towards a white, I would rag on him until he got the message."

As Jack is talking, my own memories flicker in my mind like the Hollywood version of flashbacks: vignettes of war and combat fought by two races against the third. Initially, I had kind of envied the blacks their brotherhood—not really realizing until later that their unity was as much against whites as it was against the enemy. I remember what it was like.

"I guess I shouldn't be surprised," I say, "but it just doesn't sound like you."

The bartender returns to our table with the beer and fusses around wiping our table off and collecting empties from the surrounding tables. Jack's eyes follow the bartender as he leaves. Not looking at me, his voice seeming to rise with anger—at me, at himself, at the war . . . I don't know—Jack says, "Get it straight, Andy. I hated all whites . . . believe it!"

He stares back at me. I nod.

"I may have hated whitey, but I did respect the ones that knew their shit, that could lead and listen. Our squad leader, Sergeant Lewis, was the best. Our squad had been together for almost a year, and the sarge managed to keep most of us alive."

For a moment, Jack loses himself in reverie—his mind, like mine, flipping through the images of fire-fights and blood; heat, rain, and jungle; fear and exhilaration; and for some of us . . . shame and despair.

"We went through a lot together," Jack continues. "Six weeks to the day before most of us would be on a 747 back to the world, Sarge was leading us on a patrol, saw a movement through the canopy, signaled with his hand to lower, started to raise his rifle, and a sniper blew his brains out."

Both of us take a long draw on our beers. Both of us remembering how quickly death came in the jungle.

"Boom . . . he was gone. Boom . . . things went to shit. The lieutenant assigns us a know-it-all replacement—a real green, newly promoted corporal. This buck sergeant by the name of Garrett was a total bona fide, southern-bred, redneck from Georgia. He had never done nuthin but pud duties like perimeter defense of the air base back at Danang. He didn't have any jungle experience, and he wouldn't listen to us coons."

As he describes Sergeant Garrett, the hatred that he must have felt surfaces again, and I wonder how Jack could have changed so much since Nam. I let him continue.

"Our first patrol, he takes us on a 'pursuit'—a mop-up operation through a marsh. Artillery had already blasted the area, but the wounded survivors and stragglers could kill you as well as not. We pleaded with the sergeant to wait for another squad to cover our flank—a hill rising up into jungle to the south of the swamp—but he wouldn't listen. Three snipers hidden two feet inside the tree line was all it took. They killed Dish, wounded two more, and pinned us down in the swamp for twenty minutes until the rest of our platoon circled back and chased the snipers away. We had leeches all over our bodies. At least we could pick 'em off while we lay in the goo. When we finally pulled Dish out of the swamp, he was covered with the slimy fuckers."

Jack grimaces with the memory, takes a sip of beer. "We went to the lieutenant, but it didn't do any good. Christ! We were almost finished with our tour, and this bozo was going to get us killed. We hated him. We convinced ourselves it was a conspiracy to get us killed. We made it through two more patrols only by luck. One night, about two weeks after Dish's death, we're sitting around the mess tent, and one of us said, he's got to die. We talked seriously about fragging him, even if it meant that we'd end up in Leavenworth. Better than dead. Finally, we left it that we'd cover for each other; sooner or later the sarge would get himself in trouble, and we'd just let it happen. Him or us—simple as that. But I knew what I was going to do. I wasn't going to wait."

Jack looks hard at me, maybe waiting for me to say something. I'm afraid to say anything.

"Our next patrol came suddenly. A full company of NVA made an assault on the west perimeter of our firebase. We were lucky. A FAC was working a flight of Navy A-6s near the Ashau Valley, and within ten minutes the Forward Air Controller was overhead, and minutes later the Mark eighty-two's started pounding their position. HQ sent us out in pursuit as they scattered and ran. Our squad stayed close as we worked our way down our hilltop, but eventually we got separated from the platoon, and by the time we reached the thicker foliage of the jungle, I was the only one close to the sarge. We were spread out pretty good and had orders not to pursue deep into the jungle. I came up on the bodies of some NVA. You could see where the daisy-cutter had come and sprayed a shrapnel pattern through the trees. I could hear Garrett tramping through the jungle off to my left and reached a decision: Now was the time. It was a flawless plan.

"There were four of them, all facing the same direction as if they'd tried running away when they saw the bombs falling. I quickly checked them out to make sure they were dead and was at first disappointed that none of them had any commie-made grenades, but I didn't let that stop me—in fact, it was better, 'cause I didn't trust theirs. I took out one of my own, pulled the pin and carefully wedged it under the body of one of the gooks that had some markings on his uniform—probably an officer.'"

Jack's voice is robotic now, as if he knows that if he spoke with any emotion, he'd lose control.

"'Hey, Sarge,' I called. 'Over here! We got some dead ones.' He joined me, and I pointed with my rifle to the one whose body the grenade lay under. 'That one's an officer and he's got some neat stuff if you want it.' Lots of guys stripped bodies for souvenirs and Garrett was always talking about it. As he walked over and put his foot on the body to roll it over, I moved behind a tree for protection and kablooey!"

Jack lifts his beer to his mouth. His hand are shaking and I'm afraid he's going to lose it. I start to say something, but he cuts me off with a halting motion with his hand.

"Let me finish," he says. "I fired a full clip from my sixteen into the gooks, and then just stood there, thinking, well that was easy! And then I walked up to the sarge.

"He wasn't dead yet, Andy. He wasn't dead. He was supposed to be dead!" And now Jack starts sobbing through his hands, heart rending, deep, liquid sobs.

I know there is nothing I can say. I place my hand on his shoulder and watch it bob up and down as Jack cries. The bartender approaches the table with a questioning look, but I shake my head and he departs. I wait. An eternity.

※ ※ ※

"He lay flat on the ground, on his back." Jack's voice jars me. I'm lost in thought, still stunned by his story. "The sergeant's eyes were glazed, but I could tell that he could still see me because they followed me as I moved towards him. He knew he was going to die. He knew I had set him up and his eyes were asking, why? You know how a dog's eyes look when it's been hurt, and it looks at you not understanding the pain, and not understanding why you can't help it? Imagine a human being looking at you that way. I screamed for a medic, now desperate to save his life. I screamed again as his eyes lost focus and he died."

※ ※ ※

"I told you it was bad. Now you know why I go to the Wall . . . searching for the Angel . . . searching for forgiveness."

"What if she gives you a message from the sergeant and it's full of hate and no forgiveness?" I ask.

His answer surprises me, but disturbs me even more. "That's OK, too," he says. "Then I'll know how much to hate myself."

That breaks my heart. I don't know what to say. I search desperately for words that will help. I can't find them. Instead, I say, "When do you want to go to the Wall?"

Jack smiles, then answers, "Tomorrow."

※ ※ ※

I support Jack as we walk out the door. It's bitter cold now, and the stars are brittle and hard in the clear sky. We share each other's body heat as we walk the half block to the car. I ask Jack as I open the door for him, "Do you still hate us a little?"

Jack slowly lowers himself into the car, stiffly, almost like a bruised athlete. He raises his head and looks at me, shakes his head, and says, "I don't hate anybody. I'm still angry about some things; it's impossible to be black nowadays and not be. But hate? . . . I stopped hating the moment I killed that white boy in the jungle. I never fired my rifle again."

At Jack's place, I leave the Chevy running while I walk him to the door, say goodnight to both of them, and walk back to my car. I sit shivering in the car and remember something. I walk back up on the stoop and quietly knock so I won't wake the kids. Julia and Jack's faces peer around the partially opened but chained door.

"I forgot something," I say. "I forgot to tell you that I'm still your friend."

Jack laughs his deep, infectious laugh. He unchains the door, steps out and embraces me. "I don't know why I ever doubted it, buddy."

The car starts feeling a little warmer as I drive home.

※ ※ ※

The next morning, it's so cold that I need to bum a jump from a neighbor to get my old Chevy started. I call Jack from the diner where I'm eating breakfast and make sure he still wants to go. I can't imagine his angel will be there on a day like today. But Jack says, yes, so I tell him that I'll pick him up about ten-thirty.

The morning sky turns opaque as the temperature starts climbing, and by the time I pick up Jack there is a light snow falling. I-95 is slippery, traffic is slow, and we don't reach Constitution Gardens until almost one o'clock. Now the snow is heavier, and a couple of inches of soft, dry snow blanket the park and create a dream-like monochrome of vague structures and blurred figures moving in slow motion.

We trudge silently along the Reflecting Pool and cut through the trees towards the Wall. Both our heads are down, braced against the cold north wind. Flakes flitter around our eyes like pesky insects, making it difficult to see. The fallen snow muffles the sound of traffic along Constitution Avenue. Finally, the silence, and the tension building within me, cause me to speak.

"Don't think she'll be here."

"That's OK," he says. "She might. I just feel good coming to the Wall. Thanks for coming with me, pal."

"Whatever it takes." I put my arm around him, and we walk a few steps awkwardly in the snow and almost fall down. We both laugh.

Jack turns to me and says, "You know, I think talking about it helped a lot. I've never told anyone. It just helps having it out in the open."

"I'm glad." I jocundly turn around, start walking the opposite direction and say, "I guess we really don't need to go to the Wall then, do we?"

"Get your pale ass back here," Jack laughs. "We're going, like you promised." I turn back and join him, and he says, "What is it about the Wall? Why don't you ever go? What don't you like?"

"First, I did go . . . once. I just didn't stay. Secondly, what I don't like about the Wall is everything. I don't like the design. I don't like them using black . . . the color of death. I don't like them making it a tombstone buried in the ground. And I don't like them putting the names of the dead on the Wall reminding us who died." I'm close to tears.

Jack looks at me funny and says, "Do you have someone on the Wall?"

"You stupid fuck! Of course I got lots of guys on the Wall. Just because I wasn't there during Tet, doesn't mean that we didn't get our ass kicked in seventy also." As the words leave my mouth, I'm dismayed by my anger.

Jack's like a terrier chewing on a cuff. "I mean someone special," he says. "Is there someone you were really close to that died?"

We walk again in silence. Finally I say, "Yeah, there's someone. That's why I don't like the Wall. But I'm here for you, so let's drop it, OK?"

⊠ ⊠ ⊠

As we emerge from the woods, we see the Wall through the falling snow. It looks like a B-2 stealth bomber in flight. The snow has left a white ledge above the black Wall and outlines the V so that its two tapered sides look like wings slicing through thin clouds.

Through the blowing, milky snow, silhouetted against the black granite of the memorial, forms seem to shuffle aimlessly along the length of the Wall like the ghosts of concentration camp victims. Not until we get within thirty yards do the figures assume texture and color . . . and reality. It appears that the majority, if not everyone, are veterans, judging by the array of camouflaged fatigues, military hats, and unit patches. I know enough about the Wall to know that this was many, many more people than would be here normally on a cold, January day. They have come to see their angel.

Jack and I approach the center where the two sections meet and form the tallest part of the Wall. A man separates himself from a large group of veterans and approaches us.

"Jack-son," he says as he embraces Jack. "Good to see ya. Lots of the regulars here today. Kind of figured you might show."

"Wouldn't miss it, Mo," Jack says as he and his friend separate. "Mo, this is my friend, Andy. Andy, this is Morris Watters."

I start to put out my hand, but Mo grabs me in a surprisingly affectionate hug. "Andy! Welcome to the Wall. Come to see the Angel?" Mo is a skinny black man who couldn't weigh more than one forty. He's got a wiry brown beard that is cut short and matches the hair on his head. His features have an impish look, mirroring the personality of a prankster. I can't help but like the guy.

"Well," I say, "I'm just kind of taggin' along with Jack."

Mo looks at Jack and then back at me and says, "She's gonna be here today . . . I can feel it. It's like when you put your hand close to an electric fence . . . you feel the charge in the air without touching anything. This is a snowfall from heaven, and it's bringing the Angel with it." He catches his breath and waves an arm in an encompassing manner. "Look at the Wall. Doesn't it look beautiful today?"

We all three look down the eastern expanse of the Wall. The snow is lighter now, and in the distance, the Washington Monument is visible only as a darker shadow against the chalky sky. Standing by the monument, amidst a crowd of fellow veterans, its blackness seems softened somehow. Its shiny surface reflects back faces and clothing, the bare trees, even the snow on the ground. It suddenly has a warmth and a humanity that I would have never expected from such a stark structure. I take a couple of steps closer, and for the first time, I touch the Wall. I touch names engraved on the Wall. My fingers trace the grainy lettering, and I imagine Mo and Jack's sightless angel doing the same to Danny's name. Could I be wrong about their angel?

I had been so wrong about the Wall. . . . It is beautiful!

※ ※ ※

One of the vets from Mo's group has a big thermos of coffee and pours Jack and me a cup as Mo makes introductions. Some of the guys shake hands, but most embrace like Mo had done. It seems so natural and honest. We talk and sip our coffee. I hadn't felt such a sense of camaraderie since Nam.

Mo's like a jackrabbit bouncing from one person to the next. I'm just starting to think of him as kind of the "class clown," and then I spot him comforting someone on down the Wall. Tears seem to be flowing as freely from him as from the other guy.

Fortified by our coffee, Jack and I take a walk along the Wall and stop in front the names of some of his buddies. Jack tells a story about each one. He knows exactly where each of his friends is located. We spend quite a bit of time in front of Sergeant Lewis's name. As he tells me the stories about their squad, he includes the "sarge" in our conversation like he was there with us. He would look at his sergeant's name and say something like: "Didn't we, Sarge?" or "Remember that, Sarge?" It's odd but becomes more and more natural the more Jack talks.

We don't stop in front of Sergeant Garrett.

So I ask, "Jack, do you ever stop at . . . you know . . . Lewis's replacement?"

"Sergeant Garrett, the man . . . I . . . I killed?" Jack frowns, then seems to go somewhere in his mind, and just as I get ready to remind him of my question, he says, "I do, but it's tough. It's hard looking at a name on the Wall that you put there."

Like a downfield clip from a 270-pound offensive guard, his words blind-side me, squeezing my chest, taking the air from my lungs, and crushing my heart. My face flushes with shame as I turn away from Jack.

▨ ▨ ▨

It's hard looking at a name on the Wall that you put there.

▨ ▨ ▨

Mo comes running up to us. "She's here. She's here." His voice is quiet, almost reverent. "I told you the Angel would come today. I knew it. I could feel it. Come on, Jack . . . come on."

I look over at Jack, and he seems calm. In fact, a peculiar serenity courses through the crowd of veterans. They move slowly down the gradual incline toward the apex of the Wall from both sides.

Almost in a whisper, I say to Jack and Mo, "There must be three hundred people here."

"Andy," Mo says softly, "once the word really gets out about the Angel, there will be a million G.I.s and fifty-eight thousand mothers and fathers here."

I hadn't really thought about the mathematics of their angel. I imagine thousands and thousands of people pushing and shoving to get to her. People hanging over the edge of the Wall screaming: Me! Me! Do me! I'm next! A mob of desperate people looking for answers—looking for redemption.

But here I am amidst former Marines, Navy Seals, chopper pilots, Air Force fighter pilots, Infantry and Artillery grunts. Doing what . . . ? Calmly walking toward what everyone is calling an angel, as if we're parishioners lining up for communion. The incredible thing is that we all know that the priest has only one wafer!

I start tugging at Jack and pushing forward, but Mo says, "No, Andy, that's not the way we do it. It wouldn't do you any good anyway. The Angel picks. I think she chooses the one who hurts the most—I don't know. But she'll find you if you need her."

"But it's Jack that needs her, not me," I say. *I'm desperate for Jack!*

Jack grasps my arm just above the elbow. "It's OK. If she doesn't pick me, then somebody else here needs her more. I feel so happy just to see her and know she's real. That there is someone who can heal us."

I look at Jack and see he truly doesn't care. He seems to be happy. I envy him.

We reach the fringe of the throng, but I still can't see her yet. I ask Mo, "You've seen her before then?"

Mo laughs easily and smiles. He casually unzips his parka, unbuttons his wool shirt, lifts about three layers of T-shirts, and bares his skinny belly to me and the winter wind. His chest sports only a few scraggly hairs. Almost directly over the sternum, a small, ridged, pink scar accents his sunken chest. He rotates a quarter turn and I see the larger exit scar.

"Bounced off my rib. I tried to kill myself. The doctor said I should have put the gun in my mouth." Mo starts laughing again and says, "Course, lots of guys would like me to put a gun in my mouth just to shoot my tongue off." Now Mo laughs even harder at his joke.

He tucks his underwear in and starts buttoning up. His expression turns serious. "I guess I was one of the first that the Angel helped."

That part of my mind that has denied the Angel, denied Danny's name on the Wall, denied me peace, screams to me: Mass hysteria—it's all mass hysteria.

But I'm so tired.

I want to be happy, too.

I want to believe.

"What did she say to you? What did the name on the Wall say to you?"

Mo scratches his beard and says, "You know, I really can't remember anymore. It was all so clear that day at the Wall. It's just kinda slipped away. I just remember forgiveness and healing."

If Mo had followed that up with: Do you believe me? I probably wouldn't have. But I can tell he doesn't really care whether I believe him or not.

"I do remember the Angel using words and expressions that only my buddy would have used," he continues. "She called me 'Pipper.' That's the nickname that Reggie, my buddy, gave me. We were both door gunners on Hueys, and he used to say: 'You're no bigger than the pipper on my gun sight.' No one else called me 'Pipper.' No one else knew."

🎴 🎴 🎴

I didn't expect wings or a halo. I didn't expect circling cherubs. And certainly, I really didn't expect Jack's and Mo's angel would truly be a street person, a derelict—a bag lady, my God—but she is. Her coat is a heavy, nubby-looking thing that at one time may have been cream colored. It drags on the ground, and the bottom four inches of the coat are black where the fabric has wicked up the winter grime from the street. She is wearing a thin shawl that is barely big enough to tie under her chin. Incongruously poking out from the edge of her shawl are scruffy red ear muffs. I guess she's about five-two, but her shape could be anything, hidden beneath her oversize coat. True to form, she has a paper shopping bag filled with odds and ends.

I look at Jack to see his reaction, but he doesn't seem to notice me; instead, he appears to be mesmerized by his angel. All I feel is disappointment and my cynicism creeping back.

The blind woman uses her cane to guide herself along the Wall, and very slowly, almost studiously, she runs her hand down the black granite. Occasionally she stops her hand and traces a letter or two, but never an entire name. Until, finally, as if guided to it by a sense that transcends beyond man's meager five, her hand jumps to a name, and her fingers slowly trace a name on the Wall. She turns around, and I see her face.

It is the face of an angel. I don't necessarily mean a beautiful face. I mean a face of serenity and compassion and purity. Virtue reflects from her face as vividly as the Wall reflects the images around it. Of her blindness, there is no doubt—her eyes have that particularly sunken look, and each glazed eye has its own unfocused direction that normally makes it so difficult to look at a blind person unless they are wearing dark glasses. But I am lost in those eyes and can look at nothing else.

She walks out into the mass of soldiers, and we part before her, knowing that the Angel is on her mission. She stops by an emaciated-

looking man who is wearing fatigues that look two sizes too large for
him. He wears a Special Forces beret, and on his chest are two medals:
a Silver Star and a Purple Heart. She speaks to him. Although I am
very close, I can only hear a word or two. Her voice is soothing and
gentle but seems to have an aura of confidence that is surprising in
such a small, old woman.

Like a mother leading her child, she takes his hand and "guides"
him to the Wall. As before, she slowly traces the name with her fingers, and then she speaks to him in a voice so hushed that I can't
imagine anyone else can hear. I can only watch as she speaks, and as
he listens. I watch as first he frowns, and then he cries. And then he
smiles, and then he laughs. Finally, he hugs the Angel and holds her
quietly for a long time. Releasing her, he says something else to her,
and then he does a remarkable thing: He takes her hand and kisses
her fingertips.

The Angel turns away from the Wall and again we part for her, but
she turns parallel to the Wall and walks along the path, occasionally
tapping at the base of the Wall to keep her orientation. The snow starts
falling heavier again as she reaches the point where the path and the
Wall meet at level ground, and she disappears from view.

Everyone is silent. It is so quiet that you can hear the ice crystals
mixed with the snowflakes, chatter against the smooth surface of the
Wall. Like patients coming out of anesthesia, first one voice then
another, and soon everyone is talking and laughing. Jack and I turn to
each other and embrace.

Jack says to me, "Thanks again for coming to the Wall with me,
buddy."

"Anytime!" I say with fervor. "Anytime."

Mo bounces up and says, "What'd ya think, uh, uh? What'd ya
think, uh?" He sounds just like Joe Pesci in the *Lethal Weapon*
movies.

I'm laughing at Mo, and he looks hurt. So I give him a big bear hug
and release him.

Mo's smile returns and he says, "So what'd ya think, uh?"

"I think I saw an angel today," I say.

"Amen to that," Jack says in his best Southern Baptist impersonation.

⬛ ⬛ ⬛

We get back to Baltimore in the early evening, and I pull up in front of Jack's house. I ask Jack when he wants to go back to the Wall again, thinking he'll jump at the chance, but he is pretty vague about it.

We don't cross paths either Tuesday or Wednesday, but Wednesday night Julia calls me on the telephone.

"Andy," she says, "I can't thank you enough for helping Jack. He's a different person. He's so happy—*I'm* so happy."

"I didn't do anything. It was the Angel at the Wall. Did he tell you about her?"

"Oh yes, he told me all about his angel." Her voice turns solemn. "He told me everything." There's silence between us, and then she says in a voice that sounds like it's close to tears, "What a terrible burden to carry all those years . . . all those many years. But he's going to be OK now. And, Andy . . . you're the one who got it out of him, not some old lady at the Wall."

"She's real! I saw her. If Jack's better now, it's because of her, not me." Now it's me pleading for someone *else* to believe.

"As far as I'm concerned, you're the angel. But I didn't call you to argue; I called to thank you for helping and to tell you that I love you for it. Now here's Jack, he wants to talk."

"Hey, Andy, haven't seen you at work, so I thought we'd call." Julia was right about one thing: Jack certainly sounded happy enough. "I wanted to thank you again for going to the Wall with me. For the first time, I'm really at peace. Thanks for listening . . . and understanding, buddy. You changed my life."

"You're both giving me credit for something I didn't do. It was the Angel," I argue.

"Seeing the Angel at the Wall helped, but it was talking to you and what you said the previous night that did it. *You* forgave me. And when I told Julia, she forgave me. If the two people that love me the most forgive me, then I've got a good start on forgiving myself."

I guess I'm confused that Jack has made peace with himself even though the Angel didn't choose him. I do know that now I'm obsessed with the Angel, and that my only hope for forgiveness is to keep going back to the Wall until she chooses me.

"You're still going to go back to the Wall, aren't you?" I ask Jack.

"Sure! I want to take Julia and the kids. Next time the weather is good. You come along, too. We'll spend the whole day in Washington."

"Yeah, sure, I'll be glad to go. Just let me know when," I say, trying to hide my disappointment. I had assumed that Jack would still want to go back as often as he could.

We chat a little longer and say our good-byes. Just as Jack hangs up the receiver, I say into the empty line, "But I'm going back to the Wall this weekend."

※ ※ ※

Which I do . . . and the next . . . and the one after that. I start calling in sick so I can go on weekdays. Each time I return to the Wall, the crowds are bigger as word-of-mouth spreads the rumor of the Angel who heals the G.I.s. The Angel is impossible to predict, and although I spend more and more time at the Wall, she's never there.

But she still does come; that, I know. The stories never vary: She appears almost from nowhere, reads a name from the Wall, heals a lost soul with words from a dead friend, and then departs. I know that in time I will see her again.

I would curse the Angel . . . if I could; like I did before I ever saw her face and witnessed the miracle myself; like I did when Jack was so convinced that the Angel was his only hope for forgiveness. But now I can only curse the bleakness of my life—a life that had held no hope of forgiveness. Forgiveness for a sin that, until now, I saw as only coming at the moment of death, and maybe not even then.

I remember a term from freshman Anthropology called "Relative Deprivation" that explained how primitive people were happy with what little they had in life until they were exposed to the wealth and affluence of other cultures. Then they were dissatisfied to the degree that they were relatively deprived. Not that I was all that happy before, or even at peace, but I had reached an equilibrium that satisfied me and could have continued forever.

Now I have seen the Angel . . . now I want more; now I want peace. I want what others have found at the Wall.

※ ※ ※

Early March, the East Coast gets a break in the weather and a hint of spring. Jack invites me to visit the Wall with his family that weekend.

They pick me up early in the morning. I share the back seat with the kids, and before we're fifteen miles out of town the back seat has become a trio of kids so rambunctious that Julia laughingly threatens to have Jack stop the car so that she can spank the three of us. Julia's threats have little effect on our behavior. I'm too excited.

🔲 🔲 🔲

This time it's Jack who is shocked by the size of the crowd. Over the last few weeks, I had seen Mo's prediction come to pass. There are, at a minimum, over a thousand people at the Wall this sunny day. Parked in front of the Lincoln Memorial I see something that sends a surge of panic through me: a white van with an antenna lifted above it like a child's Erector Set. The call letters of the station are partially blocked, but the network logo is clearly visible—CBS has discovered the Angel. The one-time innocuous, oversized eye is now an "evil eye" that convinces me that the Angel won't show, or if she does, the press will hound her so, that she will never return to the Wall. I feel a rage building in me at their sacrilege. It is our Wall!

Mo comes bounding up to us, and of course, gives us all big hugs. Jack's kids take an immediate shine to Mo, and Mo leads them off on some adventure while Julia, Jack, and I visit with some of the regulars. The word is that CBS is here for some reason other than the Angel. The news team was curious about the large number of people at the Wall but seemed to buy the story that it was a big unit reunion; in fact, they were rather pleased that they had a large crowd for the backdrop to whatever story they were doing. The Vets weren't talking. The consensus among my fellow Vets was, "Fuck 'em!"

But I'm nervous—hell, panicky!

Reporters are lazy, and they have no integrity, but they also are not stupid, and the good ones can sense a story. I know I don't have much time.

Mo returns with Jeremy and Rowena, a broad smile on his face, the kids full of laughter. Jack rounds up his family and asks me if I mind if he goes alone with them to show them the names on the Wall.

"I'm honored just to be here with you, Jack. I know what you gotta do."

As Jack starts along the stone path with his family, I try to imagine myself in his position. But I can't. Instead, an image forms in my mind and becomes a daydream as real and as wishful as any I had as a child. I see myself walking along the path in a heavy snowfall and the Angel coming towards me from the opposite direction. There is no one else at the Wall, and I know that she has come to take me to Danny's name. As we come together, she takes my hand, and like Jack, I'm able to walk without fear. I'm smiling and I feel so relieved that it's over.

⊠ ⊠ ⊠

A voice, as insistent as my teachers' voices were when catching me at my daydreaming, wedges itself into my consciousness and dislodges my fantasy.

"What?" I ask, looking around for the voice that had called out.

"I said, what are you so happy about today?"

Why wasn't I surprised it was Mo? "Nothing," I respond. "Just thinking."

We start walking away from the crowd, winding around small groups of vets until we find ourselves at the bronze statue of *Three Men Fighting*—though they don't call it that anymore—and find a dry place to sit on the small, circular pedestal of the bronze. From this vantage point, the crowd looks even larger, and the trailer-court TV antenna above the CBS truck reminds me that any day now I'll be watching this scene on network news.

"Do you think the press will learn about the Angel today?" I ask Mo.

Mo looks as despondent as I feel. "If not today, soon."

We both look back toward the crowd and envision the future. My vision doesn't include the Angel, and judging by Mo's face, neither does his.

"Do you think she'll even come again?"

Mo ponders my question, and his face brightens up. "Yes I do. I truly do." He lifts his wool hat from his head and rubs his short brown hair in thought. "It's not over. Whatever the meaning of all this, it's not just for a few of us fortunate ones that got a message from an angel. It's gotta be something for all of us—something good. It's gotta be!"

"I need to see her again, Mo. I'm dying inside. I thought it was all tucked away until I heard about the Angel, but now that I know about her, now that I believe in her, I can't endure living with this guilt. You've been there—you know what I'm feeling!"

For me to open up this much to anybody was a sign of my desperation. Somehow I feel like I can tell Mo. I don't think he will try to dig it out of me like Jack would. I clutch one of his bony hands. "Help me, Mo. Help me see the Angel."

Mo smiles his scampish grin. "Can you come every day this next week?"

I laugh and answer, "I'll come every day even if I have to quit my job."

"Talk to Jack, he'll clear it with your supervisor. I don't know when she'll come again, but I've got a feeling, just like the last time when we had the big snowfall, it'll be sometime soon." Mo stands up and reaches down, grasps my arm and pulls me up with surprising strength. "Come on, let's walk. I get antsy sitting still for more than five minutes."

I laugh. "Yeah, I've noticed."

Mo laughs with me as we start walking in the direction of the Reflecting Pool. "I can't guarantee that the Angel will pick you, even though it's plain to see that you're hurting bad."

"She may not, but just like you have a feeling that she's coming soon, I have a feeling that she'll choose me. I can't imagine anyone needing her help more than me."

"You feel like telling me about it?" Mo asks in a casual voice, but we both know it's not a casual question.

"I can't. . . . I just can't. It's something that if I told someone else, my shame would be that much greater." I rest my hand on his shoulder as we walk. "I'm sorry. You've been a good friend."

Mo looks up at me with piercing dark eyes. I'm reminded of the Bears' great linebacker, Mike Singletary, as he waited for the snap of the ball. Mo says, "Promise me one thing. If you don't get a chance to see her again, promise that you won't do anything stupid. Hear me?"

I laugh and promise I won't, but Mo stops and grabs the flaps of my fatigues, spinning me around. "Don't you dare laugh. Don't you dare! Like you said, I've been there. I know the shame and guilt and despair . . . and what the fatigue of carrying all that garbage around can do to you."

Mo is shaking with emotion . . . and I guess anger. He is always so full of life and laughter that I had forgotten about the puckered bullet wound in his chest. "Promise me one other thing. If you don't get chosen by the Angel, you'll tell me about it—everything."

I feel trapped. On one hand, what can Mo do to me if I don't promise? Beat me up? On the other, he has been a solid friend, a brother in shared pain, and I owe him something. But my deepest secret, my hidden shame . . . my manhood; how can I? In the end, I just trust that I really am going to get to see the Angel. I'll worry later about keeping my promise if it doesn't happen. "OK, you got my promise," I answer.

Now Mo is all smiles again and his old self. He's jumpin' and skippin' around while I try to keep pace with him. "You be here this next week," he says. "The Angel's comin'. I feel it now. . . . I surely do!"

Mo's infectious optimism is a natural high that brightens the sky and freshens the crisp air. We joke around as we walk, and at least for a while we forget about the war and our pain. Without realizing it, we find ourselves back in front of the Wall and start looking for Jack and his family. Spotting Jack, I move in his direction. Mo shakes hands and heads off toward a group of his buddies.

▓ ▓ ▓

I can see traces of tears in Jack and Julia's eyes. But I also see a serenity in the way they walk toward me, arm in arm. Whatever had transpired between them and between the Wall had healed a deep, deep wound. I feel only happiness for Jack. I guess it shows in my face, because Jack says to me, "You look like you did the day you first saw the Angel."

"Well, Jack, I'm gonna see her again . . . soon! That's why I'm smiling."

I hoist Rowena onto my shoulders, and we work our way back to the car. We stop to eat at Bob Evans, and by the time we reach Baltimore, Jeremy and Rowena and Julia are all fast asleep in the back seat.

Jack turns toward my apartment, but I ask him if he'll drop me by Birdy's instead. I figure if I really beg Jabba, he'll give me one more chance. I miss the place. Jack stops the car at the bus stop in front of Birdy's. Before I open the door to get out, I ask Jack, "So, how did it go today?"

"I should have done it years ago, man. It was emotional, and it did hurt, but for the first time in more than a quarter century I'm not hiding anything. I'm not looking back. I . . . feel . . . so . . . good!" He raises both hands in tight fists and starts laughing. "You, too? You were all smiles today."

"Me, too." I smile back. "It was a good day.

"See you Monday at work," he says as I open the car door.

"O-o-o-h, I'm glad you reminded me. I need a favor. Can you smooth things with the bosses next week if I take off—or at least until the Angel shows up at the Wall? Mo thinks she'll be there this next week, and I figure I got one last shot."

"Count on it," Jack says and waves good-bye.

▨ ▨ ▨

I walk into Birdy's prepared to sell my soul to the devil, but Jabba is easy, even seems glad to see me, and other than a short lecture and a this-is-positively-your-last-chance warning, he lets me come back. My favorite table is even open—most people don't like to sit that close to the jukebox anyway. I stake my claim with my coat over the back of the chair and go right to the Seeburg, check that Jabba's not watching, crank up the volume and start selecting my favorites.

Halfway through my first beer, Leia walks up and laughs, "I didn't see you come in, Andy, but I knew you were here by the volume of the jukebox."

My ears redden, but I chuckle also. "You mean all this time I haven't been fooling anyone?"

"Not a soul . . . only yourself, cowboy. Augie usually turns it back down when you go take a leak." Leia surprises me and sits down at the table. "We've missed you around here," she says seriously.

"I've missed this place myself, Princess. I won't screw up this time. Augie gave me one more chance than I expected and definitely one more than I deserved." I sip my beer and point the long-neck toward the Seeburg. "I missed my jukebox."

Leia does an exaggerated pout and says, "I thought maybe you might have missed me." But then she smiles.

Now my ears really burn, and I lift my bottle and drain it, giving me time to think of something to say. "Uh . . . I didn't mean it that way,

Princess. Sure I missed you. Hell, I even missed Jab—ahh . . . Augie! It's just this is the only place I listen to music, and I miss it also."

Leia is still smiling, and she gets up, grabs my empty and says, "I'll go get you another." She puts a hand on my shoulder as she walks behind me and leans over and whispers in my ear, "Relax. I'm only teasing. Be right back."

Even though I turn my head and watch her walk away, it still feels like her hand is on my shoulder. My neck tingles where her hair had brushed against it, and the scent of her perfume, or maybe only of her skin, is so delicate that I'm afraid if I exhale it will disappear. I watch her as she efficiently checks her other tables as she works her way to the bar, and I think maybe she is as pretty as Carrie Fisher. I try to remember the last time I had been with a woman, but I can't, or at least I don't want to think about it. I let my mind coast, not thinking . . . not caring.

※ ※ ※

Garth Brooks sings a melancholy song about lost love, dumb mistakes, and wasted lives.

※ ※ ※

Leia returns with my beer and again sits down. "You don't mind, do you?" She sighs. "I need a break. I've been on my feet since three."

"No . . . sure, have a seat." I look into her eyes, but she's looking back at me and I can't keep eye contact. I was more confident around girls in high school than I feel now.

Leia breaks the silence with a laugh. "So you missed the jukebox. Don't you have a stereo at home or something?"

"No," I answer, take a long pull on my beer, and sneak a look at her.

"You're kidding! Everybody has a stereo or a boombox . . . or something. And you like music so much—that I'm sure of! Usually anytime I look over at you, you're either tapping your feet or strumming an imaginary guitar—at least you do when you've had a couple of beers." She makes a goofy face and makes like she's playing a guitar.

I break out laughing at her funny face and the image of how I must look some nights when I really get into the music—to say nothing about really getting into the beer. "Do I really look like that? You're embarrassing me."

She shakes her head. "Nah, not really. Actually, you look pretty serious most of the time, like you're really concentrating on the music."

"Well, I used to play guitar in a band. I . . . I kinda gave it up."

"I knew it!" Leia's pretty face then frowns, and she looks perplexed. "But . . . but why don't you have a stereo at home?"

I hesitate. We're wandering into forbidden territory. "I made a promise to a friend a long, long time ago that I would never have music again. I guess listening to the jukebox at Birdy's is cheating on that promise. I rationalize it because I can't control other places . . . and because, yes, I do love music and I miss it."

Leia says, "That's kind of a stupid promise, Andy." Then she sees my hard look and realizes her mistake. "I'm sorry. I shouldn't have said that." She lays a hand on my arm.

Her eyes have already melted my anger. My earlier shyness is now gone. Without realizing it, I had become comfortable in just a few minutes of our easy conversation, and I look at her face, see her discomfort, and feel a momentary urge to put my arm around her narrow shoulders. For the first time, I notice the color of her eyes—blue, and I wonder how I had never noticed how her smile dimples her cheeks, or that her nose had a tiny little cleft that looked more like it belonged on a high-fashion model than a girl from East Baltimore. Only a few crinkles darting from the corners of her eyes hint that she's not that much younger than me.

I rest my hand on top of hers and say, without thinking, "Leia, it's OK. It's something that I really don't like talking about, but I'm not angry."

Leia audibly sighs. "I'm glad. It was so stupid of me." A confused look crosses her face and she says, "Why did you just now call me, Leia?"

"Whoops! Chrissy, I didn't mean to have you hear me call you that." I take a sip of my beer and grin. "I suppose now I have to tell you? You won't let me off the hook?"

"No way, buster! Is Leia some old girlfriend?" She is smiling, and her face is so radiant that I re-access my guess at her age.

So I tell her how Jack and I had nicknamed Birdy's, the "Star Wars Bar" and how we called Augie "Jabba the Hutt" for obvious reasons. Leia laughs so hard she almost chokes, regains her composure, but then looks over at Augie as he turns sideways so that he can squeeze between the bar door, and she laughs again so hard that the tears start rolling down her face.

A positively angelic look appears on Leia's face as it dawns on her. "You mean, *I'm* Princess Leia? *That's* why you always call me, Princess. That's so sweet!" She leans over and kisses my bearded cheek.

Embarrassed, I laughingly tell her how I'm "Chewbacca" and that Jack is "Lando Calrissiun." How I even call the rounded, chrome Seeburg jukebox, "R2D2."

Still wiping tears of laughter from her eyes, Leia spots Jabba giving her the high sign, and she says, "I got to get back to work. Jabba is cracking the whip . . . oh God! Augie will fire me if he hears me call him Jabba." And she starts laughing again.

As Leia leaves, she puts her hand on the same shoulder as before and leans her head so close that again I feel her hair brush my neck—this time though it causes more than a tingle, and it isn't located in my neck. She whispers to me, "Chewy, I'll check on you later."

⊠ ⊠ ⊠

I drink another couple of beers. R2D2 sings me some songs. And I daydream about an Angel, a princess, and peace.

⊠ ⊠ ⊠

My emotional high lasts only as long as Sunday morning when I arrive at the Wall and see the size of the crowd. My confidence fades during the day faster than the quickly setting sun and the falling temperature. Without Mo around to encourage me, I'm left to my own inherent propensity for pessimism and cynicism. Finally, the darkening sky triggers the accent lights at the base of the monument, casting their cold incandescence upon the even colder granite. I look one last time along the stone path, and bundling my coat tightly about me, I trek back to my car.

Maybe tomorrow, I think to myself as I drive in my musicless car to the cheap hotel room I had rented for the week.

⊠ ⊠ ⊠

That next morning the sky is streaked with bands of high, cirrus clouds that manage to always cover the wan sun. The faded blue sky gradually bleaches as the clouds thicken, until by late morning, only small patches of blue are occasionally visible as the strong winds aloft rip open a cloud. I trudge the path along the Wall in a funk. The hours at the Wall and the weight of disappointment are wearing away at me. Only my thermos of hot coffee keeps me going through the morning.

About noon, Mo shows up with a bag of sandwiches and fresh coffee. And, of course, his boundless optimism.

▧ ▧ ▧

Maybe Mo is like a witch's familiar that has to be around for the magic to work. My earlier fatigue has disappeared, and though the afternoon light is rapidly fading, I now have no doubt that today the Angel will come. The light snow that begins to fall might as well be positively charged particles . . . the electricity in the air is substantive, physical. The crowd, as well, notices. A hush settles from one end of the Wall to the other and we wait.

The Angel approaches from the east end of the Wall, slowly making her way down the stone path. The crowd parts silently, reverently. Each step she takes is more hesitant than the preceding, and I think for the first time about how fragile she seems . . . and how tired.

A sudden gust of frigid wind sweeps across the open expanse of the memorial, swirling the snow and chilling the air so rapidly that everyone pulls their coats tighter, their hats snugger. The gust causes the Angel to momentarily lose her balance, and she gropes with a hand for support. A G.I. grabs her arm and steadies her, and she continues unaided except for the occasional tap against the Wall with her cane.

Nearly halfway up the west extension of the Wall, she stops and runs her bare hand along the etched names. She takes another step. Again she moves her thin hand over the smooth stone, letting her fingers dip into the coarse grooves of the names. The Angel pauses, and then suddenly, as if drawn to it by a magnet, her hand darts high up on the Wall, almost to the limit of her reach. She carefully and methodically runs her index finger along every letter of a name.

Danny's name? Lowering her hand, she places her forearm on the Wall and lays her head on her arm.

Mo puts his hand on my shoulder and says to me, "The winter has been hard on our Angel. She doesn't look well."

I look at Mo and see his anguish, but say nothing. The Angel lifts her head and turns away from the Wall, and I see her clearly now. Mo had been right, of course. She is as beautiful and ethereal as I remembered, but some indefinable weariness, a burden carried on thin, aged shoulders, is exposed in her face. I see my dying mother's face reflected in hers, and I wonder how much pain the Angel is holding back. What price was the Angel paying to be the conduit between guilt-ridden, angry veterans and the dead soldiers on the Wall? And was it fair for me to ask her to share my shame?

"Andy. Andy?" Mo's voice breaks into my thoughts. "She's coming this way!"

The crowd parts as the Angel moves toward me, and my first instinct is to move back also. I had imagined this moment as one of peace and happiness. Instead, my heart is pounding and my knees feel rubbery. I want to flee, but all my strength is gone. As if reading my thoughts, I feel Mo squeeze the hollow part of my shoulder and hear him say something through the sound of rushing blood. The Angel comes up to me and extends a small, veined hand.

She says, "Take my hand. Walk with me to the Wall." Her extended hand beckons to me, but still I hold back and the urge to run fills my mind. "Come," she says. "Don't be afraid."

From my side I hear Mo say, "Go with the Angel. This is what you wanted."

I take her hand. It's rough and chapped, and although my hand is twice hers, she clasps it as a mother does a child's, and we move slowly back to the Wall.

Her cane nudges the vertical rise of the Wall and she releases my hand. Without hesitation she lifts her arm toward the spot where she had been earlier. Part of me is terrified and crying out for her not to have actually found Danny's name, that she had made a mistake and confused me with someone else. But as I follow her outstretched hand, I see it alight on the name, and with my heart pounding I watch as she moves her fingers along each groove as first they trace *Daniel*, then *C.*, and finally *Young*.

At last, I am looking at the name of my friend on the Wall—the name that I had put there through my cowardice. A sob escapes my throat, and I start shaking. My voice is barely audible as I say to the Wall . . . and to my friend, "Forgive me, Danny."

The Angel still has her hand on the Wall as she turns her head toward me. She releases her cane and it falls to the path with a hollow click. She says to me, "Take my hand."

I fold both hands around hers. The racing of my heart has slowed, and I'm ready to hear her words, I'm ready to hear Danny . . . *whatever* it is he has to say to me. I'm ready for an end to it.

Her lined face, though smudged with dirt, still looks soft and delicate. A thin tracery of veins runs along her cheekbones and only further accentuates the porcelain patina to her skin. Again, I'm struck by her beauty, her purity—the feeling that she is an instrument of mercy. So softly that the wind sliding along the surface of the monument almost drowns out her words, she whispers to me, "Try to understand, Andy . . ."

For a split second, her sightless eyes seem to come into focus. Suddenly, her eyelids flutter, then her eyes glaze over and roll up into her head. Before I can react, she collapses at my feet, her body slumping against the Wall, her face resting against my boots.

I'm still holding on to her hand, and I kneel down and cradle her body in my arms. Around me, I'm aware of movement and noise, voices yelling for help. Someone lays a khaki parka over her, and a soldier wraps a blanket around her exposed legs.

I stroke her cheek over and over and murmur to her that she'll be all right. Dimly, I'm aware that I'm crying. Part of it is for her. But I know, mostly, I'm crying for myself. I know I'm being selfish. I hold the Angel close to me and cry for both of us.

A few minutes pass, I think, and I become aware of arms trying to pull me from the Angel. I fight them off, and I only let go of her when I hear Mo's voice say, "Let her go. We've got a couple of medics that can help her until an ambulance gets here. Please, Andy!" I still hold onto her hand as the medics tend to her. I hear one say to the other that she's got a good pulse. In the distance, a siren wails.

　　　　　　　　　⬛ ⬛ ⬛

The ambulance arrives and the paramedics lift her onto a stretcher. Still holding her hand, I stand as they raise the stretcher from the ground. A paramedic looks questioningly at me as I stare back dumbly. Mo pulls my hand from hers and says, "I know, Andy. Let go." As I release her hand, I know that I'll never see the Angel again, that she will never give me my message from Danny.

⊠ ⊠ ⊠

Mo stands with me in front of the Wall, in front of Danny's name. His hand rests casually on my shoulder, but I feel it's the only thing keeping me standing. We both stare at the Wall thinking our private thoughts. Me, thinking about what might have been. Mo, perhaps thinking about the Angel. Finally, Mo says to me, "She said something to you before she fainted. What did she say?"

I shake my head. "Nothing, really. She said, try to understand . . . that's all. But I don't understand. It's not fair . . . it's just not fair."

"Do you think those words were your words or your friends?" Mo asks.

"How the hell would I *know* . . . she never finished. I'll never know." I turn away from the Wall and start walking.

"Maybe she'll come back," Mo prompts as he grabs my sleeve.

I turn and stare at him.

Mo lowers his eyes. "Yeah, she's never coming back; I felt it, too."

Silently, we walk into the darkening park and to the road where my car is parked. I ask Mo if he needs a ride, but he says his car is just a short distance away and we say our good-byes. I climb into my car, coax the Chevy into starting and shift into gear. Mo taps on my window and raises two fingers. I nod, thinking he's giving me the old "peace" sign, and I start to roll away. But he taps again, so I stop and crank down my window.

"Two things," he says, still holding up his fingers. "First, you promised that you wouldn't do anything stupid and that you'd tell me everything." He pauses long enough for me to feel uncomfortable. "Second, you've got friends here at the Wall—don't forget that!"

As I drive off into the D.C. rush-hour traffic and head for my hotel room to pick up my bag—I'd already decided to go home—I think two things. The first: I know I can never tell Mo about Danny. Besides, technically the promise was if the Angel never chose me, but she did. The second: I was never coming back to the Wall again.

🗱 🗱 🗱

The drive to Baltimore is a blur. No tears. No emotions to speak of; I just feel numb from the months of hope and anticipation, numb from the letdown of being so close to absolution. I replay over and over in my mind the walk with the Angel back to the Wall, and her hand moving over Danny's name, and her words to me.

🗱 🗱 🗱

Try to understand, Andy.

🗱 🗱 🗱

But I don't understand.

🗱 🗱 🗱

It's about seven-thirty when I take the Dundalk exit. I slow as I reach my apartment building, but then continue down the street and park in the side lot of Birdy's. As I enter the door, I welcome the cigarette smoke and the sweet and sour smell of the warped, hardwood floors, varnished with forty years of spilled drinks. Princess Leia waves from the corner booth where she is taking an order from four guys in bowling shirts. I stop at the bar and get a beer and some quarters from Jabba. Jabba raises a thick eyebrow when I hand him my car keys, but just shrugs and puts them in the cash register.

My beer is empty by the time I've made my selections on the jukebox. I start to walk toward the bar, but Leia intercepts me and says, "Grab your table. I'll get you another."

Leia returns with my beer and says, "Augie told me to tell you no shooters tonight. You planning to tie one on? Leia laughs, a pleasant, sweet laugh, but with a look of concern.

"Yeah, I think so, Princess," I respond, not smiling.

"Bad day at work, huh?" She leans against the paneled post next to my table. "I've had one of those myself," she adds.

"Yeah, it's been a bad day. Get me another beer," I say gruffly and raise my bottle and chug down most of it.

"Sure." She stands there at my table for a long moment, then shyly, she says, "Augie said he'd let me off early tonight. How about I join you for a drink in half an hour? You could tell me about your bad day."

"Not tonight, Princess," I say without thinking. "I don't feel like company."

I look up and can swear her eyes look teary, but she says cheerfully enough, "I understand. One cold one coming up!" And she turns away and walks to the bar.

I feel like a heel. But then, I feel like shit anyway. I drain the last drops of my beer.

※ ※ ※

Slowly the cocoon forms around me. My thoughts, the music from the jukebox, and the cold beer insulate me from the noise and bustle of Birdy's. Leia wordlessly brings me a fresh beer at regular intervals. My mind wanders relentlessly back to the afternoon, and unbidden, I keep reliving those final moments, holding the hand of the Angel, and her final words . . . over and over again. I want to scream in frustration. I was so close! I try to imagine what her next words would have been: *I forgive you, Andy; It wasn't your fault, Andy; Heaven is beautiful, Andy.*

Bullshit!

Those are just words that I want to hear. Hoped to hear. They sound so false. They're not Danny's words. They mean nothing.
And now I'll never know. I see again the Angel touching the grey letters of Danny's name, stark against the ebony granite, and I imagine my own finger's doing the same. Today was the first time to see his name on the Wall. My thoughts become unbearable as my feeble, emotional wall crumbles, and I remember our last night: Sharing perimeter defense duties on the hot, humid hilltop; and the next day, when Danny dies, in my arms, gutted by the mine that was meant for me.

※ ※ ※

From the jukebox comes the sound of a slow guitar, individual notes and chords plucked in the melody of a lullaby. Eric Clapton starts singing the first verse of "Tears of Heaven."

Clapton wrote the song after the accidental death of his four-year-old son. I imagine what it must be like every time he sings it.

And I hear his guilt in every verse.

⊠ ⊠ ⊠

I didn't play this song. Why does it have to play now?

⊠ ⊠ ⊠

The song echoes my own plea for an end. An end to guilt. An end to the tears. A finish to the relentless burden of a life that sees no hope of forgiveness . . . except in heaven.

The keyboard blends into the background with its delicate, church-like melody, and helplessly I listen, hypnotized, as my eyes fill with tears. I don't want to feel sorry for myself . . . I don't. I just want peace.

Clapton sings of time bringing him down, bending his knee, and breaking his heart. Of making him, "Beggin' please."

Beggin' p-l-e-a-s-e. I'm so tired. I want it over. I cup my hands over my face and cry; and that part of me that knows I'm making a fool of myself, tells me to stop, but I can't. I feel a hand on my shoulder and the softness of a breast pressed against my arm; I turn and bury my head in the sweetness of Leia's arms.

⊠ ⊠ ⊠

The final verse ends and something country, with twangy words and a fiddle, starts up on the jukebox. The warmth of Leia's body and the comfort of her arms is a sanctuary that momentarily protects me from my memories. The hours and days spent at the Wall have taken a physical toll on my body as well, and Leia's warmth seeps into my chilled bones like a hot toddy sipped in front of an evening fire. I start to raise my head, but Leia gently presses it back down to the haven of her bosom, as if sensing that I was not yet ready to face whatever had brought me to tears.

Another song starts playing, a slow one, and Leia is gently swaying to its rhythm. Finally, she says to me, "You OK now?" She doesn't resist as I raise my head and swipe at my eyes with the upper sleeve of my sweatshirt.

"Yeah," I answer. "Just a little embarrassed. But thanks." I find the courage to look into her eyes, not sure of what to expect, but finding only concern.

"*Nada*," she responds, and smiles.

Tentatively, I reach for her hands, realizing that I'm reluctant to lose physical contact. Leia joins hands with mine, and we sit quietly at the table like new lovers.

"I could say you don't have to tell me about it or that it's not my business, or just pretend that nothing happened . . . but I'm not going to. I've served you drinks at this lonely table for over two years and watched you crying silently all that time. Tell me about it." She squeezes my hands. "Talk to me . . ."

Suddenly, I'm overcome with the desire to tell. To share with somebody my disappointment . . . my frustration. Somebody who will cradle me in their arms and tell me that everything is OK and that things will get better. Leia is looking expectantly at me, her eyes promising me understanding, her heart open to my pain.

Not certain how much to tell her, I decide. I smile and say, "Can I have another beer first? It's a long story."

"One condition." She smiles back. "No more crying in your beer."

"How 'bout in your arms?" I reply.

"Oh, you have that without crying," she says as she gets up to get my beer, laughing, . . . leaving me to think about the meaning of her last words.

Leia returns with my beer and a drink for herself. She again takes my hand and says, "Go ahead . . . I'm ready."

※ ※ ※

Haltingly at first, I tell Leia about my tour in Vietnam and my best friend, Danny. I leave out about how Danny was killed other then telling her that it was my fault. I could see the question mark on her face, but she lets it drop as I continue my story. I tell her how the guilt had lived with me since that day and how, over the years, I had coped

. . . or tried to cope . . . but never able to settle down, never able to keep a job for long, and never able to forgive myself.

And then, the Angel. I tell her about how at first I didn't believe in her, or at least wouldn't let myself believe. I tell her about Jack and how he believes from the start, and of our trip to the Wall, meeting Mo, and seeing her give a message to another G.I.; and how Jack seemingly overcomes his guilt just by being near the Angel and seeing the miracle of her healing.

And now, I believe in her with all my soul.

I describe my obsession with seeing the Angel and having her "heal" me with words of forgiveness from my buddy; my trips to the Wall, and my alarm as the crowds get bigger, and eventual panic when week after week she doesn't return to the Wall.

Leia listens as I recount the last few days; and, how finally today, the Angel returns; and my joy, but also my fear, when she chooses me and leads me to Danny's name. In telling the story, I had—at least temporarily—set aside my earlier despair, but now, I struggle to control my emotions in telling her about the final moments.

My breath hitches in small, but audible stutters. Leia rests her head on my shoulder and strokes my arm, calming me and guiding me through the pain as I finish my story. . . .

"While holding the Angel's hand, a feeling of utter tranquility settled around me as I waited for her to speak. Very softly she said to me, 'Try to understand, Andy. . . . Try to understand, Andy,' and then she stiffened, her back arched, and she fell at my feet."

Again I struggle for control and can only do so by stopping and hiding my face in my hands. I press my fingers hard into my eyelids in a vain effort to keep tears from forming. Leia waits quietly by my side.

I take a small sip of my beer.

Drained of emotion, I finish telling Leia about holding the Angel in my arms until the paramedics arrive, and finally watching them leave with the knowledge that I'll never see the Angel again . . . that I'll never understand.

※ ※ ※

"Oh Andy," Leia consoles me, "no wonder you are so unhappy. Don't you think there's a chance that your angel will return to the Wall?"

I shake my head. "No, Leia . . . uh, Chrissy." I hesitate at my slip, but Leia just smiles. "The Angel was an instrument of healing, and the Wall used her up. Mo felt it, too. She'll never return."

We sit silently at the table for a long time. Leia finishes the last of her drink, stands up and says, "I'm getting another drink. . . . You?"

"No," I answer. "But I do have to hit the men's room."

"Meet you back here then," Leia says as she starts for the bar. "And, Andy . . ." she calls out after me.

"Yeah?" I look back at her.

". . . Call me Leia. I kinda like it. I never did like Chrissy."

🔲 🔲 🔲

Walking back to my table, I notice that the jukebox is silent, and I dig in my jeans for some quarters and start "programming" R2D2. I feel Leia's arm come around my shoulder, and she dips her head to peer through the time-darkened plexiglass at the selections.

"Would you play, 'I Love L.A.' for me?" she asks, as she gently sways to Sinead O'Connor's "Nothing Compares 2 U." I press the last two buttons and take her hand. "It's the first one I selected," I say as I lead her to the table.

🔲 🔲 🔲

We sit listening to the music. The men in the bowling shirts are arguing in the corner over the merits of Georgetown's basketball team, while Jabba effortlessly maneuvers a large beer keg into position and opens the spigot to clear the foam.

Leia breaks the silence. "How did your friend die? Why do you blame yourself for his death?"

I look into Leia's ingenuous face, and I know she is only trying to help, but she doesn't understand. "I just can't talk about that. I'm sorry."

Leia's eyes darken and she urges, "This is what the whole thing is about . . . the Wall . . . your angel . . . everything. You have *got to* talk about it."

Again, I am flooded with the urge to tell. The comfort of Leia's arms and her compassion is like a drug that taunts and promises oblivion.

But three decades of hiding my shame and the icy barrier of my resolve cannot let go. "Princess, I just can't do it. . . . I can't."

⊠ ⊠ ⊠

Leia looks at me and a frown crosses her face, but then she smiles and scoots her chair closer and says, "Close your eyes." She takes my hands and places them on top of the table. "Imagine that you are getting a second chance to talk with your angel, and it is she that is asking you to tell about your friend."

I open my eyes, but she takes her hand and with open fingers gently runs them across my eyelids like a mother coaxing a small child to sleep.

"Relax," she soothes. "Your angel has returned. Tell her about Danny."

Her voice is entrancing. I feel the warmth of her hands and think of the Angel's hand and of holding it as she slumped to the cold ground. I remember how Mo had finally pulled me away as the paramedics lifted the stretcher and the emptiness in my soul as I let go.

Now, Leia was offering me a second chance. . . . She would be my Angel.

I open my eyes again and see a single tear winding its way down her cheek. I realize the emotional price that Leia is paying. Pain must be like physics' "conservation of matter"— as one person is relieved of their suffering, another has to accept that burden . . . it must be balanced.

I lean over and wipe the tear away with my thumb. "Leia, are you sure you want to hear this?"

She sniffs, but then smiles. "I want to help you. I think it will help you to talk about it."

⊠ ⊠ ⊠

"Danny was the best friend I ever had," I start. "We met our first day at Marine boot camp. At first, I didn't like him. I'm pretty competitive and so was Danny. The two of us matched up academically and physically, so we were usually paired against each other for hand-to-hand combat training and other stuff. We'd really go at it sometimes. But one day I was playing my guitar after chow, and Danny sat down with me and started singing along. He loved music almost as much as I did; by lights-out we were friends. By the time we got our stripe, we were inseparable. We walked together to Personnel and put in our request for Nam."

I smile as I remember our good times in the States while we waited for transfer to Vietnam. I guess I must have been lost in those memories, because Leia says, "You're daydreaming."

Sheepishly, I grin and apologize, "Sorry, I was just remembering something. You know, I think I could use another beer."

Leia signals Jabba and rests her chin on cupped hands, looking at me expectantly.

I continue, "Danny, was an artist; I mean . . . a *good* artist. He wasn't drafted into the military. He volunteered, to get the G.I. Bill, so that he could go to college and get formal training. We spent a lot of time talking about his art and my music, and what we would do when we got back from Nam. Danny was the inspiration that I needed. We had big plans, and of course, we were invincible. It never occurred to us to think about not making it back."

Jabba waddles up to our table and wordlessly lays the bottle in front of me. Swiveling like a bus in a skid, he walks back toward the bar. I don't think Jabba approves of me with Leia.

I take a deep swallow.

"We found out soon enough once we got to Vietnam that it wasn't healthy to set too many goals off in the future. Better to set one at a time, the first being to survive a day at a time. It helped having each other. We were a good team as well as best friends. More than once, we saved each other's asses. It seemed like forever, but we made it through six months out in the marshlands and then rotated back to Saigon to spend another month of easy duty guarding Tan Son Nhut, the big air base."

Again a smile comes to my face as good memories come to mind. "Just before our re-deployment back out in the field, we got our R&Rs approved, and Danny and I caught a Khlong C-130 over to Bangkok for two weeks of . . ." And I almost start to tell Leia of our two weeks of what, but catch myself.

Leia says, "Fun."

I laugh, "Yeah, fun. So anyway, we come back feeling like we've almost made it, and probably a little cocky. That lasted as long as it took to get our new orders. Our battalion was to airlift north to MR I and augment forces in place that were trying to hold on to some critical firebases and LZs in the highlands. Danny and I felt pretty confident in knowing the enemy of the marshes and rice paddies, but now we'd be fighting in deep-canopied jungle."

The smell of rotting vegetation, the buzz of insects, the echoing, hollow crunch of troops on the move along the jungle floor, the relentless heat, all these remembered senses come teeming to my mind. Suddenly, I'm hot and I pull my sweatshirt over my head and toss it on a chair and take another deep swallow of beer.

Leia leans over and brushes my hair down with her hand where my sweatshirt had mussed it up.

"We had some good officers and NCOs. They rotated us in with the experienced guys, and fairly quickly, Danny and I gained the experience needed . . . we thought."

My throat is dry and I take another sip of beer. "Danny and I always stood perimeter guard duty together, to keep each other company. It meant that we stood guard twice as much, but it went faster and was not nearly as lonely. We'd talk about everything under the sun. But the night before Danny was killed, he and I, for the first time, talked about not making it back, or of being crippled or disfigured. For whatever reason . . . a premonition . . . whatever . . . something made us both uneasy. The captain had already informed us of a major sweep the next day, and as always, we could expect casualties."

Leia moves closer to me, sensing that I need her support.

"That night, Danny asked me, other than being killed . . . what would be the worst thing I could imagine? Leia, I had seen it all. Guys losing legs, arms, even castrated, but I didn't hesitate. I told Danny that losing my hearing would be the worst—the thought of a silent world with no music was unbearable."

For a moment we sit quietly. Another of Leia's favorite songs is playing on the jukebox—"Sometimes Love Just Ain't Enough" by Patty Smyth. I look at Leia as she, too, thinks of a life without song.

"I asked Danny what would be the worst for him, but I was pretty sure I already knew, and of course he answered, to lose his eyes . . . to lose his sight. That was what he feared losing more than life itself. Of course we argued about it the rest of the night. Which sense was the most important . . . blah, blah, blah. Danny was an agnostic, but he kept describing sight as God's greatest gift."

I take a deep breath and look away. I consider ending it now, telling Leia that I can't go on. Looking around the bar, I notice that if anything it had gotten busier, and I'm afraid that I might break down again.

Leia senses it. She takes the front of her blouse and wafts it back and forth and says, "Whew, I'm hot, too. Let's put on our coats and take a walk."

"Good idea," I answer gratefully and reach for my sweatshirt.

Leia asks Jabba to save our table, and we put on our coats and walk into the cold night. We join arms and slowly start walking on the lighted side of the block. The icy snow cracks and pops under our feet, and a couple of times Leia almost slips but uses my arm to keep her balance. The traffic on the street is sparse but welcome company as we leave the better-lighted block.

"Will you finish now?" Leia draws my arm closer to her body.

"Where was I?" I ask.

"On guard duty."

※ ※ ※

"Yeah, well it was about 4 A.M. when we got relieved, and both of us only got a couple of hours' sleep before we had to get up and get moving. I couldn't shake the feeling of dread. The humidity was oppressive, like just prior to a big storm, but this would last all day, and there would be no cooling breezes. As we started down the hill that protected our firebase, I realized that I was just flat-out, piss-your-pants scared. I didn't see how I was going to make it through the patrol. Once we reached the jungle, it got worse. The deeper we penetrated, the hotter it got. At times we had to machete through thick patches of elephant grass so thick that we'd almost come to a stop. Finally it cleared a little and began to show signs of a trail, so the sergeant spread us out and assigned me point."

※ ※ ※

We stop at the intersection and let a car go through and then hurry through as we hear the cracking ice of another approaching car.

※ ※ ※

"Point is the most dangerous position in the jungle. You're out front—the first to draw the sniper's fire, the first to step on a mine, the first to trigger a bungee stick. The sarge was fair about rotating the men, but he wouldn't put up with whining when it was your turn.

"I tried . . . I really tried. But my fear kept building, and I couldn't get ahead of it. Every tree hid a V.C., every clearing provided a clear shot for a sniper, and every twig that snapped under my boots was a booby-trapped shell that was going to take my legs off. I was at the point where I was about to panic when we reached a protected area, and the sarge called a rest."

🎲 🎲 🎲

I feel Leia's hand snake into my coat pocket and her fingers intertwine with mine. Her fingers are icy, and I realize that she doesn't have any gloves. "Are you cold?" I ask.

"Not now," she answers.

I know Leia is waiting for me to start again, but to tell the rest will be so hard . . . so shameful. How do you admit to anyone that you were a coward? That's why I knew I could never tell Jack, or even admit it to Mo. Someone who's been there would never forgive letting down your buddies. But Leia was so persuasive and offered the forgiveness of an innocent. I really thought I could tell her. Now that moment had arrived, and I just didn't know . . .

"Courage, Andy," Leia says softly as she squeezes my hand.

Tears suddenly rim my eyes. Nothing she could have said could have hurt more, but then, perhaps nothing else could have made me continue.

🎲 🎲 🎲

"Danny walked over to where I was resting on a thick vine," I continue, "and I told him how I didn't think I could walk point anymore, that I had never been so close to outright panic. Danny tried to reassure me and joked about how we had the gomers on the run and probably wouldn't see any action. But neither of us believed that. Too soon, Sarge rounded us up and motioned for me to get out on point. Even though I knew how bad I'd look in front of the patrol, I started to say something to the sarge, when Danny said that he'd take point. I knew Danny was scared, too, but I was just so grateful that I kept quiet as the sarge OK'd it and signaled for us to move out. As Danny moved past me to take my position, he said to me: 'You owe me one, buddy.'"

⊠ ⊠ ⊠

Leia and I walk without speaking as the sidewalk climbs a small hill. Our labored breath creates miniature wisps of clouds that dissipate almost instantly as the cold gusts off the Chesapeake lash across our exposed faces. We reach the top. Below us the skyline of downtown Baltimore shimmers in the dark, cold water of the bay.

"We ought to start heading back," I say.

Leia pulls on my arm and says, "It's so pretty here. I'm not cold. Come on, there's a stone bench we can sit on that's protected from the wind."

We brush the remnants of frozen snow off the bench and sit down. Leia snuggles close to me.

The cold air, Leia at my side, the thirty-odd years gone by, now all seems less real than that moment in the jungle when Danny said he'd take my place and I skulked back to a safe position in the middle of the patrol. I know I felt shame, but I also remember that mostly I just felt relieved—the real shame . . . that would come later.

"Go on," she urges.

⊠ ⊠ ⊠

Reality for me now is the stench of rotting leaves and the buzz of insects as I remember Danny chopping a large leaf out of his way and disappearing into the jungle.

"Danny pushed into the jungle and the rest of the patrol followed his lead as we picked up the trail. Overhead we could hear the whine of F-4s as an air strike started going in on the ridge line about two klicks south of our position; and faintly, but getting louder, we could hear the chuga-chuga of a large anti-aircraft gun. I had just thought that we'd better be careful because the gun meant NVA regulars, and for certain some kind of defensive perimeter protecting the gun, when

I heard the loud *whump* of a mine exploding, followed by screams and yells for help. The first scream had been Danny's.

"Too late, I was no longer afraid for myself, but I was frantic in my fear for what had happened to Danny. I ran forward. The air still had the peppery odor of explosives and the worse cloying reek of blood. The sarge had already reached Danny's side and looked up at me as I knelt down next to him. The sarge shook his head and lowered his eyes, telling me that he was already dead."

⊠ ⊠ ⊠

I look into Leia's face to see what her reaction is and to try and judge what she must be thinking of me. She wipes a tear from the corner of her eye, otherwise she shows no emotion.

"That mine was meant for me. Danny died for me because I was a coward. You understand that don't you," I say, puzzled that there isn't some trace of loathing in her reaction . . . or at least disappointment.

"I realize that he died in your place, and that you were afraid, but that doesn't make you a coward." Leia's voice rises in anger. "My God, you spent a year in an ugly, horrible war. What's wrong with being afraid of dying." Abruptly her voice softens. "I *do* understand, Andy. It had to be terrible, and I can see why you feel so guilty. But on another day, it might just as easily have been your friend that was scared and you would have taken his place."

"There's more," I say. "Let me finish telling you what kind of friend I was that day."

⊠ ⊠ ⊠

Silently, Leia sits next to a coward as he finishes telling his story.

⊠ ⊠ ⊠

"I cradled his head in my arms and tried to wipe the blood from his face. His lower body was a mess, and both his legs were shredded. A large piece of shrapnel had torn open his scalp causing all the blood, but his face was unmarked. He looked serene in death, almost asleep . . . he looked angelic." *Like an angel! God, I can't go on. I was so close!*

In an instant, I relive the Angel collapsing at my feet with Danny's words of *forgiveness* (?) on her lips.

I stop talking long enough to compose myself. A jet passes noisily overhead, and I wait for it, thankful for the respite.

But I must finish. "I remember talking to him. I *know* I told him I was sorry and asked him to forgive me. The sarge yelled that we had to get out of there. The CP had called in an air strike on the triple-A, and we had to get clear. I bent down to pick up Danny's body in a fireman's carry, when the sarge told me to leave him. We could hear the sounds and yells of approaching enemy soldiers and the pops of AK-47s. I hesitated a second, but he screamed at me again to move out. I grabbed one of Danny's dog tags and said to his body that I would come back for him. I promised him that I wouldn't let him rot out in the jungle. Then I grabbed the arm of one of the wounded, and we got the hell out."

⊠ ⊠ ⊠

I stop talking as another jet from BIWI banks overhead and turns back inland heading to the west. Its exhaust crackles in the cold air and echoes over the bay as first the jet lights up a low cloud with its flashing strobes and then it disappears.

⊠ ⊠ ⊠

"The next day, the sarge gave me a couple of men to go back for Danny's body. The F-4s had knocked out the gun, and the CP was pretty sure that the gooks had moved out of the immediate area. We had a good fix on the gun location and eventually we found the first rest area. It was only a matter of taking that same path where Danny had triggered the mine."

My voice is reedy and breaking as I try to tell Leia of the final horror of my sin.

"We came to the spot on the trail. Danny's body was . . . it was . . . "I gulp for air and fight for control. "His body had been mutilated. His clothes were gone, and they had . . . done . . . things to his body. Next to his torso they had stuck a long piece of green bamboo into the ground. Stuck on the end of it was Danny's head. The fuckers . . . they had—through his eyes were two sharp sticks . . . "

▨ ▨ ▨

Finally I can hold it in no longer, and in a moan that is almost a howl, I let go of my tears and bawl in deep, octave-descending jerks that convulse my body.

Leia tries to comfort me, but the image is too vivid, my memory too damning. She gets up and walks around to the back of the bench and puts her arms around me and just holds me as slowly, painfully, I reach emotional bottom. "His eyes," I sob. "They took his precious eyes. I should have never left his body behind."

Gradually, the tears slow and Leia puts an arm under both my arm pits and grunts as she pulls up. "Come on, let's walk it off and head back to Birdy's."

My knees are weak, and I lean on Leia for support as we silently walk down the hill. The wind is at our back now and the walk goes quickly. We reach the parking lot next to Birdy's, and Leia turns to me and says, "I understand now, or at least the most I'll ever be able to; and I know there is nothing that I can say or do to change the past, but you'll never be a coward in my eyes. You were a young soldier that faced a year of terror, and bad things happened, but you're not alone, and you certainly proved your courage often enough. Another day, different circumstances, you would have died for Danny . . . and you *know* it. You'd do it right now if you could." Then Leia stands on her tiptoes and pulls my head down and kisses me. Not the peck on the cheek she'd given me before; her mouth is open and her breath is sweet as I kiss her back, and her body bends against mine so that I can feel her curves even through her winter coat.

As Leia's lips leave mine, she gently caresses my face and says, "Come home with me tonight."

"Leia, I—"

"Shh-h-h," she cuts me off. "Wait here while I tell Augie we're not coming back." Before I can respond, she runs into Birdy's, leaving me as confused as I'd ever been in my life.

Leia comes out, takes my arm, and starts leading me to her car.

Suddenly, I balk. Remembering. "I have nightmares every night, Leia—terrible nightmares." I don't want to tell her how every night it's the same: Danny's head glaring at me, with bloody stakes for eyes and his voice whispering to me, *You did this to me.*

"All the more reason why you shouldn't sleep alone. Come on." She tugs on my arm and leads me to her car.

⊠ ⊠ ⊠

That night, in Leia's arms, I don't dream of Danny.

⊠ ⊠ ⊠

The next morning, I awake early and watch Leia as she sleeps. I'm still drained from the emotional roller-coaster ride of the day before, and I marvel at how at peace I feel even though yesterday at the Wall was probably the lowest day in my life since Danny died. Part of me is still crying out for one last chance with the Angel—it still hurts to have come so close; part of me is resigned to living with my guilt—not for a minute did I assume that my nightmares wouldn't return. But part of me—just a little piece—is telling me to be happy and try to go on with my life.

Slowly I pull the covers from Leia and look at her as she sleeps curled up on her side. She sighs, stretches, and rolls on her back exposing all of herself to me. Her eyes open and she smiles, realizes that I was watching her, laughs, and pulls me down into her arms. Our lovemaking is at first shy in the light of day and without the booze, and although our passion builds, it remains tender as we join and I ride a roller-coaster that I could ride the rest of my life.

⊠ ⊠ ⊠

Later, Leia makes us a huge breakfast—well actually brunch—and we joke around, play with our food, and pretty much avoid talking about Danny. Leia has to go in to work at three, and I call the docks and tell them that I'll be into work by noon. I help Leia clean up the dishes, and she drives me to Birdy's to pick up my car.

Leia pulls into the side lot next to my Chevy. We had been two jab-ber-boxes all morning long, but now, suddenly neither of us knows what to say. Finally she says, "About last night, I don't want you to think it was just a mercy . . . uh—that I did it because I felt sorry for you. I want to be your friend . . . or more, if that's what you want. I just want to help you . . . I care for you. . . . " Her voice trails off as her head lowers and she blushes.

I lean over and kiss her passionately. Still embracing, I hug her tightly to me and say, "If you had not come to me, I don't think I could have made it through the night. I know I don't deserve to be happy . . . to feel good . . . to think about the future, but I can't help it; you've changed everything. I want to see you again tonight. I want to *be* with you tonight . . . and the next.

Leia is all smiles, and to me . . . beautiful. "I work till ten," she says. "Will you come to Birdy's when you get off?"

"Nothing could stop me!" I give her a quick kiss and slide across the seat and open the car door. "I gotta run. Give me a second to make sure my car starts, OK?"

My Chevy growls weakly but catches, and I give it some gas to keep it going. I give Leia a thumbs-up, and she smiles back, waves, and blows me a kiss as she backs up and leaves. I find myself humming and smiling as I wait for the car to warm up.

⊠ ⊠ ⊠

That "little piece" of me that wants so badly to be happy is growing.

⊠ ⊠ ⊠

Work that afternoon is a pleasure. I square things with my foreman and thank him for the time off. I try to find Jack, but he's working up at the north warehouse, so I leave a message for him. The physical labor feels good after the last week's standing around at the Wall, and for the first time in I don't know how long, I feel . . . ambitious. Not only was I looking forward to seeing Leia again tonight, but out there on the horizon, far past where I'd dared look since Nam, was a future.

⊠ ⊠ ⊠

I work a full shift plus an hour of overtime, and by the time I get home, shower, and pull into Birdy's, its almost nine-thirty. As I pull open the heavy wooden door, I feel a momentary shyness, and I wonder if Leia has had second thoughts about me and will be cool toward me. But that doubt disappears as I spot her waiting a table at the back, and she waves cheerfully and a smile dimples her face.

※ ※ ※

I stop at the bar and order a beer from Jabba and he grumbles, "About time you showed up. Chrissy has been bumping into the tables all evening checking out the front door every time someone walks in." He reaches down in the beer chest and pulls out my brand and pops the top off. Then he smiles—or what passes for his smile—and says, "Here's your beer. Chrissy saved your table for you."

On the top of my table is a homemade sign that says: Reserved—Andy. A red heart drawn with lipstick is next to my name. I look over at Leia and catch her smiling as she turns back to her customers. I walk over to the jukebox and play as many songs as I have quarters for and take a seat at my table as the beginning see-saw notes of Steely Dan's "Rickki Don't Lose That Number" start to play.

Even before I feel her kiss on my cheek, I sense her perfume as Leia puts an arm on my shoulder and says, "You scared me. When I realized it was past nine, I got a little worried that you wouldn't come tonight." She pulls out a chair and sits sideways.

"Sorry, but I worked late to make up some for all the time I've been gone." I take her hand and add, "But I thought about you all day."

"Me, too." She runs the fingers of her other hand through her hair and says, "I bet I look a mess. We've really been busy this evening." She glances over to the bar. "I can't stay now, but Augie promises that he'll let me off at ten no matter how busy we are."

"No sweat," I say. "I'm happy, or I will be once you bring me another beer."

Leia smiles and rises from her chair. In a sensuous voice she says, "*Anything* you want, lover. Save my seat."

Lifting my beer to my lips, I watch her walk away and think to myself that this is too good, that I don't deserve anyone as pretty . . . and loving. For about the tenth time today, I question how I could be so lucky. Especially . . . since . . . I don't deserve to be so blessed.

Leia drops off my beer then hustles over to other tables and makes endless shuttles to the bar. I settle into my music and find myself reliving the events of the previous day. The familiar pattern, the downward spiral of unworthiness that has relentlessly flawed my life, begins its insidious return to my thoughts, and I struggle to keep it at bay. I remember the embrace of Leia's arms as we shed our clothes, and I felt the warmth of her body next to mine. But then I think about the Angel collapsing just as she is about to give me Danny's forgiveness. I think about how Leia's face lighted up when she saw me enter Birdy's, and how that, in turn, sent a warm masculine pride through me: That's *my* girl. But then I think of my cowardice and how I caused Danny's death. I try to imagine a future with Leia . . . to have a woman who loves me and understands me. I think of Jack and Julia, of Jeremy and Rowena, and how happy they are . . . to have a family of my own, even this late in life. But then I think how Danny will never have that . . . or anything . . . ever.

It becomes an emotional ratchet—a slipping gear. One cog up and two down.

Danny, give me peace.

I catch sight of Leia at a far table, and she smiles as she notices me and does an exaggerated wipe of her brow. She points at her watch and then does a "five" with her fingers, closes her hand and gives me another "five." Ten minutes.

Move one notch up.

The country-rock beat of John Mellencamp and "Cherry Bomb" lifts me another notch as I tap my foot to his distinctive beat.

※ ※ ※

"I told Mo I knew where you'd be," I hear Jack's bass voice say. I turn around in my chair and see Jack looming over me. Next to him is Mo with a huge, beaming grin on his face.

I jump up and embrace first Mo and then Jack. Flustered, I ask, "Wha— what are you guys doing here? Mo, you're a long way from home."

"Why, we came to have a cold beer," Mo says. "I heard they have the coldest beer in Maryland. You goin' to invite us to sit with you or not?"

"Hell yes! Sit!" I say as I grab a couple of chairs from another table. "Let's get you a couple of those cold ones." I look around and get Leia's attention and raise two fingers as she nods.

We sit and Jack reaches over and grasps my arm and squeezes it. "Mo told me what happened at the Wall yesterday." Jack pauses as I lower my head.

"You don't mind me telling Jack, do you? I was really worried about you, and I didn't know what else to do." Mo sounds like a little boy as he pleads with me not to be angry.

"No, I don't care. Hell, you saved me the trouble of telling the whole story to Jack myself." I look at Mo and see the veil of concern lift from his face and his puckish smile return.

"So how you doin', buddy?" Jack asks.

I smile. "OK . . . I'm doing pretty good. A lot has happened since yesterday."

Leia walks up with our beers and sets them down. She says hello to Jack and smiles at Mo but then starts to leave, and I stand and say, "Wait, Leia. I want to introduce you to Mo."

Mo pops up like a cork and takes her hand. "Leia, this is a very good friend of mine, Mo Watters. Mo, this is my girlfriend, Leia." It just slips out. I glance at Jack and see his eyebrows arch, and a smile come to his face. I look back at Leia, and I'm surprised to see her blushing. Helplessly, I shrug and say, "I told you a lot has happened since yesterday."

Jack can't contain his laughter at my expense, and still laughing, he comes around the table and gives Leia a big hug. Now even Leia and Mo start laughing, and I'm left with no option . . . I join in.

We stand chatting at the table for a few minutes then Leia says, "I'll let you men talk. Andy, I'll just help out Augie a little longer."

"No. I want you to stay," I urge. "Go fix yourself a drink and come back."

"You sure?" Leia looks questioningly at all three of us.

Mo, in character, holds out his arm in gentlemanly fashion, and says, "Let me escort the lady to the bar and see for her safe return."

Leia smiles at me, and taking Mo's arm, says, "We shall return."

⊠ ⊠ ⊠

I fill Jack in a little more on what happened the day before at the Wall and how Leia had helped me get through the rough time I had last night. Jack is sympathetic about getting so near, and I can tell that part of him still wonders what the Angel might have said to him. Leia and Mo start back toward our table, and Jack asks me, "You really going to be OK?"

Yesterday there wasn't much doubt how I would have answered Jack, but now I at least have hope . . . and I have Leia. I answer, "I

think so. I know it's not going to be easy, but yeah, I think things are
going to get better."

▨ ▨ ▨

The four of us talk and laugh over our drinks. I can tell that Mo has
another fan in Leia by the easy way that they've already become
friends. Jack and I explain to Mo our *Star Wars* nomenclature, which
sets Mo off in hilarious laughter. Then Mo acts indignant when Leia,
Jack and I all agree that Mo is C3PO. The more he complains and
argues, the more he sounds just like the "prot
ocol droid," and finally he surrenders in laughter.

Leia gets us another round while Mo checks out the jukebox, and
Jack and I go take a leak.

We all get comfortable around the table again and Mo says, "Andy,
can we talk about the Angel for a minute? Something's happened that
I think you should know about. That's why I drove to Baltimore, I
wanted to tell you."

*Oh God, I'd been so wrapped up in my own life—and Danny's death—
that I hadn't even thought about the Angel and what had happened to her.*
I feel so ashamed, and I know it shows in my face as I say, "I didn't
even think to ask. What have you heard? Is she OK?"

Mo shakes his head. "Yeah, she's fine . . . she's better than fine . . .
she can see!"

I'm puzzled. "What do you mean . . . she can see?"

Mo is standing now, unable to contain his excitement. "I mean the
angel has her sight back. She can see again. They're calling it 'The
Miracle at the Wall'! She recovered consciousness late last night and
her sight was back. It isn't quite normal yet, but the doctors say that
all her vision will return."

"Where did you hear this?" I ask.

"It's on the Washington news," Mo answers. "It was in this evening's
paper, and two stations had a small blurb on TV, but the press has been all
over the Wall today, and the whole story is coming out about the Angel
and everything. I kinda of thought you'd rather hear this from me."

"Yeah, you're right. Thanks, Mo." I guess until now I still held out
a subconscious hope that the Angel would return to the Wall. My head
is reeling, and I have trouble organizing my thoughts. I'm happy for

our Angel, but now there is a feeling of finality. I don't know how I should feel, and most confusing, I don't know what it means . . . or understand how it happened.

I look at Jack and then back at Mo. "I don't understand . . ."

Suddenly, Leia cries out, "I do! I understand. Don't you see, it's Danny's message to you!"

"What do you mean? What message? The Angel never got to finish the message," I argue.

"Your angel recovering her *sight* was his message to you." Leia is animated now. Her face is aglow and her eyes are brimming with a layer of tears. "Remember what you told me about how Danny thought that sight was our most precious gift. What if the soul of the person has the power to send only one . . . just one message through to your angel. What would Danny do if the angel was blind? Think! What would he do?"

Leia is panting with spent emotion. She clasps her hands around mine and pulls them to her cheek. The first tears drop from her eyes as she says, almost in a whisper, "Oh Andy, you know what your friend would do. He'd give her the gift of sight if it was within his power, and he'd ask you to understand. He'd say, 'Try to understand, Andy. . . . Try to understand.'"

🞖 🞖 🞖

All the cold days at the Wall when I waited for the Angel, I'd daydream about the moment when the Angel would give me Danny's words of forgiveness. I'd think about how good it would feel to know that Danny forgave me and that he wanted me to be happy in my life. Sometimes I'd smile then, because if I believed that, then I could also remember the good times we had together without always remembering the bad. Everything good I had daydreamed didn't prepare me for the open floodgate of joy and happiness . . . and love for my friend that now rushes through every fiber of my being.

🞖 🞖 🞖

"Danny forgives me. . . . Danny forgives me. . . . Danny forgives me. . . ." I say over and over, as Leia holds me in her arms and my friends sit by my side.

EPILOGUE

Jabba sets the Diet Coke down in front of me and places my quarters in a vertical stack next to it. It's summer now and rivulets of sweat trace the lines of Jabba's broad face. He leans over the table and braces his weight—or a small portion of it—with his hands and pleads, "Promise me that the two of you won't decide to stay out in L.A."

After the wedding tomorrow, Leia and I are catching an evening flight out of Dulles to L.A. for our honeymoon. Leia had warned me that Jabba would probably start working on me if he got the chance. All this last week he had been ragging on her about how terrible L.A. is with all its traffic, freeway shootings, smog, fires, and riots. She tried to reassure him, but she has also always talked about moving to L.A., and so I can understand why Jabba is concerned.

"Augie," I say earnestly, "I promise you that we're coming back."

Relief sweeps across his features, and he lifts his stained bar apron and wipes his brow. "The drinks are on me tonight!"

"I'm just waiting for Leia to get fancied up (Jabba knows I call her Leia now, but God forbid he finds out about *his* nickname). We're meeting Jack and Julia here tonight, then going out to an Italian restaurant for dinner, but thanks."

"Well, have cocktails here before dinner and come back afterwards," he adds expansively.

I laugh. "You really *are* worried that we'll stay out in L.A. aren't you?"

"Not now." Jabba huffs. "You promised." And with that pronouncement, he grins like the Cheshire cat and walks away.

※ ※ ※

What Jabba doesn't know is that I'll probably never leave Baltimore. For Jack and Mo, and for me, and all those whose lives were changed by a miracle at the Wall, we can never leave until our task is finished. That day at the Wall, Mo said to me that whatever it all meant, it had to be something for all of us, not just those who saw the Angel. As time has passed, and our memories have dimmed and blended with each other's stories, we who experienced the miracle at the Wall, we know now what her purpose was and what we must do.

I lift the can of Coke to my mouth and take a sip. I want a beer so bad that I can still hear a voice urging me to go ahead. Leia and the guys did a semi-intervention and convinced me to get some help. I may not be an alcoholic, drink was just an escape; but for the time being I'm leaving it alone. The fact that it's still calling for me, makes me think that it'll be for the best if it's for forever. I know I'm not going to risk losing Leia. I grab the mound of quarters and walk to the juke-box. Jabba has added some new forty-fives, and I laugh out loud when I see that he'd taken out "I Love L.A." No way was Leia going to put up with that! I feed the quarters and play a good mix, including several of the new ones, and return to my table.

The music starts, and I rock the Coke can back and forth in rhythm to the music as I try to again picture the Angel. Each day that passes, my memories of her seem more like a dream, so vivid in sleep, but fleeting and ethereal in the first moments of waking. All of us have experienced this same feeling, and at times we wonder how much of what happened was the work of the Angel, and how much of it was the healing of the Wall itself.

▨ ▨ ▨

Our Angel recovered her sight completely but had no memories of the healings at the Wall. The doctors said that her blindness had been caused by a tumor pressing against the optic nerve, that it had gone into a spontaneous remission, and as it dissolved of its own accord, her vision returned. She never came back to the Wall. The press made a big deal out of it for about a week, until they perceived in their omniscient judgment of what the public needs to know that it was no longer news and let the story fade.

▨ ▨ ▨

But the G.I.s kept coming. So did the mothers and fathers, the wives, and the children of the dead who now had children of their own. Word-of-mouth had spread the story of the miracle at the Wall throughout our country. They came in the thousands looking and hoping for the things that Mo and Jack and I had found. The funny thing is that most find it without the help of any "angel." The Wall itself is the instrument of healing. Mo says that our Angel was an intermediary for us hard cores whose pain had layered our souls so thick that the Wall couldn't get through. It was Mo who first suggested that now that the Angel was gone, someone should take her place, someone should help the ones who hurt so bad that they resist the healing of the Wall.

He said it should be us.

So that's what we three do. In a sense, Mo had been doing that all along. It was his gentle shoves toward facing my demons that had kept me going. And it was his understanding comfort that held me up and encouraged me when things got bad. We take turns, and each of us covers one day of one week, and the three of us all meet and cover the same day on the last week of the month, which gives us a good opportunity to get together.

Each time I visit the Wall, I still see the anguish of the families and their pain, visible even after so many years. I see middle-aged veterans, like myself, with thirty years of anger dragging at their souls. I see children who romp on the grassy area above the monument while their parents suffer and wish that their kids could have known their Uncle Joey. I see fathers who never got a chance to tell their sons that they loved them. Mothers who want only to hold their child one last time. But now I also see that all this is part of the healing of the Wall. It is the shared suffering that brings us all together and unites us.

So yeah, Jabba, I'll be back.

⊠ ⊠ ⊠

I feel a hand ruffle the hair on my neck, and I smell the subtle trace of the perfume. From the jukebox comes the first few bars of bass, then the guitar and drums joins in, and the music picks up almost a calypso beat. I stand up and turn around.

Leia says to me, "What were you so deep in thought about?"

I say nothing as I lead Leia by the hand to an open area between two tables. I put an arm around Leia's waist and pull her to me as the clear, nearly soprano voice of Johnny Nash blends into the song "I Can See Clearly Now."

"Andy, we can't dance in Birdy's!" She's laughing and she says it in a mock, shocked voice, but her body moves with the rhythm, and she contours her body with mine.

"Shh-h-h," I whisper in her ear.

She looks up at me, her eyes sparkling. "This is *our* song, isn't it?"

I nod. "Yours and mine . . ." I press my body to hers and hold her tightly. ". . . and Danny's."

Afterword: I had already written several stories about the Wall when my sister sent me a magazine article that commemorated its tenth anniversary. It was Life magazine, and I still can visualize Michael Jordan's picture on one corner of the cover, his unique smile and good looks in vivid contrast to the otherwise black cover depicting the Wall. One of the interior photos showed a mother and child touching the Wall, and the sidebar read something like: "Everyone who visits the wall touches it . . . it's as if there is a Braille-like link to those who are missing or dead."

What if that were true? And, as my character asks in the story, "What would the dead say to us?"

In the writing, the characters took a life unto their own and went in directions that surprised me. In the beginning, Princess Leia was only intended to be what writer's call a "spear carrier"—analogous to the nameless/faceless bit players in a movie. The night that Leah takes Andy home with her, I'm as surprised as he is! Though I spent hundreds of hours revising and polishing "Angel," it was an easy story to write, taking just over a month to complete, writing a couple of hours each evening.

The story was an unexpected gift. I like to think that a Braille-like connection was made. It was the Wall's gift to me.

WILLING THE CHILD TO RETURN

David Lange

It is late when he leaves.
The air in the corridors around the secretaries' desks
      is stale breath whispered   confidences hissed
a memory of electric oils and Virginia Slims. The lights are dim.
He thinks an office pouts when the workers have gone
      waits   willing them to return
as a woman sitting in twilight hopes by brooding
to remind a child that she is alone.

He spies his letters from the afternoon
      drops into a swivel chair
           half turns into the gray steel desk
              finds his pen
but then seeing the spaces for his signatures
      awaiting life like Man or Woman on the Fifth day
thinks
      Let them wait. I'm tired. It's late.

On Constitution Avenue November rain and smoke
have reached an understanding
      settle into the lungs and ride the blood home like dogs.

His home is twelve blocks west beyond the Mall.
He walks the way dogs swim
        nose high   eyes half closed
        legs chopping short strokes through the puddled waters
moving against the currents moving against him.

He remembers a rain one spring
        when the lawn had flooded in Bethesda
            a pool deep enough to swim in.
He and the boy
            seven then   small body light and lithe and tanned
     flipping in the unexpected waters
laughter spilling through the wide French doors
            first rays of watered sun . . .

. . . an April thunderstorm years later
        Standing on the sheltered balcony of his apartment
            looking across the Potomac to Arlington
his wife had asked if he could still recall
that afternoon in Maryland.
        His mind on the papers she had brought to sign
            for a moment he was dumb
then placing the question he told her the truth:

The flood coming to him in dreams
        his one best memory of the boy.
What he did not say
        no longer having any wish to hurt her
            that in his dreams the boy himself is gone.
Only the water remains
        cooling in the weak sun
waiting   *willing the child to return.*

Along the Mall Christmas lights have begun to bloom
        saplings weighted with electric ice
            windows dressed like Cardinals at Mass . . .

Children's voices touching the snows
     flown to rest against his windows
          like soft birds settling into winter nests
still bring him from his chair no matter the book or fire.
He offers candy   a small dish of it
     small against the embarrassment
        of too much or none at all.
He is no Scrooge but neither does he keep the Day.

. . . The boy died in April 1969
          (Marines crossing a River
       into a reddening sun
     caught in an unexpected rain of fire
his body light and lithe and tanned)

The telegrams had come soon after
     the body in its khaki bag
    burning best   delay   unreality
     next of kin   Command
And when at last the matter had unraveled
    and the ashes had arrived
      Christmas was at hand.
Since then he has not kept the Day.

His walk outlasts both lights and rain.
Only the smoke of hearthfires
remain to share his last five blocks.
He senses the Wall
     its dark mass rising
    a memory squeezed from earth.
At his approach its warmth brushes him like a kiss
       embrace revealing . . .

It comes to him then
how waiting things endure
    dumb or not
        in the hope of giving warmth
as an office emptied of workers waits
as a father nodding by lamplight waits
as the ashes cold in his fireplace wait
    willing the Child to return.

Afterword: I wrote this poem some twenty years ago on an impulse against a memory from a time in Chicago many years ago while the war in Vietnam was still raging. I was in law practice, and while leaving my office one rainy, foggy evening during the period between Thanksgiving and Christmas, and making my way toward the commuter train station, I happened to pass by a shop that sold color television sets, then still something of a novelty. The shop was closed, as I recall, but the sets in the window were all on and tuned to a channel on which footage from Vietnam was airing: boys engaged in combat, or emerging from combat, or being evacuated from combat—the specific incidents are no longer clear to me. But I remember thinking then, as I looked around at the Christmas lights and decorations that had sprung up throughout the city, that somewhere, someone would have a very different Christmas than I expected for myself.

My first son would still have been a baby at the time, probably less than two years old, and I imagine that the image of the child that stayed with me from that moment on the street was affected by the love I felt for him and the empathy I could feel in turn for the father or mother of any one of those boys who might not return from the war. I do not mean to exaggerate my sensitivity, though, whether then or now. In truth, it was merely a moment, and to remember it in this fashion almost certainly is to embroider it and to give it a specificity beyond what it actually held for me at the time. But if you ask how I came to write this poem, this is what I have to say.

Contributors

Paul Allen is a psychologist and writer living in New England. He is a graduate of the Clarion West 1994 Science Fiction and Fantasy Writers Workshop and the New York Summer Writers Institute 2001. His last short story appeared in the anthology *Women Who Run with Werewolves*. He is finishing a volume of memoirs focusing on overcoming loss and tentatively titled *At the Center of the Sun*.

Michael Belfiore lives in the New York metropolitan area where he runs a writing-for-hire business with his wife, Wendy Kagan, and acts on stage and in films. A graduate of Clarion West, his short fiction has appeared in *Aboriginal Science Fiction*, *Aberrations*, and *VB Tech Journal*. His work for the theater has been produced by companies in New York; Madison, Wisconsin; and Munster, Germany.

Dr. Michael Brotherton lives in Tucson, Arizona with his wife, Leah Cutter. An astronomer at Kitt Peak National Observatory, he specializes in observational studies designed to better understand quasars and their role in galaxy evolution. A graduate of Clarion West 1994, his fiction has appeared in *Talebones* and *Tales of the Unanticipated*. He has reviewed short fiction for *Tangent*.

Michael A. Burstein was the John W. Campbell Award winner for Best New Writer (1997) and has been nominated for multiple Hugos, and a Nebula and Sturgeon nomination for his story "Reality Check." He served as secretary of the Science Fiction and Fantasy Writers of America. Burstein lives with his wife, Nomi, in Brookline, Massachusetts.

Orson Scott Card is the author of *Ender's Game*, *Ender's Shadow*, the *Alvin Maker* series, and the novels *Enchantment* and *Lost Boys*. He Lives in Greensboro, North Carolina, where he and his wife, Kristine Allen Card, are raising Zina, their youngest. His Website is www.hatrack.com.

Leah R. Cutter currently telecommutes, writing technical documentation for a California software firm. A graduate of Clarion West 1997, her short fiction has appeared in *Black Hearts*, *Ivory Bones*, and *Talebones*. Ms. Cutter recently received a two-book contract from ROC. The first novel, *Paper Mage*, is scheduled for publication in Spring 2003. She reviews fiction for *Strange Horizons*.

Nick DiChario's tales of science fiction, fantasy, horror, and mystery have appeared in many magazines and anthologies. His work has been reprinted in *The Year's Best Fantasy and Horror* and, most recently, *The Best Alternate History Stories of the Twentieth Century*. Nick has been a finalist for the Hugo, John W. Campbell, and World Fantasy Awards.

Joe Haldeman served in the 4th Engineers, attached to various airmobile infantry operations in Vietnam's Central Highlands, between February 1968 and September 1968, when he was wounded and left combat. Haldeman's science-fiction novels, *The Forever War* and *Forever Peace*, won both the Hugo and Nebula Awards; he has won four other Hugos and three other Nebulas for other work. His non-SF Vietnam novels, *War Year* and *1968*, were critically acclaimed. His current novel is *The Coming* (Ace, 2000), and the next one will be *Guardian* (Ace, 2002).

David Lange is an occasional poet, fiction writer, and video producer. He is also a professor of law at Duke University, specializing in intellectual property, entertainment law, and telecommunications law and policy. He frequently lectures abroad and has served as an advisor to the Copyright Office and the National Office of Intellectual Property of the Republic of Vietnam. Professor Lange is married and the father of five children. He lives with his wife and seventeen-year-old son in Chapel Hill, North Carolina.

Barry N. Malzberg is the author of more than thirty science-fiction novels and more than 250 science-fiction stories. His first published story appeared in GALAXY magazine in 1967. *Beyond Apollo* (1972) won the first John W. Campbell Memorial Award for the best novel of the year.

L. E. Modesitt, Jr. is the author of more than thirty fantasy and science-fiction novels, a number of short stories and poems, and numerous technical articles and commentaries. His most recent novels are *White Nights*, *Shadowsinger*, and the forthcoming *Archform: Beauty*. He served with amphibious forces and was also a U.S. Navy helicopter search-and-rescue pilot during the Vietnam War, but not in country.

Rick Reaser is a Vietnam combat veteran who has far too many friends whose names are on the Wall. A multi-talented individual, Rick is a jeweler, a scientist, and a terrific storyteller. Although he does not himself write fiction, he dreams it up so well he has been Elizabeth Ann Scarborough's muse for the last couple of years, providing inspiration and imaginative flights of fancy when all she can see is a blank page.

Laura Resnick is the Campbell Award-winning author of forty short stories as well as the fantasy novels *In Legend Born* and *In Fire Forged*. She writes a regular opinion column for the *SFWA Bulletin*, and you can find her on the Web at www.sff.net/people/laresnick.

Mike Resnick is the author of forty-plus science-fiction novels, twelve collections, 130-plus short stories, and two screenplays. He has edited more than twenty science-fiction anthologies. He has won four Hugos (twenty-two nominations), a Nebula (nine nominations), and numerous other major awards from America, Japan, France, Poland, Croatia, and Spain. His work has been translated into twenty-two languages.

Ralph Roberts has sold more than ninety books and more than 5,000 articles and short stories to publications in several countries. His work includes the first U.S. book on computer viruses, *Classic Cooking with Coca-Cola*, *Genealogy via the Internet*, and other bestsellers. Roberts is a member of the Mystery Writers of America and the Science Fiction Writers of America. He lives and works in the Blue Ridge Mountains of Western North Carolina.

Robert J. Sawyer is the author of the Hugo Award finalists *Starplex*, *Frameshift*, *Factoring Humanity*, and *Calculating God*, and the Nebula Award winner *The Terminal Experiment*. He lives near Toronto. His Website is www.sfwriter.com, and his latest novel is *Hominids*, featuring more of Mary and Ponter, his characters from his story "Black Reflection."

Elizabeth Ann Scarborough is a Vietnam Army Nurse Corps veteran and author of numerous short stories and twenty-five novels, including the 1989 Nebula Award-winning *Healer's War*. She has been collaborating with Anne McCaffrey on the *Acorna* series. Her most recent solo novel is *Channeling Cleopatra*.

Michael Swanwick is the author of six novels and countless short stories. He has received the Hugo, Nebula, Theodore Sturgeon, and World Fantasy Awards for his work. He lives in Philadelphia with his wife, Marianne Porter. His newest novel, *Bones of the Earth*, was published in February 2002 by HarperCollins Eos.

Byron R. Tetrick is an international airline pilot and a retired Air Force fighter pilot. He served in Vietnam as a forward air controller, flying 187 combat missions. He is a Clarion Science Fiction and Fantasy Writer's Workshop graduate. His short fiction, including a Sherlock Holmes adventure, has appeared in recent anthologies. His first non-fiction book, *Choosing a Career as a Pilot*, has just been published. He lives with his wife, Carol, in Fishers, Indiana.

COPYRIGHTS